Asa stepped out of the shower in the cramped hotel bathroom and dried off. He twisted a towel loosely around his hips and rifled through his shorts for his cell phone, then remembered leaving it in his overnight bag just outside the door. He swore softly, then opened the bathroom door a crack and peeked out. He didn't want to disturb Kai, especially since she probably still had an attitude over him being in her hotel room. He stepped out of the bathroom to find her sprawled across the bed on her back, tangled in the sheets, and moving fitfully.

His first reaction was alarm, until he realized her moans were more erotic than fearful. Whatever—whomever she was dreaming about, she was pretty turned on. Shaking off the thought, he bent down to search for his phone.

"Asa…"

He raised an eyebrow and stood up when he heard his name, surprised that Kai had awakened so quickly. Cell phone forgotten, a roguish smile curled his lips. She was still asleep; and, dreaming about him.

He moved to the head of the bed, watching shamelessly, as she rubbed and caressed her body with lazy, sleepy strokes. He wanted to crawl into that bed with her.

After a few moments, her eyelids fluttered open in a sleepy haze.

Kai watched him expectantly, as if waiting for him to make a move. He didn't; couldn't, despite his revved up libido. So, it came as a complete shock when she pulled him down by his hair, licked her lips and laid one on him.

UNEARTHING PASSIONS

ELAINE SIMS

Genesis Press, Inc.

Indigo Love Stories

An imprint of Genesis Press, Inc.
Publishing Company

Genesis Press, Inc.
P.O. Box 101
Columbus, MS 39703

ISBN: 1-58571-184-5
Manufactured in the United States of America

First Edition

Visit us at www.genesis-press.com
or call at 1-888-Indigo-1

For Alvin

ACKNOWLEDGMENTS

Special thanks to those who helped me achieve this sometimes unfathomable, goal. First, to my aunt Costella Bowden, who raised me to believe I can accomplish anything given a little effort. Next, of course, to my critique partners (in alphabetical order): Carol, Emily, Kathy, and Shirley who've been in this with me from the very beginning. To Ann H. White, who read this work in its infancy and told me it was only a matter of time before it sold. To Haywood Smith, who shared her time and wisdom. To Carmen Green, you're truly an inspiration. To the members of Georgia Romance Writers, there's no way I could have done this without your support. To my wonderful agent and champion Michael Psaltis, whose wise counsel has kept me sane through it all. To my wonderful friend, Pauline Morin, for allowing her statue of Suzy to appear in this book. To Sandy Brewer and Sandy Shephard, who read my manuscripts and liked them. To my husband, Alvin Brewer, for babysitting, cooking and cleaning, and doing laundry so I could write. I promise I'll do some housework now; well, at least until I start the next book. And, to my beautiful two-year-old daughter Sierra, who was born three months premature, weighing only one pound, thirteen ounces, for growing so big and strong, and being considerate enough to listen to her iPod mini while Mommy completed this book.

CHAPTER ONE

At eight-thirty on Sunday night, Asa Matthews stepped out of the shower in his Savannah, Georgia hotel suite and wrapped a towel around his waist. Shoulder-length dreadlocks dripping, he tucked a second towel under them as he crossed the room in search of his robe. He looked on top of the unmade bed, underneath it, then in the closet, before he gave up and jerked on a worn pair of gym shorts instead.

In the living room, he collapsed on the couch and dropped his feet on the coffee table where his cell phone lay, mocking him, but he didn't pick it up. Didn't call Harold, his boss. Why bother, there was no doubt Harold would call any minute. There would be the inevitable lecture about Asa's recent conduct, of course. But what could he do? *What's done is done.*

He flipped from one cable channel to another without focusing on the programming. He'd had a minor slip up—well, maybe offending his foundation's biggest donor was more than minor—but still. He was a damned good archaeologist. He'd proven himself repeatedly over the past seven years that he'd been chief archaeologist at the Coleman foundation. Besides, he—

His cell phone chirped, cutting off his musings.

The number on the readout was Harold's. Asa blew out a breath and answered it.

"Harold," he said in a weak attempt to force some enthusiasm into his voice. "How's it going?"

"We've got a couple things to discuss, Asa, as I'm sure you know."

It was probably safer if he didn't comment, so Asa waited for Harold's lecture.

"First of all—"

A loud knock sounded from the door.

"Sorry, Harold, could you repeat that?" Asa tossed the towel still on his shoulders, into the bedroom and walked to the door. "Crap," he muttered when he checked the peephole. *Rachel.*

"Asa?"

"Sorry, Harold. Can you hold on a sec?" Asa muted the phone and opened the door.

"Hey, baby!" Rachel Burton, his petite, well-endowed, sometime lover, posed seductively in the doorway, a sultry smile on her face, and a tight black dress wrapping her feminine curves. She dragged a blood red nail down his bare chest and sashayed close until their thighs were touching.

"Rachel." Asa grabbed her arms before they snaked around his waist. "I thought we decided to drop this?"

Her bottom lip puffed out in a pout, with big brown eyes adding to the sad effect that used to fool him. She brushed her lips over the rise of his left pectoral muscle. "I just came to talk, sugar. You're not going to turn me out in the cold are you?"

Knowing he had to get back to Harold, Asa sighed loudly. But, since slamming the door in Rachel's face would only cause a scene, he dropped her arms and stepped back to let her in. She was part of the reason he was in hot water to begin with. "I'll let you in, Rachel, but you have to be quiet until I'm off the phone."

She smiled suggestively and flounced past him into the room and to the bedroom beyond. "I'll be good. I promise."

Yeah, right. Asa closed the door and un-muted the phone. "Harold. Sorry to keep you waiting, I—"

"Asa, baby?" Rachel yelled from his bedroom. Asa hastily covered the phone's mouth-piece.

Rachel appeared in the bedroom doorway. "Sweetheart, you're becoming a slob …"

"Rachel, damn it."

With a self-satisfied smile, she disappeared back into the bedroom. *God, when did I turn into such an idiot?* Asa turned his attention back to the phone call. "Sorry about that, Harold—"

"I think there are *three* things I need to discuss with you instead of two. That Rachel—"

"Harold, why is my private life on the table? What's it have to do with my work?" He rubbed his temple and eased back down onto the couch.

There was silence on the other side of the line. *Not a good sign.* Harold was pissed. "Asa, Alexander Duncan is the biggest donor on the Ridgeway project, and he's one of the most conservative members of the foundation's board. You know that."

"True. But I also know he thinks I'm the most qualified archaeologist in the country to excavate Ridgeway Plantation. He wants the best, and that's me."

"He's also very old-fashioned," Harold interjected. "And if he has to choose between moral values and his choices for charitable giving, moral values win every time."

"Duncan's wanted this site restored since the nineteen seventies, Harold. It's the most important slave plantation left in Georgia. He's not going to—"

"What, have you been replaced with another archaeologist? He has the clout to demand what ever he wants."

"Asa, baby?" Rachel stood in front of him wearing a black lace bra and matching panties.

"God damn it, Rachel." Asa pulled the phone away from his ear. "I told you I was on an important call. Would you please wait?" He pulled her down beside him.

"Asa … Asa …" Harold's voice echoed tinny and small from the cell phone, and Asa looked down in horror. He'd forgotten to mute the phone. He glared at Rachel. Their indiscretion had turned into one giant headache—one that could cost him his job if he didn't get his act together. "Harold, Harold. I'm sorry."

"I'm giving you fifteen minutes to take care of your business. Then, I'm calling back. At which time, I expect to have a focused and professional discussion."

The phone line went dead.

Asa stared down at the phone. Harold had just hung up on him. The man who had championed him even before he'd completed his Ph.D. The man who had mentored him as a graduate student, sponsored the excavation for his doctoral dissertation research, then brought him on-board the Coleman Foundation three years later and guided him up the ladder until he'd become the foundation's chief archaeologist. The man who only lost his cool when someone he admired and respected had completely let him down.

Asa turned to Rachel, who had discarded her bra and was playing with her breasts. Disgust at himself, and at Rachel, roiled inside of him.

Asa stood. "Get dressed and get out."

"What?" Rachel jumped up, rubbing her bare breasts over his back as he bent to pick up discarded research journals from the floor.

With his With his jaw clenched so tightly he felt the beginnings of a headache, Asa turned, grasped her by the forearms and pushed her away from him. "I-said-get-dressed-and-get-out."

A pink flush filtered through her nut-brown complexion "Nobody talks to me like that, Asa Matthews."

"I just did." He gathered more of the papers and folders scattered around the room, placing them in neat piles on the table in the corner. For the next five minutes, he continued to straighten, and Rachel didn't move. When she finally stomped into the bedroom to get dressed, Asa sighed in relief.

Dossiers for the short-listed firms bidding on the Ridgeway Plantation Welcome Center design were in his hands when a light touch brushed his back.

"Asa…." Rachel's voice was a light as her touch. "Baby, I'm sorry."

As if he hadn't noticed her, he stacked the dossiers and his notes about each firm on the coffee table. Harold would want to know his thoughts on them when he called back and Asa intended to be ready. When he turned back to grab a group of reference books, Rachel was still standing there.

"I asked you to leave."

Rachel reached for him, but he stepped back. "Baby, you don't understand … I didn't mean to—"

Asa walked to the door and opened it. "I understand all I need to, Rach. I'm not letting some petty jealously and inconsequential love affair ruin my professional reputation, or my career. I've worked too long and too hard."

Rachel walked to the door, an angry frown on her face. "So this is goodbye?"

"Looks like."

"Nobody treats me this way." The vehemence in her sneer was lessened by the glistening of unshed tears, but Asa was unmoved. He was very familiar with Rachel's tears. Too bad they didn't mean anything.

He shut the door, politely, but firmly.

Before he reached the couch, his cell phone was ringing.

Satisfied that Rachel was no longer a problem, he grabbed his notes and the phone. He knew which firm he preferred, but wanted to give an overview of each one. "Harold, thanks for calling back. Let's get down to business...."

Kai Ellis's loud yawn filled the interior of her car as she turned into the parking garage of the Kapman, Trent and Gannon building in Midtown. She'd been up late into the night reviewing designs for the Ridgeway Plantation project. Her team made their last site visit three weeks ago and completed their final proposal, but the restoration project was still, all she thought about.

If they won, the Ridgeway job would be an exciting departure for KT & G. The last two projects the firm's historic preservation studio completed were loft renovations, and since Atlanta had been going through a "loft" trend over the past ten years, everyone in the city wanted to either live in them or develop them. Drexel Development, where Kai's soon-to-be ex-boyfriend, Kenneth Roselle, worked, had bought several dilapidated warehouses near downtown and contracted KT & G to redesign them. The commissions were great press for KT & G's historic preservation studio, giving junior architects experience in renovation work, but Kai still preferred to handle more historically significant preservation jobs. Jobs like Ridgeway Plantation. Which wasn't preservation exactly, but new development, including the design and development of a new welcome center to compliment the rice plantation's Big House and slave quarters. Winning the contract for the project would be a dream come true for Kai, and meant that the partnership at KT&G was hers.

Making partner was only part of the effort. If KT & G was to be taken seriously in the field of historic preservation, they desperately needed more stepping-stones like Ridgeway.

Ten minutes later, she exited the elevator onto the fifteenth floor of the office building. Crossing the reception area, she followed the colorful post-modern corridor, before turning left into her corner office. She dropped the drawings she carried on her drafting table and put away her purse, then headed to the wet-bar in the far corner of the room.

Focused on making fresh coffee, she didn't hear Jeremy Fuller, one of her studio heads, poke his head in. Tall and slender, he hadn't yet grown into his height, but despite his slight build, with his head of closely cropped, curly ebony hair and Hershey bar complexion, he had to beat the women off him.

"Got your email. What's up, boss lady?"

Kai nodded at the automatic drip machine. Cup at the ready, sugar packet in hand, she tapped her foot impatiently. Everybody in the studio, and probably some of their relatives, knew not to expect conversation from her until she had mainlined several hundred milligrams of caffeine.

Jeremy took a seat on the couch in front of her desk. His specialization was plantation architecture, and he was one of the best young architects she'd ever encountered. She successfully snatched him from a firm in Philadelphia when KT & G let her start the preservation studio.

A smirk curled her lip as she poured liquid adrenaline into her mug. Well, Jeremy was one thing she had to thank Kenneth for. His connections in Philly had put her onto Jeremy's scent. Jeremy had been with her for four-and-a-half years now, and when she made partner, he would follow her right up the corporate ladder. She took a long drag of coffee, then crossed back to her desk.

"Guess it's safe to talk now."

"Smart-aleck."

"Yep. So, what's up? You're not still worried about the Ridgeway job are you?"

Kai nodded and set her mug on the warmer in front of her. "I'm always worried."

He rubbed his hands together. "True, but I think we've got a good shot at this project."

"Yeah, so do I; but, you know me."

"We've paid our dues, right? We've done a lot of good stuff since you started this group." He was preaching to the choir, but Kai let her studio head talk. She needed to hear the positive words, too. "Even though we haven't been the lead on any of the big ones, we've had some pretty decent jobs. That's gotta count for something."

"We can do this, Jer. They'll see that we can." She smiled when he rubbed his hands on his jeans. "You're nervous about this project aren't you?"

"The Kid?" A sheepish smile crossed his face. "Well … kinda, sorta—a little."

"You're doing great. The team you put together to do the Design Intent Documents is top-notch. I've gone over the DID's we sent Coleman in the final bid package again, and I have to say, I couldn't have done any better myself. For the rest of the week, we're going to act as if that project is already won. Tell your team to get their questions together, because we'll be heading back to Savannah for a site visit before you know it." Jeremy grinned at her optimistic attitude and relaxed in his seat, just as Kai had intended. "And make sure your decorative arts lead gets her research notes together," she continued. "Angela's role is one of the most important."

Jeremy nodded enthusiastically. "She'll have 'em."

"Good. She has to be completely satisfied with the data the archae-ologists give her, because she's our ace in the hole. We didn't bring a Ph.D. on board just to add initials to our letterhead. We want to do this thing right."

"Right."

"Great. Now—" The phone on her desk trilled. She hit the speaker button. "Yes Christine, what is it?"

"Mr. Roselle is on line one."

Kai almost rolled her eyes, but caught herself. "I'm in a meeting. I'll have to call him back."

"He says it's urgent."

She spoke before she could catch herself. "Yeah, right."

Jeremy's eyebrows shot up. "Whoa. Guess that's my cue. I'm out."

Kai waited for Jeremy to leave before speaking again. "Christine, I'm going to take this call, but from now on, I'd like you to take a message from Mr. Roselle, all right?" She hoped her voice didn't sound too strained. Christine wasn't known for her discretion.

"No problem, boss. I'll just make myself a little note," Christine mumbled. Then, her cheerful voice piped through the tinny speaker again. "Okay, got it. Anything else?"

At that, Kai used the eye roll she'd stored up for Kenneth. "Put him through, please."

"Kai … Kenneth," came his standard reply.

"Yes, I know." She reached under the drafting table to retrieve a few rolls of Mylar that fell off when she dumped her drawings there earlier. She raised her voice to make sure the speaker caught it. "What do you want?"

"Can you take me off speaker, please? We need to talk."

Kai cut her eyes toward the phone, then continued to stack drawings. "I can close the door."

"We have things to talk about. I'm not going to do it over a speaker phone."

"And I've got work to do, which I'm not getting done gabbing to you."

"Have dinner with me."

Knowing if she said no, Kenneth would simply persist until she was on the verge of strangling him, she sighed. "Might as well get it over with," she muttered.

"What?"

"Nothing, Ken. Just talking to myself. How's the Cheesecake Factory sound?" Her mouth tilted with a smirk. "At least I can get a Raspberry Swirl Cheesecake to go along with the punishment."

Silence hung on the other end of the line, then a rustle of noise. "Talking to yourself again, I take it?" Kenneth said.

"Yep."

"I'll pick you up at your office at 6:30. We can have an early dinner."

"I'll meet you there." She was already giving him a couple of hours of her time for dinner. When she was ready to leave, she planned on leaving, not waiting on him.

"But it would be simpler if—"

"I'll meet you there, Kenneth. I've gotta go."

Asa continued eating his shrimp cocktail while he waited for his older sister, Schyler, to return from the restroom of the Cheesecake

Factory in the Buckhead section of Atlanta. He glanced around for their waiter and saw Sky weaving her way past patrons and wait-staff back to their table. They'd always looked out for each other. Several years ago, when she left her corporate business career and opened her own day spa, he stood right behind her.

Hoping his sometimes remiss manners would stave off her lecture, he smiled and rose as Schyler joined him at the table. She tucked into her Caesar salad and eyed him narrowly. Asa ate his last two jumbo shrimp while he could still enjoy them.

"Well," Sky said, resting her fork beside her plate. "I want to know what's up with you. What's going on?"

"Well … Look, Sky, I just …" He stopped himself and searched for words to explain himself, then noticed her smile. "What? I thought …"

She reached across the table to pat his hand. "What's going on with you?"

He squeezed her hand. "Um …"

"You must have gone veg. Haven't I always said that meat will kill us all?"

"Veg?" Asa's hesitancy abandoned him at the thought of joining Schyler for a lunch of tofu and alfalfa sprouts. "I don't think so, lady."

"Whatever it is, I'm glad for it. A month ago, you were jumping out of airplanes and hang gliding off the side of Grandfather Mountain in North Carolina."

Leaning back in her seat, she released his hand. "Everybody knows black men don't jump out of perfectly good airplanes. Next thing you know, you'll be bungee-jumping in Guatemala or Indonesia."

"I already did that," Asa commented causally and took a drink. "Down on Key West on the twenty-seventh of last month. Didn't even have to leave the continental US."

She stared at him in amazement for a moment, then broke into a grin that turned into a hearty laugh. "Boy, you better be glad I learned that after the fact. I would have been— No." She caught herself. "I would have told Mama."

Asa groaned, but laughed. "She would have been on a plane to Miami before the bungee cord was wrapped around my ankle."

"Sho' you right," Schyler said, then sobered. "Thought I was going to jump all over you didn't you?"

"Weren't you?"

Schyler paused, a pensive hand on her chin. "Yeah," she said after a moment. "I probably was. Definitely was," she added after he cleared his throat.

"So why didn't you?"

Schyler's grin was back. "Look at you. You look ..." She searched for just the right word. "Happy. Energized. How could I fuss, when my 'Little A' has *got it going on*."

Asa winced. "I hate it when you call me that."

"I know. So are you going to tell me what—or more to the point— *who* brought on this change of attitude?"

"Why does it have to be a who?" he protested.

"Because I know you, boy. You got rid of Rachel, didn't you?" She studied him. "You don't even have to say it. I can tell. Didn't I tell you that girl was poison? I've known it since the first time you talked about her." She waved her hand idly in the air. "Bad aura."

"Sky you've never even met her," Asa said, though he didn't dispute the assessment.

"Didn't need to. I could tell she was bad news just in how she drained your positive energy every time you spoke about her."

Asa chuckled. Schyler had gone from Louis Vuitton handbags, relaxed, perfectly coifed hair and BMWs to dreadlocks that challenged his own in length, a strictly vegetarian diet, and a healthy dose of new-age spirituality. "Whatever you say, Sky."

"But that's not all of it, is it?"

"All of what?" Self-conscious now, he sipped his wine. His sister was more perceptive than he was comfortable with at the moment. *Must be the new-age stuff.* He feigned innocence and forced himself to look up.

Schyler pursed her lips. "Getting that wench out of your life might have lightened your load, but it didn't put that drive back into you."

"I don't follow."

"You talked about the Ridgeway dig the entire time we waited for our table. You've got your excitement about your work back. It's like you finally remembered your passion—to change American archaeology with your excavations."

"And I did."

"Yes, you did, A. Two books, an A&E special and goodness knows how many awards. None of that happened by accident. You made it happen. But in the last year, you lost the drive. I still can't believe you turned down that offer from CNN."

"Let's not get into that again." Asa sighed. "I'm a working archaeologist, not an entertainer. I can't commit to a three-year contract for a television series."

She held up a hand. "I'm not trying to argue over this again. It's done and past."

"Damn right."

"All I'm saying is, all that passion and excitement was gone, but now it's back, little brother. And I just thought maybe a new woman had put that kind of light back in your eyes."

"A woman?" Asa shook his head. "Not in the way you're thinking."

"No?" Schyler's eyebrow arched. A shadow passed over their table as a waiter led a couple to their seats at the table across the aisle from them.

"No," Asa repeated.

"And what way am I thinking?"

He opened his mouth to respond, when a stunningly beautiful woman sat down at a table across the aisle. Buttoned down in a very feminine pastel suit, she was all business. Like her hair—tiny jet-black coils pulled into a tight bun—the suit's discordance with her sultry eyes and wide, full mouth, and milk chocolate skin, made a man wonder just what lurked beneath such harnessed elegance and cool. Her look was professional and serious, yet sexy and alluring at the same time.

Intriguing. Even the simple act of unfolding her napkin was a pleasant distraction. So was the wide smile she gave the waiter.

So unlike Rachel. He cocked his head at the thought as he continued to watch the woman. It wasn't the first time he'd compared a woman to Rachel lately. His thoughts drifted to Kai Ellis, an architect from one of the firms he reviewed for the Ridgeway bid. He didn't have a clue what the woman looked like, but based on her dossier, she was a woman after his own heart. Upon reviewing her resume, along with other documents in the bid package presented by her firm, Kapman, Trent & Gannon, he found her professional accomplishments quite impressive. One of only a handful of minorities at the firm, she had only been with KT & G for six years. Yet, in that short time, she skillfully climbed their corporate ladder and added a few rungs of her own. Credited with almost single-handedly increasing the firm's prestige in architecture circles by adding a historic preservation studio to their stable, her hand-picked team set the bar for high standards.

Apparently, his stares hadn't gone unnoticed. Though he had distracted her, Asa didn't manage to hold the woman's gaze. She was having a heated exchange with her companion. The guy's back was to Asa, so he couldn't see his expression, but to Asa, their argument looked to be more professional than romantic—at least on her part. But, then again, that could have just been Asa's wishful thinking. Before he got too excited, Asa decided he'd better check her ring finger when she picked up her wine glass.

"Good to go, there," he muttered under his breath when he saw her bare hand.

"I give up." Sky broke into his thoughts. "You haven't heard a word I've been saying." She shook her head. "So, no more bungee-jumping, okay?"

Maybe not bungee-jumping, Asa thought as he watched the woman across the aisle. But there was one more adventure he might have to pursue. The question was, should he?

Given that Harold's lecture still rang in his head, the answer was probably a big fat "No."

Right about now, bungee-jumping seemed a safer option; and, if he were smart, he'd book a flight to Guatamala ASAP.

"It would be a coup for us to get married."

A coup ... a coup. The words echoed through Kai Ellis's mind like a death knell signaling doom, casting the commotion of the swanky Atlanta restaurant into the background. She recognized the niggling feeling creeping up her spine. She had depended on it to get her where she was in her career to date, but for some insane reason, she had always ignored the warnings where Kenneth Roselle was concerned.

She stared over the rim of her merlot and watched her business associate. She was wasting time, when she could be back at the office redlining drawings. Better yet, she could be curled up on her queen-sized bed, sipping merlot and designing ideas for the Ridgeway Plantation Welcome Center. But no, she was fending off yet another of Kenneth's marriage proposals.

Her eyes flicked to his, then back to her wine. She considered the merlot for a moment. It was her own fault and she knew it. If she hadn't allowed Kenneth to believe marriage was a possibility, he wouldn't keep proposing. It wasn't as if their relationship was anything other than platonic, even though most people believed otherwise, which was fine with her.

On the fast track, she certainly didn't need to worry about fending off male attention, or battling her own sexual urges. Focusing on her career was her passion. As she'd hoped, her relationship with Kenneth had kept the wolves at bay, but marriage? *Not gonna happen.*

Kenneth had provided an easy out for the past six years, but a wolf had finally caught up to her. Calling a halt to their fraud of a relationship was her only choice. Watching with satisfaction as he narrowed wary eyes, she calmly set down her wine glass.

A mask of panic washed over his face, and Kenneth's hand snaked out to close over hers. "Don't turn me down again, Kai."

"This has gone on too long as it is." Unable to stand a pouting man, she pulled her hand out of his grasp. On the rare occasions she allowed herself the luxury of spending time with a man, she liked him manly. Her grandmother once warned her, "A black man has to be strong to make it in this world; strong and confident. So make sure you find yourself one who won't take crap from anybody." Yet, here she was with Kenneth.

Only once had he ever fought her on anything, and that had been four years ago. The experience had revealed a vindictive streak that she'd never known he possessed, which at the time gave her pause. But, seeing no other sign of his darker side, she dismissed her misgivings.

Realizing her thoughts were drifting, she reluctantly returned to the present. Even if she wanted to marry Kenneth, the timing wasn't right.

She signaled the waiter for the check. "If my team wins the bid for the Ridgeway Plantation restoration, I'm guaranteed to become the first African-American partner at KT & G. This is my year and I need to focus. My career comes first. I've always told you that."

Kenneth nodded enthusiastically. "That's why marriage is such a great idea. We'll be more successful than you could ever imagine."

For such a smart man, she couldn't fathom Kenneth not understanding the word "no." She didn't want to be rude, but soon, he'd leave her no other choice.

Kenneth made another grab for her hand. "Look, between your work at KT & G and mine at Drexel, we would be in the stratosphere. We'd climb so far up the corporate ladder, we'd have to carry oxygen. Just think—"

"We already work together, Kenneth. We're already successful. We don't need to be married for it to continue."

Kenneth's response faded into the distance as the stunningly attractive man at the table across the aisle caught her eye, again. Even though he was seated, she could tell he was tall. Very well built, too, distinguishing himself quite nicely in a black knit shirt and charcoal slacks. The mass of long, thin dreadlocks that trailed over his shoulders were surprisingly appealing, especially since she never had a fondness for locks. His eyes, a dark, dark brown, surrounded by full, long lashes visible across the distance, held her attention. They bored through her with such shocking intensity that Kai shifted backward in her chair.

Heat rushed up her neck and into her face, traveled downward across her breasts, then further, to settle low in her belly.

"… Didn't you?"

Feeling something brush her hand, she jerked back. A moment passed before she could refocus. When her eyes landed on Kenneth, she blinked. The contrast between him and the other man was astonishing. She glanced up carefully, discreetly. The man stood to brush a kiss on the forehead of the woman joining him. *He's the kind of man who would demand his due, then take even more.*

Kai's gaze skimmed over Kenneth, who was attractive in a conservative manner, but his skin didn't glow with the same life as the man across the aisle. Nor did Kenneth's conservative cut hair beg you to thrust your hands through it the way the other man's dreadlocks did. And nothing of Kenneth's presence, though masculine, demanded attention like the man at the other table.

"Kai. I'm talking to you."

"Yes?" Helpless to stop herself, Kai's gaze drifted back to the man with the dreadlocks. He was staring at her. She could almost feel his intense, dark eyes penetrating through her. She shuddered and pulled her eyes away. *Lord, what's happening to me?* Sex. Images of hot, sweaty, erotic sex filled her mind. She hadn't thought about sex, of any kind, in such a long time, she was afraid to calculate the date. Focusing on her work had placed sex in a position of little importance. Now, her body screamed out very loud, very lewd suggestions.

"You know you could have had the decency to tell me you've met someone else."

Kai gazed down at her salad without seeing it, her wine forgotten. Kenneth's hand anxiously grasped at hers. "Kai, I'm speaking to you."

She shook him off and placed her hands in her lap. "What?"

"Why didn't you tell me you met someone else? That's pretty disrespectful, considering we're nearly engaged."

Kai's eyes flicked up to meet Kenneth's. "We've never even been close to being engaged. I don't call a dozen marriage proposals from you and a dozen no's from me an engagement. Besides, I haven't met anyone. You know I don't have time for that, I'm working fifteen hours a day."

Kenneth shocked her with a snort.

Opening her mouth to speak, she glanced at the man at the other table. He was watching her again. She ducked her head and fumbled with the napkin in her lap.

"There it is again. That's what I mean. You're thinking about him right now."

How can I help it, when he's looking at me like he wants to eat me alive? "I … I'm sure I don't know what you mean."

Kenneth leaned forward and lowered his voice. "You look like you're thinking about … about …"

With effort, Kai forced herself to look Kenneth in the eye; but, paying attention to their conversation had become virtually impossible. "What? I look like I'm thinking about what?"

"Like you're …"

"*What?*"

"Making love with him."

"What?" she croaked. Kai cleared her throat, refolded her napkin nervously.

"I've never seen that look on your face before. All that shuddering, those pouty looks. You look like you're about to climax just thinking about him."

Talk about an understatement, Kai all but screamed. An erratic heartbeat and tightly clenched thighs with moisture building between them signified just a little bit more than Atlanta's ninety-seven percent humidity. *I'm definitely losing it.* "Is that how I look to you?" she managed to say.

"Hell yes, that's how you look." Kenneth gulped at his wine. "I'm not happy about this." He paused to set down his wine glass. "You know, if you'd given us a chance, maybe I could have awakened a little passion in you."

"Kenneth!"

"What? You're surprised I actually have a libido?" He looked down at his wine glass and mumbled. "If we were engaged, I'd show you libido."

How did this conversation get so far off topic? "This engagement fantasy of yours is over. End of discussion."

"You're making a mistake, Kai. One you'll regret. But *que sera, sera.* Right?" He raised his glass. Then with great relish, he drained the last of his wine.

They glared at one another for a few awkward moments, then he turned the conversation to topics of mutual interest. They spent the remainder of the meal discussing the Ridgeway deal and the prestige it would garner KT & G if they won. Usually the subject held her attention, but Kai's eyes continued to stray to meet those of the man across the aisle. And the more they strayed, the more distracted and disturbed she became. It wasn't like her to be so easily pulled off task. Finally, with dinner over, Kai bid her "business associate" a curt goodbye and headed toward the dessert counter near the front of the restaurant.

The Cheesecake Factory's reputation for exquisite cheesecake and other delectable confections made buying a cake or pie "To Go" a normal occurrence, so Kai wasn't surprised to find the dessert counter several bodies deep when she approached. After a few minutes of waiting, she placed her order.

"Raspberry Swirl Cheesecake, please."

She certainly hadn't made Kenneth happy tonight, but it could have been worse. She would have to move very carefully around him for the next few months.

After she signed the credit slip and took her order number, Kai turned and slammed into a hard and very masculine chest. Someone bumped her from behind, and equally masculine arms encircled her as she lost her balance. Closer now than before, she could smell his cologne. The incredible force of maleness was all around her; arms, chest, and strong, hard muscle. She would have shivered if there were room.

"Well, hello." A deep, masculine voice, warm and inviting, enveloped her.

"Sorry, I'm so sorry." Kai knew she should have stepped away, but his arms seemed to fit so perfectly around her, she couldn't make herself move. Besides, she told herself, too many people were crowded into the small area. There was nowhere else to go.

"Don't move," he whispered. It was almost an order, and she found she liked the sound of it, the feeling of his lips grazing her ear, and the tickle of his breath against her flesh. The crowd around them seemed to vanish, and this time she couldn't hold back her shudder.

Her body was aroused, and all she seemed to be able to do was go with the flow. A moan leaked out. "Mmm, nice."

"I agree," he whispered, stroking her arms lightly. "I've wanted to do this all night."

He trailed his hands up her arms then into her hair. With one quick stroke, her chignon uncurled and springy, jet-black coils sprang out and around her head like a cloud to cascade past her shoulders like a heavy rain. Kai's heart pounded in her throat as the man's hands moved to the nape of her neck. He drew his fingers up through her tangled tresses, then cupped her head and dipped to brush her lips lightly with his own. As he straightened, he lifted a few strands of her hair to his nose and drew in a long breath. Then, he stepped back.

Dumbfounded into silence, Kai looked up into dark, chocolate brown eyes so intense she could almost feel herself being sucked into their depths. This was the very man she'd lusted after throughout dinner. Long, dark brown dreadlocks hung around his face, and she couldn't decide whether they were the halo of an angel coming to her rescue, or the mane of a lion ready to devour his prey.

Self-consciously, she lifted a hand to pull her unruly hair back into its bun, but his hungry eyes swept over her, momentarily paralyzing her. The man was beautiful in a dangerous sort of way, like a lion prowling the African savanna. Now she knew this man was a lion, not an angel. He was the hunter, she the hunted.

They stood that way for a while; gaze to gaze, his eyes burning into her until she felt the heat on her face. Finally, she broke and looked away. She yearned to touch him and fondle the dreadlocks that spilled gloriously over his shoulders, falling almost to his waist. Finally, her common sense returned, and with a quick flick of her wrist, she corralled her hair back into a bun.

"You should wear it loose," he murmured, his deep voice sending shivers down her spine.

The cashier called her order.

"With a shaky gesture that belied her calm voice, Kai displayed her ticket to him.

He reached a long arm over her head to retrieve the cheesecake, then presented it to her like a gift. "It's been a pleasure. But I know you're not going to leave me hanging without even telling me your name, are you?"

His charm shouldn't have surprised her, given the skill of his seductive whispers, but it did. But, telling him her name couldn't hurt. She would probably never see him again. She accepted the dessert politely and turned to go.

He was watching when she looked back, and it warmed her. "I'm Kai Ellis," she said and smiled. The slight flicker of what seemed to be shock, or recognition, in his eyes gave her pause, but Kai dismissed it. She doubted he knew her, and heaven knows she wouldn't have forgotten meeting him. "Thanks for your help."

From the rear entrance, Kenneth stepped out of the shadows. He watched Asa Matthews, who watched Kai rush from the restaurant. Now he knew who her new lover was. The question was what to do about it.

At ten-thirty the next morning, Kai was still distracted by her out-of-body experience at the Cheesecake Factory. She was more shocked by her actions afterwards, than with what she'd allowed to happen to her at the restaurant.

She had planned to return to the office and work on the final touches for the Ridgeway project plan. But last night, after being rubbed the right way by Mr. Tall, Dark, and I-Don't-Give-A-Damn, she apparently didn't give a damn either. She had gone home, downed two glasses of wine and watched the Lifetime channel until bedtime.

Now she was paying for that little segue into irresponsibility. Thankfully, she had no meetings until the afternoon, which meant she could put her head down and work steadily until her two o'clock meeting with her vice president. She had asked Christine to hold her calls as soon as she arrived, but three hours later, she was nowhere near where she should be.

Staring absently at her half-finished project plan, she chastised herself for her lack of focus.

Christine buzzed in. "Yes, Christine, what is it?"

"Mr. Roselle is on line one."

Kai turned her attention to the speakerphone. "Christine, I told you to send Kenneth's calls to voice mail."

"He said it was an emergency." She paused, then whispered, "He's called five times already."

"You do know you can see his number on the telephone display and send him to voice mail, don't you?"

"Yeah, when I'm looking at it. I've been typing up the Cooper estimates all morning. I just grab the phone when it rings. Sorry about that."

Kai couldn't be angry because her administrative assistant was doing her job. She shook off her anger. "No, I'm the one who's sorry. I'm just a little distracted today." She rubbed the crease in her forehead. "Put him through. But, I'm setting my line to go to voice mail for the remainder of the morning."

"Done."

A second later, Kenneth's petulant voice filtered through the tinny-sounding speaker. "Kai ... I don't appreciate you avoiding me all day. We have things to talk about."

It's hardly been all day, Kai thought. "I've said all I'm going to, Kenneth. We've had this same discussion enough. You should know where I stand."

There was such a long silence on the other end that Kai moved to disconnect.

"I saw you with your lover," Kenneth practically blurted out.

Kai's hand froze an inch from the phone. "Excuse me?"

"I came back to the restaurant. Figured I'd get a dessert to take home, too."

Kai seized the receiver, effectively cutting off the speaker. Her heart throbbed in her throat so hard she couldn't squeak out a sound.

"How long?" He asked.

"Ex—excuse me?"

"I suppose you think Asa Matthews can help you make partner quicker than I can."

Kai stared at the phone, dumbfounded. "Asa Matthews? What the heck does an archaeologist for Ridgeway Plantation have to do with …"

Her voice trailed off as Kenneth's laugh crackled through the telephone, sounding almost hysterical. "Screwing him won't win you that bid, baby."

I'm not screwing anyone! She couldn't even remember what it felt like, for goodness sake.

Realization finally dawned as she belatedly put two and two together. Kenneth must have seen her at the dessert counter last night and … and … Lord have mercy on her soul. Mr. Tall, Dark, and I-Don't-Give-A-Damn was Asa Matthews.

CHAPTER TWO

As the weight of Kenneth's revelation finally sank in, Kai gripped the lip of her desk, her fingers straining with the effort as she tried to think. "What ... what are you getting at, Kenneth?" She prayed her voice didn't sound as strained to his ears as it did to hers.

"How long have you been seeing him? How long, while you've been engaged to me?"

"We're not engaged. And I just ..." How could she announce she had only met the man last night? Kenneth would never believe her. Not if he'd seen her in Asa Matthews's arms. Another drawing threatened to roll off the drafting table, and Kai grabbed for it, then smacked it onto the table. "I think you've misinterpreted—"

"I guess he'll make sure KT & G wins the bid. You know how it will look, don't you?" Kai slugged back cold coffee while he continued, "Giving his lover the project."

She lowered her mug, placing it carefully back on the warmer.

"We should get married. It'll look better all around."

"Is that what this—Damn it, Kenneth." She stretched the phone cord to angle around the desk and sofa, but couldn't quite reach the door. "Hold on." She put the receiver down and slammed her office door. "I can't believe you. All this to make me change my mind about your proposal?"

"It's best we get married. If KT & G wins this bid, what do you think people will say? Your precious reputation will be in the dirt. Oh ... and you can forget about the partnership."

Kai's eyes widened at the vindictiveness in Kenneth's voice. She had known and trusted Kenneth with her reputation and her career for six years. Now she wondered whether she had ever really known him.

But there's nothing going on, remember. She was ethical, hard working. "My team is going to win this bid Kenneth, and I'm going to make partner. *And*, I'm going to do it without marrying you."

Kenneth laughed. "You just think about what I said. I'll call you in a few days."

The line went dead and Kai sat stunned, the receiver still at her ear. Her mind painted a picture of Asa Matthews. She hadn't gotten away from him after all. The scary thing was, she was beginning to think maybe she hadn't wanted to get away from him.

Later that day in Harold Ackerman's office, Asa stretched out his long legs and let out a heavy sigh. He had been back in Atlanta for three weeks now, and Harold's office was the last place he wanted to be. But, as the director of funding at the Coleman Foundation, Harold held all the cards. Harold's day-to-day duties didn't normally include oversight of projects outside of the budget, but he had championed Ridgeway Plantation since before the main house on the site had been restored, so it was a pet project of his. That had been five years ago, but time had done nothing to dampen the man's enthusiasm. The current effort included excavating and preserving outbuildings and slave cabins. The glamorous part of the project. Harold was more than excited to take the lead.

Asa liked to keep Harold happy, but he had a feeling when the director made his way into the office, the conversation would not be a positive one. Fidgeting, he opened his DayTimer. His To-Do list for the month was still a mile long, and he knew Harold would grill him about his latest manuscript. Revisions were due to his editor in less than two months, and he wasn't anywhere near completing them. If Asa knew Harold, the man had already contacted Mona to get a status and would already know the answers to all his questions before he asked them. Asa's summons from Savannah still chaffed. So he was a little behind on the revisions. He'd get them done, His vibe was just off lately.

Vibe off lately, he rubbed an agitated hand over his face. Now that he was back in Atlanta, things would get better. His career as a fellow at the Foundation was on track. Especially now that he'd gotten Rachel out of his hair. Harold couldn't complain any longer about Asa's personal life getting in the way of work.

Then again, there was Kai Ellis to worry about. He was still in shock over that little turn of events. He couldn't chalk it up to simple coincidence, so he fished through every document he'd been given by the firms bidding on the project and finally found a newsletter photo that included Kai. It was grainy, but clear enough to verify that the Kai Ellis he'd met in The Cheesecake Factory was the same Kai Ellis bidding for the Ridgeway project. The same Kai whose firm he'd already decided, when he was in Savannah, was his choice to win the bid.

He'd have to control himself around her. Damned if she wasn't smart, successful, *and* sexy. How often did a man stumble across the total package? *Never.* He thought back to the restaurant and the way Kai's body had melted against him, almost in supplication. Damn, but he loved a woman who wasn't afraid of her sexuality. Rachel had been like that, too. He wouldn't have a woman who was otherwise.

Those slightly slanted, exotically dark eyes of hers had spoken volumes to him that night. He still couldn't get the memory out of his head. The only surprise was the way she pulled back when she realized she'd been groping him. Of course, no woman wanted to appear that hot and ready, at least not with a man they had just met. The way she'd hurried out of the restaurant had given him a good look at the rest of her. She had legs that whispered sweet nothings to him, and a heart-shaped rear-end that cupped prettily in a tailored business suit. Even her fingers, twirling her hair back into that bun, had turned him on.

Asa adjusted his pants. Maybe it was a good thing Kai had run out of the restaurant. Messing with Rachael had jeopardized his career enough. He couldn't take a chance with Kai Ellis, too. They would be working together, and he didn't intend to blow things again. His career was too important.

Now, how he'd stay away from her, he didn't have a clue. The perfect woman didn't come along every day, after all.

"Sorry to keep you waiting," Harold said when he arrived. Short and stocky, in his early fifties, he sat down and slipped reading glasses on his nose. "How's the book coming?"

"Well ..." Asa tried not to squirm. "Not as far as I'd hoped, but I'm getting there." He had a tendency to put the writing off until the last minute, which often left no time for editorial review.

Harold believed professionalism and quality was the natural result of focus and efficiency. But most importantly, discipline. It had taken them nearly two years of wrangling and ego-busting, but Harold had taught Asa the value of the concept, whether he wanted to learn it or not.

When he was hired as a research fellow at Coleman, Asa was cocky, full of himself, spontaneous and undisciplined. His dissertation had been completed in spurts of inspiration, instead of consistent, sustained work. Churning out the monthly research articles Coleman expected from him demanded the kind of discipline he'd never had to learn. The research was fun and compelling, so he never had to push himself to do that. But he hated rigorous academic writing. Fortunately, Harold's attentive persistence had made Asa a better person and a better scholar. He still had times of weak discipline—now being one of those times— but Asa had nothing but respect for Harold, so he sat up straighter in his seat at Harold's cool observation.

Harold removed his glasses, tucking them in his breast pocket. "I'm sorry, son. I didn't quite catch that."

"Just behind a little, but I'll get it done. I have two months yet."

"Mona likes to have time for one last fact check."

More than he cared to, Asa knew Mona's tendencies. On his last two books, the woman almost killed him with her anal-retentive habits.

"You know, your cockiness got you into this fix; that, and your stupid rivalry with Bill Jameson."

Leave it to Harold to cut to the bone; but, truth was truth, and now Asa was paying. Stupidity and pride had Asa working with Mona on another book because of Bill's challenge. Otherwise, Asa never would have done it. Eight months ago, he'd spoken to another editor at Hyperion Press about switching when Bill threw down the gauntlet, calling him a wuss, saying he couldn't handle his own editor.

And now he was in a mess because he'd been in the wrong frame of mind when he signed his latest contract. But he had an itch about the Ridgeway Plantation. They'd discovered a slave cemetery on the grounds last year, hence his desire to write another book so soon after the previous one. The cemetery hadn't surprised him, since much of his research and early excavations pointed to it. But, after nine months of excavation work his assumptions had proven incorrect. Carbon-dating placed the cemetery at circa 1855. Another one existed, one older than what they had already found. One that was at least fifty years older, maybe even seventy-five. A discovery would be a major find, possibly making it the oldest slave cemetery ever discovered in Georgia given the fact slavery was outlawed in the state until 1750. The issue had been gnawing at him for over a month, and he couldn't finish the draft of his book until he resolved the problem. Unfortunately, resolution meant finding the gravesite. He wanted to publish a slam dunk, not a moderately important finding.

"… too cocky, and this competition you're in with Bill needs to end. I don't want to see you make a major blunder because of these games," Harold was saying.

"I'm not worried about Bill."

"Oh no?" Harold opened a sleeve of documents and handed them to Asa.

"What's this?"

"The lecture schedule for the next six months. We've got three at the Cresge Foundation."

Asa winced. He hadn't made any friends on his last visit to Philly's most prestigious historical society. In fact, he'd probably lost a few after challenging the Foundation's largest donor, Thomas Craghill, IV on the man's revisionist suppositions about the Underground Railroad in Pennsylvania. "Those crackpots up there—"

"Those *crackpots*, as you call them, are major donors and sponsors whom Coleman wants to keep as major donors and sponsors. Bill's gotten the go ahead to speak since Craghill's still miffed over your deliberate dig at revisionist historians in your last speech."

"Bill's going to go kiss Craghill's ring so he'll continue to be a Coleman sponsor?" Asa scowled. His dislike for both men never failed to get the better of his temper.

When Harold narrowed his eyes, Asa blanked his face and sat back in his chair, ordering himself to relax. The lecture circuit brought in new funding, but it was also a demotion for a scientist. Nervous, and a little concerned about the warning Harold was attempting to convey, Asa handed the documents back. "So what else we got going?"

"A dinner at the Hermitage Plantation Foundation in Savannah in a month, and a speech at Reddington House next week."

"Which have nothing to do with me."

"None of these have been assigned to you." Harold narrowed his eyes. "I don't know what's gotten into you over the past few months, but I need you back on track, son. The run-in you had up in Philadelphia was bad enough. I don't need you reneging on your responsibilities with Mona as well."

"I'm not rene—"

Harold's hand silenced him. "You're the brightest thing to come along in American Archaeology in a long, long time. But after eight years, you're not a prima donna any longer. I thought I had broken you of that anyway." He paused. "You're falling back into your old ways.

Between this rivalry you're carrying on with Bill—which I still don't understand—and your lack of progress on this book, not to mention the way you've been carrying on with women; I have to say, you're chugging down the wrong track."

Women? One woman. He decided to skirt the female issue and hoped Harold would leave it alone, too. "It's not Bill," Asa said. "And it's not Craghill. They just happened to get in the way of my mood."

"Okay, then. What's the problem?"

"The cemetery."

"You found the Ridgeway Cemetery. Months ago. You should have plenty of data to write a few chapters about your preliminary findings. The book's not just about the cemetery, after all."

Asa waved his hand in irritation. "No ... no. It's not the right cemetery. That's what I keep telling everybody. The cemetery's too young. There's another one—an older one that I want to write up in the book. I just haven't found it yet."

Harold's sigh was irritating, but not unexpected. "Asa, you don't have time for all that. Even if you found it today, you wouldn't have enough data for a write up."

"I've been gathering data for a year. I have mountains of documentation that's been pointing the way. Even if we don't have time to do anything more than a preliminary survey, I'll have enough to fill an entire section in the book. At least three chapters, maybe four or five. All I need is to find it."

Harold propped his spectacles on his nose again and studied his desk calendar. "Mona says you're almost a month behind on one of your deadlines."

"It's just the cemetery. Everything else is done."

"What if you don't find it?"

"I guess I'll have to write-up the one we've all ready found."

"Where do you stand on the text for that one? Is it done?"

"Uh ... no, not quite. But it's getting there."

"How much?"

"Fifty percent?"

"Are you asking or telling me?"

"Okay, it's about forty percent done."

Harold made a note on his calendar. "All right. I'm giving you two weeks to find the cemetery. After that, the other one goes in the manuscript. Understood?"

"Yeah, understood." Asa readied himself to leave.

"But that doesn't mean you don't have to work on the manuscript for two weeks. I want you writing up the cemetery you have right now. If you find the other one, that'll give you six weeks to get the draft completed." He peered pointedly over his spectacles as Asa headed out. "Oh, one more thing. The meeting with the Welcome Center Steering Committee's been moved up to tomorrow. You said during our phone conversation last week, you'd come to a decision."

Asa groaned. "Maybe Richard should handle that. We've already spoken."

He wasn't so sure he should be the one making the final decision about the bid. If it ever came out that he and Kai met *before* the bid was awarded—it was a disaster he didn't even want to contemplate.

"Son."

The single word was filled with warning and made Asa feel five, instead of thirty-two.

He eased off the doorjamb and dropped his arms.

"I called you in to advise you that your professionalism is in need of serious repair." Harold removed his specs and stood up. "And you stand here telling me that Richard is capable of handling project responsibilities that are clearly yours?" He glared at Asa. "I expect to see you in that meeting tomorrow, book or no book. And by the way, I want you managing this thing the rest of the way, I don't care what you and Richard worked out."

"But …"

Harold held up a hand. "You'll do it, or I'm cutting your funding. You'll be giving lectures to sponsors, just like Bill, for the next eighteen months, is that clear?"

Asa sighed. Harold didn't say it directly, and he wouldn't, but he was still angry over the phone call when Rachel was in Asa's hotel room.

"I said, is that clear?"

"Yes, sir. It's clear." What he wouldn't make clear was that he agreed with Harold. He shouldn't have suggested Richard make the decision in the first place. He could make the decision—he had already done it anyway. He was a professional and so was Kai. They could handle the situation like mature adults, and they could make it work.

The next day, the scent of freshly brewed coffee greeted Asa as he strolled down the Foundation's well-appointed halls. The meeting with the Steering Committee wouldn't start for another thirty minutes, which gave him plenty of time to grab some java and meet with Richard before hand.

Thank God for Richard. Maybe they could still fix it so Asa could focus on managing the project while Richard babysat the winning architecture firm. They had planned things out long before Harold had brought down the hammer yesterday, but there were still details Asa could finesse. He needed Richard's presence on the project for propriety's sake. He couldn't have people thinking he had something going with the lead architect, even though that's what would probably happen.

Asa opened the double doors to the conference room, where Richard sat peering critically at a calendar and notepad spread before him. An associate professor at Wilburson University in suburban Atlanta, Richard specialized in the etymology of Black English.

"Wassup, Richard." Asa greeted him with a half-hug, half-handshake, then turned to help himself to coffee from the service near the door. There was an edge to Richard's typically absent-minded grunt, but Asa brushed it aside and sat down opposite him. "So, are we cool with the plan?"

When Richard grunted again, Asa tapped him on the skull with his Mont Blanc.

"What? Huh?"

"What's up with you, man?"

The guilty look Richard gave him when he finally raised his head did not bode well. "Aw, hell." Asa jammed his Mont Blanc into the breast pocket of his shirt and sat back. "You're backing out on me."

"No, not exactly. But, there's been a slight change."

"So much for well laid plans."

"Hold up, now." Richard raised a hand before Asa could voice his protests. "Something serious has happened." Asa cocked an eyebrow, wondering whether Richard's easy agreement weeks before had merely been a pacifying gesture. "One of my colleagues had a heart attack last week. Everyone in the department has to help pick up the slack while he's recovering."

"So what are you saying?"

Richard shrugged. "My teaching load is the lightest …"

Asa added a few more choice phrases under his breath. How the hell was he supposed to get his book completed now when he still had that cemetery to find and would be saddled with a group of self-centered architects as well?

"Sorry, man, I know you need to get your book done."

That and keep the funding he needed to excavate the slave cemetery. He made no attempt to hide his irritation at Richard's news. "You've studied the firms that are bidding, toured 'em around the site. Who's your pick?"

"You've got yours figured out, right?"

Asa nodded. "I still want your opinion."

Richard tilted his head in consideration. "Well, two are at the top of my list. KT & G is pretty new to the game, but still well qualified."

Glad Kai's firm made Richard's top picks, Asa felt more comfortable. "Who else?"

"Well, there's Armstrong Cole in Philadelphia." Asa cut a sharp look in Richard's direction. The Philadelphia firm was last on Asa's list. "Yeah. Figured you wouldn't like that. Actually, Chicago's Markum and Abbot is also good."

"I don't like the idea of them being north of the Mason-Dixon Line. A southern firm might have a better connection to the subject matter."

Richard nodded. "That's why I'm also leaning toward KT & G."

"Then KT & G'll be our choice. Are you good with that?"

"I'm cool with it," Richard replied, looking up from his calendar.

Kai's firm. Asa considered the negative ramifications of having Kai Ellis in such close proximity when he wanted to do unprofessional and indecent things to her luscious little body.

Fifteen minutes later, the proposal review team, including Harold, Asa, Richard, Rod Maraguichi, Tom Fogerty, and Bill Jameson, convened in the conference room. Harold handed each of the men present a large stack of folders.

"We've narrowed the short list to five firms," Harold said. "You've seen these before, but we'll review them as a group."

The committee thumbed through the documents as Harold continued. "This has been tough, but I'm sure all of you are glad that we've finally managed to whittle down the list of seventeen architecture firms to five."

He nodded to Asa and Richard. "I know you've met representatives from all of the firms during their tours of Ridgeway, but to refresh your memory, Bill is going to take us through the proposals of the five left in contention. We'll do a round robin for comments. Then, of course, Asa, you and Richard have the final say. It's your baby after all." Harold turned and nodded to Bill Jameson who rose from his seat and approached the podium.

Bill Jameson, a short and wafer thin man with a perpetual frown, scurried from the projector, set halfway down the conference table, to the podium. "Good morning, gentlemen." Through thick glasses, he blinked rapidly, and smiled at everyone present. Everyone except Asa. His smile slipped to a flat line when their gazes met. Asa watched with satisfaction as Bill's eyes skittered away from the challenge to focus on his notes.

"I've numbered your packets. Each one contains marketing materials for the respective firms." He held up selections from one of his packets. "Included in each packet are resumes, a set of preliminary sketches of their proposed solution, and of course, a cost-estimate. We'll start with the packet labeled 'number one.'"

Asa opened the first folder, the firm from Philadelphia. Memories of their site visit were still vivid in his mind. They were only on-site for three days, but managed to damage several pieces of equipment, including an expensive self-leveling rotary laser—which they had yet to pay to replace—and they had absconded with some artifacts as if they were collecting souvenirs.

Bill turned on an overhead projector and dimmed the lights. "Armstrong Cole Architects has been in existence since 1875 and have specialized in architecture and interior restoration for the past 100 years. Their emphasis is on restoration, rehabilitation, and preservation planning ..."

Droning on about the Philadelphia group, Bill showed slide after slide of their finished work. The man might be kissing up to Craghill, Asa thought, but that was as far as his influence would go. Asa's gaze wandered back to his DayTimer where he jotted down Kai's name.

Kai Ellis. Architect. 30.

Sexy female architect. He scribbled below Kai Ellis's name, then drew a dark double line underneath it, thinking back to that night at the restaurant.

Though her animated conversation had drawn his attention, her hair demanded he linger. Pulled into a bun at the back of her head, he could tell the long thick coils—a stunning jet black—were all natural. But what he liked most was the wildness. Sexy and out of control, it made him fantasize about the person underneath. He could already see her tresses fanned out on his pillows while he made long, luxurious love to her. Even from across the aisle, he'd felt a connection cracking like lightening between them as her mouth—pinched from arguing with her date—softened when she looked his way.

He'd been fascinated, finding the transformation a pleasant surprise. But Ms. Ellis, Kai, had appeared downright startled. She obviously had no more control over the passion he saw blazing in her eyes than she did over the riot of hair that threatened to spill out of that rigid bun. Just like her hair, she seemed a mass of contradictions, and in an instant, he knew he wanted her. He had this crazy need to find out why she would tie up such beautiful hair, instead of releasing it to fly.

"So what's your take on them, Asa?"

Richard kicked him under the table. Oblivious of the others awaiting his response, he darted an angry glance at his friend.

"Ahem." Bill cleared his throat. "Your thoughts on Philadelphia, Asa?"

"Oh, uh … competent, very good work."

"Quite, quite," Bill agreed.

"But they aren't the team for us."

"Why not?" Bill's thin shoulders slumped.

Harold removed his spectacles and peered down the long conference table. "What makes you say that, Asa?"

He relayed his experiences with the group during their site tour, and the men around the table, appalled by the firm's lack of professionalism, nodded in agreement.

Except Bill who was tight-lipped. "Well, then. Let's move on, shall we? Firm number two is from Chicago. Richard, I believe you hosted them at the site."

As the presentation continued, Asa had to struggle to pay attention. With Richard's bombshell and Asa's own deadlines hanging around his neck like an albatross, he was afraid to even think about Kai Ellis's possible role on the project.

"Any comments on number two, Asa?"

"They're good. I saw some of their work down in New Orleans."

After comments from others around the table, Bill continued. "Firm number three is Kapman, Trent, and Gannon from here in Atlanta."

Asa opened the folder and smugly flipped through the proliferation of marketing materials. "This team is new to historic preservation. I know most of the premier preservation firms on the east coast, but I had never heard of this one until we started the evaluations."

Bill perked up, apparently pleased that Asa hadn't criticized the Chicago firm and equally happy that he liked KT & G. Asa smiled back at him, then enjoyed the shock and wariness on Bill's face.

"They've done well, though, considering their newness to historic preservation," Asa added.

With a nod, Bill agreed. "That's right. They've done several loft renovations, two of which were period restorations."

Lofts? Asa mouthed derisively. Why was Bill discussing lofts? Was he trying to give the edge to the Chicago firm? Because the KT & G team had certainly done more than loft renovations. "They're a little more experienced than that, Bill," Asa said. "What about their work in Milledgeville, Georgia last year? They won a national design award for that project."

Bill paged quickly through his documents, stumbling in his haste to praise the firm. "You are correct, Asa. They did restoration work at a mansion in Milledgeville, Georgia." He glanced around the room at the other committee members. "This is a very good sign. From 1803-1868 Milledgeville was the state capital, you know. It boasts over two hundred architectural landmarks, several of which are listed on the National Registry of Historic Places."

What are we, high school students? Asa wanted to ask.

Harold wheeled his hand at Bill, prompting him to move along.

"Yes … right." Bill fumbled to put up the next slides. "They've also completed three or four restoration jobs for residential customers. They are indicated in your packet." Asa sat back in his chair and crossed his arms while Bill stumbled on. "The firm has also participated in five major restoration projects with other well-established architecture firms." Bill beamed at the men sitting around the table. "It's quite a lot of activity for a firm not known for historic preservation. And all of the projects, except three, which are still in progress, have been completed over the past five years. Pretty good for newbies."

"Yeah, well … nice of you to share, Bill," Asa said, wondering why Bill was trying to make Kai's firm sound unqualified.

Bill's eyes narrowed. The tightness around his mouth was unmistakable as he glared at Asa. Asa's eyes wandered to the clock that ticked slowly—too slowly—on the wall near the door.

CHAPTER THREE

The meeting seemed to drag on and on, but Bill finally completed his review of the short list. After Harold asked for input from the others present, he finally allowed Asa to announce the decision he and Richard had agreed on. Bill was the only one displeased, but Asa hadn't expected different. Bill's accusation, during the meeting, that Asa hadn't done his homework wasn't a surprise either. It was as if he thought Asa had closed his eyes and wiggled his finger chanting eeny-meeny-miney-moe.

When Harold adjourned the meeting, Asa stood and closed the KT & G dossier with such a triumphant flourish, even Richard eyed him suspiciously. "What's up with you, man?"

"Nothing, my brother." They headed out. "Absolutely nothing."

"I know you, A. Something's up." The self-satisfied smile on Asa's face broadened into a full grin at Richard's wary gaze. "Something's up. Or you're up to something."

They paused at the elevator bank, and Richard waited expectantly.

"You remember I told you about that sexy—"

"Asa." Harold ambled down the corridor behind them. "Hold on a minute. I'd like a word before you leave."

"No problem." Asa grinned at Richard, who was swearing under his breath. "I'll catch you later, Richard."

"I know this is short notice," Harold said as they continued down the hallway to his office. "But since KT & G is local, I thought you could go ahead and meet with the lead architect."

"When? Today?" *Please.* Asa kept his expression mild and tried hard not to look anxious.

"Oh, no, no. The firms don't even expect us to make a decision until sometime tomorrow." Harold nodded at a passing executive as they entered his office suite. "Gayle will call the firms this afternoon to let them know a decision's been made." He glanced at his executive secretary to see if she'd heard. "KT & G," he told her. After she nodded in response, he turned back to Asa. "Why don't you stop back here around 4:30? I'll give you Kai Ellis's contact information so you can set up a meeting with her for tomorrow."

Asa nodded. "It won't be soon enough for me," he mumbled under his breath.

"What was that?"

"Uh ... I said 'looks like a *fate accompli'*."

When Asa walked out onto the balcony of his apartment at midnight, the Atlanta air was balmy and thick with humidity. A few lights still twinkled in the night's sky, capping Atlanta's secondary skyline—the financial center in Buckhead. He should have been working on his book, not standing on the balcony of a Coleman Foundation corporate apartment thinking about Kai Ellis. He lingered for a moment to enjoy the light breeze and the view of the North Georgia Mountains in the distance.

After a few minutes, he sat down in the closest patio chair and chugged a bottle of spring water, wondering what Kai was doing on a Monday, at midnight. Probably the same thing he was doing. The same thing he had been doing for the past eight years. Working. Fulfilling his professional dreams and loving each and every moment. Mostly.

His thoughts returned to his conversation with Harold from the day before. Just because his mouth reacted quicker than his brain at times, didn't mean he wasn't a dedicated scientist. He worked his butt off. Maybe he didn't make a deliberate show of his efforts the way Bill Jameson did, but he worked three times as hard.

Refusing to dwell on the past, he drained the last of his water and set the empty bottle on the table beside him. Things were coming together. His love life had calmed down, and now that he'd discovered mutual interests with Kai Ellis, maybe settling down was in the cards. He'd been fantasizing about taking her to bed since he'd first laid eyes on her, but now he could imagine much more. There was a lot more to the woman than a gorgeous body and great hair.

He crossed his ankles and stared out at the night sky. Kai Ellis would fit him, his life, his drive and determination. She had the same passion, the same fire. He had seen it in her eyes at the restaurant, and could see it in her professional work. She was one hell of an architect, and man, would they burn up the sheets when they finally got together.

Pre-Kai, as Asa had taken to calling the period before her employment at KT & G, the firm's founders were known as the strip mall wizards of the Southeast. They were good at what they did, profitable and respected. But strip malls were the only things they built. During the Kai Ellis era, however, they had branched into historic preservation, winning several awards and garnering impressive recognition for the quality and authenticity of their work. Even their loft renovations were exceptional.

A small measure of pride touched him. As much as he desired her physically, he was also proud of Kai and of her accomplishments.

He was equally impressed with her design team. Most of them had been with her since the beginning. They even called themselves "The Family," and they definitely loved Kai. That was clearly evident in the KT & G newsletter someone had slipped into the KT & G dossier. The issue highlighted her preservation studio. There were fan letters to the "boss lady" and even a few editorial cartoons. Evidently, her French-twisted bun was her trademark. When Asa read one cartoon, which offered a reward for a photo or reasonable facsimile of Kai with her hair loose, he laughed aloud. He had done the impossible without even realizing the significance.

The offices of Drexel Development were perched at the very top of the Crescent Building, on floors forty-five through forty-seven. Set right on Peachtree Street, in the heart of Midtown Atlanta, the onyx and chrome tower owned the skyline. Only the Bank of America Tower was taller.

Kenneth Roselle's window office was smack in the middle of a row of junior executive offices on the forty-seventh floor, and just like his office, his rank as a junior executive was neither at the top or the bottom, but in the middle; the boring, unnoticed middle. At the moment, he was standing in his middle office, in the center window, going completely unnoticed and in imminent danger of becoming invisible, if he wasn't careful. He gripped a five iron in his hands, and was terribly tempted to take a swing at the wall of glass in front of him.

He stared out over the city's skyline, where office lights were just beginning to twinkle. It was a little after six a.m., and Bill Jameson was late. Normally Kenneth would be irritated, but today he was glad for the extra time alone. He had barely begun to calm down from Kai breaking things off with him, when he discovered she had won the bid for the Ridgeway Plantation restoration. The entire situation made him sick. To his stunned disbelief, she'd been serious that night at the restaurant, refusing to hear reason and even resisting his threats.

He had even tried arguing, though they hadn't argued much in the past. But that night at the restaurant, she held firm, shutting him out of her life just when all their hard work together was finally beginning to pay off.

When he'd walked back into the Cheesecake Factory that night, he'd been angrier than he could remember being in a long time, but almost walking up on her and Asa Matthews groping each other in the middle of the freaking restaurant had him seeing red.

Kenneth's fingers tightened around the golf club in his hands. If he'd had a five iron that night, that walking can of testosterone named Asa Matthews would have a Titleist Pro V1-sized hole in his skull.

Kenneth hadn't managed to subdue his anger since, and Kai had made it even worse when he called her the next day at work. He figured scaring her about the partnership she was hoping to win would be enough to get her to see reason and finally agree to an engagement. She wanted that partnership more that anything in the world. The thought that she'd screw up her chances over a conflict of interest with a womanizer like Matthews blew Kenneth's mind. Leave it to Kai to think that her work could stand on its own. Well, he was here to tell her the world didn't spin in that direction.

Despite himself, Kenneth couldn't help wondering about her relationship with Matthews. How long had they been seeing each other? Six months? Longer?

The thought of her making love to Asa Matthews when she would never spread her legs for him made him want to puke. Six years. Six damned years of coddling her, working with her, showing her respect, kindness and gratitude. Where had it gotten him? No damn where. And God, she was so beautiful. Those sexy eyes and crazy hair. She had never worn her hair down for him. All those nights they'd spent at her place or his, developing bid proposals for joint projects, and not once had she ever allowed him to touch, only to walk up on her in another man's arms in a public place, with her hair flowing down her back and Matthews's fingers tangled in it. Kenneth swung the golf club against the glass window with all his might, then watched it bounce back, reverberating in his hands.

"Am I interrupting?"

Kenneth cursed at the sound of Bill's voice. "You want to tell me how the hell KT & G won that Ridgeway contract?" He said without turning around. "You said Chicago or Philly had it wrapped up."

"Oh, yes. That." Bill stepped hesitantly into the room.

Kenneth pitched his golf club into the corner of the office where several balls and clubs were scattered and returned to his desk. "Well, what are you standing there for? Sit down and give me a report."

"Yes. Yes. Of course." Bill sat down, his nervousness apparent in the way he glanced around the room. "How have things been going for you?"

"I don't have time for small talk. What's going on over there at the foundation?"

"Well, we gave KT & G the Ridgeway bid. They'll be submitting a detailed budget this week and will probably start sending their architects and decorative artists to the plantation in the next two weeks." Bill fidgeted with a brown accordion file he'd brought with him. After unwrapping the elastic cording, he withdrew a sheath of papers and offered them to Kenneth. "We have several other projects that we'll announce RFPs for soon. You get the first peek."

"Do I look like I care about the next projects?"

"They're great projects. One of which I've spent a great deal of time doing research on. Paulsy House. It's a townhouse in Charleston that was allowed to stand when the Union set fire to the South during the Civil War. It was the residence of a relative of General Grant's wife. She wouldn't allow it to be burned."

Kenneth's interests lay in nothing but the Ridgeway Project, but he tempered his impatience and politely took the papers. "It's an important project, you say?"

"Oh, yes. Definitely. It's a beautiful little Georgian style mansion-nette. But inside, it contains the most wonderful Federalist interior architecture and furnishings. Most of which have managed to stay in the home or within the Paulsy family."

To Kenneth's disgust, Bill settled back in his seat. The man couldn't possibly think giving him a heads-up on new projects would salve his anger. Kenneth thumbed through the papers and tried to get a handle on his temper. "So you've been researching the Paulsy?"

The man nodded rapidly, causing his comb-over to flutter. "For the past three months." He clutched at the accordion file. "Along with other duties, of course."

"Of course." Kenneth toyed with the gold-dipped golf ball paperweight on his desk, straightened his desk blotter. He didn't need to look up to know Bill was getting more nervous. Finally, Kenneth looked up, a charming smile on his face. "And what duties are those? I know I've asked before, but fill me in again. I've got so many things in my head, I tend to forget."

"Oh, the usual. Assessing properties for the Historic Preservation Society National Registry. People think their homes can be put on the registry so easily." He shook his head, pursed his lips. "But as you know, strict qualifications have to be met."

"Mmm. What else?"

"Well, um. Research. Research on the Paulsy. I published an article about it in Architectural Review. Then there was the bid proposal assessment for Ridgeway, of course. That's done now. And … and speaking engagements. Several of them."

"You've been doing quite a bit of speaking lately, haven't you, Bill?" He tossed the paperweight absently in one hand.

Bill swallowed, nodded.

"Last time I saw you …" Kenneth set down the paperweight and tilted his head, pretending to remember, then snapped his fingers and smiled. "Oh, yes, that's right. You've been doing speaking engagements for the past twenty-four months, haven't you?"

The accordion file crunched, collapsing under Bill's white-knuckled grip. "Eighteen."

"Pardon me, eighteen. I'm still surprised it wasn't twenty-four." He sat back, a little smile tipping the corners of his mouth. "The Foundation doesn't like it when scientific evidence is fabricated, do they?" Bill stared at him for so long, Kenneth wondered if the man was still breathing. "I suppose you're just lucky to still have your job. Nasty subject, your suspension. But, I'm getting off track, again. What were we talking about? Oh, yes. What you've been working on. So, they've let you start doing research again?"

Bill mumbled something.

"Sorry, I didn't catch that." He waved it off. "Never mind, it's not important. I do need a favor from you, however, since you didn't follow through on the last one."

"But, I didn't promise—" Bill took a breath. "I figured you wouldn't mind too terribly much if KT & G won the bid. You and Kai Ellis …" he trailed off, looked out the window as if hoping for support from the heavens, then looked back at Kenneth. "Won't this benefit Drexel Development as well?"

Kenneth wasn't about to admit that his failure to convince Kai to include a few retail shops in the welcome center design had cost him dearly in the eyes of the people that mattered at Drexel. He shrugged. "Doesn't matter to me, really. What I want to know is what's going on with her and Asa Matthews?"

He watched as Bill picked his memory. "Going on? I'm not sure what you mean. Aren't you two …"

Bill knew that he and Kai were a couple, or that they were supposed to be. Bill had met them a little over two years ago at a Coleman Foundation fundraiser where he was trying to schmooze his way a little higher in the organization. He'd been hungry for ways to make a name for himself then, and since Kenneth needed some contacts as well, he and Bill had connected and remained tight. Bill had been smitten by Kai immediately, just as so many of the shy, insecure men in academia were when they met her, but as usual, she barely noticed.

She didn't recognize the advantage her beauty could be, Kenneth mused. Lord knows if she did more socializing and networking, she could win more projects with her face alone than by any work the two of them did together.

Back then, he couldn't convince Kai to use her sex appeal to their advantage, but his interaction with Bill had paid off. The man had contacts galore, a network of preservationists all over the country. And Kenneth hadn't failed to take advantage of the insider connections. He and Kai had won several projects because they played to the personal strengths—or weaknesses—of committee members Bill had so naively supplied Kenneth.

Kenneth pulled his thoughts back to the present. "How do they know each other?"

"I wasn't aware they did. He's been out in the field for the past—"

"Could they have met on site? All the architecture firms made visits to Ridgeway Plantation."

"Yes, of course. How could they put a bid together without—" Bill stopped, apparently remembering something. Kenneth leaned forward in anticipation, almost swearing under his breath, but caught himself in time.

"What is it?"

"Yes. They visited the site. And Asa was there." His lips formed a sneer over Matthews's name.

Kenneth hadn't realized that Bill disliked Asa, but wasn't that a useful tidbit of information. He filed it away.

"But the other archaeologist, Richard Dunlop toured KT & G around the site. As far as I know, Asa didn't come into contact with them at all. In fact—no, he didn't. He made a point of avoiding everyone. He can't stand having outsiders on location. Just wants to work with the other researchers and graduate students. Ridgeway has always been his baby, and he hates the idea that the foundation wants to commercialize it already."

Kenneth sneered. "Look, I need something I can use against Matthews.

Chewing on his inner jaw, Bill reluctantly said, "Well, he's on the verge of being censured." He smiled cautiously.

"Come again?"

Bill's smile became smug, confident, his nervousness a memory. "The Director of Funding isn't too happy with the way he carries on with women. Matthews has them visiting him on site or at speaking engagements. It looks bad; he treats them terribly, too."

Bill apparently needed no prompting to speak now, so Kenneth kept quiet, listened, and gathered ammunition.

"He's also alienated some very important contributors." Bill stared through Kenneth to pluck at a memory. "He's very opinionated, and doesn't often know when to keep his mouth closed. Of course, Harold Ackerman is getting paid back for all the deference he's shown Asa over the years. He's finally realized that the sun doesn't rise and set in Asa Matthews's ass."

Obviously shocked by what he had just said, Bill froze.

Kenneth didn't acknowledge the blunder; instead, he picked up the papers Bill had given him. "This Paulsy House." Bill's attention shifted as if Kenneth had flipped a light switch. "I'm interested in learning more. And I'll definitely have a partner architecture firm working up a bid for it. Maybe even Kai's." He looked at Bill, carefully enunciating his words. "Perhaps a dinner meeting would be appropriate?"

Kenneth stood up, signaling the adjournment of their meeting. "The favor you owe me ..." Kenneth began, letting his voice trail off.

"Of course. Anything."

"I'd like you to keep an eye on Asa Matthews."

Whistles and applause greeted Kai when she stepped off the elevator and into the reception area of her studio. At seven-thirty in the morning, all of her studio heads, junior and senior architects, assistants and interns were crowded near Christine's desk.

"We—got—the—JOOOOOBBBBB!!!" Jeremy shouted, then everyone erupted at once.

Jeremy grabbed her into an ecstatic embrace. A champagne cork sailed through the air, and Christine passed out plastic champagne flutes filled with bubbly.

Kai shouted over the chaos. "How did you guys find out already? We weren't supposed to hear anything until later."

Christine passed her a champagne glass. "Mr. Gannon called late yesterday while you were in the post-mortem meeting for the Johnston renovation. He said he knew we'd want to know as soon as possible."

Jeremy jumped in. "I called everyone at home last night and told them to get here extra early today. We all wanted to see your face when you got the news!"

Kai lifted her glass of champagne, and the group quieted to an excited chatter. A lump lodged in her throat. She blinked hard. She wasn't going to tear up, she wasn't. No doubt stunned by her uncharacteristic loss of composure, the group went completely still. Christine gave her back a motherly rub, and Kai almost lost it.

"We're proud of you, honey. You just say what's in your heart."

Kai put a tight rein on her emotions and cleared her throat. "To the Preservation Studio, you guys put in so much hard work. You're dedicated, you're talented. You love what you do, and you bring glory to this great profession we call architecture. To all of you, I couldn't ask for a more talented team."

"To The Family!"

The cacophony continued until they'd downed several bottles of cheap champagne. Kai figured very little work would be done today, and that was fine for the others, but not for her. As the leader of the preservation studio, her work was just beginning. She continued down the hall to her office with Jeremy on her heels. She dropped her briefcase on the couch opposite her desk and went to the wet bar in the corner where she poured out her cold coffee and ran water for a fresh pot. For a brief moment, she considered joining the team for happy hour down at the Hound Dog. She had never done so before, and this was such a special victory.

She turned to Jeremy—who had flopped down on her couch with his feet hanging off the side—and grinned. "Wow."

"Wow, is right. I can't believe it. I can't tell you how excited I am that we got this job."

Kai pulled a mug from the overhead cupboard and retrieved a packet of sugar. "We must have really bowled them over with our presentation." Given the expertise of the firms they'd been up against, the decision seemed to happen too fast. Now she wondered if Kenneth had been right about Asa Matthews's influence. "This is great, but I wonder what the deciding factors were."

"We promised not to over-develop the surrounding land," Jeremy said. "That was the key. I mean, we let them know that we wouldn't be creating some kind of pre-1863 Busch Gardens or Disney World. We offered them a design that'll generate income but will also focus on what's important, the history of the site."

"Well said." Kai drummed her fingers on the counter and waited for coffee. "That was the hardest sell I had to do with Kenneth. You know how the guys are at Drexel. If they could develop every piece of vacant land into retail establishments, that's what they would do."

Jeremy gave her a sly look. "I think having Drexel on our team helped a lot, too. We knew we could count on you to get your boy on the same page."

Kai bristled at Jeremy's reference to Kenneth, knowing Drexel had no claim on this win. But she brushed aside her worries about Kenneth and his comments about Asa Matthews's influence. KT & G was well qualified; otherwise, their team would have never made it to the final cut. She clapped her hands. "Well, I can't wait to get started. I guess I'll hear from Mr. Gannon at some point about the kickoff meeting, and then we'll plan our next road trip to Savannah."

"Oh, yeah." Jeremy nodded with relish. Kai knew he was remembering the frolicking good times the pre-bid team had on prior trips. On one of them, he had made inroads with Judy Alvarez, a junior architect in the studio.

"Okay, enough talk about work. We already planned happy hour. You coming?"

"Oh, Jeremy … I … no."

"Come on, you can afford to relax a little now. The pressure's off."

She looked up. "You know better."

He waved away her concern. "I know, I know. Now the hard work starts. But you need to live a little. You're getting that partnership. We all know it. This project was the clincher. Besides, it won't hurt you to loosen up for a couple of hours."

She opened her mouth to protest.

"One hour. One drink. Promise me."

She sighed. "Let me think about it."

"I'm gonna bug you all day," he warned, then smiled. "But, for now, I'll leave you alone."

After he left, Kai poured fresh coffee and reconsidered Jeremy's offer.

She moved around to her drafting table, which was positioned at the window behind her desk, and littered with pictures of Ridgeway Plantation. She set her mug on the edge of the table and let out a satisfied sigh as her eyes passed lazily over each of the photos. How could she blame Jeremy for his excitement when she was even more excited herself? Landing the Ridgeway deal was the opportunity she'd waited for her entire career. Six long, hard years she had worked for this. The one project she was convinced would land her the partnership she'd always dreamed of, and it was just the beginning. There was a lot more good fortune in store for her at KT & G. For her, and her entire team. *And Asa Matthews had nothing to do with it.* The bid process was well on its way long before their encounter at the Cheesecake Factory.

She sat down at her desk and draped an arm atop her head. The rich smell of the Jamaica Blue Mountain coffee called to her. Raising her mug to take a sip, she caught a whiff of cedar and cologne and closed her eyes, letting the image of a tall dreadlocked warrior slip from that private space in the back of her mind and out into the open. She had the contract for the Ridgeway project now; she could afford to play a little. If not at happy hour, at least in her imagination, so Kai gave in to a sigh and let her mind's eye fill with visions of Asa Matthews. So sexy and dangerous looking in all that black, he was a walking fantasy. What wonderful games would the imaginary Asa play with her?

Hot, steamy ones, no doubt. "You're probably as good as this Jamaica Blue Mountain coffee I'm drinking, Mr. Matthews," she murmured.

Just imagining his hard lean muscles enveloping her, his strong hands cradling her head, long fingers fisting in her hair, an involuntary shiver trailed through her. A wistful sigh slipped from her lips. "It's a shame I can't enjoy you every morning along with my coffee."

"I'm sure that can be arranged."

The voice came from the open doorway. Kai's eyes flew open. Her coffee mug slammed onto her desk blotter.

She blinked. Once. Twice. A third time.

Asa Matthews, looking sinister and intense in a black knit shirt and slacks, leaned casually in her office doorway. "Now, what were you saying about enjoying me?"

CHAPTER FOUR

Asa hadn't planned to rush to first base. A smooth, skilled approach that would eventually end with the two of them wrapped around each other—preferably naked—was his normal style. But one glimpse of Kai sitting at her desk, looking business-like and sexy, and thinking about him, made him want her as soon as possible. Like maybe now. But, work came first, so he stepped into Kai's office, tossed the heavy field notebooks he'd brought along on the couch, and sat down.

He could tell she was rattled. *Good.* No sense being the only one in the room struggling for composure. She recovered enough to clean up the coffee spill with a tissue, but took her time about it, so Asa enjoyed the view while he waited. Since he couldn't see the rest of her, he concentrated on what was visible above her desk. Today she wore a conservative hunter green business suit, with a cream-colored silk shell, beneath double-breasted linen. Her hands. Slim fingers with unpolished, but manicured nails commanded graceful, economical movements. She wiped off her mug and the drips on the mug warmer, then threw the tissue away. With her game face solidly in place, she finally looked up.

It was nothing like the sexy bedroom expression she wore the first time he'd met her. None of the electricity, the lust, or the desire was in her eyes, or in the softness of her mouth. The mask of bland politeness was meant to do anything but entice. Yet, Asa was enchanted. He smothered a smile and labeled Kai's mildly upturned mouth a Buddha smile, but Kai Ellis wasn't a stone statue. He had already seen the real person underneath: hot-blooded, lustful, and all woman, and he intended to do what was necessary to see that woman again. Soon.

"May I ask what you're doing here?" she asked.

Asa employed a Buddha smile of his own, jotted down a few lines of gibberish on his pad and pretended to read the notes back. "You were speaking of how you'd like to enjoy me … uh … each morning, I think you said." He flicked his eyes up at her, then back down at the pad, but not before noticing the Buddha smile had disappeared. "Un hunh. You said, and I quote 'You're probably as good as this Jamaica Blue Mountain coffee I'm drinking.' Never heard of that flavor," he interjected before continuing. "'It's a shame I can't enjoy you every morning, along with my coffee.' End quote."

A pleasing flush rose beneath that exquisite cappuccino colored skin, but the anger in her eyes surprised him. Most women thought him charming, some harmlessly so, others hungrily. Never had he met a woman who seemed afraid of him, but there was definitely fear interlaced with the anger.

Back to business. He stifled a sigh and set down his day timer to gather the field notebooks he'd brought, dumping them all on her desk before he stood up. "You want me," he murmured under his breath, then walked across the office to the wet bar.

"Excuse me?"

The steel in her voice impressed Asa, and he had a feeling this woman could break balls if she wanted to. Made him wonder whether she hadn't already. "I said I want some coffee." In search of a mug, he opened cupboard doors. Coffee connoisseur that he was, he'd noticed the coffee maker when he arrived. Any woman for whom coffee was so vital that she had her own personal machine in her office, was a woman after his own heart. Mentally, he added a positive tick to his "Kai Ellis" list.

He looked over his shoulder. At her desk, Kai sipped her coffee, then set the mug on the warmer. Her back was straight, her chin raised, ready for a fight. Asa's mouth curled in salute. He wanted to tell her she was in a losing game, but said instead, "May I?"

Kai studiously ignored him.

"Suit yourself." He chose a mug from the cupboard. "I'm used to taking what I want."

Before he could even pour the coffee, Kai was out of her chair and at the door. She swung it open wide. "I don't know what your game is, Mr. Matthews," she said in a strained voice.

"It's doctor."

"Excuse me?"

"I have a Ph.D. It's Dr. Matthews."

"*Dr.* Matthews, then." She glared. "This is a place of business, not a pick up joint. Not a night club, not a bar."

Asa held up his hands. "My bad," he said, deciding now wasn't the time to start an argument. She was going to be one tough nut to crack, but she was well worth the trouble. In any case, he was glad she wasn't some kind of weakling, willing to make it easy on him. Rachel had certainly not been much of a challenge. Kai's body was better also. Her skirt revealed ten inches of well-toned thighs and sexy mile long legs. Slender calves that would have driven a saint to sin ended at medium-heeled pumps that matched her suit. But unfortunately, that sweet round bottom he remembered swishing away from him at the restaurant was hidden beneath her jacket.

He grabbed his coffee and headed to the couch.

Kai cleared her throat, composed herself with a deep breath. "Look. I'm sorry. I just ... I need to apologize."

"For what?"

"I ..." She stopped, then began again. "You caught me off guard the other night at the restaurant and ... I've never reacted—"

"The Cheesecake Factory? You're apologizing for the Cheesecake Factory?"

She looked at him with surprise. "Of course. What did you think?"

Confused, he studied her for a moment. He was the one who should be apologizing, not her. He shook his head, more disappointed by her sudden acquiescence.

She was so embarrassed by her own actions, Kai wasn't sure what more to say. Five minutes ago she was sipping her coffee and thinking about him—and talking way too much—and then he just materialized like a vision, acting like he was in a in club in Midtown instead of a place of business. As rude as he was, guilt for her thoughts weighed heavy. She hoped apologizing for giving him the wrong impression at the restaurant would set things on their proper course, but now he was studying his DayTimer and acting pissed off. She sighed and rose to freshen her coffee, taking time to scrutinize him while he wasn't looking.

His dreadlocks were pulled back in a leather thong at the nape of his neck, flowing past a heavily muscled shoulder when he turned to dig something out of his saddlebag. His dress was business casual: black slacks, black knit shirt, with short sleeves that showed off his impressive biceps. Kai almost chastised herself for staring, but since she'd turned him off with her apology—what difference did it make now?

Coffee in hand, she approached her desk, pushing the notebooks there aside. "What are you doing here, Mr.—Dr. Matthews? I thought Richard, uh, Dr. Dunlop would be managing this project."

A slow, suggestive smile tipped Asa's lips.

Okay, apparently he wasn't completely turned off, Kai decided, clearing her throat.

"Since I'm the lead archaeologist, I'll be overseeing your work on the welcome center. The slave quarters are my specialty, although the other outbuildings are under my supervision as well. As for Richard, he's a member of the research team. His schedule better affords him the time to show the architectural teams around the site, but I manage the projects…." He shrugged, letting his voice trail off. Kai's Buddha smile was back, and he was beginning to learn that it meant she was preparing for battle. She wasn't such a push-over after all.

"Lead?"

"Yes. You don't have a problem with that do you?"

"As lead archaeologist, you had a say in which team won the bid for the welcome center development?"

"Of course."

Her eyes narrowed suspiciously. "How did you know I was going to be at the Cheesecake Factory that night?"

Asa snorted. "What is this, a police interrogation? You think I was stalking you or something?"

"You tell me."

Asa crossed his arms. "Why don't you spit out what you really want to ask."

The Buddha smile again. "Since you seem to already know the question, why don't you do the honors."

"You think I would pick an incompetent design firm to do the welcome center just so I could get a little play?"

"Did you?"

Asa was careful not to let the insult he felt show in his smile. "Ridgeway plantation is my baby, sweetheart. I've been excavating the slave quarters and out buildings for more than eight years, starting with my Ph. D. research. It's the backbone of my career. There is no way in hell I would jeopardize that effort with an incompetent design firm."

"So if you're confident in my design team, what are you doing here now? We didn't need you before. Why should we need you now?"

Crossing his ankle cavalierly over the opposite knee, Asa leaned back. "You tell me."

Kai had that deer in the headlights look again, a cross between fear and excitement. And since she seemed afraid to answer the question, Asa answered for her. He pointed to the field notebooks on her desk. "We record all site work in those. Since the tours, your team only covered the currently preserved excavations and none of the work that's in progress. I thought you might benefit from some more detail." He stood and picked up a notebook. "Of course, if you don't need them, I'll take them back when I return to Savannah."

"No. No. I apologize." Kai's voice and demeanor softened. "We definitely want to see them. We want the welcome center design to be as informed as possible. The more details we know about the slave community, the better."

Some of the building tension eased from Asa's shoulders. "All right, then. Most of the binders contain scaled drawings of slave houses and outbuildings in various stages of excavation and preservation. A few

Order Form

Mail to: Genesis Press, Inc.
P.O. Box 101
Columbus, MS 39703

Name _____

Address _____

City/State _____ Zip _____

Telephone _____

Ship to (if different from above)

Name _____

Address _____

City/State _____ Zip _____

Telephone _____

Credit Card Information

Credit Card # _____ ☐ Visa   ☐ Mastercard

Expiration Date (mm/yy) _____ ☐ AmEx   ☐ Discover

Qty.	Author	Title	Price	Total

Use this order form, or call 1-888-INDIGO-1		
Total for books		_____
Shipping and handling: $5 first two books, $1 each additional book		_____
Total S & H		_____
Total amount enclosed		_____

Mississippi residents add 7% sales tax

have sketches of potsherds and remains of woven baskets and other domestic artifacts." He sorted through the pile and pulled out two notebooks and handed them to Kai, watching as she flipped through them.

"They have sketches of stoneware chamber pots and Colonoware, fragments of coiled basketry, and a type of pottery called magic bowls. I could go on—"

"Angela is going to go nuts when she sees this stuff," Kai said, cutting him off.

"There's a ton of data." Anger at her previous insult ebbed with the excitement Asa heard in Kai's voice. He picked up another notebook. "I only brought copies of a fraction of it. About fifteen percent of the plantation has been excavated to date, even less preserved and cataloged. There's a lot more work to be done."

"I've been wondering, with this being one of the richest archaeological sites ever found on the east coast, why on earth are they planning a welcome center before everything's excavated?"

He closed the notebook, handed it to Kai, and returned to the couch before he spoke. "First of all, it'll take the next thirty years to excavate and preserve the entire site. That's too long for our benefactors. Second of all, it's about the money."

"Isn't it always?"

Asa glanced at Kai. She must have finally realized how much she had misjudged his dedication to his work. "Have you heard of F.A.M.E?"

"The word, or F.A.M.E as in Forty Acres and a Mule Enterprises, F.A.M.E.?"

Asa nodded affirmative to the second choice.

"Why?"

"Coleman Foundation is a non-profit subsidiary."

"Um, maybe I don't need to know this stuff."

Asa eyed her with amusement, then reached for his day timer and checked a note before continuing. "F.A.M.E. has gotten some bad press. It's not some shadowy organization that operates at the edge of the law. It's mission is …" Asa waved his hand in dismissal. "Never mind, it's all a sore spot with me. Anyway, F.A.M.E. created Coleman

Foundation, and we're funded by an annual endowment. But, since one of our illustrious stewards decided two years ago that we should wean ourselves away from F.A.M.E. funding, we've become dependent on a few very wealthy benefactors. And—"

"And they want a commercial enterprise."

"Bingo." Enjoying the shoptalk, he relaxed. Kai seemed relaxed, too.

"But you said Coleman Foundation is a non-profit. You can't profit on commercial sales from a welcome center and tours?"

"True. But we could tag all the proceeds as funding for future excavation and research."

"Sounds like killing the goose that laid the golden egg."

Asa grunted in agreement.

"So why doesn't F.A.M.E. take back control of the foundation? Then you wouldn't have to commercialize anything." Kai stopped. "Listen to me. What am I saying? I'm all for the commercialization of the place. It's going to help me make partner. Forget I said anything." She smiled over the desk at him. Not the Buddha smile this time, but a real one. Talking business was what was comfortable to her. Asa vowed to remember that point.

Despite the way his day had started, and aside from their tangential discussion of F.A.M.E. and the Coleman Foundation finances, Asa was in an excellent mood. He had spent the morning with Kai, reviewing the work at Ridgeway and the designs her restoration team was developing for the welcome center. He rarely wasted his time discussing his archaeological theories with lay people, but watching Kai become engrossed in the field notebooks did his heart good. So good, in fact, he found himself confiding his hopes of finding the slave cemetery to her.

Evidently, Kai's passion for her work was transferable to whatever subject she happened to be tackling at the time, because both of them forgot about breaking for lunch as she soaked up the information he gave her and even challenged some of his theories. Asa couldn't remember a more stimulating morning that didn't involve sex. So much so, he had almost forgotten his physical attraction to Kai in favor of the intellectual-almost.

He had been considering inviting her to a late lunch, when she adjourned their meeting and unceremoniously dumped him into the hands of one of her studio heads, Jeremy Fuller, when they walked down the hall to the preservation studio.

More disappointed than he cared to admit, he leaned against Jeremy's drafting table and tried to appreciate the drawings he was being shown. He spotted Kai walking toward the back of the studio with a young Hispanic woman; his eyes latched on and followed. It was mid-afternoon, and Kai still looked as fresh as she had hours before, when he'd stepped into her office. Watching her rear-end sway seductively in that short skirt had him heating up again. Potent. That was the only way to describe her.

"… and the elephants will be housed down here at the end," Jeremy said.

"Sounds good."

"The polar bears will go right there beside them."

"What?" Asa dragged his eyes away from Kai. "Sorry, I don't think I heard you right."

The kid grinned at him and shook his head before turning back to the plans on his desk. "I was talking about polar bears and elephants."

"Yeah," Asa said, glancing up to find Kai again. "Go on. I got you, bears and elephants."

"Player."

Asa felt an elbow in his side. "Yeah, um hmm." He nodded without taking his eyes off Kai. "That sure is interesting."

A finger snapping in Asa's face blocked his view of Kai and had him scowling. He grabbed at it.

"Hey, Asa, man. Dr. Matthews."

It took a minute for Asa to realize Jeremy was speaking. "Yeah, what's that all about?"

"Just trying to get your attention, player."

His attention finally focused on the young architect, who was grinning at him. "What's so important that you have to get in my face to get my attention?"

"Hey." Jeremy peered at him thoughtfully. "Why don't you and Dr. Dunlop stop by the Hound Dog tonight? Boss lady'll be there."

Asa took a moment to glance around the studio. The corner of his mouth tilted when he found Kai again. He turned back to Jeremy. "I'll see if we can make it."

Jeremy rolled out fresh tracing paper. "Sure is fun to see boss lady trying to work while her man's walking around the studio. And, it's pretty cool to see you all messed up over her, too. It's about damn time." Jeremy tore off a stretch of paper and taped it to the table. "Judy." He pointed a drafting scale at the Hispanic girl Kai had been walking with earlier. Now the two women were seated at Judy's drafting table discussing a drawing. "She's my lady. She's been trying to get boss lady to drop Roselle and move on for quite a while."

Asa drew himself up a little and watched Kai and Judy work together. "Roselle?"

"Yeah. You know, Kenneth Roselle III, from Drexel Development." The boy's face twisted into a frown. "You might have heard of him. Drexel does a lot of work in Atlanta. Mostly strip malls. He hooked up with Kai six years ago and pushed Drexel into preservation, too."

Asa frowned. Kenneth Roselle? Kai was *dating* him? She had spark and fire. Kenneth Roselle was about as exciting as dried paint. "I've heard of him," he said.

Roselle had attended several Foundation fundraisers to network. They hadn't been formally introduced, but Asa had heard about him and wasn't impressed. He definitely wasn't the kind of guy he would have expected Kai to date. "So what's up with that? Anything I should be concerned about?"

"Nah," Jeremy said over the drafting pencil he'd stuck in his mouth as he prepped his table. "Rumor has it they were engaged."

"What?"

Jeremy pulled the pencil out of his mouth as he smoothed down his drafting surface. "Yeah, but I don't think it's true. It's probably just what Roselle wanted people to believe. The way she was talking to him on the phone a few days ago, didn't sound like they were together to me. If they aren't, Judy'll sure be happy about it. She can't stand him."

"Join the club."

"Alan Warren," a jovial voice announced itself over the phone.

"Alan," Kenneth said with the same joviality. "It's Kenneth Roselle. Do you have a minute?"

"Hold a minute please."

Kenneth heard the muffled sound of a female voice, the closing of a door, a heavy sigh.

"Roselle." The joviality was completely gone from Alan's voice, stiffness in its place. "May I help you?"

"Don't you always?" Kenneth quipped.

Silence.

"Well, Alan, how are you doing?"

Silence again.

"Ah come on, Alan. We're buddies, aren't we? You don't have to be afraid of me." This time he didn't wait for a response. Didn't expect to get one. "I hear you guys at KT & G are about to vote on a new partner." He picked up his gold-dipped golf ball, tossed it absently. "Kai's on the short list isn't she?"

If it weren't for his stilted breathing, Kenneth would have been concerned that Alan had hung up on him. Not that he would ever dare. Alan wasn't as helplessly malleable as Bill Jameson, but then again, he didn't have to be. The distinguished partner and board member of the great architecture firm of Kapman, Trent, and Gannon was cheating on his wife with his secretary, something that the ethically pure members of the upper echelons of KT & G greatly frowned upon. Kenneth knew as well as Alan, that to keep that little secret quiet, Alan would do whatever Kenneth asked of him.

Kenneth set the golf ball in its holder and straightened in his chair. Such a shame he had only discovered the tantalizing morsel a few weeks ago, he might have been able to use the information earlier to deal with Kai and her recalcitrant attitude about their marriage; but, that was then. "Alan? Are you there?"

A heavy put upon sigh echoed through the phone. "Yes, Roselle. What do you want?"

Kenneth glanced around his middle office and decided his fortune might be turning. "Yes. What do I want? Well, why don't we make a little deal, shall we?"

CHAPTER FIVE

With her stomach grumbling, Kai turned into the parking lot of the Hound Dog Bar & Grill. Since she hadn't taken a break for lunch, a Hound Dog double-stacked quarter pound burger with cheese and heavy on the ketchup sounded like heaven.

She hadn't been to the Hound Dog in over a year, but she still remembered their fabulous burgers. Thick, hot, and slathered with every condiment you might want, a burger with a side of fries was the perfect distraction. She had been in quite a surly mood since Asa Matthews' appearance that morning.

Guilt had warred with shame the rest of the day. Not only had she embarrassed herself, talking into her coffee mug like a lovesick teenager, she had insulted Asa by accusing him of selecting her firm because of his attraction to her. She might as well have called her own firm incompetent outright. Asa must have seen her insecurities flashing above her head like a neon sign.

Their meeting went on longer than expected, given their rough start. They had talked all morning—about Ridgeway, about Coleman, and KT & G; and a lot more things that she probably should have kept to herself. It was way too easy to get along with Asa, and that made him dangerous. But, his excitement over the dig was contagious. Worse yet, he was someone she could fall for, which was down right scary. She didn't want to feel that way for him—for anyone.

A loner her whole life, Kai was typically more comfortable with platonic, work-related relationships. Spending the majority of her morning with a man she was attracted to and also had a high level of professional respect for was something very different from her norm. By two-thirty, she had become so alarmed by their "fit" that she abruptly called a halt to their meeting and like a coward, pawned him off on Jeremy. She could have sat with him all day and into the evening, discussing the latest issues in historic preservation, or the newest archaeological discoveries.

Even worse, she could see herself in a relationship with him that was anything but platonic. Which, given her opportunity to make partner, would be a disaster were it to happen.

She shook herself out of her reverie, vowed to distance herself from Asa, then grabbed her purse and hurried toward the bar's entrance.

When she walked in, the hostess led her to the double booth in the back of the bar where her team was waiting.

"Boss lady!" two of her junior architects yelled.

"Hey, hey!" someone else said.

"We were wondering when you planned to join us," Judy added.

Jeremy was plastered to her side. He glanced at his watch. "What took you so long? It's six-thirty. You said you were leaving at 5:00 sharp."

"Hah." Angela, her decorative arts specialist, smirked from the other side of the booth. "We're lucky to see her at all."

Kai pushed her way into the booth beside Angela. She was used to their ribbing. They respected her dedication to her job, and it had predictably rubbed off on them. The team was a hardworking bunch, though they played equally as hard. She didn't mind though. They deserved their playtime, and happy hour was their weekly stress reliever.

She feigned irritability. "Don't talk to me until I've had a double-stack."

Jeremy immediately snapped his fingers for the server, ordered for her and poured her a beer from one of the pitchers in the center of the table. "Drink," he commanded. Only after she raised the glass and took a swallow did Jeremy speak again. "Okay, everybody. Now that boss lady's here, the partying can officially begin."

While Kai reached for a helping of chips and salsa from a bowl on the table, a few dozen or so people gathered around the booth. Others moved off to continue their partying on the dance floor,

"So boss lady," Judy said. "What's up with *El Gato Grande*?"

Mouth full of chips and salsa, Kai gave Judy a quizzical look. "*El Gato Grande*?" Kai asked after she washed her chips down with a swallow of beer.

"Yeah." Judy's eyes glinted with mischief. "The Big Cat."

Tamara, one of her interior designers, turned her attention to their conversation. "Oooh yeah, boss lady, what's up with that?"

Kai laughed. "I have no idea. Something about a 'Big Cat.'" She caught a look between the two women, then noticed Judy nudging Jeremy in the ribs.

"Hey Tam," one of the junior architects yelled from the dance floor. "Get your butt out here."

Tamara wiggled out of the booth. "Duty calls, but I want to hear more of this later."

Starving, Kai dipping another chip. "I don't know what you guys are talking about, and I'm too hungry to care. All I want right now is my burger." She could smell her hamburger approaching.

"A Quarter Pound Double-Stack with cheese, extra ketchup?" the server asked

"Lay that thing right here." Eyeing the French fries that were piled high beside the burger, Kai's stomach rumbled in anticipation. "I've been wanting to get my hands on you all day."

She sank her teeth into the cheeseburger and closed her eyes so she could really enjoy it.

"You took the words right out of my mouth." The whispered words were so close to her ear, she could feel them. Kai yelped and dropped the burger on to the plastic basket. French fries went flying. *Asa Matthews. Arghh.* Did the man get off on sneaking up on her?

"Jeremy. Judy." Asa nodded to the pair sitting in front of Kai.

"What's up, Asa?"

Kai stared at Jeremy. *Great. All I need is the two of them becoming buds.*

"Hey, Dr. Dunlop," Jeremy said when Richard walked up. "Nice to see you again."

"You, too. Thanks for inviting us."

Kai glared at Jeremy, then backed off when he smiled amicably. Why was she angry with him? It wasn't as if he knew what had gone on between her and Asa. She swallowed the lump of burger that had lodged in her throat and lifted her beer. There was no way she was going to ruin her dinner worrying about Asa Matthews.

Mouthing *"El Gato Grande,"* as she pushed to the edge of the booth, Judy waggled her eyebrows at Kai. It was all Kai could do not to sputter her beer all over the place.

Judy slid out of the booth. "Jeremy, why don't we give the boss some privacy? I'm sure she and Dr. Matthews have some 'shop' to talk—right?"

"Huh?" A jab in the ribs, courtesy of his girlfriend, cleared his thinking. "Oh. Yeah. Right ... right."

As her allies abandoned her for the dance floor, Kai narrowed her eyes at Asa. She was still starving, so she didn't confront him. After all, Richard Dunlap was there to chaperone. Surely, Asa wouldn't try anything in front of a colleague.

She took another bite of her burger, savoring it with pleasure. *Pure ecstasy.* The flavors of ground beef, gooey cheese, grease, and lots and lots of ketchup mingled in her mouth. She almost moaned in delight from the delicious burger and the delicious man that had her skin tingling as he watched her eat.

Richard slid into the seat Jeremy and Judy had vacated, and Kai gave him a smile between bites. The least she could do was be polite. After all, Richard wasn't the one making passes at her. But she made no move to invite Asa, who was still standing beside her, to sit.

After two more bites, the edge was off her hunger. Kai set down her beer glass and smiled across at Richard. "It's a pleasure to see you again, Dr. Dunlop. You'll have to excuse me. I skipped lunch." She swiped at her napkin before offering her hand. "I'm surprised to see you. My boss told me you had pressing matters at the university and wouldn't be continuing with ..." Kai's voice faltered momentarily. Asa eased his large, warm body into the booth beside her. "... the project." Kai finished and tried for what she hoped was a smile.

"You heard right, unfortunately, but I wanted to come by and congratulate the team. I had planned to come by this morning with Asa, but I wasn't able to—" Richard broke off, his eyes narrowing. "I wasn't able to make it."

It wasn't long before Kai realized what had discomfited him. Asa's arm was resting behind her on the back of the booth. *Breathe*, she told herself, though she could feel anger rising.

"Well I hope you'll have a little time to spare to come out and see how we're doing from time to time."

He gave her a warm smile. "I'll make sure of it."

Kai didn't hear another syllable out of Richard's mouth, because all her senses, except her sense of touch, had just shut down. Asa's hand was at the nape of her neck. His touch was light, barely there. She leaned forward, purposefully moving away from him to pick up her beer glass again. To her shock, his hand followed, moving to stroke her shoulder blades.

She practically pushed him onto the floor in her haste to disentangle herself and get out of the booth. "If you'll excuse me, *Dr. Matthews*, Dr. Dunlop," she said through gritted teeth. "I need to go to the restroom."

Not looking back, she started toward the ladies' room. She blew out an angry breath, "Hey, boss lady!"

Tamara was striding toward her, winded and exhilarated from dancing.

Still focused on making it to the ladies' room unimpeded, Kai skirted the dance floor.

"Something wrong?"

"I—just watch my purse for me, will you, Tam?"

Her colleague hesitated. "Uh, yeah sure, boss."

Judy and several of the studio team regrouped at the table. "What's going on?"

"Why do you ask?" Asa said.

He contemplated his next move as Judy returned his blank stare with the intuition only women seem to possess. He would have to play it cool with Judy. She wasn't one to miss much. He waited another long minute for her to decide whether things were cool.

"Is boss lady okay?" she finally said.

"Yeah. She just went to freshen up before she meets me on the dance floor."

At that, apparently all was forgiven. "All right, now."

Jeremy picked up an empty chip basket from the table and gave Judy a conspiratorial smile. He threw in a five-dollar bill.

Asa could see several of the team digging money from their pockets as he made his way to the dance floor. The pot was actually filling up to see whether Kai's bun would come down. Given the way Kai had stalked off, he had a sneaking suspicion that wasn't about to happen; at least, not this evening. He wasn't even sure whether he could get the woman on the dance floor and close enough to him to take her hair down.

She had dogged that burger and the beer, he thought with a chuckle. Definitely a surprise. He hadn't taken her for a beer drinker, nor a greasy burger eater, but she seemed to have been in heaven as she ate. He had actually been waiting for her to lick her fingers, but watching her lick her lips in satisfaction had been a pleasant concession. After all that, he had expected her to be feeling relaxed, which was why he'd put his hand on her back. But, she had been a hell of a lot more tense than he'd expected.

He stopped at the edge of the black tile floor and leaned against the brass railing that separated the walkway from the dance floor. Considering there was only one path back to the dining area, and he was standing in the middle of it, there was no way she could get past him when she emerged from the ladies' room.

A few women went into the bathroom. One came out, gave him a once over and a big smile. He responded with his wish-I-could-but-I-can't smile, but that didn't stop her from trailing inch-long acrylic nails against his chest before moving on. Any other time he wouldn't have hesitated to give the woman a tumble, on the dance floor and otherwise, but Kai Ellis was in his blood now, and every other female paled in comparison.

He glanced at the booth where the chip basket was piled high with bills. He got a thumbs-up from Jeremy, a pensive look from Judy, a murderous one from Richard.

Knowing him well, he could all but see gears in Richard's head rotating. Sometimes, he just analyzed situations way too much; to death, in fact. When Asa had finally gotten around to telling Richard about how he'd met Kai, Richard had given him an emphatic thumbs-down and warning after warning against making a move. But that was nothing compared to the way he'd hammered Asa in the car on the way to the bar, after Asa told him about the altercation in her office.

Asa hammered him right back, reminding him, quite sarcastically, that he and Kai could, as mature and unmarried, consenting adults, pursue a personal relationship outside of the office.

The door to the ladies' room opened again, and Asa turned his attention to Kai. She stepped out and glanced around. Her placid face twisted immediately into a scowl when her gaze landed on him. He was on her in two strides.

"If you don't want to make a scene," he murmured, like the lover he wanted to be, "you'll smile politely and let me escort you to the dance floor."

"What could possibly make you think I would dance with you, Dr. Matthews?"

He nodded toward the booth where her colleagues sat watching.

"Oh, thanks. Thanks a lot."

"You seem to be having a difficult time saying my name, Kai. It's Asa." He draped an arm around her waist.

He turned her and led her to a less crowded section of the dance floor, then pulled her against him. A stroke of his hand released her hair, and he threaded his fingers through the soft spongy mass and massaged her scalp. Relaxed and pliant, she swayed against him to the beat of the music. Asa stroked her back lightly as he rubbed his cheek against her hair. The rightness of Kai Ellis felt stronger and stronger each time he touched her.

Asa let himself drift and enjoy the feel, smell and sight of Kai in his arms, until Jeremy paused in front of them, breaking into the cocoon the music had wrapped the two of them in.

Kai stiffened against him.

"Oooh, boss lady." Judy approached behind Jeremy. "Your hair."

Disappointment filtered in as Asa felt Kai pull away from him. She twisted her hair into a bun and hurried off the dance floor.

That was the second time she'd run away from him, Asa thought, and he intended to stop the habit she was forming.

Judy's gaze swung from Kai back to Asa's. "She looks upset." "I think I'd better go after her."

She had to get herself together, Kai thought as she entered the cool, quiet sanctuary of the ladies room. The horror that her colleagues witnessed her melting into Asa's arms on the dance floor was bad enough. How could she allow herself to fall for him after all the misery and pain loving someone had always caused in her life? First with her father, then with Bobby back in college.

Painful memories welled up inside her; she forced them back down. They were in the past; they couldn't hurt her now. Nor could Asa hurt her. She had built a life for herself after it had fallen down around her during college, and she was on the brink of making Partner in KT & G.

There was too much to lose by giving in, falling apart, or allowing Asa Matthews to barge into her orderly life, towing chaos in his wake. It didn't matter how much talking to him for hours felt like seconds, how being in his arms made her feel safe and secure, in a way she had never experienced before.

What mattered was control. Of her life, her career, herself—even her hair. If Asa could manage to disrupt her hair within five minutes of being in the same room with her, Lord, the havoc he would wreak in her life.

With new resolve and determination, Kai wet her fingers in the sink, then finger-combed her hair back into place, sweeping it into a bun just as Judy walked through the door.

Knowing Judy probably wanted to talk about Asa, Kai hastily turned the water to full blast and splashed her blotchy face.

"Could you go grab my purse, Judy? I need to leave."

Kai grabbed blindly for paper towels in the dispenser beside the mirror. She wasn't having much luck, until Judy pressed several into her hand.

Kai took extra care drying her face. She should have felt better by now, but her face was still flaming—along with a few other body parts. Despite her previous conversation with herself, she knew Asa would force her to face their attraction. Just the thought of confronting him got her frazzled over again.

"Kai."

Kai pressed the paper towels against her eyes and remained silent.

"This is Judy talking to you. Your friend, not your employee. You can tell me what's wrong."

Kai heaved a huge sigh. I refuse to let him win. I refuse to let him *win.* She lowered the towels from her face.

Judy put an arm around her and squeezed. They were shoulder to shoulder and Kai could see the two of them in the mirror. Judy, with her olive skin and chocolate brown hair flowing in graceful waves down her shoulders, wore a reassuring smile. While Kai's hair was flying around her face, spirals everywhere, popping out of the bun she had hastily crafted, her mouth pressed into a grim line.

She scowled at her appearance. Judy's flowing hair made her look like a sexy cover girl for some national fashion magazine, while Kai's looked like she'd just stuck her finger in an electric socket. There was certainly nothing sexy about her hair. She couldn't, for the life of her, figure out Asa's fascination with it.

"I like your hair down, Kai. Why don't you wear it like that more often?"

"Now you sound like him."

In the mirror, Judy smirked and cross her arms. "*El Gato Grande?*" She laughed.

"Don't call him that."

"Well if he doesn't look like a big cat hunting down prey, I don't know what does. The two of you on that dance ..."

Not wanting to remember, Kai turned away from the mirror, away from Judy. "Could you go get my purse please, Judy? I really have to go home."

CHAPTER SIX

Asa was almost clipped by a dude driving into the parking lot as he chased after Kai, but he finally caught up with her. She hadn't made it to her car yet, thankfully. And he needed to apologize.

"Hold up, Kai."

She kept walking, pissing him off.

"I said hold up." Asa grabbed her arm and swung her around. "You forgot your purse," he said, shoving it at her. "Hey, give me a break, all right? I overstepped, but I'm trying to apologize."

She rolled those exotic eyes at him and took her purse, but didn't say thank you.

"Why are you always running?" he asked when she turned around ready to walk off.

Her feet did a military style turn that looked sexy as hell in her forest green pumps, but Asa took care to flatten his lips. She'd be off like a shot if she saw even a hint of a grin.

"Excuse me, Mr.—Dr. Matthews. I hate to disappoint you, or burst any of your delusional bubbles, but I'm *walking*, not running, away because I've had about all I can take of your childish antics." She looked him up and down as if he were scum on the bottom of her heel. "How you gained graduate degrees with your work ethic and unprofessional conduct is beyond me."

Asa stepped back so he could get a good look at her. "Unprofessional? This is the second time you've insulted my work ethic. I wonder why that is? Maybe because you can't handle your attraction to me. Yet, I'm the one who's unprofessional? I don't think so, Ms. Ellis. I work damn hard at what I do. Don't try to tear me down because you're insecure."

"Just stay away from me, and we'll do just fine," she huffed.

Asa took a step forward, knowing she'd back up. When she did, he took perverse pleasure in repeating it. Pride made her stand still this time.

"That will be kind of hard, don't you think? You're the lead architect; I'm the lead archaeologist. We have to be tight." He held up his index and middle fingers, crossed. Her eyes were blazing, and he could swear smoke was coming from her ears.

So much for getting on her good side. All his dreams of having her in his life were slowly slipping away. Where was his game? Apparently not in the parking lot.

"As far as I'm concerned—"

"As far as you're concerned, you'll work closely with me because this project will help you make partner in your architecture firm. I know all about your quest for the executive ranks, and I commend it." Her gasp of dismay had him softening his tone. The anger he was feeling only a moment ago began to fade. He trapped a lock of her hair in his fingers and brought it to his nose to sniff. "Power is very sexy on a woman."

Tension vibrated through her at his words. He could almost see it radiating in waves around her. She wanted to pull away from him, but didn't. She had guts; he had to give her that.

"Don't you know how to talk about anything but sex?" Kai finally said.

"Not when I want you the way I do. Not when I know you want me just as badly."

"I don't."

Since her eyes were saying differently, Asa dipped his head so their foreheads touched. "Don't treat me like I'm stupid. And don't lie to me." He brushed his lips quickly over hers, then raised his head. He wanted to kiss her, really kiss her, but given his batting average, he wasn't taking the chance.

Still, he wouldn't allow her to wriggle away from him. If he didn't touch her—and often—she would never get used to him. She was tense right now, but she was softening, so he held on, stroking her the same way he had that night in the restaurant. Speaking calmly, but firmly, he said, "You stand here in this sexy little business suit, pretending you don't feel or want." His stroked up her arms, brushed his thumbs over the curve of her breasts, causing her to flush, her lips to part. "You feel, baby girl. I make you feel."

Her mouth formed a trembling frown as she struggled to control herself, so Asa backed off. The last thing he wanted was for her to be upset over her reaction to him. He wanted her comfortable. The way he knew she could be when she forgot about appearances.

"It's all right," he whispered. "It's okay. Look, I know you think that little episode in the restaurant wasn't at all like you. You're probably still shocked at what you did. But baby, that's the real you, and you let it come out just a little bit that night, for me."

She turned her head away, but Asa wasn't having that. Gently, he touched her chin, prodding her to look at him.

"You're either trying to run from me or pulling away, but I'm not letting go. Not when I just found you." He gazed down at her, letting her see the desire he held in check. "Name the time and the place, Kai, and I'm yours. Anyway you want me."

She faced him with her eyes widened, almost as if she were pleading. Asa didn't know whether she wasn't used to honest feelings being spoken so boldly or whether she thought he was running a line on her, but he figured he'd take his chances and kiss her. He lowered his head.

"Well, well, well."

Kai jerked away and Asa turned around to see Kenneth Roselle leaning on the bumper of an SUV.

Damn it. Leave it to Roselle to interrupt his groove, just as he was making inroads. Kai tried to pull away, but he held on tight. Knowing her well enough that she'd rather do as he asked than to cause a scene, he draped his arm possessively over her shoulder. He'd hear an earful later, but right now it was time to take care of business.

"Well, well, what?" Asa asked, as Kenneth dusted off the toe of the Italian leather loafer he'd propped on the bumper of someone's truck.

Roselle took his time tidying himself before he looked up, as if that bit of posturing was going to give him the advantage. Kai was with Asa, not Kenneth, and that was all that mattered. Asa folded his arms across his chest and waited.

Roselle finally straightened and looked at him. Smiling disingenuously at Asa, he glanced at Kai. A surge of protectiveness filled Asa as he let his arm drop to her waist. He pulled her close to his side and gave her a quick squeeze to let her know he had her back.

"I warned you to stay away from him, Kai. I thought you wanted that partnership?" Kenneth said, his gaze moving from her head to her toes as if she were naked. "Apparently you don't want it very badly, the way you've been carrying on with this one all over town."

When Kai tried to step forward Asa caught her, shaking his head.

Asa had to check himself to keep from glancing over at her. Was this how Roselle had treated her when they were together? If it was, the woman needed to be taught some self-defense lessons so she could avoid men like him. Didn't she realize he was pure poison? If she hadn't yet, she would now. Roselle was certainly showing his true colors. What Asa couldn't understand was Kai's connection to him. She was smarter than this. How could she get involved with a man who could be so vicious to his lady?

Kai squirmed beside him, so Asa tightened his grip. "I don't think the lady's professional goals or her personal liaisons are any of your business, Roselle. So I suggest you go on where ever it is you're going."

Kenneth sneered at both of them. "Oh, I think they are, isn't that right, Kai? Her professional goals and personal liaisons are very much my business. She wouldn't be up for that partnership at her firm right now if it weren't for me, so don't think that being her lover is going to change that fact."

This time Asa had to use a visible amount of force to keep Kai tucked by his side. She obviously wanted no one thinking of them as lovers, but the last thing either of them needed was to give Roselle the upper hand by doing something stupid. Asa pulled his keys from his pocket and whispered in her ear the make and model of his car and where it was. "Go get in the car, babe. I'll be there in a minute."

She hesitated, glanced at Kenneth, then accepted the keys.

Asa waited for her to leave. "All right, Roselle. If you've got a beef with me, bring it on, but leave Kai out of it."

"With you? Who are you to me? You're nothing, Matthews, but I suggest you leave Kai alone, or you're going to cost her that partnership she wants so badly."

"Oh? And how do you propose that's going to happen? The bid her firm won to work on Ridgeway practically bagged that partnership for her. Done deal."

Kenneth smiled. "It's not done until it's announced publicly at the partnership dinner. That's weeks away. Anything can happen between now and then."

Asa straightened. Unfortunately, Roselle had a point, which had him a little worried. "I know your reputation, Matthews. And it's only going to hurt Kai."

Asa cursed internally. "My reputation is only going to *help* her. And when Kai's team designs an award-winning welcome center to showcase

Ridgeway, no one is going to be able to touch her. Is that what you're afraid of, Roselle? That she won't need you anymore? Apparently, she didn't need you to win this bid, did she?"

Kenneth stepped forward.

So did Asa.

"You stay away from her."

The corner of Asa's mouth curled at the demand. "Or what?"

Roselle folded his arms defensively across his chest. "You might be able to romance the ladies, but you should stick to the models and stay away from professional women. You can't handle Kai. You can't give her what she needs."

"Oh, and you can? I find that really hard to believe."

Kenneth gave him an incredulous look. "And what have you done for her lately? Give her the bid because you were sleeping with her?"

Asa's patience finally snapped. He grabbed Roselle by the lapels and shoved him against the SUV. "I suggest you step off."

Kenneth's face was strained, but he held his own. "Perhaps doth protest too much."

Asa tightened his grip. "You give me a reason, Roselle; just one good reason, and I'll show you just how unprofessional I can be." Shoving Kenneth hard against the car, he released him, started to walk away, then turned. "Don't make me prove I'm serious."

"I'm sorry, Jon. What was that?"

"Kai, weren't you listening?" Pete asked.

Pete Gannon, owner of KT & G, and her boss Jonathan Rojeski, sat on the couch across from her desk, peering inquisitively at her. For the past thirty minutes, they had been discussing their expectations for the Ridgeway Project, but all Kai could think about was Asa. One minute, he was a hungry predator staking his claim in her office, and then again at happy hour. The next minute, he was seducing her like a pro in the parking lot, then championing her like a knight in shining armor against Kenneth.

After the altercation at the Hound Dog, he had graciously taken her to a coffee shop until they could safely return to the bar to get her car. She figured he would try something while he had her alone, but he was surprisingly gentlemanly. Now, she didn't know what to make of the man. Suppressing a sigh, she pulled her mind back to the meeting.

"I'm sorry, Pete, my mind was wandering a little. Please, continue."

He lifted an eyebrow. "Ahem, so anyway, Kai, I know it's short notice since the kick off meeting was only yesterday, but Coleman is ready to get this show on the road."

She nodded eagerly. "So am I, Pete. What's the plan?"

"We want you to take a road trip up to Ridgeway Plantation on Friday. Stay the weekend and get a feel for what the archaeologists have uncovered since your design team last visited."

"Not a problem," Kai said. Overtime and weekend work was common in the industry and definitely expected if you wanted to be promoted. She'd do whatever was necessary. "I've been anxious to get up there since Dr. Matthews gave me copies of their field notes. They've accomplished a lot more than they discussed with us during the site visit. A trip back would give me some time to get my head around it all."

Jonathan stood and walked to the wet bar. "Asa will be accompanying you."

"A-asa? I mean … Dr. Matthews?" Kai stared at him, stunned.

His back was to her as he poured a mug of coffee and handed it to Peter. "Yes, he felt it would speed things up greatly if you had a guide to accompany you who has intimate knowledge of the site."

"I see."

"And we quite agree," Peter said after taking a drink. "After all, he and his team know the site like the back of their hands. And we haven't even seen any of the new things they've discovered recently."

"Of … of course." Kai wiped damp hands on her skirt and strained to keep her voice even. "I'll have Christine book a rental car and hotel immediately."

"No need for that," Pete assured her as he sat his coffee mug on the edge of her desk. "Coleman has taken care of all the details. Asa will be picking you up from the office on Friday at 7:00 a.m. sharp."

"Great … that's … helpful."

"Asa will be a great help on the project; an invaluable asset. The Coleman Foundation has great faith in him, you know." Pete drummed his fingers on Kai's desk, then stood to leave.

Kai stood as well.

"You've done a great job pulling all this together, Kai. I'll be anxious to hear from you next week. Revise your project plan based on what you find this weekend, and have Christine set up a meeting with me on Tuesday." He clasped her hand briefly, nodded to Jonathan, then departed.

Kai gazed at the door.

"Is something wrong?" Jonathan took Pete's abandoned mug and placed it in on the counter beside the coffee pot before coming to perch on the edge of Kai's desk, setting his own coffee mug carefully on the blotter beside him. "You seem a little preoccupied."

"Just have a lot of things on my mind, is all."

"Well, did the two of you hit it off?"

"Pardon?"

"You and Asa Matthews. Did you hit it off?" His grin had Kai wondering just what he meant by the words "hit it off."

"He's a fun guy, although he's a workaholic, just like you," he continued.

Asa Matthews, a workaholic? Right. She couldn't deny that Asa had many accomplishments, but he just didn't seem the workaholic type.

"Working with him won't be a problem, I hope?"

Kai gave a start of surprise. She could work with anyone. She had never had a problem before, and she wouldn't start now. "No, of course not. Why would you ask that?"

"No reason really, but you seemed a little tense when he joined the kickoff meeting yesterday. Did something happen on Monday when he came to brief you? Something I should know about?"

Kai's hand fluttered to her hair, afraid it might break free of its bun at the mere mention of Asa Matthews's name. "No, of course, no. Nothing happened. I … I've just been really anxious about the project, that's all."

"Well, good. We've got to keep the man happy. If Coleman got wind of any problems, it just might cost us this project. To hear them tell it, Asa Matthews hung the moon." He smiled at her. "But I have every faith in you to make things work. You always do."

I always do … "Yeah …" Kai's voice trailed off.

"Oh, and by the way," Jonathan said, as he stood up. "Regarding your nomination for partner, things are going well. You made the cut— of course that was a given—it won't be long before you'll be a full fledged partner, I'm positive of it."

At the mention of the partnership, all thoughts of Asa dropped away. Kai clasped her hands together in excitement. "Oh, Jon, I'm so happy about all this. I just can't believe it may finally come true."

"You're a prized asset, Kai. You're honest, hardworking, and innovative. We need people like you on our executive team. Look at this studio. You've accomplished unbelievable things in the six years since you've been with us, and you know I was the last person that believed KT & G could do historic preservation."

Kai smiled at that. When she first joined the firm, they had bumped heads more times than either of them could count. She was just out of school with a freshly minted Master's Degree and a drive to affect change, while Jon was comfortable, set in his ways, and wanted to maintain the status quo. Kai's eyes twinkled. "Proved you wrong didn't I?"

Jon snorted. "I'm embarrassed at my own ignorance. Not only did you prove we could do historic preservation, but you showed us it could generate revenue and prestige." He shook his head in amazement. "Who would have thought?"

She beamed.

"You called this one right, Kai. You made it happen. And you deserve to be a partner."

His pride in her meant a lot. More than he could know. "Thanks for tooting my horn to the board, Jon, I owe it all to you, you know."

"You never needed my help."

Kai stood when he turned to go.

He took her hands in his. "You're doing great work. I'll see you after you get back from your trip."

If I live through it.

"Oh, and say hello to Kenneth for me. I didn't get a chance to speak with him at the kickoff meeting, not that we owe him. I doubt having Drexel partnered with us gave us an edge."

Kai's head spun in confusion as she tried to keep up with John's rapid topic changes.

"May I speak frankly, Kai?"

She was wary, but willing to listen. Sitting down at her desk, she waited.

"I'm not trying to imply anything inappropriate. You know that."

She nodded. "Of course not, Jon. You would never ..." her voice trailed off under his dissecting gaze. "What are you not saying?"

"Just that you need to get out more," he said. He put a hand up to stop her from speaking. "Kai, we want hardworking and dedicated partners here at KT & G."

"Of course. I thought I was doing a good job of that." She took a breath because she could feel her pulse begin to pound.

"Hear me out. We want hardworking and dedicated partners. The Board wants that, of course. But *I* want hardworking and dedicated partners who are happy and well-adjusted." His hand silenced her again. "You've met Asa Matthews, Kai."

She nodded, wondering what Asa had to do with her partnership.

"Pay attention to him," Jon said. "He's got that winning combination of drive and *joive de vivre* that I'm talking about. From what I hear, he goes a little overboard with it from time to time, but still."

I'm being compared to Asa Matthews?

"He's a person you can't help but have a good time around." The brief look Jon gave her made Kai uncomfortable. "Let yourself have a good time when you're with him."

Kai gripped the lip of her desk with both hands to keep from jumping out of her seat. "Just what are you trying to say, Jon?"

He held up his hands in defense. "All I'm … Look, you've got the partnership in the bag. You've worked hard for six years. *Damned hard.* Sometimes harder than you should have. Have some fun with this project. We've won the bid. The hard part is over."

Had she heard correctly? "But what about …"

"Kenneth?" Jon waved the thought away. "You and Kenneth will never marry."

"That's not what I was going to say."

Jon leaned forward; Kai leaned back. "Kai, I've always thought of you like you were my own daughter—"

"I know that, Jon, but—"

"Let me finish. The firm may think it needs Kenneth Roselle and Drexel Development to partner with on deals, I don't. What I'm trying to say is, you don't need him, either. You never did."

Kai's face clouded with anger. "What are you saying, Jon? That I should just brush Kenneth aside? We've been together a long time. And he's been an important part of my success."

"I wouldn't go that far, though you've definitely been a part of his." Jon smiled sadly, then shook his head. "Kai, believe it or not, you would be in exactly the same place you are now without having ever laid eyes on Kenneth Roselle."

"Well." Kai blew out a breath. "Well."

"When I said I thought you and Asa Matthews would probably hit it off, I meant it. He's got a passion for his work that's equal to your own, but the man knows how to enjoy himself, too. Watch him, he'll show you the ropes."

Kai was speechless as Jon rose. She stood too and followed him to the door. "Let your hair down, Kai. Enjoy this, you deserve it."

The door clicked quietly shut behind him, but opened again before Kai could get her balance. Jon's head snaked through the crack in the door. His smile was kind. "Oh, one more thing. Have Christine add me to that meeting between you and Pete on Tuesday."

Then he was gone, and the room was quiet again.

Kai stood at the door for another moment, lost in the confusion of Jon's words. What was he trying to tell her? That she didn't have fun? That she didn't enjoy herself. That she didn't have a life? *I'm about to make partner, yet he's criticizing me for not having a social life?*

She threw up her hands. "I can't think about this without coffee."

In her office late that evening, Kai gathered the Ridgeway Plantation photos from the surface of her drafting table in a circular sweep of her arm. She shuffled and stacked until the pile was uniform, then she flipped through them, placing particular ones on the light table behind her. She switched a few, replaced others, and then after a second perusal, satisfied herself with the ten remaining photos. The rest of them she slipped into a large manila envelope for later.

She cleared the drafting table with a few swipes of her drafting brush, sprayed the surface with cleaner and wiped it off. Rolls of drafting paper of various weights were nestled in an egg crate carrier to the left of the table. A set of jewel-tipped pens, cleaned and sorted, sat nearby, and mechanical drafting pencils and leads from 6F to 6HB were separated in several slots in the drawers beneath the table.

As the cleaner evaporated, Kai rolled her chair back just enough to stretch her legs. She crossed her arms atop her head and listened to the quiet.

Nothing. Not a sound.

If she didn't already know that the door to her office was open and that it was 9:30 p.m., she would have turned to check the door and the clock. It could have as easily been 6 a.m.

She loved the quiet of the office when everyone had gone home to their families; there was simply something about the quiet that made her feel at peace. At those times, she could get comfortable and release the pent up creative energy in her soul without worrying about what her colleagues might think if they saw her in action.

Content that she had the freedom to let loose, Kai pressed her bare heels against the crossbar at the foot of the table, stretched fully and smiled.

Her design time always began quietly. She would sit for a moment to let her thoughts wander aimlessly. Sometimes, she would close her eyes and just think. Other times, she would crawl onto the couch opposite her desk and nap.

Nap wasn't the correct word, though. That was never what actually happened. Normally, she would tell herself to stretch out on the couch and take a fifteen-minute power nap, but as soon as her eyes closed and her breath became even, the ideas would flow. They would race through her mind—a whirlwind of energy, light, and pictures: shapes, smells, even sounds. Then she would jump up and rush to her table and sketch.

Sometimes she would turn away from the table, cross her arms and rest her head on her desk to get the ideas going. But no matter how she started, it was always peaceful and quiet, but then would transform itself into a frenzy of energy that she harnessed for the creative process.

The actual act of creation was anything but peaceful, more complete chaos, a total red-hazed passion of thoughts, pictures, and ideas coming together.

And she loved it.

Kai recoiled from the stretch and shoved her fingers in her hair; her curls tumbled down her back. She even loosened a button on the waistband of her skirt. Her shoes were already off.

Yes, she thought with a grin. *I'm ready.* She grabbed a roll of tracing paper and set to work.

Kai spent a restless Thursday night, wondering what the next day would bring. She had arrived at her office early on Friday; too early. It was six-thirty when she pulled into her parking space. All her tasks were in order, so there was no real reason for her to be there so soon. Her arrival just prior to Asa's would have been sufficient, but she needed some time to herself beforehand. She needed to prepare herself for him, for the onslaught of whatever he did to her by simply existing.

She exited the elevator on the fifteenth floor, flicking on lights as she moved down the corridor. Approaching her studio, she noticed the dim flicker of a desktop light. Judy Alvarez was hard at work, as usual. She reminded Kai of herself when she was just out of college, in early and out late. Determined to make a success of her career, Judy did the work of two or three people. She was well on her way to reaching that goal.

The girl's tenacity was evident as soon as she was hired. Judy even boldly approached Kai and asked her to be a mentor to her. Kai didn't hesitate. Judy was surprisingly mature for her age, and over time, they'd become close friends. And although she was six years Kai's junior, Kai eventually found herself asking Judy's advice on men and relationships.

"Mornin', Kai," Judy called cheerily from her desk.

"Good morning, Judy. I'm going down to Ridgeway, today. Looks like we'll be getting the project off the ground in a week or so."

"Great!" Judy's voice trailed off as she turned back to her work. Then mumbling, more to herself than to Kai, she said, "This is going to be so awesome."

"Stop by my office in a while. I'll update you on the latest," Kai said.

"Will do."

"Coffee, coffee," Kai muttered as she entered her office and flicked on lights. Her mind wouldn't be fully functional until caffeine entered her veins. She dropped her luggage at the door and went straight to the coffee maker.

When the brew was ready, Kai poured a cup and sipped it slowly, savoring the warmth and the jolt. She closed her eyes and drew in a deep breath. To her dismay, or pleasure—she hadn't decided which—her mind immediately honed in on Asa and what could only be described as "The Kiss." She shivered, then groaned and took another sip of coffee.

"Wow. What are you thinking about?"

The unexpected voice from the door startled her, and Kai's eyes flicked open. This time, she didn't lose her grip on her coffee cup, but she did decide she should probably take a seat. That and close and lock her door from now on. "This is becoming a pattern."

Judy entered the office and plunked down on the couch.

"Coffee?" Kai offered.

"Nah, I'm awake. I've been up since four."

"Judy, you work too hard."

"I'm sure you did the same when you started here."

"Yeah, maybe."

"And you're no different now. You just do more stuff at home."

Kai concurred as she sipped more coffee. "Well, I'm off to Ridgeway this morning."

"Okay," Judy said, crossing her legs and leaning back comfortably on the couch. "So what are you doing here? Why didn't you just get a rental car and leave from home?"

"Asa—Dr. Matthews—is driving. I'm going with him."

Judy tilted her head. "Are you okay with that?"

"Of course." Kai sounded a little too casual, a little too breezy, even as the reply slipped from her mouth. Setting her coffee mug carefully on the coaster by her telephone, she turned to rearrange the site photographs on her light table.

"Are you finally going to tell me what's going on with you two?" Judy asked.

Feigning innocence, Kai absorbed herself in the photos. "What makes you think something's going on?"

"Oh nothing, except that Asa Matthews is the most gorgeous thing that's walked through this studio since I've been here. Then there's the fact that he practically fought me over who would take you your purse at the Hound Dog."

Kai jerked around. "What?"

Judy waved away her question. "And the fact that you told me you were breaking things off with Kenneth makes you available—You did break things off with him, didn't you?"

Kai had never been able to make Judy understand why she stayed with Kenneth for so long. So, when she confided in her well-grounded protégé that she planned on breaking up with him, Judy had been ecstatic. A firm believer in soul mates, Judy felt that Kenneth was definitely not Kai's.

"Yeah. I did it at The Cheesecake Factory three weeks ago."

"Good. Now you're footloose and fancy-free. Free to indulge a little, maybe in Dr. Matthews. Lord knows he wants you. If a man that fine wanted me, I don't think I'd be running the other way. And all that hair. His locs are seriously tight."

"Who says I'm running the other way?" Kai protested. "Besides, I've never really cared for the dreadlock type, myself."

"Yeah, maybe not, but his look great. Well manicured, tidy … They just seem to fit him, you know. He looks—mmm, I don't know—dangerous."

Dangerous. Asa Matthews was definitely dangerous, but for Judy's benefit, Kai snorted derisively. "Yeah, right. Mr. Nineteenth-Century-Archaeologist in a cardigan and glasses is really dangerous. I'm so scared."

"He doesn't wear glasses," Judy said dryly. "And I doubt we'll ever see him in a cardigan. He sure looks fine in black, though. I bet that's his signature. Black. Mmm …" Her eyes rolled skyward as she raised her arms in a leisurely stretch. "He's sleek, like a cat."

"You need help, Judy," Kai said as she fiddled over items on her desk.

Sobering, Judy dropped her arms to her sides. "No seriously. I think you and Dr. Matthews would make a great couple. Aren't you the least bit attracted to him?"

When she didn't respond, Judy continued. "I'm not necessarily saying go after him. Just that he's great looking, intelligent and all that." She shrugged. "Enjoy the weekend with him. Just don't make it all business." Alarm must have flashed across Kai's face, because Judy backpedaled. "You don't have to make a move on him. But if there's a little chemistry, I say don't fight it."

There was plenty of chemistry; too much of it in Kai's opinion. She wasn't at all sure she could maintain her typical control in his presence, especially after his little performance at happy hour.

"Kai, you okay?"

With a sigh, she looked up. "Judy, can I confide something in you?"

"Sure, boss. You know you can."

Kai recounted her first encounter with Asa; the coffee spill incident and altercation in her office. Then in the parking lot at the Hound Dog, conveniently leaving out the part about Kenneth showing up, not sure if she was ready to discuss the fact that two men were fighting over her.

The smile on Judy's face when Kai finished was a surprise. She had expected disapproval. "What's that look about?"

"Guess I was right," Judy said.

"About?"

"The attraction. The chemistry."

Kai groaned. "God, it's awful isn't it?"

"Awful? Of course it's not awful. What are you talking about?"

"Well, unethical, the ..." She crossed to the bar and began straightening the already straightened sugar and creamer canisters. She wiped down the already clean countertop, then turned back to Judy. "To get involved with him while we're working together."

Judy moved to Kai's desk, propping her hip on the edge. "How do you figure that?"

"It's against my professional ethics," Kai explained. "How would it look, getting involved with people I do business with? It doesn't set a good example for others. Like you, for instance. I'm your mentor, and here I am cavorting with a colleague like I'm a common—"

"You're kidding me, right?"

"I'm not kidding."

Judy moved to stand in front of Kai. She folded her arms in reprimand. "Girl, puh-lease."

Kai put down the cloth she was holding. "Huh?"

"First of all," Judy said, taking Kai's hand and walking her back to her chair. She pushed her down in it and returned to the couch. "You're talking to a woman who is currently involved with your studio head."

"Yeah, and about that—"

"No, we'll get to Jeremy later; let me finish. What in heaven's name do you call your relationship with Kenneth? That's cavorting with a colleague, isn't it?"

"That's different."

"Different how?"

"It's purely a business relationship. We've never slept together."

Judy flung an arm out wide against the back of the couch and stared at the ceiling in disbelief. Narrowed eyes dropped down to peer at Kai. "You've got to be kidding. You're thirty years old; don't tell me you're still a virgin."

"No."

"Then what's the deal?"

"I don't know," Kai said with a shrug. "Work has always given me more of a thrill than sex. With Kenneth, there was attraction, in the beginning. We kissed a few times, but there wasn't any spark, romantically speaking. Things were working professionally, so we just left things the way they were."

"And he never pushed?"

"Of course he did. But we were just out of college when we met. He thought my reluctance was because I was a virgin. I never bothered to correct him, that's all. Eventually he gave up."

"But he still stuck with you? What man would want to be with a woman who's not attracted to him? Who won't sleep with him?"

"Kenneth is all about the money, Judy. We're a very successful team. He liked our image as a power couple."

"So you've been celibate for six years?" Judy said with wonder.

"Yep," Kai said. "It sure does help keep the mind clear."

"Yeah, right. What about Kenneth? Don't tell me he's been celibate for six years, too."

"No, of course not. Well, he thinks I don't know, but he gets his share on the side."

Judy held up a hand in protest. "Kai, don't tell me anything else. I'll lose all respect for you."

Kai's face fell, a little. "Oh Judy, you're the only one I can confide in about this."

"I'm just stunned," Judy said. "I never thought the two of you were suited to each other, but I can't believe you would stay with someone when you know he's sleeping around on you."

"Well, it's not like he was getting anything from me in that department. I couldn't deny him the pleasure from others."

"Kai, you can teach me a lot when it comes to architecture, but you've got a whole lot to learn about relationships."

Kai moved to the perch on the edge of her desk. "I need all the help I can get. School me, girlfriend."

Judy crossed her arms. "Okay, cool. My advice is to never lose respect for yourself, because the moment you do, your man will, too. And then at some point, you'll start to think it's okay for a man to be disrespectful, that you don't deserve any better."

Kai smiled confidently. "Okay. I've got that."

"No, I don't think you do."

Kai's smile fell. "Okay … I don't."

"Kai, don't ever let a man sleep around on you. It doesn't matter whether you're sleeping with him or not. If you're in a committed relationship, it should be monogamous."

Kai absorbed Judy's comments, then shook her head. "So what should I do about Asa? I get the feeling you don't see anything wrong with our being attracted to one another."

"You're right, I don't. It's only unprofessional—in my opinion, of course—if you let it get in the way of your job. But it's your responsibility to keep things professional."

Kai gave Judy a wary look.

"You're professional, Kai. I've seen you in action. You know how to keep your personal feelings out of the boardroom. You're just making excuses."

Crossing her arms over her chest, Kai said, "Okay, Miss Smartie-Pants, why am I making excuses?"

Judy looked skyward. "Oh, probably because you've never met anyone you connected with like Asa Matthews, because with one look, he can turn your knees to jelly. Because you're afraid that sex with him will give you a bigger thrill than work. Because you can't control how you feel when you're around him. Because, you—"

"Okay, okay. You've made your point. But I think I have a better one." Kai's mood turned serious. "I could jeopardize my chance at making partner. And there's no way I'm going to choose a man over my dreams."

"It's not a matter of choosing, Kai. Your relationship with Kenneth has soured your brain. You don't have to choose between having a relationship and having a career—as the old saying goes: You *can* have it all."

"I intend to." Asa Matthews's smooth deep voice drifted from the doorway to settle around Kai like a soft velvet cloak.

CHAPTER SEVEN

Judy rose to great him. "Dr. Matthews, it's good to see you again."

Kai's control over her emotions was precarious at best, so she hung back, observing her two colleagues from her perch on the edge of her desk. Asa was dressed all in black, as usual, and Kai could smell the woodsy scent that had haunted her for the past week. Was it aftershave? Maybe it was the soap he showered with. *No, let's not think of him bathing just yet.* As an image of Asa in the shower flickered in her head, Kai chastised herself sternly, then cleared her throat in a futile attempt to shake the picture of wet, soapy, hard-muscled man from her mind.

"Ms. Ellis," Asa said, turning to greet her.

Kai watched her hand disappear inside both of Asa's much larger ones. Rhythmically, his thumb stroked the soft, sensitive skin between her thumb and forefinger. He continued to hold her hand, continued to stroke.

She could feel him watching her, waiting for her to meet his gaze. But, coward that she was, Kai looked to Judy, who was shaking her head at her in dismay. *Okay I'm a coward, so sue me.* She took a deep breath, then turned to face him. His smile was warm and inviting, but beneath it, Kai could sense the raw sexuality that was ever-present. Helpless to stop herself, her gaze traveled lower, warmth spreading quickly over face when she realized Asa was waiting patiently as she shamelessly took in his powerful form.

"Sorry I missed you after the kickoff meeting," he said, an amused smile teasing his lips. "But I had to rush off to Wilburson; academic red tape concerning your team's next site visit."

"Yeah, I missed you, too." Kai gasped softly, her eyes locked on his lips. She realized too late what she'd just said.

Asa's smile widened, and he continued to stroke her hand "Anytime, anyplace," he said, giving her a sly reminder of his proposition.

"I mean, I missed you after the meeting, of course." Kai pulled her hand away with a jerk. Her brow creased with embarrassment and anger. Normally, she was very good at camouflaging her emotions, but Asa brought out feelings in her she couldn't seem to hide.

"Where are your things?" he said, breaking into her thoughts. "I'll take them down to the car."

"My things?" Kai felt flustered, discombobulated. She couldn't seem to clear her head.

"Yeah… your things? For the weekend? You did plan to wear clothes didn't you?" Asa held up a hand in surrender and grinned. "Not that I'm complaining, mind you. If you want to tour the plantation *au naturale,* I promise, I won't stop you."

He and Judy shared a laugh, but Kai ignored them. "My things … my things, uh." She turned back to the desk and drafting table, hoping that her luggage would miraculously appear in front of her. Her mind had gone completely blank. *Girl, get a hold of yourself.*

She peered into her coffee mug without seeing it. "I think I need more coffee."

Asa was grinning at her when she looked up. "It's full."

"I'm sorry. What?"

"Your coffee cup is full."

Kai stared at his straight teeth and cocky grin, a grin that was starting to get on her nerves. *What is he so God-awful happy about, anyway?* "What are you smiling about?"

"Don't answer that!" Judy burst in, with a laugh.

Kai closed her eyes momentarily and took a deep breath. Then she set her cup down and put her hands on her hips. "Are we going to Ridgeway, or are you two going to stand here all morning grinning at me?"

"I'm waiting on you," Asa said. "I asked where your things were. You never answered me."

Bristling, Kai pinned him in place with a glare, then stomped over to the door, where she had finally located her luggage, and picked up her laptop case and carry-on bag. She thrust them at Asa's chest as he walked toward her. "Well speak loud enough for someone one to hear you next time."

"Good idea," Asa said, glancing back at Judy. He gave her a quick wink, then said to Kai, "I'll make sure and try that next time. Be back in a few."

Kai watched him exit. "Can you believe him?" She said to Judy as she glared at his back. "How can I spend an entire weekend with him? He's exasperating."

Judy laughed. "You've got it bad, sister-girlfriend."

Half an hour later, Asa was speeding down the highway as the sun began to peek through the clouds. He was thankful they were going south on Interstate 75 instead of north. At six forty-five in the morning, rush hour in Atlanta had already begun. He relaxed into his seat and glanced over at Kai, who was gazing out of the passenger window in an obvious attempt to avoid looking at him.

They had stopped at Starbucks on the way out of town and stocked up on rations, blueberry muffins, croissants, and coffee—lots of coffee. Asa took a sip of java, then slipped his cup into the console cup holder, his hand colliding with Kai's in the process. When she jerked away, Asa wondered whether his teasing back at the office had been too strong. He glanced over briefly before turning back to the road. Kai's fiery curls stayed in his mind's eye.

He couldn't resist teasing her. Teasing was his normal way of lightening the mood when he was around women, but for some reason that method wasn't working quite so well with Kai. She seemed to have an aversion to letting go, having fun. Or maybe she just didn't like him. Well, the way he saw it, he really didn't have much choice in the matter. His only other option was to rip off her clothes and make love to her, which was exactly what he couldn't do. So, he stifled a groan and let the monotonous highway lines put him in a trance, dismissing the ludicrous notion that Kai didn't like him—of course she liked him. There was no mistaking her attraction or the chemistry between them. He was just going to have to modify his approach. In the meantime, maybe he'd try to figure out why the conservative Ms. Ellis was so uptight.

Kai kicked herself mentally for her ridiculous performance in the office earlier that morning. She was a confident and successful business-woman, but around Asa, she became a tongue-tied sixteen-year-old. And if that wasn't enough, she had jerked away from him just now as if she had been burned.

She closed her eyes and leaned back in her seat. Memories of Bobby Alders played like a home movie on her eyelids. She hadn't thought of Bobby in years, but since Asa Matthews had invaded her world, her experience with Bobby seemed to be foremost in her mind.

"Honey …" Asa's voice broke into her thoughts. Heat rushed to her face and chest so fast Kai didn't hear the rest of what Asa said.

She glared at him. "I know you didn't just call me 'honey.'" His games were becoming tiresome. In her anger, Kai forgot the professional politeness that typically governed her actions and she shifted in her seat to confront him directly. "Why do you think you can be so familiar with me, Dr. Matthews, when you know we have to work together." She paused to take a breath. "And let me also say this: even if we didn't work together, I would never go out with you, date you, or engage in any other activity with you. Is that clear? You may be able to charm other women with your smooth talking and all that … that … *hair*, but it doesn't sway me. So I would appreciate it if you would put your charms on hold for the duration of this project." She turned forward and waited for the barrage of accusations, questions and propositions, but Asa kept silent.

She was tempted to look over at him, but she didn't dare. Finally, a small triumphant smile crept over her face. She'd told him. Well, with some people, you simply had to be blunt. Asa Matthews was obviously one of those people. Smug, she folded her hands in her lap, lifted her chin, and stared at the endless ribbon of asphalt that stretched before them.

"Um, Kai?"

Was that cheerfulness she heard in his voice? Kai turned to Asa and blinked in astonishment. Her feeling of triumph disappeared. He was *grinning* at her. How could he be grinning? She had laid down the law in her best "I mean business voice," a tone that had never failed her. Worried, Kai wondered whether everything had come out of her mouth as she had intended. The way she and Asa seemed to mix, there was no telling what she had actually said. She groaned inwardly and steeled herself for the inevitable blow to come.

"I guess you didn't hear me clearly," Asa said. "I was asking for a croissant," he paused for effect, pointed down to the bag at her feet, and laughed, "… with honey—they usually toss in those little packs of honey. I hoped I might persuade you to spread a little over a croissant for me."

Kai fumed. "I'll tell you where I'd like to spread some honey," she grumbled, then cringed when Asa laughed again.

"I'd like nothing better, babygirl." Asa gave her a smoldering look before turning his attention back to the road. "But the cops might have something to say about that. Lewd behavior in public is probably a crime in Georgia, especially if you're operating heavy equipment."

The masculine chuckle drifting through the car's interior made Kai want to slide under the front seat. Instead, she engrossed herself in the road ahead. *Four hours. Four more hours before we reach Savannah. Four more hours to endure pure torture.*

"… but if you'll just pass me a packet …" Asa was talking, again. "… I'll spread it on myself, if I can. Sometimes it's hard, you know, when you're trying to drive and all."

Steam was spewing from Kai's ears, but Asa's laughter was infectious. She couldn't let a smile slip through. She fought it the entire way. She was making a fool of herself. "You can wipe that smirk off your face, Asa Matthews." Grudgingly, Kai picked up the bag and found the condiments he requested. She opened one, spread it on a croissant and handed it to Asa, knowing she'd never be able to look at a packet of honey the same way again. Grateful that she didn't jerk when her fingers touched his on the handoff, Kai leaned her head against the headrest and closed her eyes. She felt herself slipping into the deep, dark abyss where Asa Matthews and hot, sexy nights awaited. *Damn you, Bobby; you're the cause of all this.*

"Truce?" Asa said as he switched the croissant to his left hand.

"Huh, what?" Kai jerked back from the fog.

"Truce, okay? I'll admit, I have been coming on a little strong, but I can't help myself. You're a very attractive woman."

Kai groaned inwardly. *Now he's being nice. I'm losing this battle.*

"Yeah, yeah, I know," Asa said. "Put a hold on my game. Gotcha. Sorry."

His concession was surprising, and Kai relaxed in spite of her continued wariness.

Half of the croissant disappeared into Asa's mouth. Kai watched, fascinated, as his Adam's apple bobbed as he chewed, then swallowed. "Listen," Asa said. "All games aside. I'm not straight-laced and buttoned-down, not that I don't care about my work. I do. It's the most important thing to me right now. But I kid around quite a bit; I like to have fun." He took his eyes off the road long enough to glance her way. "You can do both, you know."

"Kid around and have fun. Really?" Wide-eyed, Kai feigned innocence.

"Oh, she's got jokes?! The lady's got jokes." Asa laughed and nodded in approval. "Good one. You should keep it up."

For a moment, Kai's breathe caught in her chest. It felt good to laugh and joke with Asa. His smile felt good. She smiled slightly herself, but it was gone as quickly as it had appeared when she realized Asa was no longer grinning.

"I don't want you to think I'm coming on to you when I'm only kidding around, all right? If we're going to work together, you've got to loosen up." He polished off what was left of his croissant and wiped his hand on a napkin. "So how 'bout it? Think we can do this truce thing? Get through this project without killing each other?"

Despite having just bawled the man out for his forwardness, Kai couldn't help but feel somewhat disappointed by Asa's concession. She took his hand anyway. "Okay, truce. And I apologize for jumping to conclusions." Suddenly, Asa's fingers tightened around hers. "Hey!"

Asa laughed at her alarm and loosened his fingers, but didn't let go. "I'm kidding, I'm kidding." He laced his fingers in hers and shook her hand and arm as if to get the kinks out. "Loose, Kai. Loose," he said, dropping her hand to grip the wheel. "Relax a little. It won't hurt you."

Yeah, right.

There was a seriousness in his expression that Kai could clearly see, despite the fact that he was concentrating on the road and not looking at her. "You know, life can be pretty interesting if you just let it happen to you from time to time instead of trying so hard to control it. You should try it."

Great, now he thought he could give unsolicited advice. Letting out a heavy sigh, Kai leaned back against the headrest and stared straight ahead. "That's a highly overrated notion."

"Sounds like you know from experience."

Kai didn't comment, and Asa let the subject drop.

Kai was pleased to learn that Asa wasn't a talkative driver. After they'd both consumed coffee and pastries, he flicked the radio to a jazz station and lapsed into silence. Kai had a lot to contemplate, and the four-hour road trip seemed as good a place as any to sort things out. Asa was at the top of her list. Between bouts of thinking about him over the past week, she had been thinking about Bobby. He was the love of her life as a junior in college. The second man she had ever trusted with her heart; the first being her father. Both had been mistakes she greatly regretted. Both men made her realize she could lose everything if she didn't take care; if she didn't pay attention and stay in control of herself.

She had been on scholarship at Georgia Tech when Bobby entered her life, and their relationship had been like a whirlwind. A senior and an art student, Bobby was as "anti" as Kai was conformist. He convinced her to kick back and have a little fun, and she rebelled in simple ways. Skipping a class here or there, taking a break to eat lunch with him or catch a movie instead of studying.

Bobby encouraged her to let her hair grow instead of keeping it neatly cut as she had for so many years. Kai happily accommodated his wishes, finding out she liked the way her thick jet-black coils swirled around her head like a dark halo.

With Bobby, she discovered sexual passion. A passion so surprisingly similar to what she felt when she designed buildings in her studio classes that it filled her with awe and wonder. She gave in to Bobby, to passion, to life, loving and playing in ways she hadn't since she was a child.

That year had been a carefree time. A glorious time that reminded her of freedom she hadn't seen since she was five years old and living with her parents. Gina and Vernon were artists, flower children of the sixties and seventies, and she was their love child.

For the first four years of her life, she'd grown up in the proverbial Volkswagen van, living at one campground or another all over the west coast and the southern U.S. They even spent a year on an Indian Reservation in Canada. Although she had only been a small child, Kai remembered the times when days were long, and her parents were always there, to spoil and indulge her.

Perhaps her memories were so clear because the day they left her was so equally strong in her memory, equally painful. She had loved both her parents with the trusting oblivion of any child, but her Daddy more so because she was considered so much like him: their hair, their coloring, their single-mindedness when they set themselves upon a path. With her parents, she had been free. Free to love and be loved. Free to be herself without worrying about pleasing others. Then suddenly, they were gone.

In loving Bobby, in letting herself be free, she had taken a big chance. One she hadn't allowed herself since her grandmother took her in. And in taking that chance, she had lost everything all over again. Because her grades slipped below the required B+ average, she lost her scholarship. Bobby graduated and left to pursue Lord only knows what. She lost her grandmother's approval, too, and outside of school and her grandmother, she didn't have much else.

A part-time job helped pay tuition, but college took a year longer than planned. And her grandmother's only wish, to see Kai graduate, went unfulfilled, because Floreen Arrington died six months before Kai donned her cap and gown.

From that point on, she kept both feet on the ground and her head out of the clouds. She won a fellowship to graduate school, then an entry-level position at KT & G and hadn't looked back since.

While the passion she had discovered with Bobby had consumed her, the experience had taught her that the power and drive she had always successfully channeled into her studies, into her designs, was uncontrollable when it came to people, destroying her personal relationships, her career goals. So she buried it, so deep that she gradually learned not to miss it. The same lessons learned kept her attached to Kenneth Roselle for too long. His passion and focus only on work was what she needed at the time. Instead of reminding her of what she'd denied in herself, partnering with Kenneth helped to keep her centered on her job.

Kai peeked over at Asa. He was so different from Kenneth, from any man she'd ever known, even Bobby. Dark dreadlocks hung luxuriously around his face, grazing his forearms as long thick fingers gripped the steering wheel. He seemed to always be there, invading her dreams whenever she closed her eyes. Cocky and proud, he would pull her into his strong embrace. Sometimes he was naked and aroused, sometimes fully clothed. But always, always, he wanted her, and that made him irresistible. Unfortunately, she always felt powerless, and completely out of control. In her dreams, Asa would reach for her openly, or with only a gesture or a smile, and just like that, she fell into the abyss.

Kai smothered a helpless groan and dragged her gaze from Asa's well-muscled physique. Knowing how much she desired the man who sat beside her, yet fully aware that she couldn't allow herself to give in to the bite of passion he ignited in her, with his raw, barely contained sexuality.

Hours later, Asa turned into the parking lot of a Days Inn on the Riverfront in Savannah. Kai had dozed off during the drive, and she stirred as the car came to a stop. He had enjoyed watching her sleep as he drove. Her features were softer, her mouth lush and relaxed. He could only hope that he could manage somehow to keep her as relaxed and warm when she was awake as she had been during her nap. Before she fell asleep, she had worried over something long and hard, her forehead creasing as she studied the problem. Asa was grateful when she finally dozed off. Hopefully, she had solved her problem.

He hesitated to wake her, but he needed to go into the hotel to see about their reservations, since check-in wasn't until twelve, and it was only eleven o'clock. At the same time, he didn't want her waking up alone in a locked car.

Now where did that thought come from?

He shook his head. He supposed he had become somewhat protective of her after their encounter with that snake, Roselle. His hand was on the passenger headrest, only inches from where Kai's head lolled to the side. She would have a crook in her neck. Then she'd be cranky and crotchety, and wouldn't want him near her. Grinning despite himself, Asa realized he liked when she was angry at him and spitting fire. She didn't need his protection. She could take care of herself.

Resigning himself to the inevitable, his fingers flexed before he reached to touch Kai's hair. Her bun had loosened while she slept, and several curls fell across her face. Asa brushed a few of them away, and Kai turned to snuggle against his hand. Desire hit him hard in the gut. God, she was beautiful, and she didn't even realize it. She was too focused on her work and career to have a clue that she was so desirable.

This was precisely the kind of woman he needed in his life, Asa suddenly realized. Someone confident, who knew what she wanted and went after it. Someone who was as into her work as he was into his. Someone who understood—completely understood, and accepted—how work could become an obsession. She was the other half of him that he hadn't realized was missing. They were two sides of the same coin, he and Kai Ellis.

A small voice in the back of his head told him that now was exactly the wrong time to become obsessed with a woman. He was skating on thin ice with Harold, and if he started something with Kai that didn't work out, he stood a good chance of losing big. Kai could lose even bigger.

But how could he think about the consequences when God had designed his perfect woman? Gently, he brushed the pad of his thumb over Kai's cheek. He had been waiting for her all his life. It wasn't logical, but simply the truth. Now all he had to do was convince Kai of the fact.

The midday sun beamed down on them through the windshield, and Asa could almost pretend they were a long married couple on a weekend road trip to one of their favorite seaside towns. As he watched her, Kai's eyes inched open, and she gave him a watery smile. Asa's stomach twisted as she stared blankly at him. The way she gazed up at him, like a lover awakening from blissful sleep, she wasn't even close to being lucid, and he'd be damned if he was going to wake her fully and remind her that she could barely tolerate him.

"Go back to sleep, baby girl," he crooned. "I'm going into the hotel to see about our rooms."

He couldn't resist giving her cheek a final stroke before easing his hand away. It was a struggle not to brush his lips against hers, but he resisted, finally letting out a sigh of relief when her eyes closed again and her head rested on the seat.

Asa got out, closing the door gently before heading into the hotel.

The matronly desk clerk smiled in greeting. "Well, hello there, Dr. Matthews. Good to see you again."

"Mrs. Sophie." He gave her a polite nod. "I know we're a little early, but you don't, by chance, have any rooms ready yet, do you?" He glanced through the plate glass window of the lobby to the parking lot beyond. Kai had just stepped out of the rental car and stretched lazily, still sleepy. His lips curled into a smile.

"Ah, the Missus needs a little more rest, I take it," Sophie said. "I'll see what we have." She clicked away on the hotel computer. "Looks like we do have a room available. Three- sixteen. Is that okay?"

"Just one?"

"Beg your pardon?" Sophie looked confused.

"We're colleagues," Asa explained when he realized what Sophie was thinking.

"Hmmm." Sophie's sideways glance told him she didn't believe a word, but his attention was snagged again as Kai crossed the parking lot toward the entrance.

"Hmmm," Miss Sophie said again.

"So do you have two rooms?"

"We'll why on earth would you want two?" She glanced at the door, her eyes making a quick appraisal of Kai as she entered the lobby, before turning back at Asa. "She'll give you a run for your money."

The desk clerk's quick summation of the situation made Asa think he had stayed at the hotel one too many times. He'd always wanted to try the Bed and Breakfast across the street. Maybe next time he would stay there.

Sophie looked down at the computer screen in front of her. "We won't have a second room until check-in. How about I go ahead and give you this room. You know, let the Missus take a nap." She winked at him. "Maybe get the ball rolling a little faster for you, eh?"

Asa was careful not to match her sly grin with one of his own, but had to like the lady's style.

Kai made a slow, drowsy turn in the queen-sized bed, snuggling contentedly against the pillow she was holding. After losing sleep over Asa the last few days, she was truly exhausted. The nap had done wonders. Reveling in the luxury of the rare relaxation time, she listened to a shower running and wondered whether she was still dreaming. Her dreams had been delicious. After riding for several hours in such close proximity to Asa, her dreams of him had become much more intimate.

As the shower continued, she drifted off, tumbling back into an erotic fantasy. She could see Asa in the shower, rippling with muscles. Black curls covered his chest and tapered in a "V" at his navel, his physique amplified by the water and soap that sluiced over him. He invited her in, pulled her to him, and grasped her bottom with both hands. His mouth enveloped hers, sucking, teasing, opening, devouring. They moved together fitfully, under the warm spray of the shower, anxious in their need for one another. Thick masculine fingers pinched and squeezed, grazed and stroked, until she could stand no more. Then feather-like palms brushed the tips of her nipples before moving lower to press into sensitive flesh, exploring the heat building between her thighs. Kai was shivering when she drifted off to sleep again.

Asa stepped out of the shower in the cramped hotel bathroom and dried off. He twisted a towel loosely around his hips and rifled through his shorts for his cell phone, then remembered leaving it in his overnight bag just outside the door. He swore softly, then opened the bathroom door a crack and peeked out. He hadn't checked his messages since last night, and he was anxious to learn whether his graduate students had discovered the cemetery, but he didn't want to disturb Kai, especially since she probably still had an attitude over him being in her hotel room.

Knowing Kai would be too polite to complain, he had let Mrs. Sophie explain the room availability problem, and smugly followed her cute, but perturbed behind to her room. Miraculously, she'd let him in the door so he could change into workout clothes. He even managed to finagle the room key from her. She could be out or snoozing when he returned from the gym, he had argued, and he had been right. She was fast asleep before he left for the gym and was still asleep when he returned two hours later.

After debating whether to get dressed and worry about checking his messages later, he decided he could listen via speakerphone while he shaved. If he kept the volume low, Kai would probably sleep through it.

Gingerly, he stepped out of the bathroom to find Kai fast asleep. His concerns about waking her had been for nothing. As he tiptoed to the bed to retrieve his phone, he stopped abruptly. Kai was sprawled across the bed on her back, tangled in the sheets, and moving fitfully. *What on earth?*

His first reaction was alarm. Until he realized, her moans were more erotic than fearful. Whatever—whomever she was dreaming about, she was pretty turned on. Shaking off the thought, he bent down to search for his phone. He stood transfixed, swallowing hard when she brought a hand to her breast and gently caressed a hard nipple. His rational mind told him to get his cell phone out of his bag and go back into the bathroom, fast. But his body thought better, and his legs refused to move. Biting back a groan, he watched Kai's hand trail lower, moving across her stomach. Reluctantly, he dragged his eyes away. If he wasn't careful, he'd do something they both might regret. With gritted teeth, he grabbled his duffle bag and fished out his phone.

"Asa ..."

He raised an eyebrow and stood up when he heard his name, surprised that Kai had awakened so quickly.

"Hey, sleepy head ..." he began. His voice cracked, and he cleared his throat nervously. "You woke up...." Cell phone forgotten, a roguish smile curled his lips. She was still asleep, and dreaming about him. Well, that would explain the ecstasy, his ego surmised.

He moved to the head of the bed, watching shamelessly, as she rubbed and caressed her body with lazy, sleepy strokes. Her hands gripped the bed sheets with tense fingers, and Asa couldn't resist the temptation to reach out and touch her. He twisted a loose curl at her temple around his finger. She had thrashed her hair out of its bun, and it lay sprawled over the pillow, a mirror of her body sprawled across the bed. Asa's eyes moved lower, quite appreciative that Kai had undressed to a camisole and panties before laying down for her nap. Her bare legs tangled in the sheets at her knees and a camisole strap had worried itself off the edge of her shoulder. Asa trailed a hand down her cheek, and she instinctively turned her face into his palm. He smiled at the habit she seemed to have fallen into with him.

God, he wanted to crawl into that bed with her, but he resisted. Kai would hate him afterwards, but it couldn't hurt to look. He laid his cell phone on the bedside table and eased a hip onto the edge of the bed so he could watch her sleep.

After a few moments, her eyelids fluttered open in a sleepy haze. She smiled, more relaxed than he had ever seen her.

"Hey," she said, snuggling in close. "I was dreaming about you."

Asa stifled a groan and resisted touching her again. He wanted her so bad he could taste it. He cleared his throat. "So it appears."

Kai watched him expectantly, as if waiting for him to make a move. He didn't. Couldn't, despite his revved up libido, so it came as a complete shock when she pulled him down by his hair, licked her lips and laid one on him.

CHAPTER EIGHT

Too shocked to do anything else at the moment, Asa fell into the kiss, but he was smart enough to pull back before it was too late. He looked into Kai's eyes, shaking her gently. "Wake up, baby. You're still dreaming."

Kai looked him dead in the eye, bit her lower lip suggestively and shook her head. At Kai's sudden and uncharacteristically erotic gesture, Asa almost went off in his pants. Something he hadn't done since ninth grade, when he was in love with his algebra teacher. Still, caution was warranted, despite Kai's encouragement. "Tell me," he demanded. "Out loud. Tell me you're not dreaming, baby." *Maybe I'm the one dreaming.*

"I'm not dreaming," Kai said softly. "I'm completely awake."

That was all Asa needed to hear. And this time, Kai didn't have to initiate the kiss herself. Asa was practically on top of her. He wasn't ashamed of his eagerness, just grateful for Kai's cooperation.

She moaned softly, flicking her tongue against Asa's. Inside he sighed with relief. Kai was lucid and wanted him. A thrill sharper than what he'd felt the night he first laid eyes on her shuttered through him. He deepened the kiss.

She had been dreaming of him. Them. Together. She wasn't as immune to their attraction as she pretended. But what turned him on most was knowing that behind that little Buddha smile of hers she was fantasizing about getting busy with him. Thank God for that, because his desire for her was becoming an obsession. As his mouth moved over hers, Kai braided her fingers into his hair. He stroked her gently, drawing her closer, felt her shudder under his hand. He brushed the camisole strap off her shoulder and moved to cup her breast.

Her entire body tensed.

Asa cursed and stilled his hand, murmuring quiet words of encouragement against her lips as he prayed she wouldn't turn him away. There was a pregnant pause, but finally, she relaxed. Asa let out a pent-up breath and lowered his head to the valley between her breasts. The pads of his thumbs circled her shoulders offering continued encouragement. Kai's body tensed slightly, then her hand was in his hair again, guiding him to her breast. He took her in his mouth and suckled gently. Realizing she couldn't yet tell him verbally that she wanted him, her soft, reluctant cry of pleasure was like a crash of cymbals in his ears, so powerful and deafening was its message.

Asa forced himself to breath, to take things slowly, but his body fought his mind for control. He dragged his mouth back to Kai's and plunged his fingers into her hair. Her timid explorations into his mouth heightened his arousal, affecting him to a greater degree than a bold and direct gesture ever would have. She tasted sweeter to him for her shyness, and his hands slid anxiously down her body, touching and teasing as he caressed silky smooth limbs. Completely in tune with her body, he could feel her need intensifying. She wanted him, and he was desperate to give her what she craved.

Again, he paid homage to her breasts with his mouth, while his hands moved lower, grazing the waistband of her panties. Already aroused from her fantasies, Kai cried out when his fingers ventured between her thighs and slipped beyond the edge of lace and silk. She groaned aloud when his whole palm met her feverish heat. Asa peeled away the moist material that clung to her skin, gently parting her desire-slick folds to stroke. She shuddered against him, a moan trembling from her lips.

Her body tensed as she struggled against the pleasure he gave her. Asa anticipated the hand that moved to push him away, and when it came, he resisted, refusing to release her, refusing to let her deny her passion. He easily batted her hand away and increased the pressure against her center. His thumb moved insistently in a circular motion, until finally a ragged sob bubbled from her throat. This time when her body tensed, it was to press her pelvis into his palm.

Asa moved lower, shifting and sliding, maneuvering until his shoulders were cradled between her thighs. He caressed her skin with his lips, tasted her with his tongue as he stripped away her panties. She cried outright when he covered her with his mouth and slipped a finger inside her. As she writhed beneath him, he increased the rhythm of his strokes, and let his towel fall away. His tongue, his fingers, his lips, led her closer to climax, her gasps growing louder and more fitful with each stroke. Until finally, finally …

She melted against him. Broken sobs spilling from her lips, her breath coming in short, quick gasps as he took her over the edge. Her muscles clinched tightly around his fingers, fluttered in butterfly spasms, then relaxed. Asa moved his hands to her waist and held her, kissing her stomach gently as she sobbed. She was still tearful as he trailed kisses up her torso, then moved to cover her.

He felt like a god, a world conqueror. Kai was his and nothing could stop the smile that spread over his face as he rose above her.

Except tears.

His face fell abruptly. She turned her head when she realized he was watching her, an anguished sob convulsing her shoulders. His heart rolled sharply. Her cries were no longer the result of pleasure. Stunned that he could have read her so wrong, Asa couldn't move for a second. He lay heavily atop her, his erection a faded memory. He wasn't sure how many minutes had passed when Kai squirmed beneath him.

Rolling way, he barely managed to suppress his sigh of helplessness. He pulled her into his arms, knowing nothing else to do, or say. Worry took the place of desire, as hot tears rolled down Kai's cheeks and dripped onto his chest.

Inside, Asa cursed. Cursed the man who had hurt Kai so much she couldn't enjoy being loved. Cursed her experiences, whatever they were, that held her in an emotional prison. Cursed himself for being so thoughtless and insensitive. But, despite the cause of her tears, what had just happened between them was not a mistake. Yet he knew without a doubt, it was exactly how Kai would interpret it.

Kai sat up and stared out the window of the hotel room. She pushed her hair back from her face and held her pounding head gingerly as her eyes adjusted to the sunlight streaming through the window. She looked down at her wristwatch and groaned. It was almost two o'clock, and they hadn't even been to the site yet. She groaned even louder when she glanced down at the sheets tangled around her legs. Heat flooded her face, then spread to her chest and down into her belly. Kai lowered her head and covered her eyes, puffy from crying, as she remembered what had recently transpired in the room.

She stilled. Suddenly alert, she listened for sounds of Asa. The way he stalked around like a cat, she might find him in a chair in the sitting area or humming in the bathroom. Hesitantly, she let a hand trail down the camisole she wore to her breasts and shivered. Asa had touched her there. Her hand moved lower and alarm bells rang loudly in her head. They had almost … She had almost … Kai drew her legs up to her chest and wrapped her arms around her knees. There she rested her chin and pondered what had happened between them.

He had been incredibly gentle. Not at all like she would have expected. The way his hands had caressed her, prodding and prompting her for a response, lifting her to heights she thought she'd never fly to again. He'd given her pleasure without seeking his own, allowed her to experience his touch, his caress, without asking for more.

Pain prickled at her eyelids as fresh tears threatened. He had wanted her, was more than ready to make love, but sensed her fear and apprehension and stopped himself. It was a reaction she hadn't expected. Not from Asa, who obviously had a healthy sexual appetite. Why he hadn't taken what she offered surprised her, almost more so than her own responses to his touch. She opened her eyes, letting her gaze flit from one object in the nondescript hotel room to another.

Why couldn't he have just given in, instead of playing the gentleman? At least, then she could be angry with him. But he hadn't. She rubbed her eyes on her knees and took a deep breath. She wasn't sure how this was going to affect their professional relationship, but she was thankful for his restraint. It was what she wanted, right? So why, she wondered, was she shivering at the thought of his touch, and wanting him all the more? Because he had graciously controlled his own needs in deference to hers. She stood up, desperate to ignore the feelings of desire that pooled in her belly.

"Get a grip on yourself," she ordered loudly. "He's probably just playing you, so you'll come begging him for it next time."

Kai thought about the things Judy told her before the road trip. She was a professional and an adult. So was Asa. They knew how to handle themselves. Kai padded to the bathroom. A relaxing shower would release some of the worry and tension that filled her. She hoped.

A few minutes later, the shower having had the desired effect, and she was calmer, if not completely decided on her course of action with Asa. She continued to ponder her dilemma as she brushed her hair and pulled on a fresh pair of slacks. She had enjoyed the pleasure Asa had given her. She would be lying if she denied it. And it was tempting to see if she could handle being with someone so worldly. He clearly wanted her in a way no one else ever had, including Bobby. She smiled briefly, then sobered. Asa was a player, used to getting what he wanted from women. For all she knew, he started trysts with women on every dig site he descended upon.

No. Reality made her decision clear. He wouldn't be honing his love-making skills on her. She had a professional career to nurture and maintain, not to mention her reputation. Kai Ellis would not become Asa Matthews's next paramour, and she would tell him so as soon as she saw him again. She retrieved a silk shell from the closet and slipped it on, then checked the time on the bedside alarm clock on her way to the bathroom.

Five minutes later, when she was done applying a miniscule amount of make-up, she glanced at the clock again. It was getting late, and she had yet to hear from Asa. Hesitant to call the desk and ask for him, she wondered where he was, assuming he had finally gotten a room of his own.

She was anxious to go to the site now, needing a distraction. Once they arrived, she'd find something to keep herself occupied. She knew that Asa's team had completed some excavations since her last visit, which he had planned to discuss with her, but after she'd practically begged him to make love to her, how could they carry on as if nothing had happened between them? Maybe she could get those field notebooks and wander the site by herself, or just sit in one of the work sheds and look over them on her own. She'd rather study the dry, scientific field notes alone than endure Asa's woodsy cologne and heavy baritone as he led her around the site. She resolved to make a beeline to work shed number two as soon as they arrived at Ridgeway.

Now that she had a plan, her courage was renewed.

An hour after Asa left Kai's room, he slipped the electronic room key in its slot and turned the latch to his room. Kai had been pretending to sleep when he left her, but she had been breathing faster than a bellows. Same as him. But if it was easier for her to pretend to be fast asleep, Asa wasn't going to make the situation worse by calling her on it. The carefree smile he'd plastered on his face for Mrs. Sophie's benefit when he went to the lobby to get another room had slipped quickly and now was long gone. He hauled his laptop case and other luggage into the room and sat down on the edge of the bed, relieved to finally be alone.

He couldn't seem to shake the feelings that had built in him earlier as he had held Kai in his arms. She had looked so vulnerable, so small and helpless. She had been utterly and completely his for the taking, but he couldn't do it. Not to her or to himself. Something in her eyes told him how much she really wanted to take the next step, but the same thing told him she was afraid to do so.

Cupping his chin in his hand, Asa contemplated his attraction to Kai, choosing to blame the physical—anything deeper or more significant he refused to face for the moment; had to be the hair. Seeing it fanned out over those bed sheets, wild and unencumbered, loose and free made him want to free Kai from the prison of propriety in which she had jailed herself. She deserved the freedom of passionate, uncomplicated sex, the freedom of wild abandon. The freedom to love and be loved. Anyone with so much drive and ambition, passion and heart for her career deserved to experience the same in her personal life.

He'd brought her to climax, had her hot and ready for him, but the tears stopped him. No matter how much he wanted her, he would never force her. His sole concern now was how to deal with the issue. She would probably try to pretend it never happened. She'd become an ice princess like before, and he'd have to thaw her out all over again.

"Brother-man," he said angrily, as he unpacked his laptop and plugged in his modem. "You've screwed this one up royally." The cell phone on his belt began to vibrate. He scowled and attached the earpiece. "What?"

"Well, excuse me, little brother."

With effort, Asa lessened the growl in his voice. "Sis. What's up?"

"That's what I was calling you about."

"Huh?"

"Cammy … UVA … Hello?"

Asa drew a hand across his face. "Sky, give me a break all right. Helping Cammy get into the University of Virginia isn't exactly at the top of my priority list. I've got a real job, you know." Normally helping friends, cousins, or colleagues' kids with their college entrance application essays was something he gladly made time for, but this thing with Kai had him so off kilter he was having a hard time concentrating on anything else.

"Unh hunh, like that ever stopped you before. Okay, boy, spill it. What's wrong?"

"Nothing's wrong." Asa bit down his annoyance and stared at a black screen as his computer booted up. Kai's reflection stared back at him, her hair loose and waving in the breeze. He almost smiled, until he noticed the shimmer of a tear trail down her cheek. *Man, I'm losing it.*

"Hello?... Hello?" Schyler called. "Asa?"

"Yeah, yeah." Kai's image faded, replaced by the blue and white of *Windows* clouds as the laptop chimed to life.

"Asa, honey. I don't mean to be a pest, but I really do need to know what's up with Cammy's essay. Her mom's bugging me. Have you had a chance to look things over?"

"Schyler, the application isn't due until Christmas, that's six months away."

"I know, baby. I know, but come on. Tell me something, anything to get Nancy off my back."

"It's fine," Asa said, stretching the truth a bit. "I've glanced at it, and it seems okay, but I need time to read more carefully. Give me until next month. I've got a lot on my plate."

"Hey, that's cool. I understand. I'll tell Nancy it's in the bag, that you're still reviewing, but—so far, so good."

Asa felt his sister's relief over the phone. "That all?"

"Well ..." Schyler hemmed and hawed a little. "It was. Until ..."

Distractedly, Asa pulled up a database listing of the artifacts that had recently been found. "Until what?" He could go over them with Kai on the site, which would give him something to look at besides her.

"Until you answered the phone." She paused. "What's going on with you? You don't sound like yourself at all."

Women. Why do they have to be so damned perceptive?

"You seemed excited about this site visit, especially since it was going to give you some time to get to know your new babe."

"She's not a babe."

"Testy, testy. Okay. So obviously she's the problem. What's up?"

Asa rolled is eyes at his sister's editorializing and scrolled up and down a list of walking sticks, vaguely noting that Jamal, one of his graduate students, had failed to date more than thirty percent of them. He grunted into the phone, not sure whether he wanted to indulge his sister's speculation about the state of his relationship with Kai.

"Little A., you heard me. What's up?"

"Things aren't going as well as I had hoped."

"What? My brother having trouble with the ladies?"

"It's a difficult concept to grasp, I know," he commented dryly. "But yes. I'm having a little trouble."

"You sure don't sound like my brother. I don't know whether I like it."

He grunted, paying more attention to his database than to Sky.

"Maybe you should leave this one alone."

That caught Asa's attention. "Why should I?"

"Oh, brother. I didn't mean it as a challenge. Look. She's obviously not your type, alright? She might look the part, but other than that, she's pretty different from your typical selection."

"What's that supposed to mean? You don't think I can handle an intelligent babe?"

"Thought she wasn't a babe."

"Look, Sky, she's just got some issues, that's all." He rubbed his knuckles over the stubble on his chin. He never had gotten around to shaving. "I've gotta figure out how I'm going to play it."

"Mmm hmmm."

He obviously hadn't fooled his sister.

"Okay, tell me what happened."

"We're riding to Savannah, right? We were eating croissants and stuff and I made a joke about honey. She thought I was calling her honey. Which I was, but—"

"I get it. You wanted her to pass the honey, too," Schyler finished. "Clever. Then what?"

"Man, she got all pissed off." He was surprised his anger was still there. The incident in the car had been minor. But coupled with what had happened later, it began to dawn on him how far her sexual repression went."

"Down, boy. She's really got you wound up."

"If you only knew."

"So she doesn't like you teasing her?"

"Sky, you know me. That's what I do." He considered his methods momentarily, doubting them for the very first time. "Part of the charm, you know. Anyway, she keeps getting bent out of shape when I'm just kidding with her."

"Like how?"

"I'll get her nice and relaxed, then she tenses up, pulls back whenever I start teasing her. Maybe she thinks I'm making fun of her or something."

"That doesn't seem so bad. It just sounds like she hasn't vibed with your sense of humor yet. She just has to get used to you."

"Nah, sis. It's more than that. I think some guy screwed with her head."

"What makes you say that?"

"Er ... well," Asa stammered and glanced back at the database he'd forgotten about. Maybe he should mark the walking sticks that Jamal still needed to date. He reached down to search his saddlebag for a pencil and pad.

"A."

"Hold on, Sky. I'm trying to find something to write with. I do have other things to do besides gabbing with you."

"You ain't fooling me. I hope you realize that."

Asa sighed loudly into the phone. "I do have work to do."

"So what makes you think somebody screwed with her head, Asa. Huh?"

"Just, something I got a sense about."

"Uh huh, and how did you get that sense, A?" Schyler's voice rose a little in pitch. "What did you do?"

"Girl, calm down. I didn't commit any crimes. We're both consenting adults."

"All right, all right. Fine."

"Yeah well, somebody's messed with her head. Bad."

"You gonna quit with that and tell me why you think so?"

"Cause I'm God-damned irresistible, that's why," he quipped, though he wasn't laughing. "And she's resisting me."

"Ha ha."

Asa sighed. "Here's the deal. I'm in her hotel room, right?" He interrupted himself before Schyler could. "Don't ask me what I was doing in her room, I was just there, okay?"

"All right. Go on."

He proceeded to tell her what had happened, her silence broken by an occasional "whoa."

"And one thing led to another ..."

"Oh, Asa, baby. Please say you didn't."

"Man, Schyler, that's the problem. We didn't. She wanted to, but she was crying by that point." A heavy breath seeped from his lungs. "Her asking for a kiss isn't asking for sex. Besides, she had just woken up, and I'm not sure she really wanted what she was asking for." Miserable, he stared at a gray dialogue box on his laptop screen. Silence stretched over the phone line long enough to let his sister know he wouldn't share anything more.

"A, you still there?"

"Yeah, yeah. I'm here."

"I didn't mean to bring you down, baby."

"It's all right. I'm cool." He wasn't, but it was what Sky expected him to say.

"You know," his sister's voice was gentle but laced with warning. "She may still be with her man."

Asa's brow raised in surprise, but then he remembered their altercation with Kenneth Roselle in the Hound Dog parking lot. He knew he didn't have to worry about taking Kai from Roselle, she'd already dropped him. But if anyone could screw up a together sister like Kai, it was Roselle. Here he thought he'd been pleasuring Kai, but he'd probably caused her more pain. Asa was disgusted with himself. Who knows the mind games Roselle might have played on her. And he had never even stopped to consider that she could have reasons other than her career goals for not wanting a man in her life right now. "Damn."

"A—"

"Listen. I gotta go, Sky. I'll talk to you when I get back."

"A—"

Asa closed the phone without saying goodbye, dropped the earpiece and went back to inventorying the walking sticks.

What was he supposed to do now when he wanted Kai so bad it was like a fist clutching at his heart? He blew out a long breath and stood, pressing his fingers against his eyelids. Well, the best thing he could do for Kai Ellis right now, and himself, was to stay away from her, he decided. She wasn't ready for what he wanted from her. Maybe she never would be. He checked the time. It was almost two. Since she had been "sleeping" when he left her, Asa decided to wait until two-thirty to call about going to the site.

At the plantation, he could finish cataloguing the walking sticks instead of having Jamal do it. Anything to keep himself busy, and his mind off Kai. Unfortunately, there was still that matter of her site tour.

He ran a hand through his locs and glanced down at his saddlebag. He had brought three field notebooks with him, and there were others in the work sheds on site. Maybe he'd just hand her an armload and let her fend for herself.

Kai reached for the phone on the nightstand and was startled when it rang before she had a chance to pick up the receiver.

"Uh, hello?"

"Kai? It's Asa."

With her heart thumping nervously in her chest, she covered the receiver and cursed herself for picking up the phone before she'd gathered herself. She counted to ten really quickly, then raised the phone back to her ear.

"Hello," she said again. "Yes?"

When she heard Asa nervously clearing his throat, she relaxed a little, and the tension that had begun to resurface in her shoulders began to seep away.

"Uh, yeah. Are you about ready to get over to the site? I thought maybe we could do a quick tour today before it gets too late. Um ... then we can ..."

Kai gripped the telephone receiver tighter when Asa paused. Her heart thudded in her chest as she wondered what he was thinking.

"... then we can go over the restoration plans in greater depth tomorrow."

The stilted conversation made Kai wish for Asa's typical flirty banter. "That, that sounds fine, I'll ... I'll be ready in five minutes." Kai hung up and searched near the bed for her shoes. He had sounded as nervous and unsure as she felt. Maybe he planned to ignore what had happened between them.

The disappointment she felt at that possibility made no sense, making Kai wonder what her reaction would have been had he done the opposite.

Asa barely spoke a word to Kai as they drove to the site. He'd planned to apologize, until she met him in the lobby looking like a shy kitten. Was she angry, or simply embarrassed? It was impossible to tell, so he figured his best bet was to keep his mouth shut.

He ground his teeth together as he parked and got out of the car, slamming the door behind him. He'd done a bad, bad thing, Asa decided as he took off up the hill without waiting to see whether Kai was behind him. "One day," his mother had frequently told him, "your rash behavior is going to catch up with you." That time seemed to be closing in fast, because he'd barely gotten in Kai's good graces, and he'd screwed up already. They still had a couple of months to work together. He stopped and looked back. Kai was trudging up the hill in a pair of dressy looking slacks and a summer top, but she had the good sense to wear comfortable shoes. As she got closer, he could see that her jaw was set.

Good, she was just as pissed as he was. That suited him fine. If he was mad at her and she was mad at him, maybe he could keep his hands out of her panties. Her hair was falling out of its French knot, and he cursed under his breath. If she didn't keep that hair tied up, he would never be able to keep his hands off her. Not that it mattered either way, he thought ruefully. If it was tied up, he'd just pull it down again. His frustration needed a release, so to piss her off he said, "Keep up slim, I don't want to have to carry you back to the hotel." He got a steely-eyed glare from her, and that made him feel fine. He turned and kept going.

Only through sheer determination and professional training did Kai manage to keep her lips tightly shut. Her latest encounter with Asa had her straining not to call a cab for the airport and take the first flight back to Atlanta. During the drive from the hotel to the plantation site, she reminded herself that she had her partnership and her design team to think of; there was no way she'd let Asa Matthews get the better of her. No matter how much she craved his touch, no matter how much her body and her heart pushed her toward him, she would not sacrifice everything she had worked for simply for a quick roll in the hay.

She glared at Asa's back as he strode up the narrow drive to the plantation grounds. She tried not to appreciate the view from behind. Today, he was dressed casually in jeans and T-shirt, but still his customary black. The man had to know how good he looked in black. So good she wasn't at all sure she wanted to spend the weekend alone with him, being tutored about rice plantations.

Determined to keep herself and her mind at a discreet and professional distance, Kai asked Asa for a tour of the greater part of the plantation. When the team had toured before, their movements were tightly controlled to minimize their impact on the excavation work in progress. She had reviewed countless site plans as the team developed their welcome center designs and hoped for a more comprehensive tour this weekend. Thankfully, Asa seemed just as determined to distance himself with business as she, and obliged her. After introducing her to Jamal, the camp supervisor, Asa brought a golf cart around for their tour.

"How much do you know about rice plantations?" he asked, after they climbed into the cart.

"Mmm, not a lot," she said. "I couldn't find a lot of books on the subject, and when we took our site tour, we focused mostly on excavation of the outbuildings and slave quarters." She paused to glance around. "But I was particularly intrigued by the geometry of Ridgeway's layout. I was hoping we could approach from the main road to start today's tour."

"Doable." Asa turned the cart, and they drove the long way around the site. "That road there," he said, pointing to a magnolia and oak-lined lane. "Magnolia Avenue. It's the main approach. When the plantation was in operation, this road stretched about two miles from the Big House and intersected with the old highway to Savannah."

They drove at a casual speed up the avenue. About two hundred yards from the mansion, Asa pointed out plotted and roped off slave quarters in various stages of excavation. "Ridgeway wasn't typical of most plantations, even rice plantations, in terms of layout," he said. "Adam Ridge, it seemed, was a fan of the famous landscape architect Fredrick Law Olmsted. He saw himself as somewhat of a Renaissance man, a gentleman planter who not only managed the business of his rice plantations, but was influential in their design as well. When he was twenty-five, the land for Ridgeway was deeded to him by his father. The father's main holdings were up river about fifteen miles." Asa stopped the cart near one of the slave quarters that appeared to be still intact. Kai started to get out, but he stopped her with a brief touch.

Asa was all business, which intrigued her. At first, she was sure that the formality was intentional, given their earlier encounter. But as he gazed down the wide plantation drive, Kai realized he had completely forgotten about their lustful hotel room interlude. His mind was totally focused on Ridgeway.

"Ridge planned the layout of the plantation with an architect and oversaw the construction himself. This plantation was considered—both then and now—as one of the most efficiently designed and profitable rice plantations in the region."

"All because of the layout of the buildings?" Kai asked.

"In some ways, but not all." Asa looked off into the distance as if imagining the plantation back in the nineteenth century. He was completely focused on their tour and the history of the place, but Kai briefly wondered whether the fleeting touch on her arm moments earlier had sent a jolt through him as it had her.

Turning slightly in his seat, he waved his hand back down the avenue they had traversed. "Take the approach, for example. Ridge was a master of psychological conditioning. That's my theory, anyway."

Kai smiled at that.

"I'm not joking. That school of thought maybe more modern, but I can guarantee you the methods aren't. Ridge wanted not only the slaves and his paid employees to know that he was a powerful man, he wanted his peers to know it as well."

He hopped out of the cart, leaving Kai to follow, and walked a few yards down the avenue, stopped, and turned to face the Big House.

"Look at this view." Asa's gaze was loving, and Kai couldn't fault him. She often felt that way about buildings she had designed, or magnificent architectural monuments she'd studied. If she had ever doubted Asa's assertion that Ridgeway was his baby, she didn't now. She and Asa had more in common than she'd wanted to admit.

"There were over seventy little slave cabins on either side of this lane," Asa said. "Each cabin was separated by huge magnolia and oak trees. The trees made the cabins seem even smaller than they actually were. And then you get to the end of the lane where the main house sits. It's already enormous, but after seeing these small two room cabins, at a glance, visitors could appreciated the contrast—in size, power, and authority"

Though she nodded, Kai didn't quite agree. "An interesting theory."

"Not a theory, fact. It's been documented by contemporaneous travelers and scholars. Even Ridge's idol, Olmsted, approved."

Kai raised an eyebrow. "I know Olmsted visited the south and studied its architecture, but—"

"Believe me, it's well documented." Asa's gaze zeroed in on her own, surprising Kai with its intensity. "But getting back to my point. As I said, the layout is unique. And it was copied in a few plantations later. But there were a lot of things about the site plan that helped increase efficiency on the plantation." He held out a hand. "Let's go into one of the cabins and I'll show you."

Not wanting to appear rude, Kai took Asa's hand and tried not to over-analyze the gesture, but couldn't help feeling a little giddy as Asa laced his thick finger through hers with an intimacy that felt completely natural.

They approached one of the intact buildings. "This cabin is one in which we'll allow small tours." Asa waved a hand. "White washed brick. Pyramidal roof, symmetrically arranged window-door-window façade, exterior brick fireplace and chimney. They baked the bricks right here on the plantation."

Opening the heavy wooden door, Asa tugged her inside. "This type of quarter was called a hall-and-parlor house. Two rooms—the hall, where the slaves cooked and worked, the parlor where they slept. One family per house."

He opened the door separating the hall from the parlor, and Kai peeked inside. There was a single window, a dirt floor, and holes lining each wall where pegs for hanging clothes had once been. Kai stepped into the tiny space. "This room's a little smaller than the main room, isn't it?"

"Yeah. Actually, I've been developing a theory about the ratio of room size as well.

Kai cocked her head. "Another one?"

"The parlor is about ten feet by ten feet." Asa smiled and squeezed her hand. "With the hall slightly larger. It's consistent with the room size of typical huts in West Africa. I think that fact, along with the industry had a lot to do with the success and profitability of this plantation in particular."

"I'm not sure if I'm with you on that," Kai said as they stepped out of the cabin. Now that Asa was treating her more like a colleague than a conquest, it seemed appropriate to debate his theories. She ignored the tiny shivers moving through her body, since Asa seemed oblivious to the effect his handholding was having on her, and debated his theory. "What does room size have to do with the success of a plantation?"

"Well, for one thing, according to a prominent archaeologist at the University of South Carolina, slaves who were housed in quarters with larger room sizes, say fifteen by fifteen feet— more like dormitories rather than homes—had a higher mortality rate than slaves who lived in the smaller sized spaces." He put up a hand at her skeptical expression. "I'm not saying that something so simple made all the difference. What I'm saying is Ridge had a brickworks on the site, which infers that the slaves most likely built their own cabins. My research tells me the Ridgeway slaves had quite a bit of autonomy because of Adam Ridge's personal beliefs as well as the nature of the business of rice growing." He paused a moment, looking down at her as if he had lost his train of thought. "We'll talk about production later. Suffice it to say, the slaves were used to making their own decisions in the course of a day's work. So my theory is that the slaves built the cabins based on what was familiar to them, what was typical in regions of Africa from which they hailed."

Marveling at how they were debating academic theories, when only a few hours ago she and Asa were practically making love, Kai almost laughed. The only thing that kept her from giving in to the urge was the fact that Asa would have demanded to know what she was giggling about. But dang if she wasn't enjoying herself.

Apparently so was Asa. He was completely relaxed, treating her as a professional colleague, instead of someone he wanted to take to bed.

More than pleased with how the day was progressing, Kai pulled her thoughts back to business. "The slaves wouldn't have necessarily come directly from Africa. They could have come from the West Indies or Virginia or somewhere else," she said, considering his theory about the size of the slave quarters. "Which means they would have been exposed to a lot of Western influences by the time they got here, wouldn't they?"

Asa shook his head. "The Ridges were a second generation rice growing family, and the elder Ridge had already learned of the rice growing economy in Africa. By the time Adam Ridge established his own plantation, he took care to acquire a great many of his slaves directly from Gambia, Senegal, and Sierra Leone, where there was a strong rice growing tradition. Besides that, we know a lot about the traditional style of housing in that region of Africa." Asa was smiling himself now, enjoying the debate as much as Kai. He was also stroking the palm of her hand with his thumb, making her think that perhaps he hadn't dismissed her as a future bed partner after all.

She shouldn't have been happy about that thought, but if she were honest with herself, she would admit that it definitely pleased her.

"So you see, if you obtain slaves who already know a great deal about the industry and allow them some autonomy in the development of their environment, you may increase their mortality rates as well as their productivity." Asa turned her to face him, brought her hand up, clasping it in both hands. "That's the theory anyway," he said softly.

A little dazed by the shift in her feelings about Asa, Kai wiggled her hand free of his grasp and escaped back to the golf cart. She had prepared for animosity and distance, even crude teasing, only to find in Asa a companionable tour guide. Despite their rough beginning, she was enjoying herself immensely.

They toured the site for several more hours, viewing the foundations of the overseer's cabin as well as the remains of the slave hospital. The next day, they spent in the remains of the rice fields where Asa shared details about rice cultivation and production.

As their intellectual exchanges continued, Kai learned as much about Asa as she did about Ridgeway. He was deadly serious about his work, as much as she was her own. He had told her as much during that first altercation in her office, but to see him in action, defending his arguments and displaying the expertise he had developed over almost a decade of study and scholarship was oddly stimulating.

CHAPTER NINE

On Sunday morning, Kai rolled her luggage to the lobby of the hotel and turned in her room key. The weekend had turned out to be a much greater success than she could have hoped, and her respect for Asa had grown as well. He hadn't attempted any more personal overtures, which made her much more comfortable, and when she got overly excited over the slave hospital, he allowed her the time and the space to design. He had cleared a space in one of the work sheds so she could set up her portable drafting table and left her alone to sketch for hours.

After completing her room checkout, Kai dropped her luggage in the lobby and her body into a comfortable upholstered chair. She was feeling invigorated and surprisingly magnanimous toward Asa. He seemed happier and more energetic, too. Apparently, Jamal had discovered a few artifacts that might relate to the cemetery Asa was looking for. It had put him in quite a jovial mood, making the upcoming ride back to Atlanta seem much less daunting. Kai had decided overnight that once she won her partnership, there just might be room for a relationship with him after all.

She flipped open her cell phone to check her office voice mail. After listening a few moments, she sighed. Her father had called and left three messages, which meant he was back in town from one of his whimsical escapades and was feeling fatherly and guilty. What would it be this time, dinner? A gallery showing? Whatever it was, Kai wasn't interested. Not that her own feelings ever mattered to Vernon. She closed the phone gingerly, wondering when she would finally be numb to her father and the faded memory of her mother.

Moments later, Kai caught Asa's profile in her peripheral vision as he strode down the hallway to the checkout desk. It was insane, but she couldn't seem to stifle her heated reactions to the man. She let her eyes pass slowly over his lean hips and long legs as he chatted with the desk clerk. How he could make a pair of plain charcoal gray Dockers look sexy was beyond her. She supposed it was the way they accentuated the firmness of his butt; or maybe, it was the way they stretched across his muscular thighs.

Kai caught herself in mid-drool. The short-sleeved crewneck sweater Asa wore was his typical black. Though the outfit brought plenty of approving stares from women passing by, it would definitely have been considered too casual for the boardroom. Considering it was Sunday and they would be on the road for the rest of the day, Kai couldn't criticize the choice. The muscles in his arm and shoulder flexed slightly as he signed the checkout form. His locs fell gracefully across his forearm, making her shiver slightly, remembering how they had felt trailing across her bare stomach.

She almost dropped the phone when he turned and stared straight at her. He was at least twenty feet away, yet she felt completely exposed. She read raw desire in his gaze, and she crossed and re-crossed her legs uncomfortably.

It was going to be a long drive back to Atlanta.

Kai put a finger to her temple and closed her eyes. She felt a migraine coming on. She didn't need any of this right now, not when she had to ride four hours in close proximity to Asa.

A hand touched her shoulder, and she almost flew out of her chair.

With a hand over her heart, she opened her eyes and turned to see Asa's intense brown eyes staring back at her. "You scared the living daylights out of me."

"Ready?"

Asa's kind smile shook her, worried her. Kai took a deep breath and stood. "As I'll ever be."

Asa pondered the woman beside him as they drove down the highway on their way back to Atlanta. Kai had been so restless to sketch after their site tour that he cleared a space in one of the work sheds for her. He had watched her briefly from the doorway. She had kicked off her shoes and relaxed completely as she got to work. The more he thought about what he had seen, the more Kai reminded him of his mother. He liked to think that in some way he had been helpful to his mother some twenty years ago when she'd finally made the decision to be herself and live her own life regardless of the consequences. He may have only been ten years old at the time, but he had been strong for his mother; she had said as much.

He glanced over at Kai as she thumbed through a field notebook. He was sure she wasn't really studying the contents, because she was sitting too rigidly in her seat. After observing the real Kai in the work shed, he knew that if her mind were racing with new design ideas, she would be more relaxed.

His anger had dissipated somewhat during the weekend as he puzzled over her. In fact, by the time they were half-way through the tour, he was thinking impure thoughts about her. Now, he simply wanted to help her. He wanted to pull her out of her shell. Free her from her self-imposed prison. He wanted to see her smile, laugh, let her hair down and not care. He wanted to experience the real Kai Ellis; all of her, all the time. Not just the dimension she let the world in on, and not just in private when she thought no one was watching.

He nodded purposefully to himself as he drove down the highway. He was just the man for the task. After all, he'd seen his mother through her tough transformation; he could do the same for Kai.

His phone rang, pulling him from his thoughts. When his sister's digits scrolled across the small amber screen, Asa attached his earpiece and answered.

"Talk to me," he said enthusiastically.

"Wow, Little A, what's up with you?" Schyler said, sounding surprised. "After that last conversation, I figured you'd still be a little stressed."

"Huh?" Asa had to think back to his last conversation with his sister. So much had occurred since then that he had forgotten he'd spoken with her.

"You know. The deal with Kai."

As the conversation came back to him, Asa's enthusiasm waned a little. "Oh."

"Oops. Sorry, little brother. Guess I popped your bubble again, didn't I."

Although the foreplay he and Kai had shared in her hotel room had never strayed far from his thoughts, he had been more concerned with her state of mind than anything else. His sister's timing was terrible, but her call had reminded him that Kai was vulnerable.

"So what's up?" he asked.

"One of my regulars came in today. I got some more scoop about your girl."

"Go on."

"Where are you? Are you alone?"

"I'm in the car. Kai and I are on our way back to Atlanta." Asa sighed impatiently. Kai was glancing politely out the window, pretending she wasn't eavesdropping on his conversation. "Are you going to tell me what you called for or not?"

"How good is your phone? I don't want her over hearing this."

"Sky, I don't have time for your—"

"Okay, okay. Listen," she continued, excitedly. "She was sitting with Kenneth Roselle at dinner that night you first saw her, right?" When she got no response, she continued. "You said they were arguing or something. You remember don't you?"

"Actually, I was trying not to, but go ahead."

"A, she tried to break up with him before, but he kept putting her off." She paused dramatically. "She finally finished him off at dinner the night you met her."

Asa perked up a little. This was solid confirmation of what Jeremy had told him. "No kidding?"

"Hey, baby brother. She's as free as a bird."

"That's real interesting." Excitement crept into his voice. "I guess I'll have to do something about that."

At his evasive answer, Kai looked over. He gave her a big grin.

"Guess what else, A." His sister was calmer now, but he could tell she was about to burst. She always did that to him. Held back, teasing him.

"Ol' boy was creepin'," she finally said.

"Really?" Asa resisted the temptation to turn and look at Kai. She didn't seem that naïve to let some guy dis' her like that.

"Yeah, but wait 'til you hear why."

"I'm listening."

"He was steppin' out on her because she wasn't giving it up." Schyler paused, then sing-songed the last part. "No hoochi, no kootchie, no nookie, no nothing."

Asa had to concentrate to keep the car on the road. He glanced over at Kai, hoping his phone conversation sounded sufficiently cryptic. "They were together how long?"

"Six years, from what my customer, Rhonda, tells me."

"That's a long time." Six years was damn sure too long to go with out sex. He looked over briefly. Kai met his gaze and smiled slightly before turning back to look out the window. Was that a part of her punishing herself as well, he wondered Considering the way she had reacted to him, she certainly hadn't been celibate for six years for health or biological reasons.

He grinned as he considered how he could possibly use that tidbit of information. "Ah yeah, you better step out of the way big sister, 'cause it's on now." He grinned into the phone.

Schyler laughed, excitement filling her voice. "Now that's what I'm talkin' 'bout. You go, little brother."

"Hey, thanks for lookin' out, sis. I got to go. I got some work to do."

"I hear you, boy. Talk to you."

At the sound of the dial tone, Asa removed the earpiece and grinned over at his single and free companion. "How you doin' over there, shorty?"

Kai studied him for a long minute as if he'd asked her a trick question. "I'm okay. Sounds like your sister gave you some good news."

"As a matter of fact, she did. Better than I could have hoped."

"Hmm."

"So what's on your agenda when you get back to Atlanta?" he asked, doing a horrible job at sounding casual.

"I've got to give Jon and Pete a report about the trip, of course. They'll be as excited as I was about all of the new excavations."

Asa nodded.

"And I've got to get back on top of the other projects I'm managing …"

"I meant socially." He was about to get this party started and break little Ms. Kai Ellis out of her shell.

"I beg your pardon?"

"Your social agenda. Whatchu got planned on your social agenda?"

Kai looked at him quizzically. "Why, nothing. I'm too busy."

"Too busy for dinner?"

Kai returned to her office after her Tuesday morning status meeting with Jonathan and Peter and slumped down on the couch. She had worried all morning that her predicament with Asa would show in her presentation. And was thankful it was over. In response to a simple "Well, Kai, how did it go?" she had an irrational fear that she would blurt out "Oh, just fine, sirs, except I almost slept with the client's lead archaeologist. We didn't, of course, all in the name of business, you know. But other than that everything went great."

She had a considerable number of phone calls to make for her other projects, and here she was waxing romantic over Asa. She sighed and picked up the phone.

An hour later, all her phone calls were complete, but before she could even cross the room to refresh her coffee, Asa was back on her mind. Despite what her rational mind told her, she couldn't ignore her attraction to him; an attraction that had grown in intensity over the weekend and morphed into respect as well. Asa was the kind of man she never believed existed. The kind of man she definitely never expected to attract.

She shuddered as she thought of the things he'd done to her in her hotel room. He had backed off considerably after that episode. In fact until the tour, he brooded as if he hadn't a friend in the world, no doubt from embarrassment. Then, in the car on the way back to Atlanta, something had happened to loosen him up again. Once again he was the playful and charming Asa Matthews she'd come to know over the past week. Funny, how she had missed his smirk and risqué remarks.

By Wednesday evening, she still hadn't decided if she'd go out with Asa. Judy had come over, she claimed for dinner, but Kai knew her real goal was to get the full details about her road trip with Asa and find out if she was going to go out him.

"I think I should wait until the project is over," she said to Judy as they sat down at her dinner table over chicken Caesar salad and white wine.

"You're a wimp," Judy said. She waved her salad fork in the air as she sipped her wine. "The project will be over, then you'll say, 'I should wait until the firm is done supervising the construction. Then you'll say—"

"Okay, okay," Kai said, cutting her off. "If I tell you you're right, will you shut up about it?"

"Nope."

Kai glanced slyly over the rim of her wine glass. "So … Will you shut up if I call him and ask him out?"

Judy almost knocked her chair over as she jumped up and dove for the phone on the sideboard.

"I'm going to regret this," Kai said with a laugh as she refilled her wine, then gulped down half the glass. "Must be the wine talking."

"Must be." Judy shoved the phone at her.

A war between reluctance and eagerness was going on in Kai's head. Reluctance was winning, but eagerness was gaining. So with a final fortifying sip of chardonnay, she dialed Asa's number.

Judy looked on, beaming encouragement her way as the phone rang once, then a second time.

"He's not answering … I told you this wasn't—"

"Talk to me." Asa's deep tenor rumbled over the phone line.

Kai covered the mouthpiece. "He answered … Oh God. Now, what am I supposed to say?"

Judy waved her on. "Talk to him, not me."

"Hello? … I'm hanging up now," Asa said.

"Um. Ahem. I mean …"

"Kai?" Her heart skipped a beat. "Is that you?"

She took a deep breath before answering. "Uh, yeah. It's me … um … Hi. How are you? Yeah … Um."

"Everything okay?"

"Okay? Yeah, sure. Everything's fine." Judy stared a hole right through her, as if that would keep her on message. "Yeah, Asa. Everything's fine."

"You sure? You sound a little …" His voice trailed off, then Kai could literally hear the grin spread across his face. "This wouldn't be about dinner would it?"

Kai covered the receiver again. "Ughhhh. He can see right through me, Judy."

Judy simply smiled. Kai gulped down the rest of her wine.

"I …" She gave up. "How'd you guess?"

"I'll pick you up on Friday at your office. How's 6:30 sound? We'll make it early and take things from there. That cool?"

"Yeah. Sure … Um …"

"Cool. See you Friday."

CHAPTER TEN

Friday night, as Kai and Asa waited in the entrance of the Rio Bravo Mexican Cantina restaurant, Kai watched a curious little machine making tortillas. Little balls of dough moved down a circular trough, like kids on a water slide. Once the dough balls reached the bottom, a metal sheet came down to flatten them, then they were pushed off into a basket to be fried up later.

"Never seen one of those?" Asa twisted a finger around a lock of hair at the nape of her neck.

"No. I always wondered if they made them by hand." She tried to slip out of his reach. Oblivious, Asa shifted closer.

The pager Asa held vibrated, indicating their turn to sit down. They walked to the traffic light—a real one—that stood on the floor at the end of the waiting area. The light was red. When it turned green, their hostess pulled two menus from the stand and asked them to follow as she led them to their table.

Once seated, Kai rubbed her hands together with relish. "I haven't had Mexican in a while, and I know exactly what I want."

Her hands froze when she looked up to see Asa staring at her across the table. His piercing dark eyes had that predatory look in them that she now knew well. "I know exactly what you mean."

Heat spread across her face, forcing her to look away. If she thought she'd be able to have a simple dinner date with him, without the night being laced with sexual innuendo, she had been fooling herself. Kai studied the menu as if there was going to be a quiz later. Thankfully, the menu was the large kind with two folds that you could really get lost behind.

She sighed. Lost was exactly where she was. She knew it was only a matter of time before she gave in. She was powerless to fight Asa; she wanted him too much. She had talked herself into believing that she would at least make the decision about when sex would happen. But no matter what her mind said, her body screamed: *Now, now!*

"So what's so good here that you've just got to have?" Asa asked.

Amazed at the direction of her thoughts, Kai lowered her menu. She considered saying he was but he might decide to take her up on it.

"What are you up to over there?" Asa asked, smiling slyly at her when she didn't answer.

"Oh, nothing. I'm going to have *carne asada*."

"What's that?"

"Mmm. You've never had *carne asada*?"

"No." Asa's eyes fell to her mouth. His voice lowered. "I haven't. But I've been wanting to try some." The visible shudder that went through Kai's body brought a triumphant smile to Asa's face.

A basket of chips and salsa were plunked down on the table between them. "*Buenos noches, amigos*," the waiter said. "Are you ready to order?"

Since Kai had yet to regain her voice, she let Asa take over. "We'll have two *carne asadas*."

"Ah, *carne asada*. You will like. *Es muy delicioso*." The waiter took down the order and left.

"*Muy delicioso*." Asa wiggled his eyebrows suggestively and grinned at Kai.

"When are you going to stop doing that to me?"

"When you stop doing what you're doing to me."

"What? I'm not doing anything. What am I doing to you?" A laugh bubbled up despite her attempt to hold it in.

"Making me want you," he said simply. "Making me want to pull that stupid little bun of yours down every time I see you and bury my fingers in your hair. Making me want to make love to you until you can't walk, can't breath, can't remember your own name."

Kai shivered again and scrambled for the chips and salsa.

"You do that again and I'll be on you so fast your head will spin." Asa's eyes were hard and dark, his threat, soft and dangerously serious.

Kai didn't risk asking him what she was doing that was so enticing, and mercifully, their food arrived before he could explore the topic further.

They ate quietly for a few minutes. Asa savored the new dish he was experiencing and Kai tried to compose herself.

"You were right," Asa said after taking a few bites of the thinly sliced, marinated beef. "This is off the chain."

Kai concentrated on cutting her meat and eating.

"So tell me a little bit about yourself," Asa said.

Surprisingly, Kai welcomed the change in topic. She didn't like to talk about her family, but it was better than matching wits with Asa about sex and desire. She took a deep breath. "What do you want to know? There's not a lot to tell."

"I don't know, about your background. Your parents, where you went to school. What kind of hobbies you have, what you like to do in your spare time. What you love, what you hate. What pisses you off."

"That's a lot."

Casually, he took another bite of food, swallowed. "I want to know more than just your last name when I take you to bed,"

Kai's fork stopped in mid-air.

Asa simply shrugged. "Baby, I want you. I can't help it."

"Are we ever going to be able to get through a conversation without discussing sex?"

"Only if we're having it."

Kai sighed loudly and rolled her eyes. Maybe if she talked he would shut up. "Okay," Kai began, "I was raised by my grandmother in East Point."

Asa nodded.

"I went to Georgia Tech, received undergraduate and graduate degrees in architecture. I like jazz, I hate rap, and I love to read and go to museums. I don't have spare time. And people who lack ambition piss me off."

"Well done," he said, grinning at her. "So, what about your parents? You said you were raised by a grandmother."

"My paternal grandmother. I don't have much to do with my parents—parent." Knowing she couldn't avoid the inevitable question, she cleared her throat. "My mother died on a trip to India when I was about six years old."

Don't waste your sympathy, Kai wanted to say when Asa reached across the table to grasp her hand. She pulled back and shrugged. "I hadn't seen her for almost a year. I barely remember her now, anyway."

"Still, it had to hurt knowing she died without giving you a chance to say goodbye."

"She did that on my fifth birthday." With forced casualness, she dipped a tortilla chip in salsa and munched. "My father lives in Metro Atlanta. Down in Little Five Points."

"No joke? He probably knows my sister. She lives in that neighborhood, too. Owns a day spa. What does your father do for a living?"

"Vernon? He's a sculptor."

"You call him by his first name?"

Kai shrugged. "What else should I call him; he wasn't a father to me."

Asa ate more of his entree, which really was quite good, and took his time absorbing what Kai had just revealed. He also made a mental note of what she didn't. He was actually surprised she had opened up so much. After being around her over the past week, he got the impression that she was exceedingly private. Why was she so talkative now? Not that he was complaining. In fact, he planned to discover as much as he could while the floodgates were open. "You don't sound all that concerned—about your relationship with your dad, or your mother's passing."

Kai looked down at her plate. "I'm not," said her words, but the sorrow in her eyes said differently. "I didn't spend a lot of time with Vernon growing up, and Gina has been dead for almost twenty-five years. My grandmother mothered me. So I don't feel I missed out on much"

"Still, it must have been hard on you growing up."

"I dealt with it. Ignored it, pretended my folks didn't exist."

Asa studied Kai's face, which she had schooled into a blank mask. There were strong feelings under that placid Buddha smile. Otherwise, she wouldn't work so hard to pretend otherwise. "Does your dad mind? You're living in the same city."

Kai shrugged again. "I was their 1970's love child, and up until I was four I was an *objet d'art*. Then, when I ceased to be cute, Vernon turned me over to my grandmother to be raised. Their hippy, free-love ways don't appeal to me. I prefer good old Republican family values, thank you very much."

Asa's eyebrows rose in surprise. "You're a Republican?"

"No, but I try to live as opposite of my parents as I possibly can."

"Interesting." He murmured it more to himself than to her and mulled over the things she'd told him as he polished off more of his food.

Kai had revealed more than she intended; much more. Very few people knew about Vernon and Gina. Her story had always been that she was raised by a grandmother and didn't have much contact with her parents.

"So in living a lifestyle opposite your parents, do you think you've denied yourself anything?"

"No." Kai thought immediately of Vernon. His passion for Gina was a badge of honor. Although they had never married—neither believed in the concept—if given the chance, he would have laid down his life for her. His love for her had been crazy, jealous, zealous, and everything in between. Kai envied him that. His passion and zest for life, for her mother. But she couldn't allow the same for herself; couldn't make herself so vulnerable. The cost was much too great.

"Mmm," was all Asa said.

"So what about you? Who is your family, what do you like and dislike. What do you like to do in your spare time?"

"Well." Asa sat back and got comfortable. "Now that you ask."

A smirk tilted the corner of Kai's mouth. His humor was growing on her.

"My parents are Asa Matthews, Sr. and Johnetta Matthews. I have an older sister named Schyler and a younger brother named Alexander."

"Okay."

"My likes and dislikes. Let's see now. This may take a minute to sort through." Asa gazed upward for a moment, then looked back at Kai with a devilish smile. "I like having sex, I dislike not having sex, and I have sex in my spare time.

"You asked," he said, in response to her stunned expression.

Asa laughed at her distress. "Didn't I tell you to loosen up, girl? You've got to chill out. You're too tense and uptight." He leaned forward and whispered conspiratorially. "You know what they say is the best remedy for tension, don't you?"

Kai gave what could barely pass for a laugh. He was way too comfortable with his sexuality.

He slid the knife she was playing with from her fingers and took her hand. Dark brown eyes held hers. "Look, Kai. You know how I feel about you. And I know how you feel about me; even if you refuse to admit it." He placed a finger under her chin and lifted her face. "Look at me."

When she didn't lift her eyes, he squeezed her hand and firmed his voice. "I said, look at me."

Reluctantly, she complied.

"I want you, Kai, really badly." His eyes searched hers. "But I'll never take what's not willingly given. Do you get what I'm saying?" He took her other hand in his. "When we make love, you'll want me just as badly as I want you. And we'll both be willing participants." He let go of her hands and dipped a chip in salsa, then lifted it to her lips. "Now, quit worrying and take a bite and pretend it's me."

The effect he was having on her was as amazing as it was magical, and Kai found herself giving in to his charm. Pretending with everything in her that the spicy mix of south of the border flavors was Asa, she closed her eyes and bit into the salsa drenched tortilla chip. When she opened them, Asa was on her side of the table, with one hand nestled at the nape of her neck.

An artful flick untwisted her bun as Asa's lips touched hers. He intensified the kiss briefly, hinting at what was to come, then brushed feather-light kisses on the tip of her nose and eyelids before withdrawing.

Kai's hair hung free about her shoulders, and Asa turned the fingers of his hand, twisting them in her hair. She tilted her head slightly from the pressure and caught the brief, but passionate flare in his eyes.

"You don't know what this does to me," he said quietly. "I can't wait to run my fingers through your hair while we're making love, fan it out on the pillow behind you. This is what I see when I dream about us." He lifted a stray coil to his nose and drew in her scent.

After a moment, Asa released her hair and moved back to his side of the table. Calm now, his eyes were clear, his body and emotions fully under control. Kai was amazed, and a bit envious of the calmness and discipline he showed. How did he master his passion so easily? Could she ever hope to do so as well? If she wanted Asa, she would have to learn.

Still gazing at her, Asa said, "You should leave your hair down. It makes you look wild. Like a lioness."

Kai's lips parted. She had always thought of him as sleek, like a cat. His black attire made her think panther, but his dreadlocks always made her envision him a lion, with his regal mane. She liked the thought of herself as a lioness to his lion. And sooner or later, the lion would take his mate.

Asa peeled his eyes away from Kai's as his phone began to vibrate. He was reluctant to end their conversation. He could tell by her expression that he had triggered something in her mind and her body, and gauging from the lack of focus in her eyes and the slackness of her jaw, it was definitely something sensuous. "Whatever you're thinking," he said softly, "keep thinking it."

He reached down, irritated beyond measure over the interruption, to retrieve his cell phone. "What?"

"Whoa, Little A. What's up with you?"

"Sky, you're disturbing my groove, baby." He'd told her about his date earlier. "What do you want?"

"Oh, my bad, I'm really sorry about the interruption, but I had a great idea. Come down to the shop when you're done with your date."

"Why?" He should have never told Sky he was taking Kai to dinner tonight.

"Well, you said Kai tenses up when you tease her. Since you want to get her relaxed, I figured I could help you out. Bring her down here to me. I'll give her a free massage. Get her all melted and soft to the touch."

Asa's mood brightened considerably. "Now that sounds like a plan."

The bell at the entrance jingled when Asa opened the door to his sister's salon.

"Well, well. This must be Kai." Schyler smiled at the woman coming toward her as she and Asa walked through the door of Aromia Natural Body Spa, watching proudly as Kai took a long sniff and murmured compliments about how tastefully decorated her establishment was.

The scents were lavender and sandalwood, to relax the body and the mind.

Crystals, candles, and assorted knickknacks were on display and for sale, but given Kai's button downed appearance—the sensible but stylish pumps, the pin-stripped business suit, and according to her brother, the ubiquitous bun at the back of her head—Sky had a feeling her shop wasn't the kind of boutique Kai would frequent, but hopefully that would change.

"That's me." Kai extended her hand. "Nice to meet you. Schyler, right?"

"Yeah. Whatchu know good? You keepin' my little brother in line?"

Asa, who was standing protectively beside Kai, pretended to look wounded.

"It's a pretty tough job."

"Don't I know it. He really knows how to work your nerves."

The two women laughed together as Sky tried to get a sense of her brother's latest love. Despite the clothes, Kai seemed fairly laid back.

"Look, I hate to rain on the parade," Asa said as he placed his hands on Kai's shoulders and kneaded. "But we didn't come here to celebrate 'Pick-On-Asa-Day.'"

"Mmmmmmm." Kai squirmed as firm fingers worked a little magic.

Asa grinned at his sister. "See what I mean."

"Oh yeah, I can see the problem." Schyler answered with melodramatic seriousness. "Doctor, we may need to operate."

Kai laughed. "You're as bad as he is."

Schyler pulled a terry cloth robe and two towels from below the counter. "Here, Kai. Why don't you take these into room number three, undress, and lay down on the table. I'll be there in a minute."

Kai looked quizzically from Schyler to her brother. "This is our appointment?"

"Don't look a gift horse in the mouth," Sky responded, giving her a little shove in the general direction of the massage rooms. "Go on, now."

As Kai began to shuffle hesitantly toward the massage rooms, she turned and looked back.

"Yes, it's free," Schyler said.

"Well, in that case." Kai practically ran to room number three and shut the door behind her.

Schyler smiled and turned back to Asa. "She doesn't look uptight to me."

"Yeah, well."

"Must be you."

Asa raised his hands innocently.

"Boy, I know your style. You come on too strong. How many times do I have to tell you that?"

"She wants me, Sky. You saw her in the Cheesecake Factory. She was all over me."

"How about—she fell on you, after you ran down there, tracking her. And then you were all over her."

"Well, she didn't stop me."

"'Cause you probably didn't give her a chance."

A rakish twinkle flickered in Asa's eye. "Some women like that."

"Boy ..." she warned. "Let me go see if I can straighten out the kinks you've jerked into your woman."

The warmer was filled with fresh towels and Sky took out a stack, then grabbed a vial of scented oil from a nearby cabinet before retreated into the massage room after Kai.

"What have you done to my brother?" Schyler's question was good-natured, so Kai didn't feel intimidated, but all the same, its directness surprised her.

"What do you mean?" she asked, her voice muffled as she peered down at the floor through the opening in the massage table.

"He needs a massage himself. He's just as worked up as you are." Schyler gently lifted Kai's arms and legs and peeled off her robe, exchanging the dry heavy cloth for warm, moist, towels.

"Really?" came Kai's distant response.

"Yeah, girl. Be careful with him, he's not use to being whipped. Might mess his head up, you know."

"Whipped?" Kai snorted. "That'll be the day." Schyler wrapped each of her feet in a warm towel. "Oh, that feels good." Moans escaped from below the table as Kai's body responded to the relaxing treatment.

"You're not his type." Schyler smoothed a towel over Kai's shoulder blades and upper back. "But, maybe that's just what he needs right now," she continued as much to herself as to Kai.

Kai wasn't sure what to make of Schyler, or her comments. They weren't said in a disapproving manner, but their conversation wasn't one she was comfortable holding with someone she had just met. In defense, she tuned Schyler out and enjoyed the massage preparations.

"My brother's a very virile man, if you know what I mean."

Kai tensed.

"Uh oh. Now I see why you're so tense." Schyler leaned down and looked at Kai under the table, then shook her head. "I put a few drops of lavender in the warmer, so just relax and enjoy the music. Meditate if you like. I'll be back in a few minutes to begin your massage."

The overhead light flicked off and a tape of flowing water began to play somewhere above her head, so Kai put aside her worries for the moment and let herself float away as the steamy towels worked their magic. She wasn't going to think about Asa, work, or her parents. Well, maybe she'd think about Asa just a little bit.

Why hadn't she ever considered having a body massage before? It made so much sense. She listened as water showered over a waterfall. Maybe she could make this a monthly event for herself. *Mmmm. Yes, that would be good.* A reward to herself after she made partner. She floated, let the aromas, the steam, and the gentle sounds take over. She felt more relaxed than she'd been in quite a while outside her design studio.

CHAPTER ELEVEN

Kai's eyes fluttered when the door opened.

She started to tell Schyler she planned on making the massage a monthly habit, when she noticed the shoes. From her position, she couldn't see above the table, but she could certainly see beneath. She knew the black Kenneth Cole Oxfords that had just walked in would fit only a man's foot. One man in particular. Asa's. What was he up to? No good, apparently, especially after their conversation at dinner. He had made no secret what he wanted to do to her, with her.

Nah, he wouldn't try anything in his sister's shop. *Would he?*

She wasn't sure. As she pondered the question, she felt large, warm hands touch her shoulders and jumped.

He would.

After promising Sky he wouldn't destroy her professional reputation by doing something crazy and foolish, Asa finally convinced her to let him give Kai her massage. Whatever Kenneth Roselle had done to cause her to shrink away from a man's touch. That was why Asa had been so determined to get close to her in the restaurant; why he was in the massage room right now. If he was ever going to convince her they would be good together, she would have to get used to his hands on her. A full body massage seemed a good step in the initiation process. He moved the towel that covered Kai's upper back and shoulder blades, then opened a vial of oil and poured a quarter sized pool into his open palm. He rubbed his hands together quickly to warm them and touched her bare back. When she tensed, he left his hands were they were, unsure what to do next. After a minute, thankfully, she finally relaxed.

Asa breathed out a sigh. As he began untying the knots from her shoulders, knots he knew he'd caused, Kai let out a soft, surprisingly erotic, moan.

This time Asa tensed. Did she have to sound so good doing that? His mind immediately slipped into a fantasy with Kai as the star. After a moment of caressing her body a little too lovingly, he realized what he was doing and almost jerked his hands away. If he weren't careful, he would blow his cover. He took a deep breath and returned to kneading her back and shoulders and tried to focus on the sound of rushing water from the CD that played in the background.

Kai moaned again.

Maybe this wasn't such a smart move after all. He clenched his jaw and worked his way down to the small of her back, applying small circular motions of pressure as he went. The third moan nearly undid him. If she sounded like this when they made love, he was in serious trouble, even more than he was right now. He was afraid to go any further. If he removed another towel, or asked her to turn over, he would be lost.

He found the towel, recently discarded from her shoulders, and laid it back into position.

"Oh, God, that feels so good." Kai's voice was husky, aroused. "Please don't stop."

Asa miserably bit back a groan. *What the hell am I doing?*

He couldn't handle this. He must have been a lunatic to think he could give Kai a massage. She was naked for God's sake, completely naked. Glistening and shiny with oil *he'd* applied.

She moaned again.

Asa almost tripped over himself as he stumbled from the room. He shut the door with a loud bang. Schyler looked up from her perch at the counter, then glanced at the clock. "That was quick ..." Then she saw his face. "What's wrong with you? You look like you just saw a ghost or something."

"Or something ... here." Asa shoved the vial of massage oil he'd forgotten he had into his sister's hands and paced nervously around the shop.

Schyler eyed at him curiously.

"Don't ask."

It wasn't until she disappeared behind the door of the massage room that his breathing began to return to normal.

Schyler entered the massage room to the sound of the shower running in the adjoining dressing room. "Kai?" she called. "Are you all right?"

"Just fine, I'll be out in a minute."

Schyler's brows crept up a notch as she heard humming coming from the shower stall. After a few minutes, Kai emerged, wrapped in one of Aromia's thick terrycloth robes, her hair, out of its bun, tumbled and curled, damp and heavy over her shoulders.

"Wow, great hair. You should wear it down."

"You sound like Asa."

Schyler leaned against the massage table as Kai shrugged quickly into her clothes. "Speaking of my brother, what in the world happened in here? He came streaking out like he'd just seen Jesus."

Feeling quite pleased with how she had handled Asa, Kai didn't mind speaking to his sister about him now. "He's made his intention clear since I met him that he wants a relationship. Tries to tempt me by saying all kinds of shocking things to see how I'll react. I figured he needed a taste of his own medicine. And I do believe I succeeded."

"You wanna tell me what's going on?" Schyler asked apprehensively.

Once Kai related the incident, Schyler was practically rolling on the floor with laughter.

"I knew there was something I liked about you." They raised their hands in a friendly slap of camaraderie. "Go on, girl, with your bad self."

Kai was dressed now, but Schyler suggested they chat for a few minutes more. "We need to stay in here a little while, otherwise Little A might think something's up."

"*Little A?*" Kai smirked. "I'll have to remember that."

"Be ready to run the first time you say it."

When they emerged from the massage room, Asa seemed jumpy and uncomfortable as he sat awkwardly on the couch in the waiting area. "Ladies." He stood as they crossed the room.

"Wow, Asa," Kai said. "I'm glad we came. Your sister gives the most wonderful massages. I didn't know what she was up to when she stepped out. But then she came back and finished me off ..." An innocent shrug lifted her shoulder. She stood on tiptoes and kissed him on the cheek. "It was absolutely great, thanks."

Asa seemed to relax at her words and gave his sister a lopsided grin before putting an arm around Kai's shoulder. She gave Schyler a conspiratorial wink as she and Asa left the store.

"So you ready to call it a night?" Asa asked as they walked to the car parked at the curb. "After such a great massage, you should be ready to fall into bed."

"With you?" Kai's eyes widened innocently. She wondered how far she could push him and get away with it. Seeing the shoe on the other foot for a change was pretty funny.

Asa looked so horrified, Kai almost laughed aloud. He raised a defensive hand. "No, no. I mean alone."

Grinning, she watched Asa's shoulders heave up and down as he tried to breathe. *This could be fun.*

"I'm having a great time," she replied airily, touching his forearm lightly to give her words more emphasis. She could barely manage a straight face. "I don't want this night to end." The doe-eyed look that spread across Asa's face was exactly the reward she'd hope to get for her inspired performance. "I'm game for anything. What do you want to do, now?"

Asa choked back a cough as he helped her into the car. He was so cute when he was flustered.

Kai was grateful for the darkness, so that Asa couldn't see the grin that had spread over her face.

Ninety minutes later, Asa stood in the plumbing aisle of the twenty-four hour Home Depot store in Buckhead. "This is it," he called over his shoulder to Kai as he picked up the 1 1/4" round PVC tubing. After the fiasco in his sister's shop, he was afraid to engage in any typical dating activities for the remainder of the night. If he couldn't control himself at Schyler's, he couldn't control himself anywhere, which meant clubs were out. So were bars, which tended to have an aphrodisiacal affect on him.

When Kai told him she didn't want to go home yet, he wasn't sure what to do. They ended up in the Barnes & Noble bookstore on Peachtree Street, where they browsed and had coffee. However, the later it got, the less Asa trusted himself to play it cool per his sister's suggestion. Home Depot seemed the least romantic place to take her, and the safest.

"This is exactly what we need for covering the cemetery on the site," he commented over his shoulder. He pulled a twelve-foot long piece of tubing from the shelf as Kai came down the aisle behind him. Once cut, the plastic rods could be threaded inside the edges of the tarp. With a little sand packed inside them, they would serve as weights to hold down the tarp coving the excavated portions of the cemetery. "One of the employees told me I'd be able to cut what I need myself if I came by tonight." He walked to the end of the aisle and turned, looked to and fro down the long corridor, where he hoped to see either the girl that had helped him, or a saw so he could get to work.

Kai watched as Asa placed the plastic rod in the teeth of the vice and tightened the handle. Her gaze fell to his lower body, then moved upward as his left bicep strained. Clad in charcoal gray micro fiber slacks and a black Armani shirt, he wasn't dressed for manual labor, and something about the contrast was surprisingly arousing.

The form-fitting ribbed shirt, and the way the short sleeves stretched taut over his muscles mesmerized her. Kai shivered involuntarily, transfixed by alternating expansion, straining, and release of muscle underneath Asa's skin. The relaxing environment of the Aromia Natural Body Spa must have sapped her defenses more than she realized. She drew in a shaky breath.

God, hurry up and finish cutting the rods. I can't take much more of this.

After feeling the crush of Asa's arms embracing her at the restaurant, she had been able to think of little else since, and even though she knew initiating an intimate relationship with him was the worst thing she could be considering at the moment, that was exactly what she was thinking. She shivered again.

"You all right over there?" Asa asked, glancing up.

"Mm, yeah. Fine." Kai hoped she sounded as relaxed as she was aroused. She folded her arms in front of her and shifted uncomfortably, transferring her weight from one leg to the other. "It's different here in the middle of the night. Seems a lot bigger than in the daytime."

Asa peered up at her, but didn't reply as he continued to turn and score the PVC tubing.

Kai was losing the battle with herself. Apparently, she had more of her father's passion than she wanted to admit, and it was starting to show itself with a vengeance. She may have succeeded in keeping herself in check since college, but she'd also been careful to avoid temptation. Now the devil was taunting her unmercifully with a dreadlocked black panther, no less. Sooner or later, she knew she would give in.

She stifled a moan as Asa reached to loosen the grip, then skillfully shove the pipe down the workbench another foot. Though her vision was beginning to blur slightly, Kai's eyes stayed trained on the tight ribbed fabric that hugged his arms. Her mouth watered.

"What the—" Kai blinked, first in alarm, then morbid fascination, as she found herself pinned between cold orange shelving and hard, warm muscle. She wasn't sure how she had come to be in such a predicament, but the feeling wasn't all together unpleasant.

Asa's lips were mere inches from hers. "That's the same look you had in your eyes when I first saw you," he said.

Kai's breath was coming too fast for her to respond intelligently. Slack-jawed, she could only stare up at him. Asa's fierce, fiery eyes, piercing in their intensity, stared back. She wasn't sure whether his gaze, or the cold metal of the shelf pressing into her lower back made her shiver, but she did, uncontrollably. When she felt the hardness and heat of Asa's insistent arousal as he shifted his weight, her eyes fluttered closed. If not for the closeness of his body, she would surely have slipped to the floor like a melted Freezer Pop.

He touched his lips to hers in a contact so brief Kai thought maybe she was imagining things. She opened her eyes, then gasped when she felt pressure, then warmth, then the flick of a tongue on her neck. Her head fell back, her eyelids closed. She sobbed out a heavy moan.

Asa's arms folded around Kai's waist as he pulled her away from the shelving just enough to slip his hands lower so that he could cup her bottom. His fingers kneaded soft flesh as he lifted her slightly. When the heat at the apex of her thighs finally made contact with his arousal, he raised a hand to the back of her head, and claimed her mouth, smothering her moan with his own.

He was on fire with wanting her, needing her. His mind wasn't listening to reason. Logic had completely deserted him. All his sister's warnings had long been discarded. Schyler was wrong, there was no reason to wait, no reason to take things slowly. Kai's body was crying out for him, crying out to be loved. Asa slipped fingers into the soft coils at her neck to release her hair. He gripped fistfuls and pulled, tilting her face upward. And when the soft, feathery silk of her hair tangled with the springy coils of his locs, the sheer eroticism of the contrasting textures nearly sent him over the edge.

"God, Kai. I want this so bad. Tell me you want it, too," Asa breathed near her ear before lifting his head to stare down at her.

Eyelids half closed, Kai looked drunk in her passion. Then with an aggression that surprised him, she twisted her fingers into his hair and pressed against him, hip to hip, tongue to tongue. She wanted him, too. Desperately.

She pulled away just as Asa was ready to crawl inside her. His hands stroked up and down, touching her everywhere he could reach without getting obscene. He lowered his head for another mind-numbing kiss.

"Damn, you girl!!!!" A yell sounded from the next aisle over, then a deafening shower of metal. Asa cursed and Kai stiffened. Coins, screws, nuts and bolts, something, cascaded to the floor. Asa looked down at her, soaked in the desire swimming in her eyes. She looked beautiful, ready, and completely his. Her hair was mussed, her lips full and red, and her eyes sparkled with desire. Their hips were fused together, and even had he wanted to, he couldn't hide his need from her. Unfortunately, the commotion had spoiled the moment and Kai pulled away. Asa ran a shaky hand through his hair and stepped back. Neither of them spoke; and, finally, Asa returned to cutting the PVC tubing.

His hands trembled as he pressed the blade against the pipe. After the first turn, he lost his grip. "Damn it. I can't do this tonight." He looked up. Kai was sagging against the orange shelves, staring straight ahead.

"Screw this." Asa grabbed the pieces of tubing and stood up. "Come on." He laced his fingers into Kai's and charged down the aisle.

He said nothing as he dropped the cut pipe onto the checkout counter at the front of the store. Ignoring the smirking cashier, he waited for the total, then slapped a twenty on the counter, grabbed the bag with his free hand and marched purposefully from the store, dragging Kai behind him.

"Hey, you forgot your change!" The cashier yelled. "Hey!"

Kai tried to catch her breath as they drove north. She glanced down at her hand. Asa's large fingers were still laced into hers, stretching them wide as he held on tight. From the flicker of streetlights, she caught his profile. His jaw was rigid, his mouth in a hard line. "Where are we going?" she asked.

"My place."

As Asa sped down the dimly lit streets to his apartment, Kai mused at the recent turn of events. This wasn't Bobby Alders beside her, and she wasn't a naïve twenty-one year old anymore. Nor was she helpless or out of control. She was strong, and she knew—for the first time, perhaps—what she wanted from a man, or more precisely, what she wanted from this virile man sitting beside her. A rueful smile curled her lip as she pondered how Asa had charmed and seduced her over the previous weeks. Always glib, always direct, always smooth, he was now trembling, so intense was his need for her. Her attempt at humor and teasing at his sister's shop had started a chain reaction of lust and passion between them, making Kai all the more aware of her power. Power so fierce, so driving that Asa wouldn't stop until he had her. The idea that a man so skilled at loving women was so out of control, that she was the cause, was shocking and arousing. A more effective aphrodisiac he couldn't have given her.

But once they reached the electronic gate at Asa's corporate apartment, he discovered he had forgotten the remote, stopping them in their tracks.

Kai took it as a sign. Maybe she hadn't learned anything from her past experiences after all. Here she was running headlong into exactly the same situation. In the course of only a few weeks, she had forgotten everything that mattered to her—the partnership opportunity, her career, her personal ethics—all because of a man and her passion for him.

Beside her, Asa swore and fidgeted restlessly, as they waited for the guard to come out and verify Asa's residence before they were allowed through the gates.

Once in the garage, he parked and shut off the engine. "Finally," he said and turned to grin at Kai. The few minutes they spent waiting to be admitted into the complex had been long enough for Kai to come to her senses, and regain control over herself. Asa stepped out of the car and moved to open the passenger door. When Kai got out, she was immediately enveloped. The barely leashed passion in Asa's kiss made her shiver. She decided to wait until they reached his apartment to let him know she had changed her mind.

Asa's fingers were still laced in hers when they stepped into the elevator. He had held her hand in a tight grip since they left the Home Depot, as if he was afraid she'd make a run for it if he let her go. She glanced at the long thick fingers that stretched hers apart, the strong as steel muscles that rippled through his forearm, the long, thin dread-locks that tangled and fell around his arms and broad shoulders. If he hadn't forgotten his remote, she would be making love to this powerful man right now

The elevator doors closed, and Kai squeaked in surprise when Asa pressed her against the back wall of the elevator and stared down at her. His eyes were dark with desire, almost crazed with lust. His jaw clenched tight. His mouth descended; crushing, assaulting, taking her breath. He was overwhelming and … too much. His tongue invaded her mouth, wet and insistent, parodying the motions and rhythms of sex. The effect weakened her knees and made her shake. His fingers tangled in her hair, pulling her closer. Husky groans filled her ears.

Suddenly panicked, and feeling as out of control as Asa seemed to be, Kai shifted her arms and squeezed them between her chest and Asa's, then pressed her palms against him. This wasn't how she wanted their first time to be. "Stop," she whispered, in a voice just loud enough for him to hear.

The steel bands that gripped her flexed for an indeterminable moment, then fell away. When Asa finally opened his eyes, they were clouded, dazed. He gulped in air and stepped back. Their eyes met, and something in her expression made him sober immediately. His expression turned from desire to pain right before her eyes.

"Aw, baby. No," he said, backing away. He scrubbed his face with his hands before shoving them through his hair. He whirled to face the front of the elevator and cursed. "I *knew* this would happen." A deep breath lifted his shoulders, but he reached back, without turning around, and wiggled his fingers in a request for Kai's hand.

"Asa, I'm sorry. It's just … You overwhelm me."

The only sound was the ding of the floor indicator and his heavy breathing.

She had made him angry, Kai thought. Maybe she should just shut up. Or better yet, leave. She checked the floor indicators above the elevator doors. They were at floor eleven, so she reached around him to press the button for the lobby but Asa grabbed her hand.

"You're not leaving." Turning slowly, he looked down at her with an expression so sad Kai almost felt sorry for him. Sorry that he was scaring her with his verve and his larger than life attitude and personality. His maleness, especially when she wanted him just as violently as he wanted her.

"We're not leaving things like this, baby girl."

Kai took a hesitant step back.

Asa's fingers gripped her hand tighter. "You think I would force you? Is that what you think of me? After this? After Savannah?"

He dropped her hand and turned around to face the front of the elevator. "If I haven't proved to you by now that when we finally make love, it'll be what we both want, then maybe you *should* go on home."

To Kai's utter embarrassment, the button for the lobby lit up. He was telling her to go. Asa, who had pursued her since the day they had met, didn't want her. She was stunned by the emptiness that came with the thought.

"Asa." She reached out to touch him and got no response. "I'm sorry … I just. Look, this is all new to me. This, this …" She struggled to find the right words. "This wanting without regard for the consequences." There was a slight, but noticeable, shift in Asa's rigid posture that strengthened Kai's resolve, encouraging her to go on. "I'll come up—No. I want to come up."

Needing to see his face, she reached for his arm, turned him around. In a gesture of truce reminiscent of their drive to Savannah, she lifted her hand. After a long moment, Asa's hand joined hers, and she breathed out a sigh of relief. "Let's take this slowly, okay?"

Seconds later, the elevator chimed for floor fifteen.

Asa dragged her out behind him. "It just better be soon," she heard him mumble. "I can't take much more of this."

She smiled at his admission, her remaining tension evaporating. This was her Asa. Exactly as she wanted him-demanding and confident. She didn't want a slow, delicately considering man. She wanted Asa, in all his power, glory and overwhelming sensuality. She just ... she just needed her partnership first. She wondered if he would be willing to wait that long.

Kai glanced around Asa's apartment while he stored the tubing from Home Depot. A photo album lay on the coffee table in the neutrally colored living room, along with scholarly journals and thick academic books. The couch was beige with several throw pillows in various shades of orange and yellow for accent. However, the blanket strewn haphazardly over the arm looked like a Navaho pattern, colored in rich wines and greens. It was worn in a few spots and was apparently a personal item, rather than a part of the corporate furnishings.

Asa didn't give her a chance to argue about being in his apartment. He immediately poured her a glass of wine, and the next thing she knew, she was sitting on his couch, sans her heels, sipping an absolutely marvelous burgundy and being fed grapes and cheese from his fingers.

Kai stirred slightly, muttered in her sleep, then woke up with a jerk. Firm hands restrained her, rubbed her tension-filled shoulders. "Asa."

"Shh, go back to sleep, baby girl."

She shook her head. How could she have fallen asleep? And with her head in Asa's lap no less.

Asa maneuvered to pick her up. "You want to stretch out in the bedroom?"

Nervous and afraid of the temptation of Asa in the same room with a large bed, Kai struggled out of his arms and sat up.

"I guess that'd be a no." He smiled at her and tangled his hand through her hair. "I love your hair, babe. You really ought to wear it down." He nipped her lips with a kiss, then sat back, watching her. She tried to keep her worries from showing on her face, but when Asa moved away from her, she knew her efforts had failed.

"What did I do now?"

Kai twisted her hair back into its bun. "I don't know what you mean?"

Asa watched her for a moment, then turned to the coffee table to nibble at the left over cheese and grapes on the tray. "Yeah, you do. But I'm not going to spoil a pretty good date—our *first* date—with an argument."

Relieved, Kai sighed. She didn't want to argue either, but she wasn't ready to explain about her hair and why she didn't wear it down. Too much was going on right now. Her emotions were in too much upheaval. So much about her relationship with Asa reminded her of the past, and then so much about being with him was different. She wasn't sure what the differences were, but maybe once she figured it out, she would have the courage to make some changes. She didn't want to think about it right now. Once she made partner, maybe then she would consider a few adjustments.

"I'm sorry, Asa. I'm just ..."

He pulled her to him, cuddled her. "Come here, baby girl. What did I say in the elevator? I meant every word. When you're ready, its gonna be on, right?"

She nodded. Would she ever be ready for Asa Matthews? "I need to get going. It's pretty late."

He seemed reluctant to let go of her. "All right, but you know you can stay the night. I can keep my hands to myself for a few hours." When she eyed him warily, he laughed. "All right, maybe I do need to take you back."

"I think that might be a good idea. Do you mind if I use your bathroom first?"

A few minutes later, as she returned to the living room, Kai glanced around Asa's apartment. It was elegant, but fairly nondescript. More field notebooks lay on a side table in the hallway, along with a few artifacts from the plantation. A framed photograph of what she assumed was Asa's immediate family stood there as well. When she approached to take a closer look, her hand stopped. A bulletin from the Hathburn Museum and Auction house lay open on the table and two pieces were marked with colored Post-It flags, both by V.L. Arrington.

Kai drew in a sharp gasp when she felt Asa's hands encircle her waist. She put a hand to her heart, then quickly laid the auction bulletin aside and leaned her head back against his chest. "You scared me." She shuddered as warm lips captured her earlobe. "Do you always sneak up on people like that?"

"Mmm."

V.L. Arrington. She didn't like the coincidence that the pages were open and the artist's work marked.

"You want to go to this opening with me?" Asa asked.

Kai turned to study him. "Why?"

He shrugged. "It's a folk art exhibit. You said you liked the genre. I'm into it, too. In fact, this V.L. Arrington cat is one of my favorites." He released her and picked up the bulletin. "He's been kind of obscure until recently, but I came across one of his pieces back about ten years ago in a shop in D.C. Not too many people had heard of him then."

Kai edged away from Asa, wary now. "You know a lot about him."

"Nah, not really, but I get a lot of auction bulletins. You'd be amazed at how many archeological artifacts are stolen, and then sold on the open market. I just stumbled across the Arrington guy at one of them a few years back. I was real pleased to see his name. Looks like he's finally moving up in the world."

Kai let out a breath. He didn't know, she told herself. There's no way he could know. "I'm ready to go."

Asa dropped the bulletin back on the table. ""Where's home, baby girl?"

"Brookhaven."

A laugh burst from him. "That's only two miles from me. I can stop by your place for a treat after my morning jog instead of my usual smoothie.

The evil eye glare Kai gave him wiped the smug smile off his face so quickly, Kai had to bite the inside of her cheek to keep from laughing herself.

CHAPTER TWELVE

"Knock, knock." Asa called, as he walked up the stairway in the rear of the Aromia Natural Body Spa the next morning. Schyler's loft above the store was her sanctuary. The eighty-foot by twenty-five foot expanse was a source of envy and one of the reasons he had decided to move to Atlanta.

"A, that you?"

"Yeah, I'm here." He stepped into the loft and looked around. Even though Schyler had lived in the space for over seven years, he still got a rush from simply being here. The loft was raw and beautiful, interrupted only by large twelve-inch square columns. There were remnants of paint on the walls, an old iron crank press sat in one corner and heavy wooden beams traversed the plaster ceiling, slicing it into massive recessed rectangles. There seemed to be acres of floor space, and at least a mile of windows cut through the worn brick walls on both sides.

"Hey, babycakes." Schyler approached and stood on tiptoe to kiss him on the cheek. "How you doing?"

"I'm doing good. Well, actually better than good."

His sister's knowing smile made him grin. He followed her to the open kitchen that seemed to have grown from the ceiling and rooted itself in the center of the loft.

"How about let's have some coffee and you can tell me."

"Sounds like a plan."

Schyler dumped ground coffee into the filter and rinsed the glass carafe.

Asa shifted on his stool and glanced around the loft. "Coming to your place calms me down. I like chillin' up here."

"Good." She busied herself with her task, then turned to the fridge. "How about some deep fried tofu?"

Asa grimaced. "Coffee's fine, thanks."

"Hey, don't knock it, baby, but I knew you were coming by, so I bought some blueberry muffins. The giant ones you like so much."

"Now, that'll work."

Asa refused to eat Sky's cooking now. Prior to her transformation, whenever he came to visit, she had to beat him with a spatula to keep him from eating her out of house and home. Now that she was a tofu-eating, wheat grass growing, vegetarian, she always had leftovers.

"If you add some salsa on top of tofu…" she licked her lips and rubbed her belly. "Boy, mmm. It tastes just like *huevos rancheros*."

"I'll take your word for it," Asa said with a shudder.

"You'll get to meet Leon today." Schyler's voice was muffled as she dug a block of tofu out of the pan of water where it rested in the refrigerator. "He's an artist that lives nearby…." She stood and went to the counter to rinse the square she had extracted. "I'm getting some more pieces from him today."

"Oh, yeah?" Asa was intrigued. "Folk or modern?" Archaeology was a discipline that uncovered the old and the ordinary more often than the extraordinary. As a result, Asa had developed a deep fondness for the ordinariness of folk art.

"Folk."

"Sounds cool. I'd like to meet him…," He grimaced as he watched his sister slice tofu into inch-sized cubes and coat them with … something. "How do you eat that stuff?"

"Yumm, yumm, yumm." Schyler smacked her lips. "I decided to display some of his pieces in the window last Christmas. Really just to give my products an interesting contrast, but all my clients wanted to buy the stuff." She pulled a wok down from the assorted pots and pans that hung above the kitchen island and poured in sesame oil and crushed oregano, then turned on the stove. "So now I'm selling some of his stuff."

Asa rubbed a hand over his clean shaven chin. He was so engrossed in Kai last night he must have missed the artwork. "I didn't notice any folk art in the store last night."

"Not that you would have. You were a little distracted, but there wasn't any. It's selling like crazy. That's why he's bringing more."

"Mmmm."

"His work's really taking off. He's got an art show coming up in a few months, somewhere downtown. Had one in New York last year; come to think of it, he's got some at auction. Hathburn Museum and Auction, I think. That's why it's selling so well. About time, too. The man has to be in his fifties." Schyler skillfully flipped the browning tofu as she talked. "He's been sculpting for—well, I guess, all his life—but never made much money. Now folk art is in, and he's becoming the toast of the art world."

"Have I heard of him?" Asa wondered at the name. He considered himself a connoisseur, and paid enough attention to art circles, folk art at least, that he was surprised he hadn't already discovered him. But he didn't think he knew any folk artists named Leon.

"Don't know." Schyler glanced over her shoulder. "Does V. L. Arrington ring a bell?"

"V.L. Arrington." Asa sat back. "You're kidding."

Schyler shook her head.

"You're selling work by V.L. Arrington? Here?" He looked at her in astonishment. "His pieces at auction start at $7500.00."

"Hmmm." Schyler didn't seem impressed.

"Girl, did you hear what I said?"

"Sure."

"Well ..."

"Well, what. It's just money ..."

"Just ..." Asa shook his head in disbelief. His sister was definitely not the same person she used to be. "I wanna meet this dude."

Schyler glanced at her watch. "No problem. He'll be here at nine-thirty. Maybe he'll give you one of his pieces."

"Give?" Asa was still in shock.

Schyler nodded emphatically. "That's what I said."

After breakfast, tofu for Schyler, muffins for Asa, they went down to the shop to wait for Leon. Schyler appraised her brother quietly as she straightened products in a display near the window. He relaxed on the couch in the waiting area near the massage rooms, with his eyes closed and his mind very far away.

Although Asa had told her about his date over breakfast, he left out some important details. He and Kai must have become intimate last night. From his relaxed manner and easier than normal grin, Schyler assumed that was what had put him in such a great mood, but he was unusually quiet about the particulars. Ever proud of his conquests, Asa always kissed and told. But not this time.

"I'm surprised you didn't give me a blow by blow description of last night, Little A." Schyler prompted. If her little brother had indeed fallen for Kai Ellis, she didn't expect to learn much more from him, today.

"Already told you everything," he said without turning to face her.

"Hmmm."

"Hmmm," he mimicked unconsciously.

"You did the do didn't you?"

"What if we did?" Asa eyes were still closed, his hands behind his head.

"Well?"

Asa sat up, his brows furrowed in irritation. "Well, *what?* You want a play by play?"

"Whoa, don't get your boxers in a wad. I was just asking."

"Well ask something else, I already told you all I'm going to about that. We had a great time."

Amazed, Schyler watched as her brother transformed in front of her eyes. His face softened and his shoulders relaxed. He stood and walked to the counter. "Sis, she's as cool as a fan. Strong-willed, intelligent, full of life, passionate. It's too bad she only lets go when she's provoked."

"Is that right?"

"Yeah. Take her hair for instance," he said, warming to the discussion. "She keeps it pulled back in that bun, but it doesn't want to stay there. Little curls are always popping out, and she tries to tuck 'em back in."

"She does have great hair."

"Her hair." Asa's eyes gleamed as he stared at Schyler. "It's like her—wild inside, if she'll just let it out."

"Oohh …"

"That's why I keep taking it down. Every chance I get I'm taking her hair down—and she hates that. I don't understand why."

"Mmmm." Schyler nodded thoughtfully. "Maybe one day she'll figure things out and let you in on the secret."

Asa looked up at his sister. "Oh, it won't be one day. I'll see to that," he assured her.

Before Asa had a chance to challenge the worried look on his sister's face, the bell at the entrance jingled, and in an instant, her eyes turned from shadowed to bright. A tall, attractive man in his fifties propped the door open with his foot, then struggled to pull two wooden crates through the door.

"Leon!" Schyler shouted. "Hold on, Asa can help you."

Asa was already at the door, easily lifting a crate and holding open the door with his shoulder. V.L. Arrington brought in the other crate and sat it down near the counter. Asa followed and placed the second crate beside the first.

"Leon Arrington," Schyler announced, "I'd like you to meet my brother. Asa Matthews, meet V.L. Arrington, sculptor, folk artist, and all around great guy."

"Good to meet you, Mr. Arrington," Asa said. "I truly admire your work."

The artist pumped Asa's arm. "Thank you, son. Thanks a lot." He eyed Asa. "But, have you even heard of me?"

They chatted briefly and Asa explained how he'd first come across V.L.'s work, then they helped Schyler set up the display of folk art and iron sculptures in a front corner of the shop.

"I'd love to purchase a piece from you, Mr. Arrington," Asa said after the display was complete. "It would make a nice gift for a new friend of mine."

"Woman friend."

"Of course."

V.L. was sharp-eyed, direct, as were most artists. Asa studied his face and dark, piercing eyes. His clothes were casual and bohemian, making him seem younger than he probably was. He had thick coarse, wavy hair that was graying at the temples and pulled into a jet-black ponytail that hung down his back. Asa doubted it was a fashion statement. He had a feeling that this man was born with a ponytail and an eclectic manner. Salt and pepper tendrils curled at his temples and forehead, framing his face like a garland of leaves.

"She has hair like yours," Asa blurted, suddenly noticing the connection. "Artistic, unruly. Kind of out of control." He watched the man lovingly tend to his "children" as V.L. fondly called his pieces, shifting one slightly, moving another to a different place. He turned and held his hands out to his sculptures. To Asa, V.L. looked as if he were accepting them as grown and was now allowing them to leave the nest.

"I think of it as my source of strength," V.L. commented about his hair, giving the salt and pepper curls a pat. "Like Samson, but I used to curse this stuff. Lord did I hate it. Made me different. But then, I learned that it was me, my soul, my essence. I let it guide me. I'm proud of it. Wouldn't trade it for anything in the world, now."

Asa listened, wishing he could introduce this man to Kai. "Could I commission something from you?"

"Surely. What do you have in mind?"

"Well." Asa rubbed his hands together. "It's for my new lady friend. And I kind of see her hair the same way you see yours." He moved his hands around demonstratively as he talked. "Her hair is her strength, who she is … inside … Just like you said. Only she doesn't know it." He paused and considered what he actually meant. "Or won't accept the fact."

"Mmmm."

"It's wild, with springy coils, like yours. Black as coal, too. And when I take it down …" Asa's eyes lost focus as he thought of Kai. Memories of the night before flooded his senses. His Kai, with her hair flowing like a river over his lap as she slept.

"So Leon, could you maybe do a piece that shows her the way Asa sees her? Full of life and all that?" Schyler said. "I'm thinking wrought iron would be good."

Asa must have zoned out or was looking stupid or something, because Sky punched him in the arm. "Ow, girl." Rubbing his arm, he stepped out of her reach and scowled at the indignity of her assault.

V.L. was ignoring the both of them, rubbing his chin as he considered Sky's suggestion. "Let me see what I can come up with—I may have just the thing." He zeroed in on Asa. "What's your lady friend do?"

"Architecture. She's an architect. Best and brightest in Atlanta. Bad as she wants to be. She'll be my wife in six months."

Schyler gasped sharply. "Asa!"

Asa shrugged. Now that he said it, he realized it was the truth.

"What are you talking about? You haven't known her a month."

"Sometimes love happens that way," V.L. said, seemingly unaffected by the announcement. He reached to shake Asa's hand. "Good for you, son. Leave life in the hands of fate. That's what I always say.

Congratulations—maybe I'll do something for your wedding as well."
He weighed Asa's dreadlocks in his hand. "I'm sure you two make a
striking couple. Seems you've got a hair thing going on yourself"

"Hey, lady," Asa said, turning to his sister. "I need to jet. I'll catch
you later, all right?"

"You'd better. We have some things to discuss, like your *marriage*."

"Nice fellow," Leon commented after Asa departed.

"Yeah, he is." But she was worried about him. Marriage? Her
confirmed bachelor brother?

"Hey, now, Schyler," Leon cautioned. "Let the man live his life.
He's grown. He knows what he's doing. Anyway, his new lady sounds
like a worthy challenge."

"That's what I'm worried about."

"How so?"

She sighed. "He's never mentioned marriage before. In fact, I'd
come to think he would never get married. He's not the type really."
She paused and shook her head. "Why am I telling you this anyway?"

"Hey, this is Leon. If you need to talk, then talk."

"Okay. Asa's an archaeologist. He's on digs most of the time. When
he's not, he's writing books about them. He likes to write down in St.
Croix; he's got a place down there. He'll leave town for six months at a
time, just to write. When he comes back, he's off on another dig."

"Okay. So …"

"So, he won't be in Atlanta long enough to build a relationship,
much less a marriage."

"Don't you think you should let him decide that?"

"Well … yeah," she confessed. "But I'm afraid he's probably not
being honest with himself."

"Mmmm."

"All that hair stuff, that's what I'm worried about."

Leon turned to look at her. "How's that?"

"I don't know her well yet, I just met Kai last night. She seems nice
enough, you know. I mean, maybe he's right about her needing to
loosen up, but how would he know? He's only known her a few weeks.

Maybe she's got a good reason for being the way she is. I like Kai, and I'd just hate to see him ruin something decent with his meddling."

"What was that name again?"

"Kai … Beautiful isn't it?"

"Yeah, just like she is, I'm sure. Her name mean's fire, I think. Might be Gaelic."

Schyler smiled. "That's tight, Leon. It fits her. When she unties her hair, she looks almost like she's bursting into flames. She really is perfect for my brother, though. I think he's met his match. I just hope he doesn't screw things up."

"Well, I say let nature take its course. The fates will decide what's best."

There was a skip in his step when Vernon unlocked the door to his studio. Things hadn't been right between him and his little girl since she was five years old. She was so much like him, he couldn't help but know that she would resent any overtures on his part to reconcile. Unfortunately, he had been proven right.

When his mother died around the time Kai graduated from college, he considered reconciliation, but the time wasn't right. Instead, he created a statue for her that would mean something to both of them only to have it thrown back in his face.

That was all Vernon had needed to learn his lesson, and he had learned it well. He would wait for his baby. He would wait until she was strong enough to forgive. Maybe not forget, but he could live with that, and he continued to hope that some day she would come around.

In the meantime, the sculpture that he had created in her image held a special place in his heart. He had always hoped that someday she would accept it. And now, he thought with a smile as he cleared away the sawdust from his work bench, now maybe someday had finally come. There was a lot of eagerness in his heart for a reconciliation, no matter how many times he'd tried to deny it.

A few days later, at his desk at Coleman Foundation headquarters, Asa tapped out Richard Dunlap's number on the phone. While he waited for someone to answer, he relaxed against the high backed leather chair and stretched his legs under the desk. As Asa had come to expect from Coleman, the office was more than adequately furnished, with a top of the line laptop, a LAN connection, T-1 line, and plenty of storage for his books and artifacts.

He peered through the open door of his office, watching conservatively dressed men and women scurry back and forth while Richard's phone rang on the other end of the line. Asa, dressed in black slacks and a ribbed v-neck shirt, was grateful of his role as consultant and fellow. He rather enjoyed his nomadic lifestyle. While scholars, like his friend Richard, desired the security of a university tenure track, Asa much preferred the flexibility his position at Coleman afforded.

"Richard Dunlop speaking."

"What's up, Richard, it's Asa."

"Yeah, A. How's it going?"

"Absolutely, positively magnificent, my friend."

Richard cleared his throat. "I'm not going to ask what's put you in such a good mood. It's got to be a woman."

"Old habits die hard."

Richard chuckled. "And why don't we skip that discussion. Whatcha' need?"

Asa laughed. Though Kai was on his mind, he didn't mention her. She wouldn't want anyone involved with the project to know they were seeing one another. He thought she was going a little overboard with the subterfuge thing. Had already told her he'd picked her team on their merit. So it wasn't as if they were doing something unethical, but he could hang with that, at least for a while, if it gave her peace of mind. Kai had her eye on that partnership, and he wouldn't jeopardize that. He got down to business with Richard. "The cemetery. I'm going to send Jamal up to Richmond to have some glass and pottery shards tested. You got anything you want the lab to take a look at?"

"Actually, I do need a couple of charts confirmed," Richard replied. "I need some information about the foliage in the region from about 1600 to 1790. It should help me verify the dates on the slave diaries, especially if the paper was milled in the area."

Asa made a note on the legal pad. "Got it, anything else?"

"Nope. I think that's all I need. When's Jamal leaving?"

"Mmm, most likely day after tomorrow. That way he can make it back by the time Kai's team gets to the site. They'll have to put up about fifteen tents and get themselves organized. Damned if I want to have to deal with that."

"All right. If I think of anything else I'll email you tomorrow."

"That'll work. When's the summer session over?"

"Next week, why?"

"Well, my book …." And there was Kai.

"Oh, yeah. Still planning to go to the islands to work?"

"That's the plan, but this restoration project's taking up a lot of time."

"Damned architects."

Asa's mouth turned up in a smirk. That was usually his line, not Richard's, but he was rethinking his attitude. "Yeah, architects." His retort didn't come out with its normal derisiveness.

"I should be up there in about a week to help you out, but you know how things go. Committee meetings, advisory groups, final exams, might be later."

"Yeah." Asa didn't have any sympathy to give. He had been smart enough to get out of academia before he got stuck and didn't understand why anyone would willingly endure the torture. "I'll take independence over tenure any day."

"Rub it in, why don't you."

After a few minutes more of conversation, Asa hung up and continued doodling. He had printed Kai's name in block letters in the margins as he talked to Richard. She was something of an enigma. He understood her desire to become successful in her field and could even buy her suppressing some of her personal desires to get there. But, it disturbed him to think she was letting the professional Kai erase the real person underneath. There was a story behind it all, he was certain.

Surprised at his internal musings, he sat back in his chair. Normally, his relationships didn't intrude so much on his thoughts, especially during the workday. Sure, when he was out in the field he allowed personal visits, but that was always after his work was done. And he certainly had never been so infatuated with a woman that he would consider marriage. Yet he had blurted it out to his sister and V.L. Arrington, a perfect stranger.

What did he know about love? Nothing. He hadn't even figured Kai out yet, and he'd only made love with her one time. Well, not completely, but that little show she gave him in Savannah was enough to let him know the real thing would be spectacular.

He lifted an eyebrow as he relived her response to him and felt a heaviness growing between his legs. He shifted in his seat and cleared his throat, then put the legal pad and his thoughts of Kai aside. He needed to focus. He made a couple of notes in his DayTimer, which lay open on the desk. He needed to look into scholarships and work-study information for Cammy before he talked with his sister. That brought him back to Kai once again.

She didn't like the fact that he was helping Cammy get funding for her education. Lord knows, she'd made her disapproval of his involvement more than clear in their ride from the restaurant to Sky's shop. Based on the intensity of her reaction, Kai must not have gotten any help with her own college tuition. Why else would she want things to be so hard on someone else? Maybe she had had a tough life. That didn't appear to be the case, though tough was a relative term. Maybe she had been a shy child. Or maybe ... hadn't she mentioned being raised by a grandmother? Maybe the woman had been very strict and pious. Or perhaps it was her parents. She certainly didn't seem to have respect for them as artists. Maybe they were the cause of her conservative bent and rigid, puritan work ethic.

Lost in thought, Asa stepped into the hallway.

Someone brushed by him. "Excuse you."

Asa looked up. "Bill."

"You might want to look where you're going."

Asa didn't bother pondering what Bill's problem was today. He simply sidestepped him.

"Hey, I was coming to see you, Matthews."

"Have a seat in my office," he said over his shoulder. "I'll be back in a minute."

Asa returned from the restroom to find Bill quickly pulling his hand away from the legal pad he'd left on the desk. "What can I do for you, Bill?" He decided to take the high road and keep things on a professional level. The quicker he dealt with Bill, the quicker he could get back to work.

Bill smiled dimly, looked as if he was about to say something, then thought better of it. "I just came by to tell you that the board—Harold—decided that this new cemetery thing is worth funding of its own. If you find it, he wants to start a separate project."

Asa considered the idea. He was using what was leftover in the general excavation budget to do the artifact testing up in Richmond. It wasn't very much, and he had been prepared to pay Jamal's travel expenses out of his own pocket so they would be able to continue digging a little while longer. Harold's enthusiasm could be both good and bad. Bad if you were on your own with a theory, because he usually left you blowing in the wind with no funding and very little in the way of encouragement until you could prove it to someone other than yourself. Asa waited for Bill to spell out which.

"Harold's giving you money to continue the dig. But ..."

Asa saw the glint in Bill's eye. The guy just couldn't wait to drop the other shoe. Asa stilled himself for what was to come. He blanked his expression and folded his arms across his chest.

The glint in Bill's eye dimmed. "He's excited about the new cemetery idea, so he wants to restore the old slave church in conjunction with the excavations."

"You mean to tell me he wants more architects milling around during the middle of excavations? You've got to be kidding me."

The smug Bill was back. "Nope, not kidding. Guess you'll have to deal with those architects a little longer than you planned."

Asa crossed his arms. "Okay, Bill. What's the deal? You'd normally have your assistant give me this kind of message. What else do you want?"

"Nothing much to say, except Harold's letting Chicago take the new project."

Asa raised an eyebrow. Bill seemed just a little too pleased with his statement. "Is that a fact? And why is that?"

"You're not upset?" Bill asked, apparently upset himself. "I thought you wanted KT & G to have the job."

"When the KT & G team gets to the site in a couple of days, they'll be busy enough with the welcome center. Besides, I've got a book to finish, and Richard will be there to help." Asa smiled as Bill's enthusiasm over being the bearer of bad news faded. "He can deal with the Chicago team."

"But, Harold wants you to do it."

"And how would you know that, Bill?" He leaned forward. "You wouldn't happen to be spying on me, now would you?"

"I ... No, of course I'm not spying on you. I have ... I have quite enough to do, thank you."

"Right." Tired of the conversation, Asa stood up. "Let me set you straight, Bill, so you won't have to keep spying. What Harold wants from me is a finished manuscript. That's my focus right now, and that means finding and excavating that cemetery, not managing the preservation of the slave church. Now, if you don't mind, I need to cut this meeting short. I don't have time to waste on you or your petty vendettas."

Bill stood reluctantly, then glanced down at Asa's desk, his gaze lingering on the legal pad. A frown tugged at his mouth before he brought his attention back at Asa. "Apparently you do."

Asa sat back in his chair after Bill left and looked at his legal pad. Kai's name was on it surrounded by the doodles he'd made during his phone call with Richard. He smiled slightly, thought of her, then frowned. He didn't mind that Bill might suspect something was going on between them, but he knew Kai wouldn't be happy with the exposure. He just hoped it wouldn't cause her any trouble.

CHAPTER THIRTEEN

Bill Jameson hurried to his office and quietly shut the door. Too upset to sit down, he paced. *What to do, what to do.*

He glanced over at the pictures of his wife and children displayed proudly on his credenza. He loved his wife, he did, but Kai Ellis was such a lovely thing. So ladylike and polite. Just the kind of woman he would have married when he was younger. Not that his wife Miriam wasn't just fine. She certainly was, but sometimes, she could be a little bossy.

He shook his head to clear it. He was getting off track. He and Kenneth Roselle had been right about Matthews setting his sights on Kai. Upset at the thought, he grabbed the phone, but set it down again without dialing. Roselle wasn't one of his favorite people any more than Asa was, but he would make things hard for him if Bill didn't contact him. Worse, Kai could be ruined associating with Matthews.

Bill picked up the phone again, took a deep breath, then dialed Roselle's number.

"You were right," he said when Roselle answered. "I was just in his office, and her name was doodled all over his notepad."

He paused, then squirmed a little as Kenneth asked more and more probing questions. There was only so much spying Bill was comfortable doing, but it didn't seem to be enough for Kenneth.

Bill glanced nervously at his closed door, wondered how clearly he could be heard from the hallway. "They're leaving for Savannah in the next couple of days. The entire team will be there for two weeks, maybe longer."

After receiving a laundry list of instructions from Roselle and no thank you, Bill hung up. He hoped he was doing the right thing. Feeling shaky about it, he picked up the phone and dialed again.

"Hi, sweetheart," he said when his wife answered. "I just wanted to say I love you."

Miriam asked about dinner, and he promised to be home by six.

UNEARTHING PASSIONS

On Wednesday, Asa stood just outside of one of the slave cabins and looked west toward the work camp. The KT & G team had been on site for a couple of days now and seemed to be adjusting well to camp life. Amusement tilted his mouth as he watched them mill around. The little tents between the live oak trees and low hanging moss resembled slave quarters in their positioning. They were organized in exactly the same fashion, with his larger tent at the head and other work tents and sheds beyond that. He, an African-American archaeologist, descendant of slaves was, in a sense, the master of the plantation. Correction, he decided, as he thought through the analogy. Maybe not master, more like overseer. Harold, who was still cracking the whip on him about that manuscript, was the master.

Asa had been off-site, in Savannah, for the past two days doing research at the Georgia Historical Society Library and wasn't at Ridgeway when Kai and her team arrived, and he couldn't wait to see how Kai handled camp life. Searching her out among the small throng of graduate students and architects that moved about, he found her standing near one of the work sheds where two or three of her team members hovered as she explained or delegated, a thermal coffee mug in her hand. When Asa arrived, Jamal mentioned that Kai was having trouble with her tent. She looked well rested, so he supposed whatever the problem, it wasn't interfering with her sleep.

When the other two architects moved off to start their assigned tasks, Asa walked over. He knew the exact moment Kai felt his presence, because she froze. "Glad I have an affect on you," he said stepping closer. "Miss me?"

Asa hadn't realized he missed her himself until just now. He missed the aroma of Jamaica Blue Mountain coffee wafting from her mug, the way curly strands of her hair hovered just past her temple. He even missed the little frown lines that appeared between her eyebrows when he annoyed her, as he was doing now.

He brushed a thumb over them. "I missed you, sweetheart."

She whipped around and checked to see if anyone was close enough to hear them.

"Want me to check inside the work shed?" he offered. "There may be some spies in there ready to out us."

"Very funny." But despite her nonchalance, her eyes moved to the door of the shed.

"No one's in there, babe. Relax. And no one's gonna tattle on us, either. But so what if they do? We're both adults." He paused, looked her over. He wanted to tell her how good she looked, but she was still scowling. "What? Jeez. You need to lighten up around me, Kai. I told you this is just how I am."

"And I told you how important my partnership is to me. I can't carry on with you in public."'

He grinned and took a step forward. "So does that mean we can carry on in private?"

"Asa, I'm serious."

"Hey! Dr. Matthews! Dr. Matthews!" Jamal Rogers came rushing up.

"What's going on Jamal?"

"We found it! We found it!"

"The cemetery?"

Jamal nodded.

"You found the cemetery?" Asa grabbed the boy and pounded him on the back. "Well don't just stand there. Show me where it is!" He grabbed Kai's hand. "Come on!"

Jamal led them down Magnolia Avenue, away from the Big House. About halfway down the row of slave cabins, he turned ninety degrees. They passed the small garden plots behind the cabins, then another few outbuildings and took a meandering path through the brush, finally stopping about a thousand feet from the cabins.

"We started finding grave markers in this direction." Jamal pointed eastward and gasped quickly, taking a breath. "When you told us to start looking in all the areas on the old site plans marked for refuse, we found it."

"Why would you look for refuse?" Kai asked, startling Asa.

He squeezed her hand. "God, I forgot you were there. Genovese. Eugene Genovese is a renowned historian. His specialty is slavery and its theological roots. He and his team uncovered some slave cemeteries in the Tidewater area of Virginia back in the 1980's, and then lost half of the find because they thought it was a garbage dump. That's what got me thinking about our cemetery. We couldn't seem to find it in any of the usual places. The later one was much too westernized, too Christian. It had standard headstones, a walkway straight to it, and everything was laid out symmetrically. Then I thought about the strong superstitions of the slaves who came directly from Africa and—"

"Genovese," Kai finished.

"You're quick." He studied her for a moment, her eyes twinkling with delight, probably mirroring his own. She had a big smile on her face and seemed just as excited as he was about the discovery. Oh how he wanted this woman. He took a step forward, and her smile faded abruptly. *Crap. Jamal.*

Asa stepped back and turned to his student who was picking up pottery shards from the weeds. He cut his eye back to Kai and whispered, "He's not even paying attention to us."

"It doesn't matter."

Despite Kai's brush off, Asa's jovial mood returned, and since he was still holding her hand, he pulled her closer and tucked a stray curl behind her ear. "I'm gonna get you, girl. Keep playing with me." He chuckled when she gasped, but turned her loose to kneel down beside Jamal and pick up more of the pottery shards. "I knew it was here. I knew it." They had finally found the cemetery. *Thank you, God,* was all he could think. As soon as they roped off the area and conveyed the good news to the camp, he would call Harold. Now he could finish his manuscript, Harold would be off his back and he could even stick it to wussy Bill Jameson.

Asa took a breath and looked around. Kai was standing to one side, peering with interest at where Jamal had pointed. Maybe, just maybe, he could wine and dine Kai now that the majority of his worries were over. Jamal was studying a fragment he'd just found.

"We need to get things organized so the other students will be able to help dig," Asa told him. "Why don't you go get some stakes and cord from the supply shed, and we'll get the area roped off." Jamal handed over the fragment and hurried away.

"This wasn't marked as a cemetery on any of the site plans we looked at." Asa fingered the pottery shard. "But it makes sense, given the superstitions of the earliest slaves."

He turned around. It took him a moment to focus, then Kai smiled at him. "I know. You forgot I was here, right?"

Though he wanted to touch her, he checked himself. To his surprise, she came to him.

"No one's watching," she whispered, then leaned in and gave him a quick kiss. "Congratulations."

Asa watched her for a moment; absorbed her.

She looked down nervously. "Do you know how old the cemetery is?" she asked. "You said it was older than the one you've already excavated."

"Guessing, I would put it at around 1785. We found some artifacts near the quarters that date back that far." He stepped gingerly around the area, studying the weeds and overgrowth.

"Asa, look at this." Kai held up a pitcher handle from where she had crouched nearby, then gathered shards and small fragments of pottery as if it were buried treasure. If he hadn't already been excited, he would be just from watching her.

Kai's head was bowed as she searched the grass, oblivious to anything else. Amazing. This was the woman he had been searching for before he realized he needed her. She hid all that fire and determined passion behind her French twist, but in moments like this, he could see through it all, just as she had slipped and revealed herself to him the first night he met her. She might be able to fool everyone else with her no-nonsense business façade, but Asa wasn't fooled. He felt as if he were seeing her for the first time, seeing her in all her many dimensions: as a professional, as an equal, as a woman—his woman.

At that moment, he gave up the fight to stay away from her until her partnership was secure. It was futile to even try. He would respect her need for discretion and keep things on the down low, but that was all. Behind closed doors, they were taking things to the next level.

Asa crouched beside her and found more of the pieces in a sweep of his hand. "Hold yours here." Together they assembled a pitcher, fitting pieces crudely together. The only ones missing were on the very bottom and a patch on the side.

"The slaves believed that the deceased needed the same things in death that they did in life. So they put personal articles on top of the grave during the funeral to keep the spirit in the graveyard, and they always broke the items. Pots, cups and pitchers were always broken on the bottom. Just like this one."

With a nod, he gestured to the ground, and together they lowered the pitcher to the grass. Asa looked around with a more practiced eye, his archaeologist cap firmly in place. "You see all these brambles." He pointed a little farther away, sat back on his haunches and gazed out at the thorny shrubs and scrawny trees that dotted the area a few feet away. "Early slaves tended to place their graveyards in places where there was overgrowth. If there wasn't any, they would plant trees and shrubs in a meandering path and bury their dead beyond it."

Kai looked around. "It looks like that's exactly what they did here. Only they probably didn't have to plant the brambles themselves. Looks as if they were already here. But why? You sure can't get to the cemetery very easily in the middle of all that mess."

"Exactly the point. A straight path from the graveyard to the plantation could lead a restless spirit right back to the living." He gazed at her, only just realizing that he would normally be having such a conversation with Richard or one of his grad students.

Yes, she was definitely his woman; or would be very soon.

Later that day, while Kai was working with her team, Asa and Jamal checked out her tent, which appeared to be properly staked from the outside. Asa peeked inside. Very little dirt and sand had gotten under the tent walls. The cot was neatly made up. A small stand of toiletries and an alarm clock were set near the bed. On the other side was a crate of drafting supplies.

Asa backed out of the tent. "It's neat as a pin in there. I thought you said there was something wrong."

Jamal shrugged and walked around the outside of the tent. "Looks fine to me, too. But she told me last night she thought she was missing some pieces."

"Architects."

Jamal grinned. "Guess she's not used to camping."

As Jamal walked away, Asa leaned against the tree that shaded Kai's tent. He wondered if she realized she had pitched her tent so close to his.

"What's up, Asa?"

He turned. "Jeremy. How's it going? Getting a lot done?"

"You know it." He glanced at Kai's tent. "Figured I'd help you out, my brother."

"Come again?"

Jeremy laughed. "I pitched boss lady's tent for her. That's yours over there, right?" He pointed across the small makeshift avenue of the camp to the large tent at the head of the row.

Asa tried unsuccessfully to hide his smile, then gave up all together. He put a friendly arm on the shoulder of his new best friend. "Come on, man, I think I owe you a drink."

They walked toward Club Ridgeway, a six hundred square foot area of the work camp where the students had erected a large tent. It was big enough for a few hammocks, plastic lawn tables and chairs, and a makeshift bar. An inexpensive stereo system sat in one corner, a disco ball hung from the ceiling along with plastic streamers and Christmas lights. As the group's traditional gathering place during the summer excavation season, the students took turns playing bartender and deejay and enjoyed drinks, card games and dancing in the evenings.

From the crowd inside the tent when Asa and Jeremy arrived, it was apparent that the KT & G crew had taken to the tradition with ease.

They sat down on two rickety bar stools. "I'll have a Corona, T.C.," Asa said to the stocky, barrel-chested student behind the bar.

"You?" T.C. asked Jeremy.

"Corona's cool."

T.C. set the beers on the bar.

Jeremy eyed his bottle critically. "What, no limes?"

"This isn't Atlanta," Asa said. "Drink your beer."

"Drinking."

"So, everyone settling in okay?"

"Yeah. Actually, it's kinda cool living out here on-site. I figured we'd stay at hotels like we did the last time. But since Savannah's almost an hour away, not to mention more expensive, I can see how it makes more sense to be here. We're pulling twelve-hour days as it is trying to gather all the details we need to take back to Atlanta. No way would I want to drive all the way back to Savannah every night." Jeremy took a swig of his beer and slanted a look at Asa. "'Sides, Judy's kinda getting into camping life. Know what I mean?"

Asa snorted. "Drink your beer, man."

"Drinking."

Asa peered around the room. Students and architects filed in and out. A rowdy group of card players disturbed one of the kids sleeping in a hammock. He got up, groused at them for a while, then retired to his tent.

"So, is boss lady taking to camping life?"

"Why you want to be all in my business?" Asa asked. "You sound like a woman."

"But you're smiling. She must like it just fine."

"A gentleman never speaks ill of a lady."

Jeremy made a big show of looking around the room, eyes wide. "Gentleman? Where's the gentleman? Anyway. I'm just trying to take care of you, brother-man, look out for your best interests."

"Uh, I think I can handle things myself, thank you."

"Yeah, but now things are easier with you sleeping just across the way. Boss lady can sneak over after everybody's asleep, and sneak back before anyone gets up. No one'll ever know."

Asa put his beer down slowly. He wondered whether Kai was aware of how well her studio head knew her.

Jeremy nodded sagely. "Yeah, I know the deal. Judy and I want to see Kai happy. She sure as hell didn't need Kenneth Roselle. But you're cool people. I know you'll treat her right."

"You don't even know me."

"Nah. But I'm a good judge." He gave Asa a long assessing look. "You'll do."

"Thanks. I think."

"Seriously, though. Kai is like my big sister. I've been working for her for almost six years, and I'd do anything for her. She's always been in my corner. I intend to be in hers." He signaled the bartender for another drink.

"Like you were when she got so tight with Roselle?"

Jeremy looked hard at him.

Asa was careful not to raise his eyebrows in surprise, but his opinion of the young brother rose a few notches.

"I've got her back." Jeremy said.

Judy entered Club Ridgeway a few minutes later, so Asa left Jeremy to her. Jeremy had given him quite a bit to think about. Apparently, Jeremy and Judy could see through Kai's professional façade as well. He walked absently through the little tent city, speaking briefly to the few students milling around. He was restless and he wanted Kai. It was after dinnertime, but with the excitement of the cemetery find and all the work to be done prior to excavation, he hadn't eaten. Maybe he could talk Kai into taking a ride to Savannah with him. Unfortunately, she was nowhere around.

That simple little kiss she had given him at the cemetery, ridiculous as it seemed, had meant a lot to him. Even more than the grope in the Home Depot. Not that he had minded, of course, but in the Home Depot, as every other encounter between them before today, Kai had been out of control. He wanted her lucid and in possession of her senses and feelings, and her rational mind when he made love to her. He wanted her to come to him the way she had today when she kissed him, of her own free will. And he wanted her to have no doubts about what they would do when the time came.

He took a meandering path through camp, then walked toward the work shed where he noticed the light on inside. Surprised to see Kai, he stopped short at the door. Dressed in lightweight navy slacks and a silk blouse, she was pacing around the shed. Her hair was loose, tumbling gloriously down her back to contrast boldly with her cream-colored blouse. Asa stepped, away from the door as she turned and paced in the opposite direction. He needn't have worried about being seen; she was in her own world. Bright eyes flashed as she stared into oblivion. Creating. What, he couldn't fathom.

He moved back to the doorway while Kai turned to march the other way. Both hands were in her hair now. She'd just placed the drafting pencil she'd been holding in her mouth and was plowing her hands through her hair as if she were giving it a thorough shampoo. Asa's libido kicked in, his groin tightened. He blinked a few times to make sure he wasn't seeing things. It was the first time he had seen her *voluntarily* take her hair down. The first time he'd seen her really let go. He blinked a few times as he tried to put the Kai he took out to dinner a few nights ago with the Kai who helped him piece together pottery shards in the cemetery, and now the Kai who was furiously creating in the work shed. Then he remembered her actions during their last site visit. She had taken her shoes off and was pacing then, too. Maybe if he had waited a few minutes longer, he would have seen the same scene he was witnessing now.

She stalked across the floor toward the door again, then came to an abrupt stop. She turned and rushed over to the drafting board she'd set up on the table in the far corner. Asa put his suppositions on hold and just watched. She whipped the drafting pencil from her mouth and began sketching furiously, with broad strokes. After a few moments, she stepped back, reviewed what she'd come up with, then made a few notes on another pad. She bent down to rummage through her satchel and brought out colored pencils and Pantone© markers. The stool at the table must have interrupted the smooth flow of ideas through her right brain, because she shoved it irritably out of her way and began her pacing again. This time, as she marched blindly toward the door, she scratched her head with one of the markers. Four others were gripped tightly in the opposite hand.

She turned swiftly and rushed back to the table. Asa watched her march and sketch, dash and note, for a full fifteen minutes. He wasn't sure when or if it would stop. When his stomach growled, reminding him he was still hungry, he stepped into the room, but was stopped again in his tracks.

He stared in disbelief. This time, instead of marching to the drafting board and marking up the paper with firm strokes, then prancing away again, Kai pulled up the previously ignored stool and sat down. Asa stepped back a pace or two. He thought he'd finally determined the method to her madness, but she surprised him again.

Calmly now, as if her fifteen minute fit of inspiration had never happened, Kai carefully removed the layers of tracing paper she'd taped down to the drafting board. Gone were the wild, excited strokes and long sweeps of her arms. Her movements were precise, stilted, fastidious. She moved the sketches to her right, spreading them so that she could see each one clearly from where she sat.

She unrolled a fresh stretch of tracing paper, tore it expertly from the roll, then taped it to the drafting board. She put away the colored pencils and markers, and brought out a leather pouch of what looked like very expensive drafting implements. She laid them carefully on the table, and then one by one brought out an assortment of drafting triangles and architect scales. Each was laid to her left, next to the one previously placed, her movements as careful as a surgeon's. Even though her current actions seemed more typical of her professional persona, Asa was still reeling from her earlier, frenzied exhibition.

How. *Why,* had she reeled in such powerful spontaneity.

What she did next made him scowl so fiercely he had to step out of the room completely.

Outside the shed, Asa leaned against the wall. His mouth was fixed in an angry line as the last images of Kai's performance replayed in his mind like a VCR stuck on rewind. He closed his eyes briefly, then opened them and returned to the doorway to watch her again.

Once her drafting implements were laid out, her paper affixed to its board, Kai put a hand to her head, flicked her wrist and pulled her hair back into its bun. Then she carefully smoothed the curls at her temples, moving both hands carefully from her forehead back toward her nape. Then she took a deep breath and picked up a drafting pencil.

And like the swish of a magician's wand, her carefully crafted façade was back in place.

Asa turned and walked away from the shed. He had known all along that Kai's professional face was a sham. Had been acutely attuned to the real Kai from the start. He had assumed she was afraid of the spontaneity and passion he seemed to bring out in her, that he was demanding too much, that he needed to take his time and bring her along carefully, gently.

He was disgusted at how wrong he had been. Kai wasn't afraid of that side of herself. She wasn't fearful that it would come out at the wrong time and betray all she had worked for as a professional. Hell, she had harnessed that power, that passion and intensity. She'd used it to create beautiful buildings and to become the next candidate for partnership in her architecture firm.

Once back at his tent, Asa realized he had lost his appetite. More than that, he realized he was angry. Angry at himself for not demanding more from Kai. Angry for not demanding to see the woman he met at the restaurant that first night instead of accepting her demure requests for patience. But mostly, he was angry with Kai for deliberately trapping herself in some kind of professional purgatory, hiding behind her bun as if it was a sin to let people see the gifts she used to create and design.

He plopped back on the cot in his tent and closed his eyes. Images of three different versions of Kai float behind his eyelids. He couldn't shake off the anger. Slowly, Kai's face began to morph into his mother's, reminding him of the days during his early childhood in the Caribbean. For years, Johnetta Matthews struggled to please her in-laws. It was a losing battle. One in which his mother was willing to sacrifice herself and her spirit to win.

Maybe Kai's similarities to his mother was the reason he was so attracted to her. His mother had made herself miserable during her first ten years of marriage because she loved her husband and thought she was doing what was right, but eventually found the courage to be who she was in her heart.

When she had finally convinced her husband to move them to the United States from Martinique, they settled in Charlotte, North Carolina, only a few minutes away from Salisbury, where she had grown up and where her parents and siblings still lived. She had been like a flower seeing the sun for the first time. Asa saw, even through his young eyes, how his mother bloomed and flourished. Freedom was her sun. The entire family thrived. His father landed a job as an engineer in an aerospace company, and realized for the first time, that he could be successful without his father's wealth and power to support him. Asa's mother raised her kids in bare feet and bellbottoms, teaching them to be proud of themselves as individuals.

A sigh leaked out, and Asa opened his eyes. What was Kai's reason for imprisoning herself? For the life of him, he couldn't fathom her forsaking her entire being for her career. She seemed much too bright for that. But all he could see was images of Kai bent over her portable drafting table, drawing precise lines on a crisp clean sheet of paper. Kai as she picked up one architect's scale and put down another, replacing it in the exact spot from which it had been removed. Each pencil, when she was done, was placed back into its predefined slot in the leather pencil case. Every motion, every action she seemed to have trained herself to control and restrain. If he only knew what she was battling, whom was she fighting to win over, what group she was trying to fit into. Why she pinned her hair up and wore conservative business suits, when she had a passion that belied it all. If only he knew the source of her struggles, maybe he could help.

He wondered what she really wanted out of life. Maybe partnership in her architecture firm wasn't what she really wanted. Maybe she wanted something else; something she thought she couldn't have and therefore replaced it with what she knew she could attain.

"Now you're starting to think like Schyler," he said to the nylon tent walls.

Bill Jameson let out a gasp when he ran into Kenneth Roselle as he entered the lobby of the Coleman Foundation building just after lunch. He glanced around nervously. "What ...what are you doing here?"

"Oh for God's sake, Bill. Get a grip on yourself." Kenneth jerked him by the arm and marched over to a seating area near the elevator banks.

"Did ... uhem. Did you need to see me for something?" Bill danced nervously around, shuffling from one foot to the other.

Kenneth sat down. "Must everything be about you, Bill? You tire me out with your nervous ticks. No, I didn't come to see you. And no, I didn't come to discuss you either. In fact, I was just on my way out, so calm—"

"What?" Bill swiveled to see what had caught Kenneth's eye. *Ah. Rachel.* She looked in their direction, smiled at Bill and wiggled a wave as she headed for the elevators.

"You know her?" Kenneth demanded. "Who is she?"

"Oh, I ... um."

"Well?"

"That's Rachel Burton. She's probably here to see Matthews."

They watched with great appreciation as the slender young woman walked gracefully to the elevator bank, her ebony hair swinging in a gentle bob at her chin.

"Why?"

Bill snorted. "Why do you think?"

"You mean to tell me she's one of his— "

"Don't say it," Bill warned. "Ms. Burton is a very nice young lady. She's just misguided where Matthews is concerned. And—"

"Didn't you tell me Matthews was in Savannah this week?"

Rachel entered the elevator, and the doors closed behind her. Bill hoped she'd get over Asa soon. Heaven knows Asa had already gotten over her. Kenneth poked him in the ribs. Scowling, he rubbed his side. "What?"

"Did you hear me? I thought Matthews was in Savannah this week."

"Yes, he is. Next week, too."

"So what is—what's her name, again?"

"Rachel Burton. Ms. Burton."

"What's Rachel doing here then? She got some kind of dealings with the Coleman Foundation?"

"No. She's just here to see Matthews. Poor child."

Kenneth stood up quickly, grabbing Bill by the arm. "Come on. Let's get up to your office."

"Weren't on your way out?" Bill protested.

"Was. Now I've got some business to tend to."

"But you said you already completed your business."

"I just discovered I have a little more. Come along, Bill."

Unhappy with the direction in which the day had suddenly turned, or the licentious gleam in Roselle's eye, Bill allowed himself to be dragged along.

CHAPTER FOURTEEN

Early the next morning, Kai padded the short distance from camp to Club Ridgeway. Luckily, the sleep tents were shaded under the huge magnolia trees that lined the property, but Club Ridgeway wasn't as fortunate. Once she stepped from the shade, Kai was assaulted by the thick humidity typical of a Low Country summer.

When she stepped into the large tent, it was cooler, because of the industrial-sized fans that sat in each corner. There was a cook-top in Club Ridgeway, but breakfast in the excavation camp was a continental affair and didn't require heat. All camp members, including visitors, were required to help with meals. This morning it was Kai and Judy's turn to prepare the food.

A prep table stood just outside the tent where Kai organized croissants and muffins, jams and jellies, tea, coffee, and milk, in addition to cold cereal, fresh fruit, and yogurt.

Content to take care of the mindless activities while her thoughts wandered to Asa and the date they'd shared before coming back to Savannah, Kai sliced and cut melon, then arranged it on trays. Judy carried them over to the picnic tables as camp residents straggled over in ones and twos from their tents.

"How you doing back here, boss lady?" Judy said on a return trip.

Kai grinned. "Doing just fine."

Judy stopped before picking up the tray of strawberries and bananas. "More than coffee's put you in such a good mood." She came closer. "What's up? Something good must have happened between you and *El Gato* on that date. You never did tell me."

Kai pursed her lips. Obviously, she wasn't keeping her emotions in check, if Judy could read the contentment on her face. Studiously, she cut up fruit and placed it, with exaggerated attention, on to serving trays. "Maybe I'll tell you about it later, but it was just a date."

"Just a date. Right."

Kai looked up. "And what makes you say that?"

"No reason. Unless it's that unusually wide smile of yours. Or that really pleasant attitude you're not known to have before you've had coffee."

A laugh bubbled up. "Oh, yeah. I need to get the coffee started. What was I thinking?"

"I'd say you were thinking about *El Gato*."

Kai deliberately brushed Judy aside with her shoulder and slipped into the Club Ridgeway tent.

Judy followed, saddling up close to her. "Y'all did a little bumping and grinding that night, didn't you?"

"No. Of course not." Kai avoided Judy's eyes, retrieved coffee beans and a grinder from behind the bar, then filled the automatic drip coffee maker with water. She busied herself making coffee as if she were in a top-secret chemical laboratory.

"You're not going to tell me are you?"

"Doesn't look like it."

"So what else did *El Gato* excavate after you two found that cemetery yesterday? Tell me, Kai. You're driving me crazy."

With Judy dogging her heels, Kai finally finished the breakfast preparations and sat down to eat with the rest of the group. She laughed and talked with several of the graduate students whom she had gotten to know over the past couple of days. It was amazing how quickly people bonded when they had to live together.

She felt as if she had bonded with Asa somewhat as well. Discovering the cemetery with him the day before would definitely be the highlight of the trip. She was so happy that he had found what he had been searching for. Seeing the excitement on his face as he studied the site, watching him become completely engrossed in what he was doing to the exclusion of everything and everyone else around him had awed her. His elation had become her elation, and she had stayed up half the night sketching and planning modifications to the welcome center designs as a result.

They had parted on positive terms, the sexual vibes humming sharply between them. So even with her back turned, she knew the instant he arrived at breakfast. Something intense radiated from him this morning. Maybe they hadn't bonded as much as she'd thought, because she couldn't determine whether his intensity was good or bad. She brushed it aside. She was in too good a mood to assume the worse. How could she when everything was going so well?

For the remainder of breakfast, she chatted with the students, whose excitement over the cemetery find was just as great as Asa's. As she downed a few cups of coffee, her light-hearted mood increased. She glanced dreamily about, but stopped short when she caught Asa watching her. He had moved from the tables to the entrance of the Club Ridgeway tent and was leaning casually against a support. She attempted a small, discreet smile, but it faltered when he didn't smile back.

"He's been watching you like a hawk all morning," Judy whispered beside her. "Did something serious happen between you two yesterday?"

Puzzled, Kai shook her head. "Just the cemetery. We were all so excited; him, me, Jamal. He told me all about the slave superstitions and why they made finding the cemetery so difficult, and we found most of the pieces of a water pitcher that had been a grave offering."

"Hmm." Judy munched thoughtfully on her yogurt and granola. "That's it?"

Kai glanced up, then looked back down quickly. So much for bonding. Asa was still staring, studying her. "I don't know what I could have done to put that look in his eyes."

"You did something, girl. That man looks like he could eat you alive."

Kai didn't dare look up again. "No, he looks like he wants to break me in half."

Judy chuckled. "Boss lady, I've got a lot to teach you about men."

"All I did was help him piece together that pitcher. I didn't see him again for the rest of the day. I was in one of the work sheds until past midnight working on those new designs."

No longer in the mood to eat, Kai poked at her fruit. Several of the students left to begin their morning tasks. Two of the KT & G people collected trash and coffee cups to be washed.

Judy finished her granola and wiggled her eyebrows. "You sure he didn't come pay you a little visit in that work shed? Maybe y'all worked on a few of those designs together."

"I told you nothing happened."

Judy stood up. "Well something's about to 'cause he's coming this way. I'm outtie."

Kai pushed sliced strawberries around on her plate and picked her memory for an incident from the previous days that might have set Asa off. Maybe she had done something earlier that he had just remembered. But no, he was off-site for the first two days after the team's arrival. She wasn't the type to gossip, so he couldn't have over heard something she'd said about him. No, she thought, her eyebrows wrinkling into a frown. She had done nothing, nothing at all to upset him. She slugged back her coffee and gave him a cool, stony look when he straddled the bench beside her.

"We've got some unfinished business to take care of," he said.

His dreads were unrestrained this morning; they hung around his neck and shoulders, giving him a ferocious look that seemed to suit his mood. Kai steeled herself not to lean away from him, looking him dead in the eye instead. "Apparently we do. I've obviously ticked you off, but pouting doesn't become you." With what she considered quite a regal exit line, she started to rise, but he grabbed her arm in a powerful fist and hauled her back down.

Appalled, she looked around, horrified that someone may have seen him manhandling her that way. "You don't have to get rough, Asa. A polite 'I'd like to talk with you, could you please wait' would have sufficed."

"Maybe I don't feel like being polite." His said, his eyes hard and angry. "Maybe I don't feel like continuing this little game we've been playing, either."

"Game?"

"Yeah, sweetheart. This little pretend 'I'm so concerned about my career. I have to do things just right, be just so or I won't win this partnership' thing."

"What?" Unbelievable as it was, Asa Matthews was dismissing the importance of her career. What was left of Kai's jovial mood seeped away entirely. "My career damn well is important to me. I'm not going to flaunt myself to you, whenever and wherever, just because I feel the urge. I'm not sacrificing my career. I told you that from the beginning." She blew out a breath, livid at him. She jerked up before he could restrain her, looking down her nose at him with the most condescension she could convey. "You're acting just the way you did when you showed up in my office a few weeks ago. Like you're at some downtown club picking me up. Well, I'm not one of your women. I don't drop everything for a man. Not even you." Her chest heaved as anger whipped through her.

Asa stood up to tower over her, grabbed her wrist and pulled her close. She glanced around. Thankfully, most of the others were gone or too busy attending to other things to notice them. Asa's other hand touched her chin, holding it so she could only look at him. "You weren't worried someone would see you last night."

She opened her mouth, but nothing came out.

Asa's gaze dropped to her mouth. "Yeah, I saw you in the work shed, pacing up and down with your hair flying everywhere while you pulled your design ideas together. You had the same wild look in your eyes last night that I saw in that restaurant, and you're going to look at me that way again. I'm tired of waiting."

His fingers loosened to lightly stroke her wrist. "Don't frown, baby girl. You know you want this as much as I do. I was trying to take it slow, give you some room. I didn't want to jeopardize your work." He shrugged. "But you know what I saw last night? I saw a woman that knows how to control her emotions, her passion, her body." He released her to burrow his hands in her hair. Curls tumbled down her back. "Her hair." He tightened his grip, tugged her head back and lowered his own She tensed when his lips made contact with her skin, shivered when she felt the scrape of teeth on her neck.

He nuzzled closer, licked with apparent delight, making a low growling sound in his throat. With mercurial quickness, his mood had changed from anger to arousal. Kai was unprepared for the force of it, and a moan escaped her lips before she could stop it.

This was not happening. Asa was not standing in broad daylight with his hands and mouth all over her while his students and her employees milled around everywhere. He claimed her mouth, pressed her to him in an iron grip, assaulted her with his tongue, then abruptly let her go. Kai stumbled back in a stupor.

"Contrary to your delusions, no one cares that we're together. In fact, your team is probably wondering what's taking us so long." Asa's voice was husky, full of the same pent-up desire he surely would have heard in her voice had she been able to speak. Broad shoulders moved up and down as he took each breath. "We're two grown, consenting adults, you know. But, since you're so worried, we'll head to Savannah. Tonight."

Kai sat in her tent as evening approached. She had hidden there all day. At first, she was mortified that someone may have seen the episode between her and Asa after breakfast. But if anyone had, no one was talking. Several people stopped by her tent during the day, concerned. She feigned a migraine and eventually was left alone. The lie was almost the truth, and she was surprised that the worry that sat heavily in the pit of her stomach hadn't brought one on.

She had spent much of the day doodling and sketching when she wasn't thinking about Asa. Yes, she wanted him, with a desire she had never felt for anyone else. Yet the feelings he incited in her scared her senseless. She was desperately afraid that her ironclad control would be no match for the flames igniting between them.

At noon, when someone pushed a wrapped sandwich and a Coke inside the entrance of her tent, she grabbed it like a starving refugee. She had gulped down half the soda before she realized she was being watched.

"I hope you're that hungry for me tonight." Asa stood just outside her tent, his voice low and menacing. "We're leaving at seven. If I have to, I'll drag you out of this tent kicking and screaming."

Her appetite vanished abruptly, and she abandoned the half-empty drink and the unopened sandwich.

As evening approached, Kai filled up page after page of her sketchpad. Her mind wandered, twisted and turned over the idea of being Asa's lover. She had come close twice, now. Very close, but had pulled back just before it was too late. She analyzed the consequences of letting go, of finally taking what he wanted to give, giving what he wanted so badly to take. Would Asa know how to be discreet, or would he be an overly demonstrative lover, taking pleasure in touching and petting her in public? She shivered at the thought of his hands on her, shuddered at the idea of becoming his woman.

She sketched some more while she debated the point with herself. Would it be so terribly wrong, to give in just once? Just this once to feel, to live and experience with wild abandon, the way she had in college all those years ago, or with her parents when she was a child.

She looked around her neat, orderly tent. The cot she sat on was neatly made, an army green sleeping bag borrowed from one of the graduate students lay folded at the foot. The little night stand by the bed included her alarm clock and a small notepad for jotting down ideas or sketches in the middle of the night. In another corner sat a crate full of architectural supplies. The only personal item in the room was her satchel full of pencils and leads and jewel tipped drafting pens.

She scooted to the end of the cot and dragged the satchel to her lap, opened it and pulled out a few of her supplies. Her fingers brushed over the cover of heavy stock paper. Sketches and notes about Ridgeway plantation fluttered by. She stuffed it back, grabbed a leather pencil roll and opened it. Her sketching pencils lay in their individual compartments, each neatly sharpened and ready for the next use. Carefully, gingerly, she rolled up the leather case, retied the strings that held it closed and placed it back in the bag. She leaned back on the cot, held the satchel to her chest and gazed through the tent flaps at the waning light.

In the career she had fought so hard to build, where was *she*, Kai Ellis? Had she sacrificed too much? Punished herself too harshly because her parents hadn't loved her enough to keep her, paid penance to her grandmother for years since her death in apology for the shame she'd caused by losing her scholarship?

The silence surrounding her heart, her life, was louder than she had ever realized. She replaced the satchel beside the crate of drafting paper and stood up. Her grandmother was gone, her father living his life, enjoying his career. Vernon's was certainly flying high, she thought wryly, remembering the auction she had refused to attend. Her parents had had each other. Who did she have? *What* did she have? Her career? The partnership at KT & G? No, not even that. She had a *chance* at a partnership. Just a chance; nothing more.

What would happen if she didn't make partner at the firm? She had never honestly considered not making it, had simply assumed she would; the end result of a sacrificial quest. She had never even entertained the possibility of failure, and wasn't sure why she was questioning her actions now. But what if it didn't happen? Then she would only have herself, and her job. No family, no man in her life.

She glanced sadly at her satchel. She would have her drafting supplies, she thought ruefully.

"I give up." She picked up her purse and stepped out of the tent. She was denying herself a chance to be with the most exciting man she had ever met for drafting pencils. Well things were about to change.

She left her tent and marched with renewed purpose to the picnic tables. Judy was crouched at one of the tables studying photographs when she approached and sat down. "Well, hey, boss lady. You feeling better?"

Kai let out a heavy breath and smiled. "Yeah, as a matter of fact I am. Asa and I are going to Savannah tonight."

Judy grinned. "All right now." She gathered her photos. "Speak of the devil."

Kai looked up. Asa stalked toward them, regal, graceful, like a panther on the hunt. She let herself enjoy the image without hesitation or worry for the first time since they began working together. His dreadlocks flew behind him on the light evening breeze, his eyes intense and focused on her. Clearly, her readiness had both surprised and soothed him. When he reached the table, the menacing look she remembered from that morning was long gone. All she saw was a man hungry with need. Hungry for her. She decided to enjoy it, and him, in their entirety, tonight.

"I'm ready," she said quietly, to herself as much as to him.

Asa held Kai close as they walked down Magnolia Avenue to his rental car. After checking her tent at precisely seven o'clock, he had assumed she was hiding somewhere else. He hadn't quite believed his eyes when he approached the picnic tables to find her waiting. He didn't know what had changed her attitude about coming out with him tonight, but was grateful she had. The idea of dragging her out of her tent hadn't necessarily appealed to him, and forcing a woman wasn't at all his style. He wouldn't have been able to pull it off anyway. Thank God, in the end, he didn't have to.

He squeezed her to his side and let out a little sigh. God, he wanted this woman. More than he had ever wanted anybody, and he had things perfectly planned. He was taking her to the riverfront first where they would dine at the River Grill restaurant. Then, they would take a river-boat ride, maybe on one of the gambling boats. And finally, he had made reservations at a charming Federalist style Bed and Breakfast a few blocks away, where they offered chocolates on your pillow and a glass of sherry before you retired.

After a week of sleeping in a tent, Kai would be positively drooling. While she drooled over the accommodations, he would do a little drooling himself. All over her. They would make love all night, wake up to breakfast on the back balcony of the B&B, then spend the entire day taking in Savannah like tourists.

"Asa?" Kai's steps faltered, and he pulled himself from his thoughts. He smiled down at her, giving her waist a reassuring squeeze. "Yeah, baby girl?"

She nodded toward the parking lot where a woman stood, hands on hips, staring at them. "She looks ready to murder somebody."

Asa stopped in his tracks. "Rachel?"

Moments later, after Asa neglected to introduce them, after the woman had placed a possessive hand on Asa's arm, Kai turned away. It wasn't difficult to size up the situation. His lover had come to pay him a visit. Cursing herself for being so stupid, Kai brushed a hair from her cheek as she rushed up the drive. When she brushed a second lock of her hair away, she realized Asa had yet again taken her hair down. He'd become so adept at the practice she hadn't even been aware. Awareness had obviously abandonned her in more ways than one. No man developed as much skill at seduction as Asa possessed without collecting a bevy of women in the process. Angry with herself for being one of the many in Asa's flock, she twisted her hair into a tight knot at the back of her neck and headed back to camp.

How could she have been so stupid, so gullible? She had known Asa Matthews for what, four weeks now? Hardly time to get to know someone well enough to sleep with them, but there she was, ready to traipse off with the man at the snap of his fingers. Her breath was coming in angry heaves by the time she reached camp. She ran into Judy again, but one look stopped any questions.

Back in her tent, Kai flopped down on her cot and called herself every synonym for stupid, idiotic fool she could come up with. She told herself not to think about what had just transpired, what would have happened if that other woman hadn't shown up, but she did it anyway. Asa's lover had known where he was, and obviously, she visited often enough to assume an unplanned stop was acceptable. But was it really an unplanned visit?

Kai snatched up a sketchpad and pencil. How the heck would she know whether the woman's visit was unplanned? Asa could have known for days, even weeks, that his lover would show up.

Her hand flew over the sketchpad as she analyzed, rationalized, tried to understand. It should have made her feel better that Asa was so attracted to her that he would forget about his lover, but it didn't. What it made her feel was foolish and naïve.

When she looked down at her sketchpad and found Asa's face staring back at her, she flung it against the tent wall. Her ears were peeled, listening for his angry footsteps. She had ignored his calls begging her to wait, expecting him to come after her. He hadn't. And as minutes stretched out and the sun began to set, she realized he wouldn't be coming back to get her.

Kai stared at the empty blue walls of her tent and realized she felt just as empty. She had fallen in love with Asa Matthews. She didn't know how it had happened or when. She hadn't known she was even capable of the feat, but there it was. Asa had opened her up, making her think and feel things other than those related to her work. It was the reason she had agreed to go with him tonight. Because he had opened a place in her heart that, for so many years, she had been afraid to ever expose again, until now.

Maybe she believed he would take care of her, protect her. He seemed to possess enough courage for both of them. And now, now she felt afraid and empty. Afraid because he wasn't there to catch her if she fell. Empty because she had finally admitted to herself that something was missing in her life and she wanted to fill the void.

Miserable, she curled her knees under her chin and rocked for comfort.

Equally miserable, Asa lay alone in the queen-sized pedestal bed at the Riverview Bed and Breakfast a few blocks from the Savannah riverfront. He had tried Kai on her cell phone, but got a hang up for his troubles. When he called back, she had turned it off. Though he knew she wouldn't answer his calls, he left a message for her to call him.

Rachel had ruined everything. He couldn't even rush after Kai because Rachel was hanging all over him. If he had peeled her off of his arm and headed back to camp, she would have followed, and there was no way in hell he would subject his Kai to a cat fight in front of her own employees.

In the end, he had followed Rachel, who had high hopes of staying with him in town, back to Savannah. It had taken two hours, over a dinner he had planned to share with Kai, to convince Rachel that he had not left a message at the Coleman Foundation asking her to meet him at the site. He pressed her about the source of the information, but she was so angry with him she refused to reveal anything. So as he lay in bed, trying to figure out how to make things right with Kai, he also tried to determine who hated him enough to set him up.

Bill Jameson was the only person whom Asa felt disliked him enough to want to cause such trouble. But it didn't make sense, Bill liked Rachel. And Rachel, for some odd reason, thought of Bill like an uncle.

Aside from Bill, Asa could come up with no answers. The only thing he knew for certain was that he was going to have a hell of a time convincing Kai that he hadn't spent the night—their night—with Rachel Burton.

Kai was up early, a few days later, and ready to face the day. She was immensely pleased with the fact that she had managed to avoid Asa for two solid days. After she finished feeling sorry for herself the night he'd left camp with his lover, she came up with a plan for how she would deal with him. Since she and Judy had completed their responsibilities for preparing breakfast for the team, she didn't have to eat with everyone else, so she raided the pantry in Club Ridgeway and had granola bars in her tent each morning. Coffee, however, was a different matter. There was no way she could do without caffeine, so she rose early, prepared a pot and filled her mug before the others arrived. Asa generally showed up late for breakfast, so thankfully, she had never run into him. During the day, Asa would be hard at work on his book draft or excavating the cemetery, which allowed her to work in one of the work sheds without fear of crossing his path.

Today was her third morning in hiding, and as she hefted her drafting supplies to the work shed, she congratulated herself on her clever subterfuge. The team's site visit would be over in one more week. She could keep it up for that much longer. It wouldn't be hard at all.

She was smiling when she stepped into the shed, until Asa's anger-laced voice brought her back-patting to a halt.

Kai fumbled her leather satchel before dragging it securely to her chest. "Excuse me?"

The look Asa gave her made her want to cringe, but she gathered her courage. It was inevitable that their paths would cross; there was no need to get nervous. She could handle this. She summoned all the lady-like training her grandmother had instilled in her, sat down on the bench opposite Asa's worktable and began preparing her table.

He didn't speak, but she could feel him watching. She took great care cleaning the surface of her drafting table, tore off a fresh sheet of tracing paper and taped it down. She arranged her pencils neatly, carefully, on the right side of the table and breathed a quiet sigh of relief when Asa turned his attention back to the computer where he'd been entering data into a spreadsheet.

Apparently, he wasn't going to push it, and for that she was immensely grateful. A tentative smile spread across her face as she began to work. Her bliss lasted about a minute.

Behind her, Asa shut down his computer, punched the off button on the monitor and stood up. The wooden stool he'd vacated scraped loudly across the floor, obliterating the heavy silence surrounding them.

"Aren't you going to prance around and shake your hair out?" He propped his stool a few feet away from her and sat down, arms folded. "Come on, baby girl. I want to see the show."

After she was the one dropped for his current floozie, he had the nerve to chastise her? Kai tried desperately to harness her anger and shoot back, hard. Instead, she stared down at the blank drafting table, blinking back tears.

He didn't say anything else, thankfully. It gave Kai a much-needed moment to gather her composure. When she answered, her voice was calm and steady. "There's no cause for you to make fun of me. I suppose hoping that we could both act like mature adults would be too much to ask?"

Asa barked a laugh. "You call hiding in your tent and living on granola bars the actions of a mature adult?"

Kai twisted around. He had the gall to call her childish? "I'm sorry. I suppose inviting your lover to the campsite where you're trying to seduce me is?"

"Rachel's not my lover. She hasn't been for months now."

Kai snorted in disbelief and turned on the stool so she didn't have to twist to face him. "It doesn't really change anything, though, does it? I've always told you that starting something between us wasn't a good idea. She just reminded me, that's all." Kai took a deep breath and raised her hand to offer a handshake of friendship. She hadn't managed a cordial relationship with her own father after he'd hurt her so many years ago, so her gesture to Asa was something, wasn't it? He should be grateful she was offering that much. "I hope we can maintain a friendship. If not that, we can try for professional courtesy, at least."

"Aw, hell naw." A combination of anger and desire darkened Asa's face as he stood up. He strode menacingly toward her, spread her legs with one knee and stepped between them.

Kai caught her breath, recoiling in surprise, but the gesture only succeeded in pressing her back into the edge of the wooden table behind her.

Asa braced his palms on the tabletop on either side of her and stared down. His chest rose and fell with heavy breaths. Kai focused with fascination on the pulse that throbbed at his throat.

"Scared?"

Her heart pumped so hard against her ribs, Kai was convinced he could see it thumping through her blouse, but she refused back down. "I'm not afraid of you."

His eyes raked over her, undressing her. "You should be." He stepped closer, his body blocking out the sun. "Do you want me?"

"I …"

He stared at her for a long moment, then trailed an index finger down her cheek. His voice was soft but commanding when he spoke again. "Unless you do, I suggest you stay the hell away from me. As far as you can get."

He stepped back, moved to the door, then stopped. "Because I promise you, the next time you invade my space, we're finishing what we started."

The next day as evening fell, Asa stood at the entrance to his tent and watched Kai. Her customary French twist was frazzled and drooping from the drizzling rain that had been coming down for the past hour. In the last couple of minutes, it had started raining harder, though she didn't seem to take notice. He couldn't figure out what the hell she was doing, marching around the outside of her tent with what looked like a roll of drafting tape. She probably had a tear in her tent somewhere, but he wasn't about to go over to find out. After the ultimatum he had given her the day before, the ball was in her court.

Rain fell harder, and he took a step backward into the shelter of his tent, but still kept his eye on the tent only yards away. Kai's hair was a soggy mess, now. Her clothes as well. It appeared she was trying to tape up the top of her tent. That made absolutely no sense to him. Each of the regulation tents had a rain fly that easily hooked into place to cover the ventilated opening in the top. Asa gave in to his curiosity, ignored the fact that he was still pissed at her after the whole situation with Rachel, ignored his declaration to stay away from her, and crossed the short distance from his tent to hers.

"What are you doing?"

Kai jumped, then stiffened. Her chin went up in defiance, but she didn't acknowledge him. She just continued with what she was doing, or trying to do. She had a roll of drafting tape in her hand and was trying, without success, to tape over the mesh opening in the top of her tent. She couldn't even reach the top, much less apply tape.

"That tape isn't going to stick." Even he knew that drafting tape, though it looked like masking tape, didn't have nearly the same tack. "You're better off using duct tape."

Kai continued to ignore him. Asa considered letting her stew out here in the rain. He looked down the row of tents that were staked among the magnolias. In another time and era, they could have been slave cabins. And in that same time and era, he wouldn't have let Kai struggle in the rain out of spite. Times would have been hard; people would have helped each other. He would have helped her out, no matter what his personal grievances.

He studied her, tongue tucked into the side of her mouth in concentration, ignoring him. Hadn't he told her to stay away from him if she didn't want to continue their relationship? Was that why she wouldn't accept his help? He doubted it. Even if he hadn't said as much, she wouldn't have asked him for help—or anyone else, for that matter.

"Where's your rain fly?" He finally asked.

Kai didn't respond, so Asa stepped closer, grabbing her arm. She promptly jerked it away. He decided to give her a little of her own medicine and ignore her. He bent low and stepped into the entrance of her tent.

That got her attention.

"What do you think you're doing?"

He glanced at her cot, which was positioned right under the dome opening and getting rained on. She didn't even have the sense to attach the tent's rain fly. He rummaged around near the entrance and found the nylon tent bag, then shook it out. "Where's your rain fly?" he asked again when he didn't find it in the tent bag. He stepped back out of the tent with the bag in hand. "Kai?"

Her arms were folded protectively across her chest, the drafting tape looped around her wrist, her stance belligerent. "I don't know what you're talking about."

"You know, I could let you stay out here and get wet."

Her mouth was a firm line, and she didn't give an inch. Asa sighed and called on his self-control. "Look, there's supposed to be a rain fly in your tent bag. You hook it over the mesh opening on top of the tent when it rains, so you don't get rained on." He pointed to the small plastic hooks on the tent's dome.

"I don't have any idea what you're talking about. I don't know what a rain fly is. I've never heard of it. Nor have I seen one in that bag."

"No need to get snippy, Ms. Ellis." Asa crossed his arms and looked at her, then glanced down the rows and rows of tents in their little village. There were a few people still moving around, but it looked as if most of the camp had bedded down for the night. He tossed the bag back inside her tent. "Against my better judgment, I'm going to make you an offer."

Kai shrugged defiantly, and that finally pissed him off. "You know, you were a whole lot more friendly a few days ago when you wanted me to take you to bed."

Her head jerked up, her eyes full of fire and temper.

"What?" He asked. "Go ahead, Miss Thang. Talk to me. But whatever you say won't change things. You want me as much as I want you. You're just too stubborn to admit it." He turned to leave, then stopped himself, sighed and looked back. "Come on over to my tent until it stops raining."

"You told me to stay away from you unless ... unless." She took a deep breath. "If I come over there, does that mean I consent to sleep with you?"

"If you think that's what it means, that's what it means."

"I'd rather stay wet," Kai mumbled. She turned back to her tent.

This time, instead of trying to keep the tent dry from the outside, she stepped into the interior to work on the inside. Asa could hear the rip of long strips of drafting tape being torn as he walked back to his tent.

"Well, that went well."

Under the dim light of a Coleman lantern, Asa stared at the same page of notes he had been looking at for the past hour. He couldn't stop thinking about Kai. Damn it, but she was as stubborn as Schyler. Outside, thunder rumbled. Rain began to pour in sheets. Lightning as well. He had expected Kai in his tent fifteen minutes ago, and she hadn't come. So much for bullying her into submission.

He closed his notes and shoved them into the crate at the foot of his cot. Hell, he'd have to go after her. He'd be damned if he'd let the lead architect on this project lay in her tent getting rained on just because he couldn't keep his hands to himself. He did possess a little self-discipline. Besides, the last thing he needed was yet another black mark on his record, especially after that fiasco with Rachel, and he could only pray that that embarrassing episode didn't get back to Harold.

He'd swallow his pride and go get Kai. He would let her know upfront that she didn't have to worry about being ravished in her sleep.

Asa rubbed a frustrated hand across his face. He needed a drink—or something, damn it. Something that would give him the self-control he would have to call on if he brought her into his tent.

Maybe she could bunk with Judy. He shook the thought aside. His tent was larger than anyone else's. He even had a double cot. Everyone else had singles. Even if Kai was willing to sleep on the floor with someone else, there simply wasn't room—except in his tent.

"I'm going to live to regret this," he muttered as he slid to the edge of the cot and fished under the bed for his shoes. Just as he toed them on, a shadow crossed the nylon and mesh of his tent.

Kai.

Asa closed his eyes and took a breath. She'd come on her own. Did that mean he was off the hook? That she would let him touch her?

He watched her hesitate outside and smiled. It had taken her over an hour, but she had finally made up her mind.

Asa stood up and opened the tent flap to let her in. "So why are you here, Kai, because of the rain or me?" Asa asked, wanting to set the ground rules from the very beginning. If she didn't want him, he wanted to know right up front.

She shrugged, eyes defiant. "It's wet."

Asa didn't speak for a minute, just studied her. "You or your tent?"

"What do you mean by that?"

"What do you think I mean?" Asa folded his arms and rocked back on his heels. She might be angry, but she was also nervous, he decided. Still, she was going to have to make herself clear.

Asa stepped forward, tilted her chin up with a finger. "You know what I mean. Don't you, Miss Thang?" Her lips parted innocently, seductively. "So tell me. Are you here because your tent is wet or because you are?"

Kai still didn't move, but Asa could see her mind calculating, estimating, considering. He wrapped his arms around her. "Kiss me, Kai. Show me, if you can't tell me."

Kai couldn't decide what she was doing in Asa's tent. Especially since he had shed his shirt and jeans and was now only attired in a pair of khaki shorts. If she gazed at his beautiful chest or piercing eyes, she would surely lose all of her self control. Instead, she stared at her shoes, mentally berating herself for her back and forth maneuvering. Of course she wanted him. Hadn't she admitted that to herself when she decided to go to Savannah with him? Until his most recent paramour appeared on the scene.

Her body always reacted too quickly when it came to Asa. She had never been able to control herself around him from the beginning. So, to pretend she was in his tent just to get out of the rain was a lie of which even she couldn't convince herself. She took a deep breath and replayed the decision she'd made three days ago.

"Come on, Kai." Asa brushed his lips gently over hers. "Take what you want. Give me what I want."

She saw hunger flash in his eyes the moment she decided to give in. His hands fisted in her hair a split second later. He was rough, intense with this kiss, a prelude to what she had wanted so badly for so long. She knew he would be—had suspected it from the first. She wanted it. Needed it—as he had told her so many times. But could she handle it?

She was afraid that maybe she couldn't.

He must have sensed her hesitation, because he raised his head. "Un unh, baby. Don't get shy on me now. We're finishing this thing. Tonight."

His hands moved from her hair, caressed her face, then moved to her shoulders. He had maneuvered her so deftly she didn't realize she was so dangerously deep in his tent—trapped in the lion's den—until it was too late.

His hands moved to the chambray shirt she'd thrown over her rain-soaked T-shirt.

Gentle fingers caressed her as he slipped the shirt off her paralyzed arms.

She should stop him; give herself a moment to think with a clear and rational head, but slowly, ever so slowly, her resistance ebbed away.

"Oh, yeah," Asa breathed as he took in the sight of her breasts. They were clearly visible through the wet cotton of her Clark-Atlanta University T-shirt. Her nipples peaked and strained toward him.

He pulled her toward the bed, but instead of laying her down, Asa sat down facing her as she stood before him. Strong fingers spread her thighs so that they straddled his knees. Then, without warning, he zeroed in on her breasts.

Kai let out a shocked squeak. It wasn't his hands caressing and palpitating her nipples but his mouth, wet and hot, that touched her. His dreadlocks fell like a roped curtain to cover his face, while mouth, lips and tongue suckled hard and strong. Long fingers reached up to nip and squeeze her other breast, and Kai arched her back and moaned in helpless supplication.

She didn't know what to do with her arms, or hands. Should she touch him, hold him? Thread her fingers through his exotic hair? Asa made the decision for her, and Kai forgot all about her hands.

His mouth slipped from her breast and moved down, further and further. Past her breasts. Past her ribs. To her belly button and the snap on her damp shorts. He paused when he reached the "V" of her thighs.

Kai gasped and grabbed onto his hair for balance. Even through the lightweight cotton, she could feel the heat of his mouth on her. He suckled her there—right through her shorts and underwear—just as he had her breasts. He pressed his tongue against her center in a wicked imitation of the act they would eventually perform. Kai moaned again. Louder this time. Her pelvis rocked against him, once, twice, then a third time before Asa grabbed her hips in both hands and tumbled back on the bed, pulling her with him. He lifted her thighs to rest on his shoulders.

His hair hid the movements of his mouth and hands, intensifying every erotic stroke and caress. Large hands palmed her rear end, massaged and squeezed, rocking her against his demanding mouth at the same time. And suddenly, it was too much, too intense. Too Asa.

Kai's body went rigid. She flailed in frustration as the tension and friction combined to electrify her body. She cried out. Whimpered. Tried to get away from his hands, his powerful arms and seductive mouth. But Asa held fast. His hands shot up to her breasts to pinch and squeeze, and everything went black.

Kai swirled helplessly—in a vortex of sensation. She didn't like the loss of control. Too many feelings. Too much intensity. She twisted frantically, afraid to give in, but the more she fought, the more Asa kept doing whatever it was he was doing to her.

All Kai could do was feel. Asa's touch, his hot breath. The breeze of the storm through the mesh openings in the front of his tent. And she could hear him murmuring his approval, encouraging her release.

Until finally, she gave in to the sensations.

A few moments later, Kai lay, still panting, on the bed. Her body limp and liquid from Asa's mouth and hands. She could hear him breathing beside her, and she was afraid to look at him. She squeezed her eyes tightly shut. He had turned her inside out without even taking off her clothes. She shuddered at the knowledge and the memory, then tried desperately to slow her breathing.

When she was finally calm, finally still, she tried to think.

She had never ... no one had ever ... God, what had just happened?

The unmistakable sound of a zipper broke the silence in the tent. Kai's eyes flew open. She turned. When her eyes focused she gaped at Asa.

"My turn, sweetheart." His shorts and briefs were at his knees, his erection in his hand.

CHAPTER FIFTEEN

She was paralyzed at the sight of Asa reclining beside her. A well-muscled arm cradled his head, and his hair spread like a fan behind him in sharp contrast to the white bed sheets. His legs were bent at the knees, his feet firmly planted on the floor. Heavily muscled thighs were spread wide as if in invitation. Kai's eyes fixated on Asa's hand, tightly clutching his massive erection. She wanted to look away, but couldn't. She couldn't keep from staring as he pleasured himself with long firm strokes of his fist.

"Come here." Asa's lust-heavy voice jolted her, and Kai dragged her attention from his hands to his face. His eyes were lazy with desire, but intensity radiated from him, pulling her toward him like an invisible beacon sucking her in. Helpless, she shook her head.

Back up. Leave now, while it's still possible. The frantic call from somewhere inside her rational mind refused to be heeded. Her body, her limbs refused to move.

Asa's husky voice called to her again. "Come here, baby girl. Help me."

"I ... I can't." But this time, her muscles moved for her, propelling her forward instead of back.

Asa shifted to one elbow, then sat up completely. Kai moved to sit beside him, but he shifted, so that she stood between his legs. He pulled at her arm, making Kai think he wanted her to kneel in front of him. Alarm caused the immobile synapses in her brain to finally fire and she resisted.

"Shhh," he crooned. "I just want you closer, baby. I wouldn't ask you to do that." He nuzzled her neck. "At least not yet."

Kai tensed and Asa chuckled. "Loosen up, baby girl. Don't be shy. Come on, crawl up here with me."

Nervous now, Kai lost her balance and fell forward. Asa took the opportunity to touch her, kneading her breasts, touching her hips and bottom. "Oh yeah," he breathed. "You don't know how much I've been wanting to touch you, like this." He positioned her knees so that she straddled him. "There," he said when he was satisfied. "Comfortable."

Kai shook her head and whispered, "I don't know what to do."

Asa lifted her hands, kissed each one, then placed them on his bare chest. "Just touch me, baby girl. Anywhere you want."

Kai gazed down at his body, greedily consuming him with her eyes, and she touched. His firm, hard pecs flexed under her hands; his nipples peaked. She dragged a fingernail over one of them, fascinated. Smiled when he shivered.

As her hands moved lower, Asa leaned back, returning to his reclining position. Kai touched rippling abs, traced a scar near his navel.

"How did this happen?" When she looked up, Asa was staring at her, eyes dazed with desire. Another time, she decided. Another place. Though she couldn't very well ignore the jutting erection directly below her questing fingers, she skipped it to first comb her fingers through the springy curls at his root. She shuttered when she finally touched him, marveled at the heat emanating from him. She curled one hand loosely around him, stroked gently.

A grunt from Asa made her look up. His face was contorted, and she sprang back. Had she hurt him, done something wrong?

His eyes flicked up to hers. "Something wrong, baby girl?"

"No—I ... I thought I hurt you."

He reached for her hands, fisted both around him, one above the other. "Like this." His hands closed tightly around hers, and he showed her how to touch, how to stroke him. Timid at first, he continued to guide her. When she finally gained confidence, had the rhythm, his hands dropped away, and Asa leaned back to watch.

Kai shivered as she stimulated him. She could feel the roll and coil of muscles as his arousal built. The flex of his thighs under her bottom reminded her that she was still very much aroused. Feeling strong and powerful, she squeezed and released, stroked and touched as Asa tensed and convulsed in a way that was magnificently male.

Then suddenly, his hand was behind her head, dragging her down flat against him. They were belly to belly, her hands still wedged between them and fisted around his erection. "Harder," he commanded. "Harder." Then he crushed her mouth to his. His kiss was an assault. His hand twisting in her hair, the other firmly clutching her bottom was battery, as he shuttered out his release into her hands.

He clutched her in a vice-like grip for several moments, even after his kiss gentled and his breathing slowed. Both hands moved to her thighs, and he pressed her hard against him, rolled her hips in erotic stimulation.

Kai was overcome by what had just happened. She should have been shocked, appalled even, but instead, she was awed. Awed that such a powerful man would give her such intimate control over his body. She dislodged her hands from between them to brace herself on the bed, then pushed against him, rocking with the shove and pull of his hands.

She closed her eyes, letting her mind drift. Her body tightened as her desire began to rise again.

"Just as good as I knew it would be," Asa murmured.

Kai didn't open her eyes, didn't know how to respond. She had only been intimate with one other man, and she wasn't really sure about this pillow talk stuff. Only that she was more turned on than she had ever been in her life. Asa was practically naked, and she was fully clothed and grinding her hips on top of him. What in the world was she doing?

Sated and relaxed, Asa watched Kai as he rolled her tight little butt against him. She was getting turned on again, but he wanted to know what was going on in that head of hers. "Hey." Gently shaking her, he watched as her eyes flutter open. Pleased that her focus wasn't quite as sharp as usual, he decided to have a little fun with her. "What's going on in there?"

"Huh?"

"Don't 'huh' me." He trailed a finger through her hair, skimmed over her cheek, then returned to clutch possessively at her bottom. "You've got some nasty thoughts in your head."

Kai opened her mouth to protest.

"You're thinking 'Damn, we haven't even done *the do* yet. I can't imagine what that's gonna be like.'" He shifted her just enough so he could reach the wooden crate at the edge of his cot. *Touchdown.* The musical crinkle of a condom wrapper had to be about the sweetest sound in the world right about now. "Un hunh. See. I know you, baby girl," he said as he got comfortable again. You might be a lady on the outside. But you're a tiger on the inside. You just need the right cat to bring it out, that's all."

Kai's eyes narrowed.

"What?"

"You said cat."

"Yeah. So."

"Are you referring to yourself as a cat?"

Asa grinned. "Isn't that what your team calls me? *El Gato*?" When her mouth gaped open, he laughed and slipped the condom into her hand. "Tell me what you were thinking just now."

"Oh … hmm. Well." As Kai's fingers clasped and unclasped the condom in her palm, just the thought of her nimble fingers rolling the rubber down the length of him had him growing long and strong again.

He pulled her down for another mind-blowing kiss. This time Kai was ready for him and gave as much as she got, which was all he needed to remind him to get those clothes off her. She lay flat against him now, and he nipped at her neck, sniffed at her hair, and toyed with her ears. A few more strokes and he had her purring like a kitten.

"Now," he said in her ear, "go one and slip that thing on me, girl. Then tell me what you were thinking just now."

He felt her shudder, then bury her head shyly in his hair. After a minute, she fumbled to unwrap the condom, stumbling over her words to hide her embarrassment as she shifted away from him to roll it on.

"I was thinking that was the most erotic experience I've ever had. The most intimate, too. And I …" Asa gasped as her fingers glided down to his root. "… I still have my clothes on."

Asa snaked his hands underneath her shorts and panties to palm her rear end. He squeezed it affectionately. "Don't worry, baby girl. I'mo fix that right now."

Kai gasped in shock when Asa flipped them over in a swift, acrobatic move. She was flat on her back. He was gloriously naked as he kneeled above her, and she couldn't resist the urge to reach out and touch him again.

He glanced at her from where he was intensely focused on slipping her shirt from her arms. "Oh, not scared anymore, huh?"

Kai shrugged casually. "I never was."

"Right."

"I wasn't," she insisted. "I've been with a man before. Done 'the do,' as you call it. Plenty of times."

Asa moved quickly to her shorts, stripping them, along with her panties, with astonishing speed. His eyes devoured her, his hands quick to check her attempts to cover herself. "Oh, no. This is all mine tonight, Kai. I want to see it all. Do it all." His eyes never left her face as he spread her thighs, then knelt in front of her. "God, I can't wait to be inside of you."

A flutter of nerves welled up inside. "Wow, listen to the rain," she said as his head began its descent between her thighs. She puffed out a sigh of relief when Asa paused. It wasn't that she didn't want him. She did. She just … well. Now that she had him, she wasn't exactly sure whether she was ready or not. Though, to his great credit, Asa had taken things fairly slowly, especially after that disaster a few days ago. She half expected him to ravish her in her tent the previous night, given the level of his pent-up frustration.

Coming back to the present, Kai realized Asa was studying her with a feral grin on his face. She was suddenly more worried than she had been before. "What?" she asked nervously.

He leaned back on his haunches and spread her thighs with his hands. "You like the rain, baby girl?" His fingers stroked and petted.

Kai clamped her teeth tightly to keep from moaning. *Breathe. Just breathe.* "Y-yes. I like the storms."

"Just don't like to get wet in them, huh?"

Where was he going with this? Kai's stomach clinched as his fingers fluttered over her, kneading and pulling.

"Hear that? That's a pretty fierce storm outside. About as fierce as I'm gonna be when I get inside you."

Two fingers plunged deep.

Kai wailed and clutched the bed sheets. Her pelvis bucked against Asa's hand. Heavy and thick, his fingers slipped and slid inside her, slick from her wetness as he lowered head and his mouth clamped down. Her thighs clutched tight around his neck, and she lost herself in the sensational storm Asa was creating inside of her. On and on he stroked her, licking and nibbling until she cried out her release, then finally lay limp, drenched and trembling.

Kai moaned softly and covered her face as Asa moved up onto the bed beside her. "I can't believe this," she said from underneath her forearms.

Asa's palm came down over her breast and she shuddered. "What?"

"We haven't even made love yet. And …"

"No? Don't think so, huh."

She lowered her arms. "We have?"

Asa nodded sagely.

"Then …"

"Ahh … doing *the do*." Asa leaned in close.

Kai's eyes widened as he whispered very explicitly, very profanely what he would do to her next. Before she could calm herself, he scooped her up in his arms and stepped out of the tent.

Kai shrieked in alarm. Rain poured down in sheets outside, thunder clapped and lightening flashed in the distance.

"Shhh. You don't want the whole camp to wake up do you?"

She lowered her voice to a stage whisper. "We're naked. We can't …I can't … You're crazy!"

"About you, baby girl. All about you." Asa set her down on one of the picnic tables near Camp Ridgeway.

"Someone will see us."

Asa looked over his shoulder, then back at Kai, a wolfish grin on his face. "My tent blocks everybody's vision on this side. The only other person who could see directly would be Judy. And she's probably down in Jeremy's tent getting a little something-something herself."

He stood at the end of the picnic table between Kai's legs, looking confident and regal as the rain coursed through his locs and down his chest. His arousal was strong, urgent and seeking. As her eyes adjusted to the darkness, a flash of lightening silhouetted his magnificent body. He was stunning, and everything Kai wanted.

When he stepped forward, rain dripped from his hair onto her stomach. Focused in his need, oblivious to the rain, he hooked her legs over his forearms and plunged.

Rain dripped, showering them both, and a sharp breeze made the night cool, but Kai's body was so overheated she didn't notice. She was oblivious to everything except Asa as he thrust into her, stroke after powerful stroke. She reached to grasp thick biceps, but her hands slipped. She wanted to touch his beautiful body and the dreadlocks that whipped around her with the wind and his exertion, but then her body arched like a bow and all of her senses exploded.

She saw a lion before her, ravishing her body. Taking. Giving. Taking some more. He quenched a thirst she hadn't known. Dreadlocks cascaded over her breasts, igniting pleasure points in a thousand places. He growled out her name, grunted his need. She inhaled his scent, hers as the smell of feverish and desperate sex floated on the rain-drenched wind between them. And when he leaned close, she tasted his lips and tongue. She savored him, feeding and suckling, as their mouths joined.

Too needy at the moment to worry or care about what that could mean, she let the thought slip aside as Asa drove her body to the edge. Hoarse cries ripped at her throat with each vigorous thrust, and she willingly absorbed the bruising drive of his assault.

Under Asa's lustful gaze, she shivered, and tried to keep her heavy eyelids from closing in rapture as he pushed into her again and again. Her body opened to him, inviting him deeper, ever deeper, with each thrust of his powerful thighs. She wrapped herself around him and matched his movements, rhythm for rhythm. Thrust for thrust, stroke for stroke, she took and she gave. She craved him with a fierceness that shook her to her core.

Then she was tumbling over.

Shuddering waves rolled over her. Kai reached for Asa in desperation, dragging her nails down his back. His hands tightened on her bottom, pinning her in place as he slammed into her. Then, like a bow drown against its arrow, just before release, he stiffened, his thighs tightened. Then he thrust, hard and deep, filling her completely.

Kai's body clinched violently, then burst apart in a vicious detonation that splintered her, body, mind, and soul. A throaty groan erupted from Asa's lips as he followed her with his own release.

The lion had claimed his mate.

In his workshop, a day later, Vernon lovingly covered the bottom half of a wood and wire statue with a heavy cloth and fastened it carefully into the vice. He used a crowbar to pry off the pieces of the three-tiered base that hadn't already been broken away. When that was done, he unscrewed the statue and placed it gently down on his work table. One of the inch thick pieces of wood he had detached fell to the floor. He reached down to pick it up just as the phone rang. He fingered the wood thoughtfully as he walked across the dusty studio to the phone. He still remembered the day Kai had broken it in a fit of anger, ruining the already fragile strands of their relationship.

Suzy Sunshine, as he had come to quaintly refer to the colorful wooden statue, was a piece of art he had loving created for his only daughter, to represented the beautiful fiery spirit he saw in her. But for the past six years, Suzy had only represented pain. The pain of loss, regret, and what could have been. Suzy had been in a back closet gathering dust since her unfortunate accident. The bittersweet memories of that fateful day had kept her there until now.

None of it mattered, however. The angst Vernon had carried around, heavy on his shoulders and in his heart, was completely gone. His heart beat faster now, his hands were surer, and his desire to make things right with his daughter was stronger than ever. He had never questioned the fates, and he wasn't about to start. He simply thanked them for giving him a second chance. Soon Suzy Sunshine would be back with his daughter, where it rightfully belonged.

Susie was tall, almost four feet in height, her head the size and shape of a Robin's egg. Her hair, which shot up fiercely from her scalp, was made of four discarded pieces of coat hanger wire twisted into spring-like coils. What he loved most of all about Suzy, however, was her arms. They each measured over two feet long and were raised gleefully, straight and high over her head. He liked to think that she was shouting "Hello, world! I'm here and life is fabulous." Just as his baby girl had on that final trip to the carnival on her fifth birthday.

That same morning, thermos in hand, Kai wandered down the path toward the work sheds with a dreamy smile on her face. Asa had surprised her when he didn't show up for breakfast. She tried not to be obvious as she watch for him, but Judy knew her well, and had commented. And as hard as she tried, she still couldn't keep the silly smile off her face. To her horror, several of her colleagues commented

about her jovial mood, and so in the end she was grateful that Asa
wasn't there to hear about it. Besides, she had lots and lots of work to
accomplish today—if she could manage to keep her mind on business
and off Asa.

The man was incredible, both in bed and out. And now that she
had finally made the leap to intimacy, she couldn't say she regretted it.
They had talked afterwards about keeping the relationship discreet,
and to his credit Asa had agreed. Kai smiled. She had a wonderful man
in her life now. Her career was coming together, and with any luck, the
partnership would be decided soon.

Kai yelped when she was physically jerked out of her reverie and
behind one of the magnolia trees that lined the path to the work sheds.
When she got a whiff of Asa's scent, she relaxed and allowed herself to
be enveloped in solid, warm arms. His kiss was ferocious and greedy,
and it made her heart pound. Kai was lost for a moment, but then she
heard footsteps on the path and tensed. Not that Asa was aware of her
distress, or even cared for that matter. He was too busy wallowing in
her hair, which he had tumbled down the moment he grabbed her.

"Asa," she whispered, fisting a hand full of dreadlocks to drag his
head back.

"Mmm, I love it when you get down and dirty, baby girl" Asa
licked her chin like a contented cat.

Although she shivered at the erotic gesture, Kai forced herself to
keep a clear head. "Asa," she started, but he had gone back to nuzzling
in her hair.

"Yeah, baby, I'm listening."

Kai rolled her eyes and pulled his head up yet again. "You're too big
for me to try and wrestle. Now would you please pay attention?" She
hung on precariously to her thermos. "If you make me drop my coffee,
you're really going to be in trouble."

She didn't know whether it was the threat of spilled coffee or the
determination in her voice, but Asa finally straightened up and seared
her with a look, then flashed a grin. She almost melted right then and
there. "Oh, for heaven's sake." She shoved the thermos at him so she
could twist up her hair. "Hold this a minute and stop looking at me
like I'm a piece of chocolate cake."

Asa chuckled. "My favorite kind."

She glared at him, took back the thermos. "We agreed to be
discreet, Asa."

He leaned his hard body against a magnolia tree, legs crossed at the ankles, arms crossed loosely at his chest and studied her with a patronizing smile. When he didn't respond, only continued to appraise her, Kai began to fidget.

"Say something."

His gaze moved to her mouth, then made a lazy trail down her body and back up to her face. "Let's go get naked."

"Could you be serious for one second? If you keep—"

He pulled her to him, wrapped his arms around her and palmed her rear-end. He hitched her closer, against a formidable erection. "Feels pretty serious to me—God, I can't get enough of you." He pressed her tighter against him and kissed her again. "If I had come to breakfast this morning and saw you sitting at the picnic table we made love on last night, I would have dragged you off into the woods."

Kai's breath hitched on a gasp. Was this really real? This man and his need for her. No one had ever wanted her in such a way. She pulled back so she could see his face. He read her questioning gaze easily. "I want you like nobody ever has or ever will, baby girl." Kai's eyes fluttered down and Asa nudged her chin up. "No. Look me in the eye. I need you to see that I'm not just feeding you a line. I want this—us—everything."

Kai's eyes widened, then she shut them tight. She wasn't even going to ask him what he meant by that declaration. If it wasn't what she hoped—what she hadn't realized she wanted—she'd feel like a fool. She shuddered as his hands moved from her thighs, slowly up to her neck and shoulders, kneading and caressing as they went.

"You feel like heaven in my arms, Kai. I don't ever want to let you go." He kissed her lips gently, then added. "Let's sneak into Savannah. No one'll even know we're gone."

Kai almost chuckled at the thought, it was thrilling to have someone—especially a man like Asa—want her so much. It was tempting to throw her hands up and say "What the hell." Then her senses returned. Judy was waiting for her in work shed two. "Discretion, remember?"

"Discretion, my ass," Asa responded. He grabbed her hand and folded it over his erection. "Big A says to hell with discretion."

And before she realized what she was doing, Kai was petting Asa, and his head was back against the magnolia tree, eyes closed in satisfaction. His soft groan brought her to her senses. She jerked back. "How do I let you do that to me?"

Asa's eyes opened slowly, his grin lazy. "You want me."

"Yeah, too much," she murmured. "I've got work to do, Asa. And so do you."

"I'd rather work on you."

The boyish tone surprised her and she looked up.

"I'm crazy about you, baby girl. How many times do I have to say it?" He glanced at his watch. "So when are you done with your work? It's eight-fifteen. How 'bout we meet for lunch at twelve."

"Not a chance. If we do that, I won't get back in time to finish up this afternoon."

"That would be the plan."

Asa's casual mood was getting to her. It was a new feeling, this playfulness. But as much as she liked it, she pulled back. "Yeah well, I think someone has a book they need to work on."

"Book? What book?"

The smile left her face. "Please don't put me before your work."

He frowned and stood up straight. "Is that what you think I'm doing?"

"Isn't it?"

"Baby girl, you've got a hell of a lot to learn. I don't put anything before my work. But I do include other things—other people—in my life."

"Oh."

"Yeah, oh." He glared out at the campsite, softened his expression before he looked back. "I'm making you a part of my life; a part that has nothing to do with work. I expect you to do the same." She opened her mouth to speak, but he waved her away. "And don't start with all that discretion stuff. I know how to be discreet. But I won't hide our relationship, if that's what you're thinking. When we get back to Atlanta, I expect to take you out to dinner, dancing, the movies, whatever, without you worrying about who'll see us." He stared down at her, making her uncomfortable with the force of his renewed anger. He took a menacing step toward her his jaw rigidly set. "Or would you rather we just fucked—discreetly of course."

Kai wanted to whimper at the verbal assault, but she maintained her control. She would not lose control of this situation, or relationship, or whatever it was. Right now, she wasn't sure just what she had gotten herself into.

"Oh, did that hurt?"

Kai glared up at him. "You know it did," she whispered.

"Well, join the club."

"What?"

"Have you stopped to think how it would make me feel not to be able to have you on my arm in public because you don't want to be seen with me? That maybe I have some feelings about this thing we started as well?"

"Well, I ..."

"No, you haven't. All you've been thinking about it yourself. And your—"

"My career? Is that what you were going to say?" It was her turn to express a bit of outrage. "Of course I've been thinking about my career. I told you the first day you stepped into my office that my career means everything to me. I won't jeopardize it."

"I'm not asking you to."

"Yes, you are."

"Okay, okay. Since we live on the Northside, we'll go to dinner on the Southside. All right?" He pulled her into his arms, with a heavy sigh. "I'm not just going to meet you at your place after the sun goes down, then leave before dawn. But I'm willing to compromise, if you are."

She nodded her head against his shoulder.

"All right, then. So that means you've got to realize we can have a relationship along with our careers." He pulled her away from him and stared down into her face. "You got me? We're having this relationship, baby girl, one way or another." He turned her around, swatted her bottom. "Now, scoot. But I'm coming to get you at seven."

During the remaining days on the site, Kai spent more time with Asa than she ever dared. And despite his warning that they would be visible as a couple in Atlanta, he was more than discreet at the excavation site. Only Judy and Jeremy seemed aware that something was going on between them.

Asa made a point of not coming to breakfast, for which Kai continued to be grateful. Especially since she quite often rolled out of his tent an hour before the group gathered near Club Ridgeway to greet the day.

Until Asa, she hadn't known how much she was missing of life. They both worked independently during the day, Asa on his book and the cemetery excavations, Kai on her designs and with her team, and yet there still seemed to be plenty of time to be together. Even more surprising, she discovered she possessed a sexual appetite that equaled Asa's. She should have been embarrassed, but Asa had such an immodest attitude about sex that even the thought of embarrassment seemed silly. Instead, she enjoyed their remaining time at the site and looked forward to seeing what their days together in Atlanta would bring.

"Thank you, Jonathan." *Deep breath. Deep breath.* Kai calmed herself as best she could under the circumstances and leaned back on the cot in her tent. "Thank you so much. Yes. I'll see you tomorrow. We're flying back to Atlanta tonight."

Kai hung up and clamped a hand hard over her mouth to hold back a scream. She closed her eyes and squeezed them tight, until the impulse subsided.

Somewhat dazed, she opened her eyes and stared at her cell phone, then at the blue nylon walls of her tent. She had done it; she had finally done it. Her six long years of hard work and sacrifice had finally paid off. She was going to be a partner at Kapman, Trent, and Gannon. And that wasn't the only thing. She would receive a substantial pay raise, profit-sharing, and full control of the historic preservation studio.

It was everything she had ever wanted in her professional career. The only thing she had ever truly needed had been given to her. She hugged herself, rocking with pent-up excitement. She wanted to shout her triumph to the rooftops. She wanted to yell aloud, at the top of her lungs that she, Kai Ellis, had finally arrived.

But she didn't.

"Take a deep breath and pull yourself together," she told herself. She smoothed her damp palms on her shorts, then raised them to her head, tucking in stray tendrils of her hair. "Calm. I'm calm."

"Whatchu being so calm about, baby girl?"

Kai nearly jumped out of her skin. Asa's head poked through the opening in her tent, and he grinned at her.

"Hold still, babe, I think I see feathers in the corners of your mouth."

She could barely hold in her excitement. But she did, choosing instead to rock with agitation and grin up at Asa like a loon.

He stepped into the tent and studied her quietly. "Well, I could take that expression as appreciation for my well-honed skills as a lover, but—" He checked his watch. "It's been a couple of hours, so I suspect the passion's probably worn off by now. But I'm not mad at you. What's got you ready to burst?"

Kai couldn't stand it any longer. She dragged him down onto the cot beside her. "I did it!" she whispered loudly. "I did it! But you can't tell anyone. It's not official. Promise me you won't say anything."

Asa grinned with her and pulled her on to his lap. His fingers moved to take her hair down. He nuzzled at her neck. "I promise," he murmured near her ear. "But I don't know what the hell you're talking about."

"The partnership," she said, still whispering. "I got the partnership. Jonathan just called. He couldn't wait to tell me. He just returned from the board meeting where they took the final vote."

Asa pulled her away and looked into her eyes. "No joke? Well, damn." A driving kiss came next. "Not that I didn't think you could do it," he said when he released her. "But—well, all right! We've got to celebrate!"

"No!"

"Why not?"

"We can't. Not yet. It's not official. They won't make the public announcement until the partnership dinner."

"When's that?"

Kai's shoulders sagged. "About three weeks from now."

"Hell naw, we're celebrating."

"Asa, we can't."

"Hell, yes we can. My baby takes the biggest step she's ever made in her entire career, I'll be damned if we're not!"

Kai clamped her hands around his face. He eyes were more excited than she'd ever seen them, except maybe when they were having sex. He was breathing hard, and his face was set with determination, all for her. And at that moment, she realized how much she loved him. Somehow, her heart had opened up to him and the world hadn't collapsed around her.

Her eyes prickled with tears. She stared at Asa, her ferocious lion, ready to take on the world on her behalf. She longed to tell him how she felt, to speak the words aloud, to ask whether Asa felt similarly, but she had already been blessed with so much. More than she ever dreamed could be hers, more than she'd ever thought she deserved. Her career was moving in exactly the direction she had always dreamed and planned, and she had a wonderful relationship with a wonderful man, that she hadn't dared dream of or plan for.

She sniffled quickly and gathered herself. No. She wouldn't reveal her feelings and risk what she and Asa had. She had learned that lesson a long time ago from her parents. Maybe if she didn't say the words aloud, just kept them inside, her wonderful world would last. At least for a while.

Asa was staring down at her. "What?" she asked.

"We're celebrating. In our own way," he said quietly. "Are you packed?"

Kai slipped off his lap and sat beside him on the cot. "Yes. I'm riding back to the airport with Jeremy and Judy."

"Nope. You're coming with me. I'm driving back to Atlanta. We'll celebrate on the way." She started to complain, but Asa's hand came up. "You're riding with me. Get your stuff, and I'll carry it to the car." With that pronouncement, he stepped out of the tent.

Kai stared after him, took a few deep breaths and gathered her resolve. She would keep it together, she would take care not to let the words slip out. Carefully, she wound her hair back into its bun and picked up her luggage for the trek back to Atlanta.

CHAPTER SIXTEEN

They stopped at a quaint southern-style diner half-way between Savannah and Atlanta to celebrate. The specialty of the house was fried catfish and shrimp. Kai and Asa indulged in seafood, ice tea, and sweet potato pie until they had to be rolled out of the restaurant. Thankfully, Asa knew of a Victorian-style bed and breakfast a few miles down the road.

They registered, then bedded down to sleep off their lunch. Night had fallen when Kai woke up. At first she was startled, because Asa wasn't there, but he soon reappeared, bearing a bag full of goodies from the nearest grocery store. After a leisurely lovemaking session, they reclined on the couch with an assortment of wine, cheese, and grapes.

Much later, Kai found herself more content than she could ever remember being. She swallowed a piece of cheese and sipped wine, letting her tongue curl around the wonderful flavors. She leaned back into the couch pillows and closed her eyes with a sigh. Satisfaction settled around her like a soft cloud and she just breathed. She started when her feet were lifted off the floor. Her eyes fluttered open.

Asa pulled her onto his lap as he slid down onto the sofa. After a moment of surprise, Kai welcomed the rightness of being in his arms. Lulled by the warmth of his embrace, she allowed him to feed her. First grapes, then cheese and wine, until they were both relaxed and slightly aroused.

Despite the wine, she was lucid enough to know she was falling in love with Asa Matthews. So much in love with him, she thought as she watched him return from the kitchen, it scared her. Was it safe to love someone so much? In her experience, safety wasn't a guarantee. In fact, it was the opposite when it came to love. Safety, security, it came in what you did for yourself. Like her career, and her partnership. Asa reached for her hand, and she pushed aside her worries and allowed herself to be led to bed. Allowed herself to be loved.

Love making with Asa was always a surprising adventure, and this time was no different. As he moved against her, she found that the wine had softened the wildness of their mating, but the intensity was still just as strong. Kai saw it in Asa's eyes, felt it in every touch and stroke.

When she reached for her climax, he stroked her deeper, stronger, holding her tight when she finally came apart. Then his strokes continued, strong and deep, but relaxed and easy as Asa pushed toward his own release.

His fingers tightened in her hair. He kissed the top of her head. Once. Twice. His fingers kneading her scalp like a kitten. Then he let out a long growl. "… Love you," he murmured. "I love you, baby girl."

Kai's thighs clenched as she felt a climax building again.

"Come with me, baby girl," Asa demanded, his slow rhythmic thrusts picked up speed, but amazingly the same relaxed motion infused them. "Come with me."

She felt herself falling, shattering into tiny pieces. Asa grabbed her thigh, pressed her knee into the crook of his arm, and shoved it higher. He pushed into her, pumped in furious thrusts, groaning out her name as he met her release with his own.

Later, when Asa was breathing deep and sleeping soundly, Kai lay awake beside him trying to comprehend what he'd said when they were making love. He had said the "L" word. What she wanted to hear, but not when she wanted to hear it. Limited though her experience was, even she knew not to believe what a man said in the throes of passion.

As much as she wanted it, as much as she wanted to believe that a man like Asa Matthews could love her, she wouldn't allow herself to trust it. She would pretend it hadn't happened and that was that. At least until he said it under more normal circumstances.

She rolled over and to her surprise, Asa reached for her in his sleep. He pulled her close and spooned himself around her. It would have to be enough, for now. With a soft sigh, she let her breathing fall into rhythm with her lover's and finally drifted off.

The next day, Asa was happily engrossed in manuscript additions and revisions at his office at the Coleman Foundation. Finally taking his relationship with Kai to a new level had given him renewed energy and a renewed focus on his manuscript. Certainly finding the old cemetery played a huge role as well, but making love to Kai had taken the edge off his mood. His concentration was back and his fingers skipped over the keyboard at lightning speed. He flipped through his notes, easily finding the quotes he needed, then added them to his text.

The noise at his office door jerked him out of his zone. He looked up in surprise. "Harold?" His boss rarely came down to the research floor. When he wanted to see you, you went to him. Curious, Asa waited for Harold to lower his stocky frame into the chair in front of Asa's desk. "What's up?"

Harold removed his spectacles and tucked them into his breast pocket. "I was hoping you could tell me."

That didn't sound good. Not good at all. "I'm not sure I know what you mean."

"We talked about your conduct when you came back to Atlanta a few weeks ago, and—"

"Yes, sir. We did." Asa thought quickly. Harold obviously wasn't talking about his professional conduct. This was personal. But he had done nothing with indiscretion—not recently anyway. Kai had made sure of that, and there was no way Harold could know about him and Kai. Jeremy and Judy were the only people who knew they even had a personal relationship, and they were both very protective of their leader. Nothing else had happened at the dig site that should have caused alarm. Except that time when Rach—*aw, hell.*

For one panicked moment, Asa was alarmed. But then he remembered that Kai was the only person other than himself that had even seen Rachel when she showed up at the plantation and even then, Rachel hadn't made it past the parking lot.

Harold broke into his rapidly escalating thoughts. "It's come to my attention that there was some sort of altercation at the camp site in the past two weeks. Someone who came to visit you."

Asa's jaw clenched tight. Obviously who ever sent Rachel to the site for an impromptu visit was the same person who provided Harold with his information. He intended to find out who. But for right now, Asa figured it was best to play dumb. "The dig and the site visit by the team from KT & G went extremely smoothly. In fact, the cemetery we found is turning up even more artifacts than we had hoped. We didn't have any major problems."

"We'll talk about the cemetery later. What's Kai Ellis have to do with all of this?"

Asa almost lost his composure with that one. It took everything in his power to stifle the expletive that burned in his throat. Harold was studying him closely, and Asa knew some one had been talking. He didn't know who—or why—but Harold had been told something regarding him and Kai. Man, she would have his head if their little affair came out in the open. Especially just as she had been awarded that partnership.

Harold was waiting patiently for him to answer—or slip, maybe. "Sir, you know Kai Ellis." Harold nodded. "Her professional reputation is flawless."

Harold mumbled something about Kenneth Roselle, then waved it away and waited for Asa to continue.

"She's as professional as they come. Believe me. Nothing happened at the site, especially nothing involving her that should cause you any alarm."

Harold continued to watch him, long enough to make Asa want to fidget, but he managed to hold himself still. Harold glanced at the papers scattered about his desk. "So the cemetery find is what you hoped it would be?"

Asa breathed a huge sigh of relief. "Even more."

"And the book?"

Asa couldn't hide his enthusiasm. He waved his hands over the notes he had been working through when Harold came in, and grinned. "Right on track. Like I told you, it's writing itself."

Harold stood up. Asa followed. "All right, Asa. Glad to hear it." He moved to the door, turned. "Kai Ellis is a good woman; needs a good man. Put her stock in that Kenneth Roselle fellow over at Drexel for too long. I've never liked the fellow. A little too slick for my tastes. It's about time she found someone of a higher caliber."

Asa was completely confused, and it must have shown on his face.

Harold's smile was gentle, fatherly. "Glad to see you finally found a woman that's worthy of you. Be good to her."

Asa wasn't aware of Harold's exit, didn't know how long he stood staring after the man. He was too busy trying to unhinge his jaw from where it dangled precariously close to the floor.

On the forty-seventh floor of Drexel Development, Kenneth rolled his eyes as he took the call from Rachel Burton. *God, women.* Why had he ever thought she would be useful? She murmured a sullen hello, and he remembered. It was that mouth. She had a mouth that no red-blooded man could resist. And a sexy little, horny body to go with it. He smiled at the thought. She was irritating, but at least she pleased him physically.

"Yes, Rachel. How may I help you?"

"You lying S.O.B. Why I trusted you to tell the truth about Asa, I'll never know."

"Pardon?" Kenneth said. With a tired sigh he picked up his gold-dipped golf ball paperweight and examined the finish. "It's been how many days, Rachel? Since I hadn't heard from you, I figured you and Asa were on your honeymoon or something."

"Honeymoon?" She practically spat disgust through the phone at him. "I have a job, Kenneth. And clients to keep happy. Especially after I abandoned them to go to see Asa. Because *you* told me he wanted me back."

"Yes, I did. I was under that impression. I gather I was incorrect on that point."

There was silence on the other end of the phone. Rachel Burton hadn't become a successful attorney by being stupid, but her expertise with men, it seemed, was a different story entirely. "I don't appreciate being used, Kenneth."

"How's that?"

"You used me. I don't know how or what you've gained, but you sent me back to Ridgeway plantation on a wild goose chase. Asa was on his way to Savannah with one of those architects on his arm just as I arrived."

Kenneth sat up in his seat. The contented smile left his face. "Who was he with?"

"How should I know? He made me leave not ten minutes after I got there. Escorted me back to Savannah himself."

Kenneth pressed his lips together in irritation.

"You made a fool out of me."

"No. I believe you managed that all by yourself. Where are you now, Rachel? I'd like to see you." He'd like to see those luscious lips of hers on him, those thighs tight around his waist as he screwed her again. "Where are you?" He asked again when she didn't respond.

"I'm in Atlanta, not that I'll be seeing you. I don't appreciate your tactics. And I won't be used again."

Kenneth smiled at her bravado. "I beg to differ."

"You're an ass, Roselle."

"Maybe. But I think I want to see you." He checked his watch, then his desk calendar. "Yes. I'd like to see you in about an hour. Here in my office."

"You may have taken advantage of my fragile state once, Roselle. But it won't happen again."

A second later, an angry dial tone buzzed in Kenneth's ear.

Whatever. He checked his watch impatiently. Now if Bill would just get here so he could learn what affect Rachel's little visit had had on the two lovebirds and their reputations.

For once, Bill didn't disappoint him. He was on time today. *Must be good news.* Kenneth rubbed his hands together eagerly as he waited for Barbara, his secretary, to escort Bill into the office.

He frowned as soon as Bill sat down. The man was his same, nervous self. Kenneth had expected at least a small spring in Bill's step, but he seemed more jumpy than usual. Instead of the crunching according folders he seemed to tote everywhere, Bill carried a battered black briefcase that had certainly seen better days.

Kenneth didn't waste time with pleasantries. "I just spoke with Rachel Burton."

Bill's eyes flashed with unease.

"She wasn't very happy about her excursion to Ridgeway last week."

Bill frowned. "The poor girl has suffered enough at the hands of that man. It was terrible of you to lead her on that way. Matthews finds a new woman in every port. He doesn't want her anymore."

Kenneth waved his hand. "Please, spare me the protective uncle bit. Rachel Burton isn't a 'poor girl.'" He painted a telling leer on his face. "She's no girl at all, if I do say so myself. She's every bit a woman, Bill." He waited for the notion to set in with Bill, then adjusted his crotch for effect. "Yes. She's every bit the woman. You might want to give her a try sometime. She might like that, I think."

Bill looked horrified. He grasped at his briefcase, white-knuckles bulged as he gaped at Kenneth. Kenneth shook his head. The man across from him was as naïve as—hell, he was as naïve as Kai Ellis.

"Life is a bitch. Isn't it Bill? Now, as I said, Rachel just might enjoy being with you. You two have that father/daughter thing going on, and all."

"You're disgusting."

Kenneth chuckled, amused at himself—Bill, too. "Ah. So they tell me, Bill. So they tell me." He picked up his golf ball, tossed it from one hand to the other. "I've gotten Rachel's side of things. What's your report?"

Bill's hands grasped and released the briefcase which held in front of him like a shield.

Kenneth rose. "You're looking a little shaky, Jameson. How about a drink?"

"Water," Bill croaked.

Kenneth replaced the decanter of scotch he'd just picked up, poured a glass of ice water instead, and handed it to Bill. Bill released his death grip on his briefcase to gulp it down like a man dying of thrust.

Kenneth poured himself two fingers of scotch and returned to his desk. "Now, Bill. Let's hurry things up."

"Sorry. So—so sorry. My report. I—Well. After Rachel called me that night—humiliated and in tears." Kenneth kept a stern eye on Bill, daring the man to fault him. Hesitant, Bill continued. "She told me what happened. So I let the information slip to my administrative assistant. Of course it only took a day for it to get back to Harold."

Kenneth smiled. But when he realized Bill didn't share his pleasure concerning the situation, he waited. Watched.

"Harold confronted Asa this morning. But when he told him about the cemetery …"

"Who cares about the cemetery? What about Rachel's visit? How did he take that little bit of news?"

Bill sighed. "Apparently, Asa knows how to handle Harold Ackerman. He told him about the cemetery discovery and all was forgiven."

"All ... all was—" Kenneth sputtered. "God damn it. Do I have to do everything myself?" Furious, he downed the remainder of his scotch. "Get out of my sight, Bill. Before I decide not to protect you any more."

Bill nearly leaped at the door in his haste to leave the office.

When he was gone, Kenneth grabbed a golf club and slammed a ball against the tempered glass window. It ricocheted back, nearly taking out his eye. That was a little too close to the reality of his current situation for comfort. Every gambit he had taken had fallen flat, and he sincerely hoped nothing came ricocheting back in his direction. He was taking too many chances. If he manipulated many more pieces in this little game, he might find himself dodging more than wayward golf balls.

Angrier than he could remember being in a long time, he dropped the club and poured himself another scotch.

Back at his desk, he flipped through his Rolodex, then dialed Alan Warren's number. As he waited for the man to answer, Kenneth soothed himself with the notion of how easily people could be manipulated. Some human beings were so susceptible to their baser needs. Bill, in his greed for fame and glory had set himself up so obviously that a child could have blackmailed him.

The phone rang for the third time on the other end. "Mr. Warren's office. May I help you?"

Kenneth announced himself and heard the pleasant secretary's voice go cold.

"I'll put you through," she said curtly.

Yes, most people were so easily manipulated. Kai was quite a surprise, however. She had been so squeaky clean all the years he had known her. All about business. Even he hadn't managed to sweep her into his bed. Nor had he managed to pull her into any of his gray back-room deals to the point where he could use them against her without damaging himself in the process. But now, now his precious Kai would fall just like the rest. And then she would need him. She would realize she wouldn't move any higher in her career without him by her side. The phone clicked and Alan Warren finally answered.

"Alan," he said jovially. "How are things going, my friend?"

"What do you want?"

"Tsk, tsk. Alan. Temper doesn't become you." He sipped at his single malt scotch. "I need a bit of information about our dear friend Kai Ellis."

"I have nothing to give you, Roselle. Kai is doing a fine job. Everyone knows it. And since this Ridgeway contract is going so well, she's the employee we decided to elect as the new partner this year. The board's final vote was just a couple of days ago, so whatever you've been trying to do to her didn't work."

Kenneth drained his scotch and almost slammed the tumbler onto his desk blotter before he managed to catch himself. *Careful. Calm,* he told himself. *Calm.* He set the glass on the desk soundlessly and bit his lip hard to rein in his temper. He tasted blood in his mouth and bit down harder. "Since I haven't heard the news from anyone else," he said once he could speak clearly, "I take it no formal announcement has been made?"

"Of course it hasn't. Only Kai has been told. We'll make the announcement at the annual partnership dinner as we do each year."

His lip throbbed, but Kenneth smiled anyway. "Good. That's good. Then it won't be difficult to rescind that offer, now would it. No one knows—except Kai, of course. So no one will be embarrassed."

"Except Kai."

"Ah, yes. Kai," Kenneth murmured. Very soon, she would need him. Very soon, she would be willing to do anything at all to make him happy. Because there was one thing he knew about his dear squeaky clean Kai Ellis. She wanted that partnership more than she wanted anything. It was worth even more than her pride and self-respect.

And wasn't that a good thing? He had treated her with kid gloves for much too long. She wouldn't have any pride or self-respect left when he was done with her. But, he would be the one to get her that partnership. In his own sweet time, he would get her the one thing she wanted in life.

"If there's nothing else." Alan's irritated voice echoed through the phone. Kenneth shook himself from his wayward thoughts.

"As long as we're on the same page Alan. You get the board to rescind that partnership. Immediately."

"But—"

"Do it."

"I can't—I don't have the power to. Besides, there is no reason, absolutely none to warrant such a move. Kai's earned this spot."

"Alan. Dear, naïve Alan," Kenneth chirped. "Must I explain everything to you as if you were a child?" Alan's angry sigh sounded through the phone. "Alan, would I send you on such a mission with out the ammunition to fight?"

Alan's breath hitched.

"Of course I wouldn't."

"You don't have dirt on her."

"Oh, but I do, Alan. I have plenty. Definitely enough for your board to rescind that partnership."

"Well, what is it?" Alan said through gritted teeth.

"She screwed Asa Matthews to get his vote for the Ridgeway bid."

Silence. A long silence.

"What? You don't believe me?"

"No. I don't."

"Is that a fact?" Kenneth couldn't have been more pleased. He had shocked the man out of his shoes. He ran down his pet theory about Asa Matthews's relationship with Kai for Alan, embellishing where it suited him. Alan had no way of knowing where he got his information. And Kenneth was confident the man was too afraid of exposure himself to try and find out who was spying for him.

But Alan didn't bite, so Kenneth thought quickly, rolling out another lie with the sincerity and anger of a jilted lover. "Kai's a good-looking woman, she knew if she laid it on him right, Matthews would be thinking with his dick instead of that Ivy League brain of his." He paused for effect. "You know how it is when you think with your dick, don't you Alan?"

Silence.

"Take care of things, Alan. Or I will."

CHAPTER SEVENTEEN

It was Wednesday morning, and Kai Ellis, the soon-to-be partner at KT & G, was in heaven on the drive in to work. She could have floated to the office after all the excitement of the previous days. Jonathan had encouraged her to take some time off, the entire week if she wanted, so that she could come back fresh and excited the next week. She had taken Tuesday off and spent some time with Asa. His appetite for pure decadence was amazing. In fact, he seemed to have made her a special project to help her make up for every day of her six years of sexual abstinence. She shivered pleasurably as she recalled the interestingly wicked experiences he had introduced her to.

Asa's image was planted firmly in her mind as she turned into the parking deck of her building. He had left for Ridgeway earlier that morning, but would be back on Friday night. "To pick up where they left off," he had said. Kai smiled wryly, wondering if her body would be able to withstand the strain of it all. She parked and got out.

She started toward the elevator, then stopped in alarm. She had nothing but her purse on her arm. She turned back to her car and opened the rear door to peer in. The back seat was completely empty. She shook her head in amazement. For the first time in her professional career, she had taken nothing, absolutely nothing home to work on after hours. *Unbelievable.* She locked the car.

At the elevator, she pressed the up button and waited. Strangely, only a month ago she was standing at the rear of the Cheesecake Factory berating herself for falling into the arms of a stunningly attractive man. She had warned herself that she didn't need any entanglements; said she couldn't possibly handle them anyway. But here she was, hopelessly, helplessly in love with the sexiest man she'd ever laid eyes on, and she was also a partner at KT & G. All her dreams had come true, even some that she had never realized she desired, like Asa. Judy had been right all along. She could have it all, and she did. She hugged herself at the thought.

"You goin' up or you just gonna stand there, lady?" An ill-tempered man in a maintenance uniform stood in the elevator with his hand holding open the door. The nametag on his shirt said "Ray."

Kai gave herself a mental shake, dazzled the man with her smile, and stepped into the car. "As a matter of fact, Ray, I'm going up!

"How are you doing this fine …" she began as the doors shut.

It was hot and muggy that morning down at the plantation, and Asa had his laptop set up in work shed three. He didn't notice the heat, he was so deep in concentration, until his cell phone rang. He was tempted not to answer it. He was flowing with the new cemetery chapters, and he was determined to get the last portion of the draft completed before he headed back to Atlanta and Kai. Lord knows he wouldn't get any writing done once he got there.

He glanced at the digital read out on the screen. It was V.L. Arrington. He jerked the phone from his belt. "V.L.?"

"Asa, son. How are things going?"

"Perfect," he said, a smile in his voice. "Absolutely perfect. And if you tell me you've got that sculpture done, I'll know all is right with the world."

The older man chuckled. "Sounds like things are moving right a long with you and your lady friend."

"Ah, man. You don't know that half of it." Asa sighed. He didn't normally tell every Tom, Dick, and Harry his business, but he just felt too damned good to hold it inside. "I think she's the one, V.L. I'm dying down here in Savannah without her."

"Then why don't you come on back to Atlanta, son. Give her this statue and tell her how you feel about her."

Asa rubbed his chest. His eyes felt funny. Prickly, almost painful. And his throat hurt so much for a second that he couldn't speak. With effort, he cleared his throat. "I think I'll just do that."

"Good. Good. When do you want to come by and see the piece?"

Asa thought a moment. "Do you think you captured her, from what I told you about her?"

The man was quiet for a long moment. He coughed, as if emotions had overcome him as well. "Actually, I think so. I think so."

"Great. I didn't really give you much to go on did I? Just the thing about the hair and her personality."

"No, you didn't." There was a smile growing in V.L.'s voice, now. "But your sister said you brought your lady friend by the shop. I got a great description from Schyler. So yes, I think I captured Kai's essence."

Kai. My Kai. My woman, Asa thought. Maybe his crazy prognostication to his sister and V.L. that day in the shop hadn't been as farfetched as it had seemed. Maybe he would propose to her after all. He'd make it an elaborate surprise. The book could hold another couple of days. "I'm coming back to Atlanta tomorrow, and I'll probably want Kai to myself for a few days. How about if you bring the sculpture to Sky's shop on Saturday morning, before she opens? I'll bring Kai, give her the statue and all that."

"And I'll get to meet her?" The man sounded almost wistful.

"Oh, yeah. You'll definitely get to meet her."

"You're a good man, Asa Matthews," V.L. said, quietly. "I think Kai is lucky to have you." He paused. And when he spoke again, his voice cracked with emotion. "I'll see you and Kai on Saturday then."

Kai rolled lazily over the bed, stretching like a feline laying in the sun. Asa had returned on Thursday, and she made sure her weekend was free. She had worked diligently; and despite her day off and frequent lapses into daydreams, she was able to leave the office at the office. It was a new skill she had acquired from Asa. Amazingly, the world continued to turn. She had made it home by six o'clock, and Asa was waiting at her door.

They had lazied away the evening making love and snacking, and then making love again. By Friday, the armload of food they purchased from the market was practically gone. She smiled and rolled over, hugging her arms around herself. She had stopped questioning her good fortune and simply prayed that it wouldn't end. At the request of her growling stomach, she rolled over to look at the clock. It was almost ten.

Shocked, she sat up quickly, trying to blink away the haze. Then she smelled coffee and smiled. She turned to get out of bed when Asa appeared in the doorway. He looked delicious in the pair of worn cargo shorts that rode low on his hips. A few locs fell across his bare chest, drawing Kai's eyes to the firm pectorals that she had strained against the night before. He smelled delicious, too, but more importantly, he was holding two steaming mugs of Jamaica Blue Mountain coffee.

"Morning, sleepyhead." He approached the bed, carefully. "I seem to recall a statement you made about a couple of things you'd like to enjoy in the morning."

Kai's mouth curled into a grin as she remembered the day he appeared in her office doorway. "Oh yeah? And what about it?"

"Well." He presented her with her morning java. They both paused momentarily to drink.

Asa set his mug on the nightstand and turned back to her. He kept his eyes glued to her hers as he removed his shorts, his erection jutting proudly upward. "Let's see what I can do to oblige." He crawled on to the bed, took her coffee mug and set it aside.

Later, in a sex-sated state of relaxation, Kai luxuriated in the feel of Asa's weight stretched carelessly across her on the bed.

"Hey, when was this taken?"

Kai followed his gaze. He was looking at a framed photograph on the nightstand. It was the photo of her at the carnival on her fifth birthday.

She sighed when he sat up and grabbed the photo to take a better look. It had been taken by her mother and showed her sitting atop her father's shoulders. She was laughing gleefully, with her hands stretched high in the air, her long curly hair flying in the wind above her head. The photo had been cropped into an artful composition and her father wasn't even visible. It looked as if she were floating in mid air. It was one of her favorite photographs, and she often pondered why, given that it represented both the happiest time and the most painful time of her life. Her mother had given it to her the day they dropped her off at her grandmother's house, promising they would be back for her when they "made it." A year later, her mother was killed in a car accident in Delhi. And her father assuaged his own guilt and pain by roaming southern Asia for another five years.

Even though she learned of her mother's death almost immediately, Kai still remembered her words, "We'll be back when we've made it." It had been her lifeline for years afterwards, pacifying her between birthday and Christmas visits by her father that soon dwindled to nothing, save the occasional greeting card. She was fourteen years old before she finally accepted that Vernon wouldn't be coming back for her, but she had always kept the picture by her bed.

Kai's smile was bittersweet as she answered. "I was five years old, and my parents and I were celebrating my birthday at the carnival."

Asa studied the photograph quietly, traced a finger over her wide smile. "I love it. It really captures your spirit."

"Yeah." Kai cleared her clogged throat.

Asa set the photograph on the nightstand and turned to look at her. "What's the deal with you and your folks—um, your dad?"

"I already told you." Kai shrugged off the question. "We don't get along. He wants me to be something I'm not. It's not something I agree with, so I keep my distance. End of story."

"Doesn't sound like it to me."

Kai turned to face him, anger coloring her cheeks. "I don't want to talk about it, all right."

Asa relented and pulled her gently into his arms. "All right, then let me tell you a little about my folks, then." He tucked his arms around her waist, and Kai relaxed against his chest.

Asa's poignant story about his parents' early married life took her thoughts away from her own family. Kai turned and hugged him tightly, marveling at the sensitivity and protectiveness of his entire family. Asa's father, even Asa and his siblings, rallied around his mother, showing her their faith in her. Backing her up against Asa Senior's powerful family. As a family, they decided to leave it all behind and start fresh in the States, for Johnetta. If only Kai's family had had the same tight bond, maybe her own life would have evolved differently. Maybe her parents would have returned for her, or perhaps not left her to begin with. She pressed her face hard against his warm chest to hold in the tears that threatened, but Asa must have sensed something and pulled her away to peer into her face.

He brushed her wet lashes with his thumb, pulling her close again. He didn't ask her why she was crying, for which she was grateful. How could she admit that she had fallen in love with him when she was afraid he didn't feel the same, or maybe even leave if she told him. Her life and what she expected out of it had turned a full 180 degrees in little more than a month. It was overwhelming. She sighed heavily, and vowed desperately to enjoy the warmth and protection of Asa's arms for however long it lasted.

Later that morning, outside the Aromia Natural Body Spa, Asa opened the car door for Kai and helped her to the curb. She was exquisite, so gracefully wild. Her face seemed to glow as she stepped out into the sunshine. Willful curls framed her face, but most them were pulled into a chignon on the nape of her neck. He smiled at Kai's image. Until he could convince her to wear her hair down, he would settle for the tendrils that played at her temples. But for once, at least, she'd been willing to discard her typical uniform of pressed slacks and silk shell for a sundress on the balmy Saturday morning.

Was it the radiance of her cocoa-colored shoulders and the bewitching curls at her temples that made his stomach tighten when she met his gaze? Maybe it was simply the memory of their frenzied love making earlier that morning that made him feel feverish. It didn't matter, much, and he didn't really care. Not one to suppress his desire, Asa put a heavy hand to the back of Kai's neck and pulled her close. Their lips ignited as they touched. He had been prepared for the chemistry, the all-consuming passion of their lovemaking. But the rightness that had come along with it still surprised him.

He decided not to over-analyze. He just enjoyed the kiss, enjoyed what was his. Let himself fall willingly under Kai's spell. She was his, and he hers. His arms went around her, fingers curling into the dangling tendrils that grazed his hands. Her fingers combed through his hair and clutched his locs as her desire rose. It was an unconscious act that he'd come to recognize in her, one that he wouldn't chance to reveal for fear she would refrain from it in the future. Her soft murmur of contentment made his heart skip.

A couple standing in a nearby storefront clapped appreciatively as they broke the kiss. Asa smiled down at Kai's blissful expression and chuckled. Her eyes betrayed the constant battle she fought with herself. She may be able to control her rational mind, but he had her heart, her body, and her soul. "Come on, baby girl, I've got something to show you." He linked thick, long fingers into her graceful, slim ones and strolled down Moreland Avenue to his sister's shop.

"Where are we going?" Kai inquired, pulling on his hand. "You're being mighty secretive this morning."

"Mmm hmm," he agreed, not giving an inch.

In the back room of Schyler's shop, Vernon heard the bell tinkle when the shop entrance door opened and swallowed nervously. He peeked out and almost gasped aloud. It had been months since he had seen his girl, and she was gorgeous, radiant and beautiful. More so than he had ever seen her since that last birthday they shared when she was five years old.

"Hey, guys," Schyler yelled to Kai and Asa from another corner of the shop. "Give me five minutes, okay?"

"No prob, sis."

Vernon smiled and brushed a hand over his heart as he watched Asa, with love in his eyes, corner Kai near a display of aromatherapy bath products.

Asa cupped Kai's face in his hands and pressed his lips to hers. "Maybe we should have stayed in bed," he whispered as his mouth moved to nibble at her ear. He reached back and freed Kai's hair as his lips returned to hers. By the time Schyler entered the room, they were both breathing heavily.

"Ahem," his sister interrupted. "If you guys have something better to do …"

Asa grinned and tucked Kai into the crook of his arm. "What's up sis. We ready?"

"Mmm hmm."

"Oh, wait." Asa held up a hand. "My baby girl has an announcement to make." He stepped back dramatically, giving Kai the floor.

"I've just been made a full partner at KT & G."

"Get out, girl." Schyler hugged her. "You go!"

"Bad, ain't she?" Asa laced his fingers in the curls at Kai's back as he drew her to his side. "This was supposed to be just an …" he stopped, realizing what he had been about to say an "I love you gift." He gazed down at Kai, who was smiling up at him, waiting. What the hell, he thought. It was true wasn't it? He cleared his throat and started again. "This was supposed to be just an 'I love you' gift." Kai gasped, and he put a finger to her lips before she could say anything more. "I had it commissioned before you made partner. But now, it also applies to your making partner, as well."

He turned to his sister, who was smiling wistfully at them. "Sky, you want to bring it in?"

Schyler turned to walk to the storage room, then stopped. "Congratulations, A. I'm really happy for you. Both of you."

Asa nodded and turned back to Kai. Her eyes were glassy, tears threatened to fall any moment. "Asa? I … I …"

He kissed her tenderly and tucked her hair behind her ear. "I love you."

He turned when he heard the wheels of a service cart. His sister pushed the statue out into the middle of the shop floor. "I haven't even seen it myself," he commented to Kai. "I just described what I wanted the artist to do." The statue was covered with a heavy, pale colored tarp. "You ready?"

When Kai nodded, Asa signaled his sister to remove the tarp.

Kai gave a sharp gasp and put her hands to her face. Asa smiled triumphantly at his sister, until he realized she wasn't smiling back. She was watching Kai.

Asa turned. Kai's eyes were wide, and staring straight at the statue, which he had yet to look at, so anxious he had been to see her reaction to it. He turned to look at V.L.'s piece and his mouth gaped open. Before he could recover, Kai was rushing out of the door.

"Just what the hell is going on?" Asa practically shouted.

A harsh sob filtered through the shop.

Asa turned around to see V.L. emerge from the storage room. Asa's mouth gaped again and he twisted quickly to stare back at the statue.

Unbelievable. It was Kai. An abstract version of her, but Kai none the less. "Kai …" he murmured and looked back to V.L. "At the carnival…."

V.L. stood in the storage room door, looking devastated and too upset to move. Asa gave his sister an angry look. "You knew about this?" He turned to rush out the door, not caring about Sky's response. He had to find Kai.

"I didn't, Asa," Schyler yelled at his back. "Not until today, when I … I didn't know V.L. was her father."

Asa glanced both ways down the sidewalk. Kai was two blocks away, walking erratically, blinded by tears and frantically trying to pull her hair back into place. He rushed to catch up to her.

"Baby …" he reached for her arm, but she pulled away, and continued her rapid pace.

She stopped finally, turned around. "How could you do this?"

"I didn't know, Kai, honest. I didn't know, I'm sorry." As much of her hair was in its bun as was out. He put a hand on her up-stretched arm as she tugged at her hair in frustration. It frustrated him to watch her. "Why don't you just leave it down," he said in a tone sharper than he intended.

He watched in amazement as Kai's eyes narrowed and an incredible façade of calm washed over her face. It was as if a sudden realization hit her. "You can't change me when I don't want to be changed. I was perfectly happy with my life—and myself—before I ever met you." Her hands no longer trembled in anger. Her fingers were nimble and sure, calm and steady. She stared daggers at him, daring him to speak, as she deliberately flicked her wrist and crafted a neat bun. "How you can claim to love me, then bring that man back into my life is beyond me."

She pressed her hands to her temple, just as he had seen her do in the work shed at Ridgeway. It seemed like ages ago. Slowly she drew her fingers from her forehead to her nape, smoothing curls back from her face. The enigmatic Buddha smile he hadn't seen since that first day in her office reappeared. "Goodbye, Asa."

Dumbfounded, Asa stared as she turned and walked down the street.

When Asa returned to the shop, the excited voices of his sister and Kai's father stopped abruptly. They stared wide-eyed at him. "She's gone," he stated flatly.

V.L. turned away to stare absently at the plate glass window of the storefront.

Asa walked over to the statue where it still sat in the middle of the shop floor. His fingers moved over the wooden arms, then gingerly touched the spirals of coat hanger wire that made the hair. His face twisted in pain. Heat and fury surged in him.

He continued to stare at the statue. "Why didn't you say something, V.L.?"

The other man sighed. "Look, Asa …"

"This is her," Asa said interrupted him, looking up. "Isn't it? At the carnival." The look of sadness in V.L.'s eyes told him he was right. "How could you do this to her?" He looked down angrily at the piece of folk art. He wanted to throw it across the room. "How could you be so cruel."

"I …"

"Don't you realize what this means to her? It was the most painful time of her life!" He was shouting, but he didn't care. Kai was hurting and someone would pay for bringing her such pain. Asa marched angrily toward the other man, his hands clinched into fists at his sides.

"A, hold on now." Schyler stepped in front of him. "This isn't any of your business."

He turned his angry gaze on his sister. "The hell it's not! If it's to do with Kai, it's my business."

"Fine," his sister said with more force. "Have it your way. But you're going to sit down and talk about this like a reasonable person. Now I've got a business to run, so you and Leon go upstairs."

Asa gave V.L. a challenging look, but Sky's scowl sent them both up the stairs.

The anger inside Kai still hadn't subsided, even after the long cab ride back to her condo. She purposely went to her bedroom and picked up the photograph on the nightstand. She stared at it, willing the anger, the pain, and the joy the image conjured back down into the box she'd sealed it in for so many years.

She sat on the side of the bed for thirty minutes before she finally let her shoulders sag. It wasn't working. Not like it had all those other times. By the time she was fourteen, she had learned to look at the picture without emotion. But it had all come flooding back when she went off to college. For a year or two, she managed to suppress it. Then she met Bobby and the pain was back again. She dampened it back down yet again, and it looked like she would have some peace.

But then Vernon created Suzy and tried to give it to her. Kai snorted and set the picture back on the nightstand. It was amazing how much Suzi Sunshine looked like her, even in its rustic abstraction. However, having the picture to remind her of all her joy and pain was quite enough. She didn't need a statue representing it at as well.

Suzi was Vernon's attempt to show her how to be the "proper" daughter of artists. They wanted her to be a wild, free spirit, not the placid, law-abiding, social conformist that had made her a success in her field. He had brushed aside her fearfulness and told her she needed to open her mind and live life. Never once had he given any thought to the fact that she was the way she was because all of her love of life had been drained away in those years when she was between the ages of five and fourteen.

Suddenly it dawned on her that Asa had been trying to change her just like her father had. To her chagrin, he had made much more headway than Vernon. He'd plied her with sex and loving words, and she had done just as he demanded like a puppet on a string. As for her work at Ridgeway, instead of working late into the evening as was her custom, she was sneaking off to Savannah with him or relaxing with the team at Club Ridgeway.

Now that they were back in Atlanta, she was taking days off work, leaving the office by six o'clock, and carrying only her purse out the door. Well, no more. Asa Matthews might be cut from the same cloth as her parents, determined to have his way despite the cost to Kai, but it didn't mean she had to be.

Would Asa leave, just as her parents had, because she chose not to conform? She smiled ruefully. If she couldn't trust her own parents to fulfill their promises to her, how could she trust anyone else in her life?

She forced Asa to the back of her mind. He would be gone from her life soon enough. But she still had her father to contend with. Her father, who had knowingly given Asa the statue despite the hurt he knew it would cause.

The statue had been the *piece de resistance* of his attack against her and her life choices. She had knocked the statue off its pedestal in an uncharacteristic fit of anger when her father presented it to her back in college. It had only been in the past two years that she had even begun speaking to him again.

Kai sighed and glanced at the picture once more on her way out of the room. Why had she still hung on to it after all this time?

In the kitchen, she found little left in the pantry other than snacks. After she rounded up some chips and salsa, she went to sit on the balcony. The partnership dinner was two weeks from Monday night, she realized as she stared sullenly down into the jar of salsa. She had planned to invite Asa to accompany her. The board of directors would be making the formal announcement of her partnership at the black-tie event, and she had wanted him to share it with her. Now, she was grateful the date had never come up.

Asa had planned to do all his talking from Kai's doorway. After the fiasco with her father, which still had him reeling, he was surprised she even let him in her home. She was still wearing the sundress, and her hair was still tightly coiffed. Yet, it was the way she looked at him when she opened the door that made him want to take her to bed. Her eyes raked over his body as if she was a cat, and he was a canary. And all he wanted to do was hold her, touch her and take the pain away.

Yet instead of saying as much, his temper returned. The memories returned. Memories of the old Kai who was afraid to feel and afraid to experience. The Kai who was willing to give up so much just for a career. He brushed past her into the living room. "We need to talk."

"We don't have anything else to say to each other, Asa. I'd rather you leave."

He tugged at his shirt collar and turned to look at her. To his dismay, she was glaring at him as if she wished he were dead. "We've got a lot more to say."

Kai folded her arms, defiance written all over her face. "You've turned my life upside down. You've tried to change me to suit you." She waved her hands as if she were getting off track, then clasped her hands as if to calm herself. "Look. It was fun while it lasted, but I've got a career to nurture. I've wasted enough time on fun and games and—"

Asa stared at her in disbelieve. Her hands were prim and properly folded in front of her, her face calmly set, and he couldn't stand it. "What happened to you?"

"I beg your pardon?"

Asa took a step toward her and bit back a curse when she stepped away from him. "You're not afraid of me, so stop it."

Defiantly, she backed up again.

"What happened to *my* Kai?"

"*Your, Kai?*" She shook her head and looked past him, away from his face. Away from his eyes. "It wasn't me, Dr. Matthews. It was someone you wanted to turn me in to. Sorry to disappoint you."

Asa's face twisted. At first Kai thought it was in pain, but then recognized it as ferocious anger. Anger at her. His biceps twitched as he clenched and unclenched his fists. She took another step back, this time cautionary instead of defiant.

Well, she decided, determined to preserve her dignity, she wasn't going to let him bully her into … She couldn't look at him, couldn't deal with him right now. Not when she knew she still wanted him as much as she ever had. Not when she knew that she'd never love another as she still loved him. She whipped around and marched into the kitchen. Anything to put some space between them.

She figured he'd follow, but he didn't. Kai peeked into the living from the pass-through at the breakfast bar. Asa still stood in the middle of the room, still flexing and relaxing his fists, as if he was trying to pull himself back together. In the kitchen, Kai decided to do the same. She found a pitcher and decided to make some lemonade, to give her something to do with her hands.

A few minutes later, as she placed the pitcher in the refrigerator, Asa stepped in the doorway.

Kai took a breath before turning around. "Oh, Dr. Matthews. You're still here?" Her taunt was pleasantly delivered, and just enough to tick Asa off.

He stepped into the kitchen, and studied her as she turned to face him, her back to the fridge. "So it wasn't you I made love to in your bed, this morning; brought coffee to?"

"No, I don't believe it was."

"And the woman I made love to at that bed and breakfast halfway between Atlanta and Savannah, that wasn't you, either?" Asa said as he moved closer, boxing her in against the refrigerator.

Her chin lifted. "No."

"Hmm." His thoughtful pause sounded innocuous, but the glint in his eye wasn't. He lifted his hand, touched the tendrils of hair at the nape of her neck. "The woman that likes me to take her hair down …" His hands moved to do just that. "That's not you either, then?"

Kai wasn't sure she liked the mixture of lust and sarcasm that laced the smile forming on his face. She shook her head.

"The woman that likes to be caressed." His hand dropped to her shoulder, then trailed lightly over her breast. "Like this."

She shook her head. But when his hand closed over her breast, gently kneading it the way he knew she preferred, Kai couldn't suppress the moan that leaked out.

"Hmm." He paused thoughtfully again.

Kai closed her eyes. She wouldn't allow this to happen. Couldn't succumb to his so familiar touch.

"I think it is you, baby," he murmured, pressing his erection against her. "I think it's you."

Kai sensed him before she felt his lips touch hers. She tried to turn her head, to resist, but her muscles wouldn't cooperate. His mouth sank down over hers, and it felt like a homecoming. He buried his hands in her hair, and she felt like weeping.

His tongue whipped in and out of her mouth. He bit her bottom lip gently, then licked away the hurt. He held her face in place, angled her mouth to suit, caressed her chin, her ears, her collarbone with his thumbs. Her entire body throbbed for him, for everything they had shared together. For all the gifts he had given her, all the lessons he'd taught, both in bed and out. And as lovely as it all felt, somewhere deep inside, she felt as if she were betraying herself and what she had worked so hard for, for so many years.

She glared at him, but her body melted.

"You don't want me to stop," he said, his mouth at her throat.

His hands moved to where he had just kissed her, fingers strummed lightly over her sensitized skin. Then to her shoulders, where he brushed away the thin straps of her sundress. He pushed it down, baring her to the waist. "You don't want me to stop, do you, baby girl?" He leaned down to take one of her breasts into his mouth. He thumbed the other, making her squirm under his touch.

Kai whimpered as he made love to her breasts. She felt herself slipping, her legs and knees betraying her, just as the rest of her body already had.

Asa didn't stop her, but followed her to the floor. He pushed up her skirt, fit himself between her thighs and stared down at her. "This is my Kai." He palmed her breasts, then dragged his hands down her ribs to her waist, where her dress was scrunched. He smiled when her back arched. "Yeah, it was you all those times with me, baby. You can't go back now. You liked it then, you like it now. Don't you?"

She shook her head in denial, but her eyes drifted close as he pleasured her breasts. Her chest was heaving when he lifted his head. Firm, sure hands moved to her thighs, and dragged her panties down. His fingers found her flesh, hot and wet. Kai shook her head again, this time from the torture of his touch.

"You like the way I touch you, don't you?"

Kai couldn't answer. Her body, her nerves, all of her attention was focused on Asa. His hands, his touch. Until he stopped.

Kai's eyes flicked open to find Asa staring down at her, watching. Waiting.

"You like it?" He asked. "Tell me, and you can have all you want." She whimpered helplessly. "Tell me."

Kai nodded, then almost instantaneously, the pleasure was back. He filled her with his fingers. Stroked and caressed her until she was on the brink. "You liked it on that picnic table in the rain, too?" His fingers slipped out of her. "Didn't you?" Then plunged back in. "Didn't you?" Over and over he asked and demanded, his fingers following the rhythm.

And over and over, she heard him. Heard his demands, his pleas. But all Kai could do was feel and be pleasured. Until finally she tumbled over the edge.

By the time the tremors slowed, Asa had peeled off his clothes, rolled on a condom and carried her into the bedroom.

"This is my Kai," he told her as he petted and caressed until she was flying high again. "You can't go back, sweetheart." He thrust into her with a groan.

Had his wits been about him, he would have worried about hurting her in his feverish need to feel her around him, but as it was, he needn't have. Kai was slick and wet and received him easily. Her name tumbled from his lips as his body slammed into hers, bringing her body bowing up to meet his. Eyes glazed with passion, she grabbed his hair in her hands and pulled fiercely, bringing his head backwards. His neck arched, along with his back, and he closed his eyes against the fury of his need. Stroke after powerful stroke, he gave her as he had never given before. Her body clinched tight around him as she sobbed out his name with the rhythm of her hips. Her next climax started with a tiny flutter, then built, clutching and grasping at him. He went tumbling over the edge after her. With one final gasp of her name, Asa surged upward, hard and fast, driving himself toward what surely must have been heaven.

CHAPTER EIGHTEEN

Later that night, Kai lay beside Asa in bed and watched Jay Leno's latest monologue about the president. It was hard to maintain a constant state of anger when you felt so sexually satisfied. Her head was on Asa's chest and she twisted one of his locks, which had fallen into her eyes, around her finger.

"How did you get in here?" she asked, to herself as much as to Asa. His chest was warm and it rose and fell in a steady rhythm beneath her head.

"Hmmm." He was distracted by the television, but he stroked her arm affectionately.

"I said, how did you get in here?" Kai said, pulling on the loc of hair in her hand to get his attention. "In my heart. I was supposed to be mad at you, remember?" He seemed to be rather good at diffusing her anger; maybe there was hope for them after all. She couldn't really blame Asa for her dysfunctional family. He hadn't known V.L. was her father. It wasn't his fault her father had tried to take advantage of the situation.

"I guess it's just my overwhelming charm and sex appeal."

Kai gave a delicate snort.

"Girl, you know I'm right."

Kai sat up. "Look, about this statue business...."

"I talked to your father about that. I commissioned a new work from him, you know, not something he did years ago."

"I ... I don't want the statue." Kai looked down at her hands; thinking of how she'd heaved it at her father the day he'd given it to her. "I can't take it."

"Baby, I understand. I know it's painful. But it's you in so many ways." His finger tugged at her chin when she looked away. "Sometimes you have to let go of the past, baby girl. And move forward with your future."

Anger began to crease her brow. "What's that supposed to mean?"

Asa brushed her lips with his. "Don't get mad, okay?" His eyes were pleading when he looked up. "I talked to your father."

The hair rose on the back of her neck, she could sense their conversation beginning to deteriorate. "You already said that."

"I talked to him about you and him. Your mother."

Kai stared, incredulous. "You … you talked about me, and my family … I can't believe …"

"Look, I don't agree with what they did to you. What they put you through…."

She turned and faced him directly. "I can't believe you've put yourself in the middle of my private family matters!"

"Calm down."

"I will not calm down. How dare you? *How dare you?!*" She got off the bed.

"Kai."

"This is my business, Asa. My family. Not yours. You have no right to interfere."

"I love you. That gives me all the right I need." He shrugged. "You're stuck in the past, living half a life. You work, and you go home. Work, home. Work, home. You're all business. That's no kind of life. You deserve more than you're allowing yourself to have. That's all I'm trying to tell you."

Kai backed away from the bed, continued to, until she bumped into the bedroom doorway. Anger twisted her face into a pained grimace as her ears struggled to take in the abuse Asa was spewing at her.

"I've thought about this, Kai. Long and hard. Very long and hard. You're letting your past dictate your future, and you need to let it go."

Kai stared.

"Kai?"

Her eyes didn't waver. Didn't blink.

"Kai? What's wrong?" Asa stood up and started toward her.

"Get out." She kept her voice low, forced a calm she didn't feel.

"Kai…."

"I said get out."

"But, Kai, I …"

She blanked her face. "I don't need fixing, Dr. Matthews. Your work is done here. Please go."

She watched, stone-faced as Asa dressed. Stiff muscles clinched his jaw firmly shut as he made his way through the bedroom doorway where she still stood. She didn't move as he brushed past. "And please stay away," she said when she saw him paused at the door of the apartment.

His clear and articulate "I love you" was the last thing she heard before the door clicked shut.

Then he was gone.

Kai let out a breath and crumbled to the floor like the broken doll she had insisted she wasn't. Hot tears flowed down her cheeks, and she told herself this was what she wanted. This was the way it had to be. She wasn't some kind of experiment, Asa's latest fix-it project. Let him find some other woman to change, since he seemed to have some sort of need to do it. She wasn't some sort of animal that needed freeing from a cage. She was free to do exactly as she pleased, and she was doing just that.

She drew in a trembling breath and tried to fight back the tears. "I don't need you, Asa Matthews."

She dragged herself to the bed and crawled into a fetal position. Tears sprouted anew as she laid her head on the pillow that was still warm from his body, still held his scent.

"I don't need you, Asa Matthews." She repeated her mantra and eventually fell into a fitful sleep.

Kai walked into her office on Friday with a heavy and conflicted heart. She had hoped she was all cried out, but the tears had welled up again this morning on her drive in. She couldn't even manage wearing her contact lenses today, given the state of her eyes. But it was just as well, she decided as she poured cold coffee down the sink and started a fresh pot, the glasses would hide some of her misery. At least she hoped it would.

She took extra care making the pot of coffee. Carefully measuring each scoop, then the water. Once the coffee was brewing, she took just as much time cleaning up the stray grounds from the counter. She didn't have Asa, now. But at least she had the partnership. Finally, she had the partnership. It had been enough before Asa had drifted into her life. She supposed she'd figure a way to make it be enough now that he was gone.

It's going to have to be enough, a voice in the back of her mind told her. *It's going to have to be enough.*

Uncharacteristically tense, Jonathan Rojeski jumped when Christine's voice echoed over his speaker phone. "Mr. Rojeski, Kai just came in."

"Thanks, Christine. Thanks for letting me know." He gathered up a yellow legal pad and a pen to take with him to Kai's office. It wasn't necessary for their meeting, but he would need something to do with his hands while he broke the news to Kai. He scrubbed his hands over his face in dismay. Damn it, but this was going to be the hardest thing he had ever done in his life.

"Um, Mr. Rojeski?"

He jumped again. "Jeez, Christine. I didn't know you were still on the line. What is it?"

"It's Kai. She didn't look so hot when she passed my desk."

He stopped nervously rearranging papers on his desk and glanced at the blinking red light on the phone that was Christine. Did Kai already know? "What was that?"

"She looked pretty bad. Like she'd been crying, maybe. Her door is closed, so you might want to give her a few minutes before you go down."

"Thanks, Christine. Thanks for the heads up."

Jonathan punched viciously at the speakerphone, then stared at it, helplessly. *Damn it*. He was angry enough to quit the Board of Directors over all this. How was he going to tell his best employee, a woman he had mentored, that the board had rescinded her partnership offer?

How could he tell her she was losing what he knew she wanted most in her life, because she had chosen to want a few other things in life as well, like a man who cared about her? Hell, he was the one who encouraged her to relax and have fun with Asa.

He didn't know whether he could turn back the clock or whether his efforts would matter at all, but he would find out who had done this to her. He would find out, and he would fix it—at least he would try. He owed Kai that much.

He sighed heavily, picked up his pen and pad, then stepped into the corridor.

Kai didn't hear her office door open, but when she turned solemnly away from the coffee maker, Jonathan was standing in the doorway. A little relieved to see a friendly face, to be reminded that one thing was still going right in her life—her career. She smiled. Then she noticed the strain on Jonathan's pale face, and her expression wilted. It wasn't like Jonathan to be timid, or sad for that matter. He was generally outgoing and even-tempered. Something was wrong.

She crossed to her desk, set her mug on its warmer and sat down. Jonathan still stood in the doorway. "Well, at least come in and tell me what's wrong." Kai couldn't help the irritation in her voice. It had been a long couple of days; and whatever it was her boss had to say, she wanted it said, bluntly and to the point.

A heavy sigh lifted then dropped Jonathan's shoulders. He finally closed the door, stepped into the room and sat down on the couch. He fumbled with the pen and pad in his hands as if he didn't know what to do or where to start, which only added to Kai's own frustration and distress. But, still he said nothing. Didn't even look up at her.

Kai took a fortifying sip of her coffee and leaned back in her chair, waited. Jonathan scrubbed a hand over his face and shook head. Speculation and wonder eddied through her mind. If he was in her office, if obviously had to do with her. And what was so pressing and upsetting to him that he couldn't even look at her, couldn't manage speech?

No. Her sharp gasp echoed plaintively off the walls.

Kai sat down her coffee mug. "Jonathan?" Her soft voice barely carried over office noises outside her door. The pain in his eyes was mirrored in hers.

"No," Kai said aloud this time. "Please. Not my partnership. Not …" Her voice faded to a whisper. "It's all I have left." She covered her face, knowing she couldn't stop the tears. How could she have thought all her tears had run dry.

Jonathan looked on, helplessly. Kai was quiet in her grief, but her shoulders shook as muted sobs wracked her body. He couldn't stand to see her in pain. It was like watching one of his own children self-destruct. And finally, finally, he found the strength to move. He pulled Kai from her chair, held her like one of his own kids and let her cry.

When she had quieted somewhat, he still held her. Still wanted to relieve her suffering. "I'm going to get to the bottom of this, Kai. I promise you."

Kai lifted her head to stare up at him, and tears welled in her eyes again. His dear precious Kai had always been strong, always capable. Always fearless. But now she looked as helpless and lost as a child. Her eyes were rimmed red and puffy, her cheeks tear-stained.

"Why?" she asked. "Why would they do this when I've worked so hard. For so long. Why?"

He patted her back as much to comfort himself as her. Finally, after a few more minutes of sniffling, she lifted her head.

Misery clouded her eyes in a way that Jon had never seen before. If it were just the partnership, she would have been furious and ready for battle, not ready to surrender. The fire that usually lit her eyes wasn't there. Only the dim flicker of dismay and pain.

He caught her elbow and led her to the couch. "Do you feel like talking about it?" Her startled look almost made him chuckle. Had the situation not been so depressing, perhaps he would have. He smiled gently at her. "You forgot I have two daughters. Tears may paralyze me for a moment, but I know how to handle myself. And I also know that the pain on your face isn't just about the partnership." He waited a moment, then said. "So tell me about Asa. What happened between you two?"

She hesitated.

"Kai, you know I've always thought of you like one of my own."

She grabbed his hand and squeezed. "And since I don't really have a father, I've always liked to think of you that way."

"Kai."

She waved away his protest, and Jonathan let it drop. She had enough worries at the moment. He wouldn't add any more.

"Okay, I'll tell you about Asa." She looked up at him, eyes shining, a watery smile on her lips. "He's a wonderful man, Jonathan. Not like anyone I've ever met before. He admires me. He's proud of me. He was so proud of me when I told him about the part ..." The light winked out of her eyes, and she dropped Jonathan's hand, sat straighter in her seat. "We had an amazing, a wonderful time over the past few weeks.

He made me feel like a caterpillar that didn't know it could become a butterfly."

Her smile was back, and Jonathan smiled with her. "I always knew that," he said. "I've been waiting for you to figure it out." He paused, decided to try again. "Your dad knows it, too."

"Don't. Please. I can't deal with that right now. He's the reason Asa and I aren't together now."

He listened as Kai described the scene at Asa's sister's shop over the weekend. It hurt his heart to hear it all. Jonathan didn't know Vernon, personally. She had told him years ago about her relationship with him, or lack thereof. He held out hope for some kind of reconciliation, so he always tried to point out that Vernon loved her, unconditionally. But she would never have it.

"You're not saying Asa knew your father already and was trying to force a reconciliation?"

"No. He didn't know. That was all Vernon's devious doings."

"Then why push Asa away? Why blame him?"

She stared at him with blank surprise. "He's trying to change me, Jonathan. Anyone can see that."

"No. You've changed yourself." When she started to protest, he took her hand in his again. Patted it. "You've discovered how to love again, how to open yourself up to be loved again. That's what's changed, Kai."

She shook her head. "You don't understand."

"I do." He laughed. "You don't think everyone in your department has noticed? I know I've noticed that you're not here at nine or ten o'clock every night working on one of these restoration jobs." He patted her again when she tried to respond. "No, no. I'm glad you're not. I've always told you I want well-rounded, well-adjusted team members. It tickled me to see you humming while you worked, excited to leave at five or six with everyone else because Asa was in town."

Kai's mouth fell open. Jonathan smiled again. "You're so like my Cindy. Remember how she hated Eddie when she first met him. It must have taken him six months to convince her she was really crazy about him."

"More like nine," Kai said.

"Probably," Jonathan said, chuckling. "And now my first grand-baby is on the way."

That got a smile out of Kai. "When did you hear?"

"Just yesterday. The baby's due in February."

"Oh, Jonathan. Congratulations. I'm happy for you, really I am." She sighed. "But I'm not Cindy. And the situation isn't the same at all. And I don't agree with you about my changing. I may not have been staying at the office as long as usual, but that's only because the team has done such a great job prepping for the Ridgeway design that I—"

"Believing that makes it easier, I know. But know this. You changed because you wanted to change. You were ready to change. Not because Asa made you change."

"You don't understand."

"I understand enough to say this. I don't know the entire story with the two of you. I just know that you've been happier in the last few weeks than I've ever seen you. And if Asa was the catalyst for it—"

Kai shook her head.

He ignored her and continued. "If Asa was the catalyst for it, then I'd say what you two have is worth fighting for." He stood up. "Which brings me back to the partnership. Don't get the idea that you've lost it. It's just on hold. The board wants to satisfy themselves that there is nothing to these allegations before making the final announcement."

Kai's groan made it clear she didn't believe a word he was saying.

"We had an emergency board meeting about this. And much more was made over Asa than you. It made me think that the person who brought your relationship to the attention of the board had it out for Asa Matthews, not for you. There were questions about why KT & G got the bid. The timing of it all."

"Timing?"

"When you and Asa started dating and when the bid decision was made."

"But, I didn't know him before—Oh no."

"What?"

"Kenneth. Kenneth Roselle. He saw us."

"Whoa. You lost me."

She gave him a run down of what happened at the Cheesecake Factory and how Kenneth had threatened her the next day.

Jonathan rubbed his chin thoughtfully.

"Kenneth told me it would be better for the both of us if we were engaged, then he threatened to make me regret our break up if I didn't go along with him." She glanced at Jonathan who looked as surprised as she had been. "I didn't take him seriously, Jon. I've always known he had a vindictive streak, but he's never done anything to hurt me."

Jonathan grunted. "I've heard a few things about him. But I didn't put much weight behind them. Apparently, we both misjudged him."

"Apparently. In any case, he accused me then and there of sleeping with Asa to win the bid. I was livid about it, and hung up on him. I just thought he was trying to force me back into a relationship with him. After that day, I put it out of my mind. Until after we won the bid, and Asa showed up in my office." She tried to suppress a smile but Jonathan saw it.

"Ah, the plot thickens."

"Well, let's just say, it was a little like Cindy's first encounters with her husband. Asa clearly knew who I was when he came into the office. And he thought we could pickup where we left off. I let him know in no uncertain terms that that wouldn't happen. And I accused him of picking our firm because he'd met me already."

Jonathan sat up straight at that news. "What did he say?"

"He was furious that I would insinuate such a thing. He told me that Ridgeway was his baby, he'd made his career on it. And he wasn't about to jeopardize it by picking a firm that couldn't do it justice, or didn't have enough talent and experience to do the job." She shrugged. "It made sense to me. He's very serious about his work, even if he doesn't come across that way initially. That was enough for me, and I let it go. But I made sure the team wouldn't disappoint him."

Jonathan stood up. "I think the people at the Coleman Foundation need to know about this. And I'm going to talk to the board as well. We're getting your partnership finalized as quickly as possible and I'm going to find out how close Alan Warren is to Kenneth Roselle."

"Alan?"

"He's the one that brought all this to the board's attention."

The day had begun overcast and cloudy, just like Asa felt. It was hard enough facing the fact that he had ruined his relationship with Kai, when he thought he would be strengthening it. But to learn that he had probably cost her the partnership she had worked years to attain as well …. Suffice it to say, he had come over to Sky's for breakfast—

had even been willing to have some wheat-free, gluten-free toast with soy butter and sugar-free jelly, so he didn't have to face being alone.

She had tried to cheer him up, even offering to watch one of his favorite 1970's kung-fu movies, which he had declined. At ten o'clock, he was still feeling sorry for himself. So much so he made a trip to the convenience store on the corner to buy a beer, which he had been nursing for the past fifteen minutes, while he wallowed in self-pity and waited for Sky to come down stairs to open up the shop.

"Boy, I know that's not beer you have down here in my shop."

Asa scowled at his sister. She was at the door of the shop, turning the open sign in the window.

"It's only ten o'clock Asa. What are you drinking for?" Schyler said, interrupting his thoughts.

"It's Saturday."

"Drink that upstairs or pour it out. There's a sink in the storage room." She returned to the counter. "I've got a business to run."

He had been upstairs wallowing in self-pity all morning and he wanted, no, he needed to be around people.

Kai wouldn't see him or talk to him. She had made it clear that she didn't want him in her life. At least not right now. She had told him she had some issues to deal with. But it was probably just her way of kicking him to the curb.

Asa leaned back against the wall. "I screwed this whole thing up with Kai. Damn it. It's my fault she lost the partnership, Sky. Because of me."

Hands on her hips, Schyler's gaze was scorching. "I thought you said they just postponed the announcement. Besides, I wanna know how you figure this is your fault? Y'all are grown, fully consenting adults. Neither of you is married, so it's not like either one of you is cheating on anybody."

"No. It was my fault. She called yesterday and left a message on my cell phone telling me that Kenneth Roselle told someone on the KT & G board about us. That I had picked them for the project because I was sleeping with Kai. If I had held off until she made partner...." He paused for a minute. "She begged me to leave her alone, Sky, until her partnership was secure. But I didn't do it. I kept on pushing and pushing."

"Okay, I got it," Sky said. "Since you think it was your fault, why not do something about it?"

"I did. I went to see Kai's boss and told him what was up with us."

"And?"

"He said he already had an investigation going. That he wasn't going to take a single person's word after Kai had been such a loyal employee for so long." He shrugged. "He says it should be cleared up in a day or two."

Schyler smiled then and patted his shoulder. "There. You see? You've done all you can. Her boss'll get things squared away. Besides, stuff happens, A. Eventually, Kenneth Roselle was going to screw her for breaking up with him. You just happened to be a convenient way to do it sooner, rather than later. Now I'm tired of looking at you moping around. Why don't you go home?"

CHAPTER NINETEEN

On Monday morning, in the KT & G parking garage, Kai dragged herself from her car and made her way to the elevators. Fifteen-hour days of work and dinners and association meetings, in addition to her regular duties on proposals and projects no longer gave her the joy it once did. She didn't go home and fall into a hard, but happily exhausted sleep, confident of herself and the direction of her career now that she knew things could be different. It had been a week since her break-up with Asa, three days since her partnership was put on hold, and she was working long hours, only to go home and fall asleep, fitful and miserable. She didn't know whether the hollowness that filled her waking hours was caused by her lack of sleep or whether it was because a lack of a life in general.

For the first time, Kai realized she had no life. Maybe a shell of one, but it was darn lonely. Empty and lonely. Work used to be adequate to fill the lonely spaces. Back in college, her studies acted as a balm for the hollows in her life and her heart. Friends weren't important, and since those she met didn't share her ambition, she didn't have many. Her grandmother had been her compass, helping her maintain balance and focus. Gran had been the one to remind her to make friends. To go to church. To eat. But when she died just before Kai entered graduate school, what little dimension there had been in her life disappeared completely.

The only break in her asceticism came in the form of Bobby Alders. But after that love affair had turned into a fiasco, she was even more determined than ever to push aside outside distractions. It was what her life had become.

But then came Asa. He had stopped calling a few days ago. Stopped begging for attention and recognition.

At first, she told herself she was grateful. Then, all she felt was pain. Until Asa had appeared in her life, dragging out all her demons, forcing her to look them in the eye, pushing her to overcome them, she thought she was content, but he had shown her another way. And perhaps Jonathan was right. Maybe Asa was the catalyst for her change, instead of the blame. After all, she hadn't done anything under duress. The changes had made her happy. They were scary, but she was happy nonetheless. And for the first time in eight years, her life had dimension again. She liked it. Loved it, in fact. And she loved Asa Matthews. He had shown her rainbows, when before all she ever saw was the rain. And no matter how much she tried to go back to the monochrome world she had so carefully crafted for herself, she would always remember the rainbows.

And she ached for him.

That afternoon, Kai had a few suspicions why she hadn't heard from Asa; the statue of Suzy Sunshine, which now sat in the corner of her office, had arrived that afternoon, to mock her. Arms stretched up with coat hanger wirehair flying, Suzy was in a state of bliss.

In the note that had come with it, Asa had asked that she not destroy it, but to return it to her father if she didn't want it. Kai's eyes wandered to the statue time and time again through out the day. There was no way she could destroy it. It symbolized too much. Her past, her dreams, her father ... her.

"Hey, boss lady."

Kai straightened her back and transferred her gaze to the doorway. "Judy."

"Well, don't sound so enthusiastic."

Kai gave a quiet sigh as Judy sat down on the couch in front of her. "Why don't you just go see your dad?"

Pain creased Kai's brow into a frown. Judy knew more about Kai's parents than she had ever told anyone, except Asa. She had always assumed her friend understood. Perhaps she didn't. After all, Judy had a perfect home life, with loving, supportive parents who loved her. "I can't Judy." She lifted her hands and shrugged helplessly. "I can't."

When Judy stood and closed the office door, Kai felt the tears prickle behind her eyelids. She willed them not to come, but Judy's caring touch on her back brought them to the surface, and they spilled down her cheeks. Judy rubbed her back. "It's okay. Things are going to turn out all right."

Kai's shoulders shook with emotion. "It hurts so bad," she whispered. "Why?"

"I know."

Kai sighed and reached for a tissue and tried to calm herself. "You told me once I could have it all."

Judy nodded and sat on the edge of Kai's desk. "Yeah, and you still can. Which is why I don't understand why you aren't fighting for your man."

"After the way I treated him? Besides, I thought making partner would be enough. I always did before. But ..."

"You realized there were other things just as important," Judy said simply.

"Something like that," Kai said as she twisted a tissue in her hand. Why did Judy seem to know so much more about life than she? She was so much younger, yet so much wiser. "Asa is important to me. My father is important to me." She had always known Vernon was a fascinating person—Gina, too—while at the same time she had felt embarrassed by them. It embarrassed her to tell other kids that her parents were artists, that they didn't live with her, only sent the occasional Christmas or birthday card as they globe-hopped from one exotic part of the world to the next. But despite it all, she was proud of them. They weren't like typical parents, the kind she'd yearned for much of her life, they were rebels. But they were still her parents, her flesh and blood.

Kai threw the tissue she held in the basket under her desk and sighed heavily. "You know. All those years with Kenneth, I never really thought about my life. Or maybe I just blocked it out. I just worked. There wasn't anything else, because I didn't think I needed more."

Taking Judy's silence for agreement, Kai continued. "It was too painful to think or hope for anything else."

"I get the feeling that there's a lot more to what happened to you in college than you're saying."

"Mmm. It's a family thing. God. You know I kicked Asa out of my life because he told me I was letting my past control my future." She looked up at Judy. "He even talked to my father about it."

Judy raised an eyebrow.

"I thought it was pretty presumptuous, and I told him so. But he said it wasn't just about family. It was about moving forward ... living for the future instead of the past. And ... and he was right." The statue in the corner drew her gaze. "Maybe I'll tell you about Suzy Sunshine someday," she said to Judy. "But, I need to talk to my father, first."

Kenneth whistled as he entered the Drexel Development building the next morning. He was later than usual. It was almost eight-thirty; but, hell, he deserved to take some extra time, given his grand success the previous week. He winked at the cute little temp who did the filing for the commercial division's office manager as he stepped into the elevator.

The plush elevator cab was crammed with people, but for once it didn't bother him. He was too high from the excitement over the past few days. It had been nearly a week since Alan had called him to let him know Kai's partnership had been snatched back. That had made him happy beyond belief. His company had just won a bid to do a themed commercial development, thanks to information Bill Jameson had funneled to him the previous month. What man wouldn't have a bounce in his step and a song in his heart? He was completely in control of his universe.

He stepped out onto the forty-seventh floor, still smiling. He might be a middle manager in a middle office today, but it wouldn't be long before his star rose higher. Why, just last week, Antonio Ramirez, the head of business development, complimented him on his most recent projects. And those had been done without Kai Ellis's help, thank you very much.

In his office, he dropped his briefcase on his desk. Too much energy flowed around him to get down to business right away. Instead of sitting, he walked to the corner of the room, retrieved a golf club and balls, and practiced his short game.

He was still putting and whistling fifteen minutes later when Barbara poked her head in.

"Yes, what is it?"

She bounced in, as was her way. A way Kenneth could greatly appreciate. So much to jiggle, so much to look at. Not that Barbara seemed to mind. She apparently liked the wolfish looks and small touches he gave her from time to time, though he hadn't yet laid her out on top of his desk.

At that thought, he straightened, took a good look at his secretary, who blushed and stammered before looking down at the floor. She was top heavy, startlingly so. In fact, he'd been so taken aback when she came in for an interview a year ago, he'd hired her on the spot, before she had even introduced herself. Hell, she could have been a project manager visiting from a partner company for all he'd known. But to his delight, she hadn't been. And now she was all his.

He was feeling better today than he had in months, maybe even years. Maybe Barbara would get lucky today. No, there was no maybe about it. She would get very lucky today. He pondered his morning schedule quickly. After lunch, he decided. He smiled slowly at her already imagining that fleshy plump bosom bared for his inspection. "Well?"

"Oh, umm. Oh yes. I forgot why I came in here. Mr. Ryan has scheduled a one o'clock meeting, in the conference room. Attendance is mandatory."

Kenneth gave Barbara another appreciative once-over before turning back to his putting, but Barbara giggled and he turned toward her again. She was smiling. No, actually she was grinning. He smiled back at her, took a step forward. Maybe he could clear his calendar for the morning and get started with Barbara sooner rather than later. "Wanna let me in on the joke?"

She giggled again. "No. I mean, I'm just happy that's all."

He raised an eyebrow, waited.

"Mr. Ryan said all the directors in commercial will be at the meeting today. You're the only manager they invited."

"Is that right?" Maybe Ramirez had put in a good word for him already. Well, well, well. Things were looking better and better. He walked to his desk, casually brushing against Barbara's ample breast as he went. He checked his calendar, wondering which of his morning meetings could be most easily cancelled.

Barbara ventured closer and he caught a whiff of her perfume. A breast brushed his forearm. Well, he decided. He wouldn't have to coax her to spread her legs, at least. "I think you're going to get a promotion," she whispered excitedly.

He turned to face her, touched her narrow waist, ventured around to trace her rear end. She didn't retreat, just smiled up at him. "You'd like that wouldn't you?"

"Only if you take me with you."

He chuckled. "Oh, I'll take you with me all right." He brushed his hand down her thigh, then back to her rear. "There's somewhere else I've been wanting to take you, too."

She stepped closer, and he gathered the skirt of her dress in both hands, raised it and pressed her hard against his erection. He leaned down to sniff the perfume behind her ear, then whispered, "Why don't you give Stanley Mercer a call, tell him I have to cancel the nine-thirty meeting." She nodded and stepped away, already reaching for the phone.

Kenneth unzipped his pants and sat down behind his desk. "Oh, and Barbara?" The gasp she made when she looked at him was arousing. A small tremor shook her hand as she held the receiver to her ear. Very arousing. Surprisingly innocent she was, which was even better.

"Yes?" she murmured.

Kenneth fondled himself absently as she stared, wide-eyed. "Lock the door before you undress."

Kenneth took an early lunch. From eleven to almost one, he had a Philly Cheese steak, fries, and Barbara. He found himself whistling again as he entered the building on his way to the conference room filled with his boss and all the commercial directors. At lunch, while he enjoyed Barbara's ample cleavage, he decided she was right about the promotion. Throughout their sexual acrobatics, he'd reviewed all the major projects he'd had a hand in over the past year, with and without Kai Ellis. And given Ramirez's backing, the meeting couldn't be about anything other than a promotion. So with a soaring heart and a satisfied dick, he waltzed into the conference room at one on the dot.

His steps faltered when he saw his boss, Phil Ryan, seated at the head of the table. The seven directors of the commercial development division stared silently at him as he stepped into the room. None were smiling. In fact, Phil looked stern. Angry, even. "Kenneth, there's a vacant chair here. Please sit down." He gestured at the chair to his left.

Hell, there were vacant chairs at the other end of the conference table, too—three of them. All were closer to where Kenneth was standing than the one next to Phil at the other end of the room. Suddenly, Kenneth knew the chairs close to the door would have been preferable. He walked toward Phil and had a sick feeling in the pit of his stomach that he was walking toward his doom.

"Joseph, close the door, please."

Joseph Callahan, a director in the commercial sales and marketing group rose to close the door. Kenneth didn't miss the look of disdain Joe aimed at him before he took his seat.

"All right gentleman, let's get started."

Kenneth watched and listened in horror as Phil recounted some of Kenneth's private conversations, some almost two years old. Most were people no one at the conference table should have had reason to believe he was even acquainted with. His dealings with Bill Jameson were revealed. His blackmail of Alan Warren at KT & G came up, too. His hands shook as he tried to look professional and calm. Cool, composed. Twice, his damp fingers dropped the expensive gold pen he'd brought in specifically to sign his new executive employment contract, so he finally set it aside.

He couldn't look at them. None of them. Anger boiled inside him. Rage made it hard to make out the lines on the notepad in front of him. As accusation after accusation was raised, he couldn't take it anymore and finally tuned out.

"… and Kai Ellis …"

Kenneth's oblivion came to a screeching halt. His attention snapped back to Phil. "What did you say?"

The sneer that moved slowly across his boss's face—a boss who had always shown him deference, kindness, and encouragement—was more than a little unnerving, but Kenneth breathed in deeply, slowly, and waited.

"When? Just now, or ten minutes ago, when you tuned out."

Kenneth turned helplessly to the other directors who all looked on without concern. Kenneth turned back to Phil. "Just now, sir."

"Ellis? Kai Ellis, is who I was speaking of. Your former fiancé."

Kenneth hung his head and groaned, indifferent to the fact that everyone at the conference table heard him.

The accusations against Kai barely registered, and Phil went on. But Kenneth heard loud and clear that he was no longer an employee at Drexel Development, that criminal charges would be brought against him if he didn't leave the premises with all his belongings immediately after the meeting.

Fifteen torturous minutes later, the meeting was over, and he was being escorted back to his office to box up his things. The little piece of ass he'd screwed over lunch was conveniently nowhere to be found. He wouldn't forget the slight and he'd make sure Barbara knew it. A building security guard marched him down to the lobby as promised, and to add insult to injury, Asa Matthews had planted himself just inside the revolving doors at the entrance.

The man gave him a smug nod as he was paraded through the doors and off the premises. Kenneth wouldn't forget about Matthews and his interference, either. It might take him a while to come up with a suitable revenge, but he would definitely come up with something.

"Your key card, Mr. Roselle," the fat-faced security guard said when he got to the curb.

Kenneth jerked it from his waist, then threw it in the man's face and marched away.

"Thank you, God." Jonathan cradled the phone and rolled away from his desk at two o'clock that afternoon. He took a long, deep breath and released the tension he'd carried since Friday. This morning after the board reviewed the report he and Philip Ryan had put together on Kenneth Roselle, they had voted immediately and unanimously to reinstate Kai's offer of partnership. The hours that had passed since the vote had been excruciating. But he'd finally been given the go-ahead to break the news to Kai.

CHAPTER TWENTY

Quiet and pensive, Kai observed her father from the in the doorway of his studio. He was totally oblivious to the world. A thin, well-worn T-shirt clung to his back as he sweated at his chore, and his thick black braid hung down his back. Soft, salt and pepper curls stuck to his temples as thin streams of perspiration trickled down his the sides of his face. His lips were pursed in determination as he tussled with the block of burled wood.

Over the past five years, Vernon had become known worldwide for his art. Though Kai had not followed his progress closely, she was aware of it. As she watched him work, memories of her childhood over came her. She acknowledged how much she truly loved him. She remembered sitting underneath his worktables when she was three or four. She used to catch chips of wood in a bowl and pretend they were snowflakes. When she had accumulated enough, she would dump the entire bowl over her head. But unlike typical parents, Vernon and Gina never chastised her for her actions. They would laugh with her and join in the pretense. She was their little snow princess.

Gina would spend a few indulgent hours picking wood chips and sawdust from her curls. Kai always did it for the attention, just to be next to them. Maybe that was the reason she had felt so angry and hurt by their abandonment for so many years. She had felt betrayed by people she had idolized. But remembering the snowflakes made her remember the love and the caring.

Her greeting came out as a whisper. "Daddy?"

The chisel stopped mid-stroke as Kai walked across the concrete floor. Her father looked up. Joy lit his face, even as tears welled in his eyes at her endearment. Shame enveloped her. It had been twenty-five years since she had last said the word "daddy."

Her father dropped his tools and grabbed her roughly around her waist, squeezing her into a tight bear hug. "Princess, princess." He released her to stare into her face. "Is it really you?"

Kai reached around him to grab a handful of wood chips. "It's really me," she said as she pulled her hair from its bun, a shake of her head sending strands of ebony tumbling about her shoulders.

Heavy thick hands, tussled her jet coils, making Kai smile. "It's really me, Daddy." She dumped the handful of wood chips onto her head. "See?"

Kai squealed in surprise as her father lifted her off her feet and twirled her around.

Half an hour later, she sat crossed-legged on the floor of her father's living room, brushing woodchips out of her hair. Kai's heart beat furiously in her chest. She had been so terribly afraid of stepping into the studio, but her father hadn't seemed angry, only surprised to see her. It was strange, as if he had been waiting for her all these years.

Kai sighed with relief as Vernon stepped back into the room with a tray of lemonade. She had always had a special bond with him. She hoped rebuilding her relationship with him wouldn't be a strain. He set the tray on the coffee table in front of her.

"Baby?" He handed her a glass and raised his own in a toast. "To us. To family.

Kai looked down, fingered the glass in her hand. She was reluctant to join in.

Her father took a seat. "Kai. I'm not going to make any excuses for your mother or me, but I want to explain." He breathed in deep, let it out. "I. We—"

"You abandoned me." Kai blurted out before he could continue. Her hand shook as she brought the lemonade to her lips and concentrated on drinking. It was the first time she had ever expressed that feeling to anyone. The hurt she had felt when they left her. The yearning and pain she felt every Christmas, every birthday. Especially birthdays. When she only got a present or a card in the mail, or nothing at all. Kai blinked her eyes hard, willing herself to maintain control. She wouldn't cry. She had cried enough as a child and definitely enough over the past few days. There couldn't possibly be any tears left.

"Your grandmother. We took you to see her all the time when you were a baby," he began. "At least twice a month, when we were on the east coast." A wistful smile lit his face. "She loved those visits. She always knew you were bright. Even at two, she thought you would be a genius. Or some kind of prodigy."

Kai listened quietly as she sipped her lemonade. Vernon needed to get his feelings out, and she needed to sort through hers.

"I always thought you'd be an artist." Vernon sighed heavily, and set his drink on the table. "We took you to see her the weekend of your fifth birthday. She hadn't seen you for about six months, and she was so excited."

Kai thought about Gran. Such a proper woman. The prim school-teacher must have been shocked to have raised an artist for a son. Kai knew her grandmother had loved her only son, but she had no patience for artists or the lifestyle they chose to live.

"She was appalled that you could only count to three."

Kai glanced up at her father in surprise.

"You couldn't tie your shoes. Couldn't really talk very clearly either." He looked at Kai, defiance in his eyes. "You may not have been able to count, tie your shoes, or say all of the alphabet," he said vehemently, "but by God, you could draw. You could paint, and you could build the most wonderful sculptures with your Lego's."

Kai finally spoke. "I'm sure Gran was more mortified by that than my speaking and counting skills."

Vernon chuckled. "We couldn't keep you in clothes. You hated wearing shoes and dresses. You used to tear them off as soon as Gina got them on. Your grandmother didn't think too much of us letting a little girl run around in only her bloomers."

He brushed a hand quickly over his face. "She threatened to take you from us … legally. She loved you, and she was old-fashioned. She thought you'd do better with her instead of us. If we hadn't let her raise you, she would have taken you away and never let us see you again."

Kai sat her lemonade on the table but said nothing as she tried to absorb what she was hearing.

"After Gina died …" Vernon shrugged. "What man—an artist, without a stable income-is going to be given custody of his baby girl?" His eyes were glassy now, filled with unshed tears. "Baby, I'm not trying to make excuses. In fact, your Gran was probably right. No. She was defi-nitely right. Your mother and I didn't have the sense or the money to take care of you at the time. We were young and foolish, and we had these crazy notions in our head about free love and spirituality. We felt it was the only kind of lifestyle we could lead to develop as artists. After a while, I thought it was best that you were with Mama. You were blossoming, you were learning. You learned like a sponge, soaking up knowledge. I was very proud of you."

Kai's face warmed, and she pursed her lips to keep them from quivering. A roaring started in her ears.

"Your grandmother did right by you," she heard her father saying as the roar got louder.

Kai broke down completely and let her head fall into her hands. Her body shook with her sobs as she struggled to drag air into her lungs. Gasping, she raised her head, and brushed back the hair that stuck to the wetness on her cheeks. "You ... you still abandoned me." Her eyes met her father's, and his tears mirrored hers. "You stopped coming to see me ... on my ... birthday." Sobs over took her, and she couldn't continue.

Her father understood her unspoken question. "The carnival was your Gran's idea. We had planned to spend your birthday with her, then we were all going to India for a year. She couldn't bear it. Couldn't believe we would take our child, her grandchild, to a third world country. She thought you would die of a disease or something."

And yet, Mama died instead. Kai took deep breaths, tried to calm down. It was a part of the story she hadn't heard.

"She wasn't going to let us leave the country with you," Vernon said. "She told us to make your birthday memorable, because we were going to India without you

"So we took you to the carnival. I can't tell you how many photos Gina took that day. You were happy. So happy, but you were only five. How can you tell a five-year-old that you have to leave her?"

"You stopped coming to see me." Kai couldn't look at him, so she picked up her lemonade again, studied the condensation on the outside of the glass. "You just sent presents or cards." She paused, her voice cracking. "Or nothing."

"Kai, you stopped wanting to see me by the time you were ten, and your grandmother didn't do much to discourage your behavior."

"Gran never said a word against you!"

"My mother's dead, Kai. Dead and buried nine years now." Vernon stood and turned toward the plate glass window that stretched from floor to ceiling. "We're here to start over." He turned and looked at her. "The universe has given us a second chance. We're not going to blow it now." He held a hand down to Kai, and she took it as he pulled her to her feet. "Kai, your mother and I made a lot of mistakes. Yes, we abandoned you. A ten-year-old doesn't know better than their parents, and I should have stuck it out regardless of what you were feeling about me at the time. I was supposed to be the adult, but I'm afraid I was the one acting more like a child."

Tears threatened to well in her eyes again as Kai allowed herself to be pulled into her father's arms. She was surprised at how warm and safe she felt.

"I love you, baby." He kissed her on the top of her head. "And I'm glad you're here. I'm glad you're willing to let me back into your life." He pulled her away from him and looked down at her. "Now I might try to rush things a little, trying to make up for lost time. Like I did when you were in college. But you just tell me to back off, alright? You let me in when you can. I'll accept that."

Kai gave her father a watery nod, and he pulled her back into his arms.

They stayed that way for a while. Crying. Feeling. Reconnecting.

In her office, Kai pressed her fingers into the small of her back and stretched. She had been bent over blueprints all day, but her mind was focused on Asa instead of her work, daydreaming about the time they'd spent down at Ridgeway. The fun they'd had. The wonder and pleasure on his face when they discovered the cemetery.

Was that when she'd fallen in love with him? When she realized she could enjoy something—someone—more than she enjoyed her work. onto her drafting table. She missed Asa. His laugh and his smile. His carefree attitude. His passion for his work. Most of all, she missed the pushy encouragement he never hesitated to offer. It was amazing, but his words finally seemed to have sunk in.

He had always told her she could have everything—a great career, a great romantic relationship, even a great relationship with her father— she hadn't believed him, hadn't given herself the chance to believe him. But she had taken a step toward reconciliation with her father—something she never, ever expected she'd be able to do. They had a long bumpy road ahead of them to fix all the broken threads that bound them as father and daughter, but Vernon had always been willing to try, and now so was Kai.

If she could have a proper relationship with her dad, then why couldn't she have a relationship with Asa and have her career as well? Why couldn't she, indeed, have her partnership and Asa, too?

She knew from Asa's own lips that her firm had gotten the partnership on merit, not because of his attraction to her. And she and Asa were consenting adults. There was no reason for their relationship to affect her opportunity for that partnership. And she intended to tell the board exactly that. If they had a problem with her explanation, she would quit and go to a firm that could appreciate her.

A swivel of her office chair brought Kai back around to her desk. Asa was rightfully hers as well, and she would fight for him. Given the way she'd treated him, she wouldn't blame him if he were angry.

Her growling stomach reminded her she'd missed lunch. A glance at her watch told her it was almost three. Clear in her purpose to win back her future, she opened the bottom desk drawer to grab her purse.

"Hrmph...." Kai glanced up to find Jon leaning against her office door with a big grin on his face.

"Jon. I didn't know you were there."

"Apparently not. You look pretty busy, and pretty happy. Mind if I come in?"

"No, no. Of course not. I was about to take a break anyway." She counted change into her hand. "I missed lunch again. I was heading down to the newsstand."

"That's what put that smile on your face?" He held up a hand. "Not that I'm complaining, mind you. I'm definitely glad to see you smiling again."

"Oh, I'm smiling all right. Because I've decided that Asa was right— oh, and so were you, of course—I deserve that partnership. I've worked way too hard to let Kenneth's lies and petty jealously take it all away from me." Jonathan's encouraging nod kept Kai talking. "I've also decided that I won't let it take Asa away from me either. I love him. Like I've never loved anyone else. And if I have to choose between him and this firm, then it's going to be him."

"Now wait just a minute." Jon wasn't so encouraging now.

"No, Jon. I've made up my mind. Asa has helped me learn to live in a way that I didn't believe I could. It's not enough to just have my work. I thought it was. I thought it was all I would ever need or want. But if Asa isn't in my life, I can't go back to things the way they were. I like watching the clock, waiting for five. Battling anxiously through rush-hour traffic to meet Asa for dinner. It's a hollow existence when all you have is work—believe me, I've finally learned that."

"Well," Jonathan said, with a crooked smile.

Kai wasn't sure what to make of Jon's reaction. Heck, she was a bit surprised by it herself. "I won't go back, Jon. I'm serious about this."

"That's definitely clear. I just want to be sure I've got this right. You're willing to give up the chance at partner if it means choosing between the firm and Asa."

Kai nodded.

"And what if you aren't asked to choose?"

"What do you mean?"

"What if Asa isn't in the picture? What if you meet someone else?—Hypothetically speaking."

"Jon, I'm willing to fight to win my partnership back if that's what you're asking me. And I'm going to fight to win Asa back, too. But I'll give the partnership up for him if the board has a problem with our relationship. I'm a great architect. I can do anything I set my mind to. If I can't work for KT & G, I'll work elsewhere. I—"

"Got it. Got it," Jon said, cutting her off. "But just so you know, you don't have to fight for your job. You've got the partnership back, kiddo."

Kai's head jerked up. "But … but …"

"Don't ask questions, Kai. Just say thank you."

"Um … thank you. I think." She sat back. Blew out a breath.

Jonathan jumped up, surprising her. "I'm not going to go into all the details, my dear. But suffice it to say, it didn't take much of an investigation to satisfy the board that you're the kind of person we want at KT & G. And I wasn't willing to lose you over a love affair, even if I had to resign myself. You've earned this. By the way, Asa came to see me. He did his part as well. There was a lot going on with Kenneth Roselle. More than any of us knew."

He walked to the door. "Take the day off, kid. And go make things right with Asa."

That was the plan, Kai thought to herself as Jon closed her office door. If Asa cooperated, that is.

On Monday night at nine o'clock, The Tara Ballroom at the Georgian Terrace Hotel was filled. Jonathan Rojeski addressed the crowd. "And it is with great pride I present to you Ms. Kai Ellis, the newest partner at Kapman, Trent, and Gannon." He led the audience in applause as Kai rose from her seat.

Her father squeezed her hand in support before she made her way up to the dais. When she reached the front, Jonathan began describing Kai's many accomplishments over the past six years. She blushed in embarrassment, sure that everyone could see. She was deliriously happy. Yet at the same time, she was incredibly sad. Her hair was flowing in charcoal rivulets down her back for the first time. She had never had the guts to wear her hair down in a professional setting until Asa had given her the courage. Yet, Asa wasn't there. At the most important moment of her life, one of the most important people in her life wasn't there to share in her joy.

She had tried for three days to contact him, then vaguely wondered whether he was deliberately snubbing her. Then she ran into Dr. Dunlop who was in the studio earlier in the day consulting with one of the decorative artists on her team. According to Richard, Asa had taken off for a few days to clear his head and had refused to give anyone contact information—including his sister.

As Jonathan continued his introduction, Kai focused on her father's face in the audience. His hair was pulled back into its typical thick braid, but several strands rebelled to curl at his temples. Kai smiled, wondering if that was how Asa saw her. Seeing her father this way, in an elegant tuxedo and white shirt seemed, so incongruent with the wild and thick hair adorning his head. For once, she could understand Asa's fascination with her hair. Her father's curls made her want to see his hair tumbling over his shoulders, just to glimpse the contrast against his black tuxedo.

This was the moment she had waited for forever. The moment she thought would be the happiest of her life, and yet it wasn't. Kai marveled at the changes that had occurred in her over past few months. Kenneth wasn't beside her as she had always expected him to be, her father was instead. Three months ago, she would have sworn a relationship with her father would never be possible, yet here they were. And not only that, but she had proudly introduced him to her friends and colleagues as they mingled before dinner. It was the first time she had ever been proud to be his daughter, and it made her feel wonderful.

And who would have ever expected her to fall in love, and not just any old love, passionately in love. She hadn't thought herself capable of it. Yet, Asa had made her see that it was possible; had insisted on it.

Well, she might have struck out with Asa this time, but no way was she giving up. He was worth fighting for, and she was going to make sure he knew it.

Vernon hadn't given up on her. He'd fought all these years hoping she would finally come around, and his perseverance won in the end. Kai intended to do the same with Asa.

Kai was startled from her reverie by the sound of clapping. "Ms. Kai Ellis," Jonathan was saying. She painted a stiff smile on her face and took the podium.

"Thanks, Jon." Kai looked out at the audience, and a genuine smile lit her face as she saw her father sitting up proudly, anxious to hear what 'his baby' was going to say. "Well, first of all, I want to do something I haven't done in a long time." She cleared her throat. "I want to thank my father, V.L. Arrington." As the crowd applauded, she motioned for him to stand. Her eyes misted a little as she began to speak. "This has been a long road for me to get to this point. And he's a big reason that I made it, though he probably doesn't believe it. He is really special to me, and tonight is even more special because my father is here with me."

After the clapping subsided, Kai continued, giving Jon Rojeski and her team accolades. But the longer it went on, the more anxious she was to leave. The more anxious she was to find Asa.

It was eleven o'clock and the Aromia Natural Body Spa was quiet. Schyler had spent the evening completing her biannual inventory and was shutting down for the night, when Asa came through the door and set the miniature version of Suzy Sunshine that V.L. had given him on the counter. He had taken the study model to the north Georgia mountains with him a couple of days ago, thinking it would make him feel closer to Kai, only it had made him more miserable and lonely than ever.

"When did you get back into town?" his sister asked as she shut down the register and turned off the lights from a panel under the counter. "I hope you're feeling better." Her voice was slightly muffled as she spoke from under the counter.

"I could be better," Asa admitted. "Here." He gestured toward the mini statue as Schyler's head popped back above the counter and she stood up.

Giving him a quizzical look, she turned the statue to face her, then looked up at him. "V.L. gave this to you. Don't you think he'd be offended if he saw it for sale in the shop?"

"I didn't say sell it," Asa groused. "I just need you to keep it for me. I can't stand looking at it."

Sky shoved it back in his direction. "Asa. Take the statue and go home."

He pushed it back. "Please, Sky."

She thrust her hands on her hips and glared up at him. "No. Take it home. You and Kai will work this thing out, if you'll stop being so stubborn. She called Richard looking for you, you know."

Asa's gaze switched quickly from the statue to his sister. "She did not."

"She did. He told me himself. Now, you see. She wants to sort things out. So give her a call."

"She doesn't want to sort things out. She probably just wanted to tell me she got that partnership."

"She did! Oh, A, that's wonderful! How did you find out?"

"The partnership dinner was tonight. I was supposed to go with her, remember? I snuck in and watched the presentations from the back." He turned and roamed the aisle in front of the counter. "V.L. was there. She thanked him. Said she was proud of him. Proud of the fact that he helped make her into the person she is today. She thanked her team, too. Praised them for all the hard work they'd put in, all their support and championing of her, and blah, blah, blah."

"And you ..." Schyler said.

Pain lanced through Asa. He had been stunned as he listened to Kai give her emotional speech to the KT & G crowd, even a little angry. But the pain hadn't started until he left the banquet hall and drove home. The miniature statue was on the glass pier table in the foyer of his apartment, the very first thing he saw when he walked in. That's when he knew it was time to give it up.

"My name didn't come up," Asa told his sister. "She always said her job came first. I guess I didn't believe she really meant it until tonight."

Schyler came around the counter and put her arms around her baby brother. Her head barely reached his chest, but Asa let his shoulders sag and his heart sank as she enveloped him. He leaned on her for support and rested his head on her shoulder, just as he had when he was a kid. But this was more than just a skinned knee. This was real pain he was feeling. They stood there for five minutes before Asa took a deep breath and straightened up. He gave Schyler a helpless shrug.

"How about a massage, baby brother?"

"Body massages don't fix everything."

"Maybe not, but at least you'll be relaxed."

"Fine, Schyler. If it'll make you happy. But just take the statue." He glanced back as he headed to the massage room. "Unless it morphs into Kai, I don't want to see it again."

Schyler watched with sadness as her brother shut the massage room door. She felt strongly that he and Kai should be together, but what could she do? Tempted to jump in and fix things herself, she found herself dialing Kai's office number several times over the past few days. But she had always caught herself, in time. Asa would never forgive her if she interfered. Still, it was hard to see him so heartbroken. With a heavy heart she walked to the front of the shop and knelt at the door to turn the bottom latch.

The knock that rattled the glass rattled her nerves even more, and Schyler clutched her chest. When she realized who stood on the other side of the door, she fumbled to unlock it.

"Kai!"

"Schyler, please, can I come it?" Kai asked breathlessly.

"What did you do, run over here?" She pushed the door open.

Kai caught herself smiling. "Just about. Is he here?" she asked haltingly. "I called his apartment. When he didn't answer, I took a chance he was at your place." The strange look on Schyler's face gave her pause. Maybe this was a mistake.

But, she shook off her doubts. If she was going to fight for her man, she couldn't let anyone's disapproval stop her, but she had to blink hard at the prickle that started behind her eyes. "I'm sorry, Sky, apparently I'm intruding, and I know Asa probably doesn't want to see me, but ... I have to see him. I love him." Courage filled her chest and gave her strength. "I ... I have to tell him how I feel."

"No." Schyler said. "I mean, wait. He's in the massage room. I was just going to give him a full-body." Schyler locked the door, then moved to the counter. "He's in massage room three. Here." Dumbfounded, Kai stared at the miniature version of Suzy Sunshine.

"Your dad gave it to him when you guys broke up."

"But ..."

"Look, he just brought it in to give to me. I guess he got tired of staring at it wishing it was you. Now I'm going upstairs. Tell Asa to make sure he locks the door when you guys leave."

The statue that she had once disdained, now meant so much. Kai gripped it tightly and walked confidently to the massage room. She entered and closed the door behind her. For a moment, she simply stood where she was and admired the image before her. Asa lay naked on the massage table, with only a towel covering him from waist to thigh. His head was turned away from the door, and long dreadlocks fell across his back. Without saying anything, she sat the statue on the table in front of him and lifted Asa's hair, moving the heavy mass aside so that it hung over the table. She reached over him for the bottle of oil on the side table and poured some into her hands.

With a deep breath, she closed her eyes, and placed her hands on the muscular brown back before her. She shuddered at Asa's moan when she began kneading away the tension in his shoulders.

"Mmm. That's great, Sky. Just what I needed."

Kai didn't respond, but couldn't help wondering at the irony of the situation as she remembered when their positions were reversed.

Nimble fingers moved down his back, and Asa grunted his appreciation. Kai felt him tense and glanced up from her ministrations. He had turned his head and was staring at the miniature of Suzy Sunshine. She wasn't sure what to do, so she continued the massage. Asa didn't look up, but seemed to freeze for a full minute.

Then he grasped the edge of the towel and turned. Clutching the towel to cover himself, Asa sat up. And it wasn't adoration on his face when he looked at her.

Kai's stomach did a hard roll, but her determination didn't falter. "I was hoping to talk to you," she began.

Asa scooted a polite distance away from her. "So talk."

"I ..." This was a little harder than she expected it to be. She had expected to have to deal with resistance from Asa's relatives and friends, but Asa was a different matter. What if he no longer loved her as he'd proclaimed. She glanced around, casting for a way to say what she needed to, and her eyes fell to the miniature of Suzy, her arms up-stretched, reaching toward the sky, embracing life. Telling Kai to reach for it, too.

She blew out a breath, then said, "I love you, Asa. And I came to apologize to you for how I've treated you. You mean more than anything else in the world to me, and ... I want ... I mean, I was hoping we could start over."

Emotionless eyes studied her, roaming from the hair that cascaded over her shoulders, down past the elegant turquoise evening gown to her matching pumps, then back to her face. "Guess that's easy to say now that you've got your partnership back."

Kai's mouth dropped open. "My ... how could you—"

"You told me enough times a relationship wasn't going to get in your way," Asa said, cutting her off. "Thanks for the offer, baby, but no thanks. I don't do well playing second-fiddle. Especially not to a job."

Kai had to step back as Asa slid off the table and picked up his clothes from the table in the corner. Without another word, or even a look back at her, he stepped into the tiny changing room to get dressed.

Kai's hand flew to her mouth and barely muffled the sob that she couldn't hold back. He didn't want her. She was too late. Tears slid down her face as she slumped against the massage table. Kai had finally discovered what truly mattered in her life, had finally opened her eyes, and her heart. And it was too late.

Trying to calm down, she grabbed a towel from the stack on the shelf above the corner table and patted her face. "You said you wouldn't give up," she muttered to herself into the towel. "You said you'd do anything. You told Jonathan you wouldn't choose the firm over Asa. You said ..." Her voice trailed off. There was only one thing that could win Asa back, if he wanted her the slightest bit.

With renewed determination, she knocked on the bathroom door. "Asa." There was no answer. She cleared her throat and knocked again. "Asa."

"Leave, Kai, and take that statue with—"

"I'll quit, Asa," she broke in, speaking loudly to drown out the last of his sentence. "If you want me to, I'll quit the firm. I'll give up the partnership. It doesn't matter to me if I don't have ..." A sob broke her voice as the changing room door creaked open. "You mean everything to me, Asa. Everything. I—"

The rest of her words were cut off when Asa stepped forward, pulling her into his grasp. "Shhh," he whispered as he stroked her hair. "You looked beautiful tonight." She started to lift her head to question him, but Asa's stroking hand kept her from it. "I watched you from the back of the ballroom."

"I wanted you there."

"And I was, baby. I was." He stood her away from him and looked into her eyes. "I was so proud of you. There's no way in this world I'm going to let you give up that partnership. It means too much to you."

Tears swam in her eyes, making Asa no more than a blur in front of her. "No. I told Jon. I told him I would quit. It doesn't mean anything if I don't have you."

Asa's lips brushed hers. "You've got me, baby. You've got me," he whispered.

ABOUT THE AUTHOR

Pursuit of graduate degrees in architecture and engineering provided **Elaine Sims** the opportunity to work on an archaeological excavation in Hallas, Greece and was the inspiration for *Unearthing Passions*. She worked in the field of commercial architecture for eight years before putting it aside to pursue a second career in computer programming. Now she's working on her third career as a novelist.

Elaine lives in Atlanta, Georgia with her husband and daughter.

She loves to hear from readers and can be contacted via email at elainewrites@elainesims.com.

Please visit her website http://www.elainesims.com.

AUTHOR'S NOTE

Researching slave plantations was enlightening, exciting, and heart-wrenching all at the same time. The features and characteristics of the fictitious Ridgeway Plantation mentioned in this novel are based on facts about real slave plantations in the Deep South. Although I used several sources of information, my primary texts are listed below. If you would like to know more, you can find them in your local library or order them online.

Uncommon Ground: Archaeology and Early African America, 1650-1800 by Leland Ferguson. ISBN: 1-56098-059-1

Back of the Big House: The Architecture of Plantation Slavery by John Michael Vlach. ISBN: 0-8078-4412-8

Rice Gold: James Hamilton Couper and Plantation Life on the Georgia Coast by James Bagwell. ISBN: 0-86554-651-7

By the Work of Their Hands: Studies in Afro-American Folklife by John Michael Vlach. ISBN: 9-70813-91366-7

The Afro-American Tradition in Decorative Arts by John Michael Vlach. ISBN: 0-8203-1233-9

Excerpt from

SIN AND SURRENDER

BY

J.M. JEFFRIES

Release Date: April 2006

CHAPTER ONE

"Bless me, Father, for I have sinned." Isabel Robinson wrapped the wooden rosary beads around her palm so tightly the hand-carved rosewood balls cut into her skin. The confessional was small and stifling and she felt as though the weight of the whole church pressed down on her. A sob started in the back of her throat. "It's been a month since my last confession."

"Tell me, child," the priest invited in a world-weary voice, as though nothing he heard in the confessional would ever shock him. "What have you done?"

Father Munoz had been her parish priest since she'd moved to West L.A. His softly-accented voice usually gave her comfort and strength, but not today. Her transgression against God weighed heavily on her soul.

After almost two weeks of daily Mass, she'd finally found the nerve to confess her sin. Isabel crushed the rosary beads in her fist as tears trickled down her cheeks. "Forgive me." She choked back a sob. "I killed a fifteen-year-old boy. His name was Jamal Atkins."

Isabel unfastened her seat belt as her partner, Mike Scanlon, parked the car at the crime scene. The house was seedy-looking with paint peeling from the clapboards and windows so dirty it was impossible to see inside. Set back from the street, the house had once been painted a bright California pink but was now faded to a washed-out gray, like all the other little houses on the tired-looking street.

Isabel swallowed nervously, thinking about what waited for her inside. You're a cop. You can do this. She took a deep breath, steeling herself for the inevitable. Seeing all the uniformed officers hustling around the dingy front yard caused anxiety to knot in her stomach.

"You want this one, Isabel?" Mike queried as he opened his car door. He was big man, with hair going gray and dark brown eyes that had seen everything life could throw at him. He'd been a cop for almost twenty years, Isabel only ten. They'd been partners for four years.

"Are you sure?" Isabel stepped out of the car into the rabid Los Angeles heat. August in L.A. was like a roaring furnace in hell. Heat radiated from the concrete in undulating waves that swirled around her and made her clutch her purse nervously. The sidewalk under her feet had buckled and a tree root peeked out between the broken slabs. Sweat popped out on her skin.

Mike had offered her the lead on the homicide. If she didn't take it, would she look ineffective? If she did, could she handle the case? Maybe she should have taken an extra month off. Her mother had urged her to, but Isabel had been anxious to get back on the job. Anxious to prove she could still do it.

"A couple bounty hunters," Mike said, frowning at the term bounty hunters, "on a fugitive re-take did the shooting. I don't see anything complicated about this." The grimace on his face told her how he felt about bounty hunters. As they approached the sagging front porch, he removed his sunglasses and tucked them into the pocket of his summer weight sports coat. Isabel wished he'd take the jacket off, but he wouldn't, no matter how hot. Mike believed in looking professional no matter what the weather. He smiled at her. "A good way to slide back into the job." He walked toward the open front door of the house.

Normally she would have checked the scene first, trying to get the feel of the place, but this time she kept close to Mike. Until she was more at ease, more confident that she could do her job, he was her lifeline, even though she desperately tried not to cling to him. "In and out, no sweat. All we have to do is file the paperwork. I'm good for that." She forced her voice to remain light, even though the bounty hunters really made for more of a mess. Most cops didn't like them, especially when they were involved in shootings.

"Works for me." Before entering the house, Mike stopped and faced her. Concern reflected in his dark eyes as he leaned closer. "You gonna be all right?"

The afternoon sun beat off his head. August was turning into a scorcher due to a high pressure area that had stalled just off the coast and wasn't moving. "I'm okay. Really." She didn't feel okay, but she could fake it. "Sure, I'll take lead." She told herself she could do it, yet a little spiral of fear threaded itself through her.

A uniformed officer she knew walked over to her and extended his hand. "Good to see back you on the job, Robinson."

She shook his hand, grateful for the sympathetic look in his eyes. The jury was still out as to whether she was glad to be on back on the streets. "Thanks, Nelson. What do we have?" He flipped open a notebook. "Leroy Swain. White male. Age 31. Shot once in the chest. He's dead."

"The shooter?"

He pointed toward the driveway. "Over there."

Isabel followed the direction of Nelson's finger and saw a man leaning against the trunk of black and white squad car parked on the driveway. Even with his back to her, she could see he was a brother. A shaft of sunlight bounced off his close-cropped brown hair and wide shoulders. Seeing that he was dressed in a black kevlar vest over a black t-shirt and faded black jeans, Isabel had to smile. Only an out-of-towner would wear black in Los Angeles in August.

Mesmerized by the strong set of his shoulders, an exotic awareness ran through her. Squashing it down, she dragged her gaze away from him and saw a woman sitting in the back seat of the squad car. The guy's partner?

A uniformed officer stood nearby, watching the pair. She would have plenty of time to question them later. Right now, she wanted to check the scene and talk to the coroner.

Jordan Chandler smelled Opium. The musky, sensuous scent washed over him and sent his pulses thudding. Even with the blanket of L.A. smog and rotting garbage piled in the street, he could always identify the scent of Opium. He took a deep breath, savoring it.

He slid away from the fender of the squad car and turned around. Shading his eyes, he saw an African-American woman talking to a uniformed officer. Five feet, eight inches of woman could do that to a man, especially if she wore Opium. Opium did it to him every time.

His eyes narrowed, wondering who the temptress was and why she was here.

She tucked a strand of shoulder-length, raven hair behind her ear, then put her hands on her hips, pushing back the lapels of her light-weight grey silk blazer. Something gleamed against the waistband of the matching trousers. A gold and silver shield. She was a cop. A detective. One of L.A.'s finest. If he'd known she'd be the investigating officer, he'd have shot Swain himself for a chance to get in her handcuffs.

He took deep breath, but the Kevlar vest he wore restricted his chest. He wanted out. He hated wearing the vest, but it was a tool of his trade. Sweat trickled down the sides of his chest and he felt an itch starting along the neck of his t-shirt.

Detective Sexy took off her jacket and slung it over her arm. Lush breasts filled out her white, sleeveless turtleneck. This goddess was loaded for bear. Why was a woman who looked like she could be a Victoria's Secret model working as a cop?

On her hip, a nine millimeter Beretta was secured in a holster. She carried some pretty serious firepower. He liked a woman who could handle trouble.

His gaze wandered to her face. She was handsome rather than pretty with large eyes, beautifully-sculpted cheekbones and a wide, sensual mouth. She wore no makeup on her honey colored skin. She didn't need to. She was perfect without it.

Jordan was used to the perfectly-groomed Cinderellas of New Orleans. But this gold-skinned goddess snared all his attention. She looked sultry, passionate, and she wore Opium. That's all he needed to know.

She spoke to a uniformed officer and he nodded, then grinned. She pulled a pair of latex gloves from her back pocket. Her movements were slow and deliberate as she slipped the gloves over long slender fingers. For a split second, Jordan fantasized about her hand son him. Jordan Chandler, you are a dog.

The lady detective walked into the house, her round, tight butt swinging. With shoulders straight and her head held high she acted as though she owned the whole street. She had a bad girl walk that was like nobody's business. He watched her until she disappeared into the house. Then disappointment settled over him.

Jordan glanced through the car's back seat window at his partner, Sula De Leal. Her long brown fingers rotated in tiny circles on the side of her head. Poor kid had another migraine. Jordan sympathized. The dry heat sucked all the moisture out of his skin, making him feel as if he were turning into a prune.

How could people live like this? Everything was brown. He glanced down the dirty street at the trees coated in heavy summer dust, at the brown and parched grass. In the distance a spiral of smoke reached for the sky. Another fire had started somewhere and with the sight of the smoke came the distant wail of sirens.

Jordan couldn't wait to get back to New Orleans, his hometown. He hungered for the lush greenness, the heavy humidity, and his cool house with its wide veranda and fragrant magnolia shading the yard.

He drummed his fingers on the car trunk. This was taking too long. He and Sula should have been on their way by now. The shoot was legit. What the hell was the hold up?

Sula's head lolled back against the seat. He should have left her in New Orleans. But she had pleaded and begged in that pretty manner she used when she wanted her own way. He'd caved in and brought her along, despite the fact that she just didn't have enough experience for a hard case like Leroy Swain or Race Parnell. All she'd gotten for her trouble was a dead body on her slate and a killer headache.

He hoped Sula would be okay. He'd tried to prepare her for this kind of situation, but he hadn't thought it would come this soon.

Tension vibrated through him and he rubbed the back of his neck. This day wasn't working as he'd planned. He and Sula should have been on a plane to New Orleans with Race Parnell either in custody or dead.

Jordan would have preferred dead. Then his sister Darcy would have been avenged and Jordan's conscience might be a little lighter. However, Darcy's murderer had once again escaped. Jordan chaffed to get back on the road, track Parnell down, and return him to Louisiana where he would stand trial.

Before Jordan got too deep into his reflective thoughts, Detective Sexy came out on the porch, spoke to the uniformed officer at the door and then headed over to him, descending the sagging stairs with her come-hither sway, and legs so long Jordan found himself fantasizing all over again.

Watching her strut across the dying grass, he nearly forgot his name. How was he supposed to defend himself against a walk like that?

He jumped off the car and extended his hand. "Hi. I'm Jordan Chandler."

She ignored his gesture. "Are you the shooter or the partner?" Her voice was seductive and sultry, like a hot summer breeze off the bayou. But her eyes held a dangerous glint as she looked him up and down.

An arctic breeze blew down his boxers. If she cut him off any higher, his hopes for continuing the Chandler dynasty would be shot to hell. "I'm the partner." Though this babe was all business, he nonetheless found himself focusing on her scent. The Opium swirled around him, setting his libido on fire.

When the woman narrowed a tantalizing set of raven black eyes, he couldn't help smiling.

Sula struggled out of the car, straightening to look at the lady detective. "I shot him." Straight up, Sula was a tiny woman with short brown hair and compact, athletic build. She looked frail but had the endurance of an Olympic athlete.

Detective Sexy turned to Sula. "Would you step over here, please?"

The two women walked out of earshot. Although Jordan strained to keep his eyes on Sula, Detective Sexy blocked his view. He settled for studying the detective's slender figure and flaring hips. After a few minutes, Detective Sexy called another cop over. Jordan watched the uniformed officer escort Sula to a squad car waiting at the curb.

He pushed away from the car, frowning. Wait a minute. What the hell is going on? He and Sula had done everything by the book, so why were they being treated like back alley thugs? He stomped over to the sexy woman detective. "Detective, I didn't catch your name."

She turned and gazed up at him, her dark eyes cool and distant. "Detective Robinson."

"Is something wrong with the shoot?" He couldn't imagine what could be off about the shooting that required Sula getting a police escort to wherever she was being escorted to.

Robinson raised one neatly formed eyebrow, but said nothing. Sula glanced back at him, a sheen of sweat on her mahogany skin. Third time on a job and she pops Swain. Tension kinked his shoulders. "Detective, this was a clean shoot."

She tilted her head at him. "Clean or not, I want you downtown to answer a few more questions."

"Wait a minute." He held up his hand. "We're licensed bail enforcement agents."

She lifted her chin and stared at him. "I don't care who or what you are. I don't care why you're in my town. What I care about is figuring out why there is a dead body in this house and what the hell went down. This is my show. We play my way, my rules."

Jordan swallowed his irritation. He didn't have time for this crap. He didn't care a hoot about Leroy Swain because Race Parnell was still on the street and getting further and further away.

Detective Sexy had just earned a spot on his hit list. He didn't care if she was the sweetest piece of woman he'd seen in a long time, she'd just taken over position number seven on his top ten hit parade—right below the vicious wife abuser he'd just nabbed in Tampa and right above a Dutch arms dealer he planned to track down once Parnell was behind bars. "Happy to cooperate, Detective."

A glimmer flashed in her eyes but quickly faded. Jordan smiled. He knew heat when he saw it. Detective Sexy was feeling some chemistry.

"Thank you, Mr. Chandler."

"Jordan." He uncorked all the Southern charm his mama had begun teaching him when he was still in diapers. He refused to let this cop get the better of him.

"Thank you, Mr. Chandler." Robinson pulled out a small spiral-bound notebook and jotted down a few sentences.

Jordan noticed her handwriting. Each letter was perfectly formed in the Palmer method. Instantly he pegged her as a Catholic school grad. He remembered something his Baptist granddaddy had said about his parents' decision to send Jordan to a Catholic boys' school. "The boy is only going to learn three things from those Jesuits. Guilt, obligation and good penmanship." Jordan still had good penmanship. One out of three wasn't bad.

"Officer Nelson," Detective Robinson said, "please take Mr. Chandler to the station with his friend, but in separate cars."

"Wait a second, Detective Robinson," Jordan objected. He could get to the station under his control.

"Mr. Chandler, play nice, or else I'll arrest you." She smiled innocently while her fingers gently caressed the handcuffs hanging from her belt. "The choice is yours."

Jordan knew he should just play along, but he couldn't. "I have papers from the State of Louisiana giving me the authority to return Race Parnell for trial."

She held up a finger. "One more word, Mr. Chandler, and you're in handcuffs. Either way is fine with me. Understand?"

"No problem." Though he said it quietly, Jordan raged inside. He'd hunted bail jumpers from New York City to Bogota, and he'd never had a cop question any of his methods. While this cop was making him dance, Parnell would be out of the country before Jordan could pick up his tracks again.

I failed you, Darcy. Again. Forcing himself to remain calm, he held up his hands. "Take me, Detective, I'm yours."

She tucked her silver pen into a pocket. "Thank you for all your cooperation." She turned and left.

Detective Robinson might look like a woman built for a good time, but she had a rock inside her chest where her heart should be.

Jordan asked to see Sula before she left and the cop, Nelson, took him over to check on her. "How you hanging, kid?"

Sula closed her eyes and rubbed her temple harder. Her face had developed a gray under cast which told Jordan her headache was increasing.

"Why," she whispered, "are you treating this like a joke? I shot a man."

Jordan took her hand and squeezed. "You killed scum. Swain's hands are as dirty as Parnell's. Don't waste any feelings on him. The guy isn't worth it."

She clutched his fingers. "Sometimes you scare me."

Sula was a good kid. Someday she'd be a great bounty hunter. He was sorry his quest for revenge had led her to kill, but he couldn't dredge up any emotion for the recently deceased. "I won't let anything happen to you, baby girl."

"You said we would be square with the cops." Sula ran a hand over her hair.

"If she wants to give us a hard time, we'll let her. When the paperwork is done, it's going to come off as self-defense. Right now, she's gotta look good in front of the fellas." He reached out and massaged her shoulder. "You did the right thing, Sula. Parnell had a gun. Swain just got in the way. Nobody could have predicted what happened. You did your job."

Sula tried to smile. "Thanks, Jordan." A second later, another cop came and got in the car and started the motor.

Jordan closed the door and Sula sighed. As the squad car drove away, he tried corral the feeling of dread in the center of his chest.

His knee started to throb, but he resisted rubbing it, not wanting Detective Sexy to any weakness. He needed to be tough for Sula and keep his cool in front of the hard-as-nails, built-for-sin cop.

As the squad car disappeared, turning down a side street, Jordan wondered how he was going to explain to Sula's daddy that he had just dropped his daughter into a world of trouble. Jordan would be lucky if Moses De Leal didn't nail his hide to the wall of his den and feed his intestines to Big Mama, his pet alligator.

"Mr. Chandler, would you come with me?" Nelson asked.

California cops were so polite. Until running into Robinson, he'd loved L.A. It had been a long time since he'd been called into an interrogation, and the prospect didn't thrill him.

As Mike drove back to the station house threading his way through the dense L.A. traffic, Isabel worked on her notes. She had a command performance at her parents' house later, and didn't want to be late. As far as her mom was concerned, murder was no excuse for tardiness. The same rule had applied to her dad when he'd walked a beat and after he made detective.

No one in the family had the stones to get on her mom's bad side. Besides, by keeping her mind on her notes, she wouldn't have to think about Jordan Chandler, who in the course of an hour, had burrowed his way under her skin. She couldn't afford to be distracted. If she didn't get back up to form soon, she would have to quit the force. She didn't know what else she could do. Being a cop was all she knew.

"Hey, Pristine?" Mike pulled up to a stop sign.

She hated that nickname. Why was it that just because she made sure her job was done right, the guys in the squad room had to give her a hard time? "You only call me Pristine when you have a problem." She faced him. "You have a problem?"

He grimaced. "Not exactly."

Another one of Mike's lectures was coming up. She smiled. They'd been partners since she'd transferred to robbery-homicide. Sometimes he knew her thoughts before she did. "Yes?"

"Don't you think you gave the bounty hunters a hard time?"

"You mean more than usual?"

"This is your first day back."

"Mike, this is my case. I'm doing my job." She knew if she didn't work harder at it than before, the doubts would surface and she'd be paralyzed.

"The shoot looked by the numbers to me."

"This case is hinky. It doesn't feel right." She hated loose ends and this one had too many. She frowned as she glanced through her notes. "I hate hinky. I want everything nice and tidy before I sign off."

"This Chandler guy bothering you?"

"I don't like suspects treating my investigations like party time."

Mike frowned. "Chandler's not a suspect."

"Chandler and his partner are both in my sights until I sign off on this case." Again that niggling sense that something wasn't right rose in her.

He sighed. "You came back too soon."

Isabel's palms began to sweat. She'd had to return to work when she did, otherwise she might never have come back. "I'm fine." She couldn't talk about Jamal's shooting. The pain was still raw, her guilt still fresh. Her only hope was that in time, she would be able to put the incident behind her. The department psychologist had signed her fit for duty. Why did everyone else keep telling her to take more time off?

"If you need to talk," Mike said, "I'll listen."

Isabel smiled, appreciating his gesture. "I know, Mike. Thanks." She pushed aside her misgivings and went back to finish her notes. If she thought about other things, maybe Jamal Atkins wouldn't haunt her.

Isabel walked into the interrogation room after talking to her lieutenant. Her captain had agreed that something wasn't quite right on the shooting and told her to follow up on it. Public confidence in the department was at its lowest level ever and Isabel knew that even the death of a scumbag like Leroy Swain would put the department under more scrutiny. She had to make sure all the answers matched.

She opened the door to the interrogation room and stopped short at the sight of Jordan Chandler. A rush of heat pulsed through her as she studied him and wondered why she was reacting like a school girl just because he looked good.

Jordan Chandler had propped his big black alligator boots on the interview table. Black jeans encased his long legs, molding to his muscular thighs. One large hand rested on his flat stomach, the other one dangled at his side. His black t-shirt hugged his broad chest. A pair of black oval sunglasses rested on the bridge of his nose. From the top of his head to the tips of his boots, he was gorgeous. Never before had she felt the least inclination to drool over a man. Obviously, today was a series of firsts.

Looking around the small room, she noticed Chandler had discarded his black leather jacket and the Kevlar vest. She hated wearing her vest, too. The damn thing never fit right, making her feel as if she were stuffed into a straitjacket.

Chandler sighed.

The deep sound sent shimmers of heat down her spine. Stop that, she commanded herself. This man was the last man in the universe she could afford to be interested in. Isabel walked to the table, grabbed the toe of one boot, and yanked his foot off the table. "Get your big hick stompers off my table."

"Hey!" Chandler snatched the glasses off his face.

"Does this place look like a hotel?"

His brown eyes sparked. "I have a suite at the Hotel Bel Air. Trust me, I know what a hotel looks like and this isn't even close." He glanced around and then shot her a crooked grin. "Come over tonight for a complimentary massage—it's a great stress reliever."

If he wasn't going to cooperate, she wouldn't either. "Mr. Chandler, if we get started now, you might be on a plane back to New Orleans tonight." She walked to the opposite side of the table and pulled out a chair.

"I'm not going anywhere. I love L.A."

Despite all his easygoing charm, Chandler was a hard sell. Any hopes for an easy solution faded, along with her patience. Opening a file folder, she studied her preliminary reports. She didn't want to look at him and risk the temptation he offered. "What happened at Leroy Swain's house?"

"Do I need to call my attorney?"

She shrugged. "That's entirely up to you. Once you call in a lawyer, however, you know there's nothing I can do to help you."

His golden brown eyes danced with laughter. He appeared boyish despite a light stubble on his square jaw. Isabel usually didn't take a suspect's behavior personally, or let their conduct get to her, but he annoyed her. After six years in homicide, she'd run the gamut of reactions. Suspects didn't joke. Jordan Chandler was a mite too casual. "I'm happy I can amuse you."

He planted his elbows on the table and rested his chin on his inter-locked fingers. "This is only the beginning."

"Do you think if you flirt hard enough, I'll let you out?"

"Never hurts to try."

His deep voice hit her like a brick. The Southern cadence rolled off his full lips with the smoothness of twenty-five-year- old whiskey. That voice alone could send her into fits of ecstasy. "You could try being cooperative."

"Don't you like playing games?"

She fought a smile. This guy didn't let up. "You're on the wrong side of the table."

He pointed to the chair next to her. "I could move."

Isabel sat back in the plastic chair, trying to figure out just when she'd lost control. Was it when he'd flashed that crooked grin? The way he talked stirred something in her. His words were spoken slowly, with the lusty rhythm of the Mississippi Delta. Her brother had sounded the same after spending three years at the Ole Miss law school. Jordan Chandler was "to the plantation born." Her brother had only pretended.

Stop thinking about his voice. She'd lost perspective. This had to be the first time she'd gotten hung up on a suspect. She used to be a better cop.

What should have been a garden variety shooting had turned into something that didn't quite add up. Neither the shooting nor the victim was special. In L.A., a dead body in the wrong place at the wrong time tended to be a cliché. She pursed her lips, trying to control the wild pounding of her heart. "What happened at Leroy Swain's house?"

He leaned back in his chair. "It was a meat and potatoes re-take warrant. It should have gone down easy. Race Parnell, the rat I was after, skipped New Orleans on a million-dollar bail. The court should never have let him out on bail. Even I could have told them the guy would be on the first plane out of there. We had intel that—"

"Intelligence?"

"Yeah."

"Ex-military?"

He grinned. "Navy SEAL. You never leave the lingo behind."

"I understand. My dad's ex-Special Forces." She smiled, remembering her father's stories of his days 'in country.' "He always talks in code about his time in Viet Nam."

"You think war is funny?"

Isabel noted his clenched fist. She'd hit a nerve. Picking up her silver pen, she tapped it on the table. "If I did, I would've written this off, and you'd be on your way to shoot up another neighborhood."

Chandler's jaw hardened, but he said nothing.

Isabel wondered if she was getting anywhere with him. If he was a trained SEAL, the only way she'd force him to spill his guts was to maybe shove bamboo shoots under his fingernails. She wondered if she had time to run to the nearest Chinese market. "Do you have anything to say, Mr. Chandler?"

"So tell me, Detective, is it me you don't like, or all bounty hunters in general?"

UNEARTHING PASSIONS

2006 Publication Schedule

January

A Lover's Legacy
Veronica Parker
1-58571-167-5
$9.95

Love Lasts Forever
Dominiqua Douglas
1-58571-187-X
$9.95

Under the Cherry
    Moon
Christal Jordan-Mims
1-58571-169-1
$12.95

February

Second Chances at Love
Cheris Hodges
1-58571-188-8
$9.95

Enchanted Desire
Wanda Y. Thomas
1-58571-176-4
$9.95

Caught Up
Deatri King Bey
1-58571-178-0
$12.95

March

I'm Gonna Make You
    Love Me
Gwyneth Bolton
1-58571-181-0
$9.95

Through the Fire
Seressia Glass
1-58571-173-X
$9.95

Notes When Summer
    Ends
Beverly Lauderdale
1-58571-180-2
$12.95

April

Sin and Surrender
J.M. Jeffries
1-58571-189-6
$9.95

Unearthing Passions
Elaine Sims
1-58571-184-5
$9.95

Between Tears
Pamela Ridley
1-58571-179-9
$12.95

May

Misty Blue
Dyanne Davis
1-58571-186-1
$9.95

Ironic
Pamela Leigh Starr
1-58571-168-3
$9.95

Cricket's Serenade
Carolita Blythe
1-58571-183-7
$12.95

June

Cupid
Barbara Keaton
1-58571-174-8
$9.95

Havana Sunrise
Kymberly Hunt
1-58571-182-9
$9.95

2006 Publication Schedule (continued)

July

Love Me Carefully
A.C. Arthur
1-58571-177-2
$9.95

No Ordinary Love
Angela Weaver
1-58571-198-5
$9.95

Rehoboth Road
Anita Ballard-Jones
1-58571-196-9
$12.95

August

Scent of Rain
Annetta P. Lee
158571-199-3
$9.95

Love in High Gear
Charlotte Roy
158571-185-3
$9.95

Rise of the Phoenix
Kenneth Whetstone
1-58571-197-7
$12.95

September

The Business of Love
Cheris Hodges
1-58571-193-4
$9.95

Rock Star
Rosyln Hardy Holcomb
1-58571-200-0
$9.95

A Dead Man Speaks
Lisa Jones Johnson
1-58571-203-5
$12.95

October

Rivers of the Soul-Part 1
Leslie Esdaile
1-58571-223-X
$9.95

A Dangerous Woman
J.M. Jeffries
1-58571-195-0
$9.95

Sinful Intentions
Crystal Rhodes
1-58571-201-9
$12.95

November

Only You
Crystal Hubbard
1-58571-208-6
$9.95

Ebony Eyes
Kei Swanson
1-58571-194-2
$9.95

Still Waters Run Deep –
    Part 2
Leslie Esdaile
1-58571-224-8
$9.95

December

Let's Get It On
Dyanne Davis
1-58571-210-8
$9.95

Nights Over Egypt
Barbara Keaton
1-58571-192-6
$9.95

A Perfect Place to Pray
I.L. Goodwin
1-58571-202-7
$12.95

UNEARTHING PASSIONS

Other Genesis Press, Inc. Titles

A Dangerous Deception	J.M. Jeffries	$8.95
A Dangerous Love	J.M. Jeffries	$8.95
A Dangerous Obsession	J.M. Jeffries	$8.95
A Drummer's Beat to Mend	Kei Swanson	$9.95
A Happy Life	Charlotte Harris	$9.95
A Heart's Awakening	Veronica Parker	$9.95
A Lark on the Wing	Phyliss Hamilton	$9.95
A Love of Her Own	Cheris F. Hodges	$9.95
A Love to Cherish	Beverly Clark	$8.95
A Risk of Rain	Dar Tomlinson	$8.95
A Twist of Fate	Beverly Clark	$8.95
A Will to Love	Angie Daniels	$9.95
Acquisitions	Kimberley White	$8.95
Across	Carol Payne	$12.95
After the Vows	Leslie Esdaile	$10.95
(Summer Anthology)	T.T. Henderson	
	Jacqueline Thomas	
Again My Love	Kayla Perrin	$10.95
Against the Wind	Gwynne Forster	$8.95
All I Ask	Barbara Keaton	$8.95
Ambrosia	T.T. Henderson	$8.95
An Unfinished Love Affair	Barbara Keaton	$8.95
And Then Came You	Dorothy Elizabeth Love	$8.95
Angel's Paradise	Janice Angelique	$9.95
At Last	Lisa G. Riley	$8.95
Best of Friends	Natalie Dunbar	$8.95
Beyond the Rapture	Beverly Clark	$9.95
Blaze	Barbara Keaton	$9.95
Blood Lust	J. M. Jeffries	$9.95
Bodyguard	Andrea Jackson	$9.95
Boss of Me	Diana Nyad	$8.95
Bound by Love	Beverly Clark	$8.95
Breeze	Robin Hampton Allen	$10.95

Other Genesis Press, Inc. Titles (continued)

Broken	Dar Tomlinson	$24.95
By Design	Barbara Keaton	$8.95
Cajun Heat	Charlene Berry	$8.95
Careless Whispers	Rochelle Alers	$8.95
Cats & Other Tales	Marilyn Wagner	$8.95
Caught in a Trap	Andre Michelle	$8.95
Caught Up In the Rapture	Lisa G. Riley	$9.95
Cautious Heart	Cheris F Hodges	$8.95
Chances	Pamela Leigh Starr	$8.95
Cherish the Flame	Beverly Clark	$8.95
Class Reunion	Irma Jenkins/John Brown	$12.95
Code Name: Diva	J.M. Jeffries	$9.95
Conquering Dr. Wexler's Heart	Kimberley White	$9.95
Crossing Paths, Tempting Memories	Dorothy Elizabeth Love	$9.95
Cypress Whisperings	Phyllis Hamilton	$8.95
Dark Embrace	Crystal Wilson Harris	$8.95
Dark Storm Rising	Chinelu Moore	$10.95
Daughter of the Wind	Joan Xian	$8.95
Deadly Sacrifice	Jack Kean	$22.95
Designer Passion	Dar Tomlinson	$8.95
Dreamtective	Liz Swados	$5.95
Ebony Butterfly II	Delilah Dawson	$14.95
Echoes of Yesterday	Beverly Clark	$9.95
Eden's Garden	Elizabeth Rose	$8.95
Everlastin' Love	Gay G. Gunn	$8.95
Everlasting Moments	Dorothy Elizabeth Love	$8.95
Everything and More	Sinclair Lebeau	$8.95
Everything but Love	Natalie Dunbar	$8.95
Eve's Prescription	Edwina Martin Arnold	$8.95
Falling	Natalie Dunbar	$9.95
Fate	Pamela Leigh Starr	$8.95
Finding Isabella	A.J. Garrotto	$8.95

Other Genesis Press, Inc. Titles (continued)

Forbidden Quest	Dar Tomlinson	$10.95
Forever Love	Wanda Thomas	$8.95
From the Ashes	Kathleen Suzanne	$8.95
	Jeanne Sumerix	
Gentle Yearning	Rochelle Alers	$10.95
Glory of Love	Sinclair LeBeau	$10.95
Go Gentle into that Good Night	Malcom Boyd	$12.95
Goldengroove	Mary Beth Craft	$16.95
Groove, Bang, and Jive	Steve Cannon	$8.99
Hand in Glove	Andrea Jackson	$9.95
Hard to Love	Kimberley White	$9.95
Hart & Soul	Angie Daniels	$8.95
Heartbeat	Stephanie Bedwell-Grime	$8.95
Hearts Remember	M. Loui Quezada	$8.95
Hidden Memories	Robin Allen	$10.95
Higher Ground	Leah Latimer	$19.95
Hitler, the War, and the Pope	Ronald Rychiak	$26.95
How to Write a Romance	Kathryn Falk	$18.95
I Married a Reclining Chair	Lisa M. Fuhs	$8.95
Indigo After Dark Vol. I	Nia Dixon/Angelique	$10.95
Indigo After Dark Vol. II	Dolores Bundy/Cole Riley	$10.95
Indigo After Dark Vol. III	Montana Blue/Coco Morena	$10.95
Indigo After Dark Vol. IV	Cassandra Colt/	$14.95
	Diana Richeaux	
Indigo After Dark Vol. V	Delilah Dawson	$14.95
Icie	Pamela Leigh Starr	$8.95
I'll Be Your Shelter	Giselle Carmichael	$8.95
I'll Paint a Sun	A.J. Garrotto	$9.95
Illusions	Pamela Leigh Starr	$8.95
Indiscretions	Donna Hill	$8.95
Intentional Mistakes	Michele Sudler	$9.95
Interlude	Donna Hill	$8.95
Intimate Intentions	Angie Daniels	$8.95

Other Genesis Press, Inc. Titles (continued)

Jolie's Surrender	Edwina Martin-Arnold	$8.95
Kiss or Keep	Debra Phillips	$8.95
Lace	Giselle Carmichael	$9.95
Last Train to Memphis	Elsa Cook	$12.95
Lasting Valor	Ken Olsen	$24.95
Let Us Prey	Hunter Lundy	$25.95
Life Is Never As It Seems	J.J. Michael	$12.95
Lighter Shade of Brown	Vicki Andrews	$8.95
Love Always	Mildred E. Riley	$10.95
Love Doesn't Come Easy	Charlyne Dickerson	$8.95
Love Unveiled	Gloria Greene	$10.95
Love's Deception	Charlene Berry	$10.95
Love's Destiny	M. Loui Quezada	$8.95
Mae's Promise	Melody Walcott	$8.95
Magnolia Sunset	Giselle Carmichael	$8.95
Matters of Life and Death	Lesego Malepe, Ph.D.	$15.95
Meant to Be	Jeanne Sumerix	$8.95
Midnight Clear	Leslie Esdaile	$10.95
(Anthology)	Gwynne Forster	
	Carmen Green	
	Monica Jackson	
Midnight Magic	Gwynne Forster	$8.95
Midnight Peril	Vicki Andrews	$10.95
Misconceptions	Pamela Leigh Starr	$9.95
Montgomery's Children	Richard Perry	$14.95
My Buffalo Soldier	Barbara B. K. Reeves	$8.95
Naked Soul	Gwynne Forster	$8.95
Next to Last Chance	Louisa Dixon	$24.95
No Apologies	Seressia Glass	$8.95
No Commitment Required	Seressia Glass	$8.95
No Regrets	Mildred E. Riley	$8.95
Nowhere to Run	Gay G. Gunn	$10.95
O Bed! O Breakfast!	Rob Kuehnle	$14.95

Other Genesis Press, Inc. Titles (continued)

Object of His Desire	A. C. Arthur	$8.95
Office Policy	A. C. Arthur	$9.95
Once in a Blue Moon	Dorianne Cole	$9.95
One Day at a Time	Bella McFarland	$8.95
Outside Chance	Louisa Dixon	$24.95
Passion	T.T. Henderson	$10.95
Passion's Blood	Cherif Fortin	$22.95
Passion's Journey	Wanda Thomas	$8.95
Past Promises	Jahmel West	$8.95
Path of Fire	T.T. Henderson	$8.95
Path of Thorns	Annetta P. Lee	$9.95
Peace Be Still	Colette Haywood	$12.95
Picture Perfect	Reon Carter	$8.95
Playing for Keeps	Stephanie Salinas	$8.95
Pride & Joi	Gay G. Gunn	$15.95
Pride & Joi	Gay G. Gunn	$8.95
Promises to Keep	Alicia Wiggins	$8.95
Quiet Storm	Donna Hill	$10.95
Reckless Surrender	Rochelle Alers	$6.95
Red Polka Dot in a World of Plaid	Varian Johnson	$12.95
Reluctant Captive	Joyce Jackson	$8.95
Rendezvous with Fate	Jeanne Sumerix	$8.95
Revelations	Cheris F. Hodges	$8.95
Rivers of the Soul	Leslie Esdaile	$8.95
Rocky Mountain Romance	Kathleen Suzanne	$8.95
Rooms of the Heart	Donna Hill	$8.95
Rough on Rats and Tough on Cats	Chris Parker	$12.95
Secret Library Vol. 1	Nina Sheridan	$18.95
Secret Library Vol. 2	Cassandra Colt	$8.95
Shades of Brown	Denise Becker	$8.95
Shades of Desire	Monica White	$8.95

Other Genesis Press, Inc. Titles (continued)

Shadows in the Moonlight	Jeanne Sumerix	$8.95
Sin	Crystal Rhodes	$8.95
So Amazing	Sinclair LeBeau	$8.95
Somebody's Someone	Sinclair LeBeau	$8.95
Someone to Love	Alicia Wiggins	$8.95
Song in the Park	Martin Brant	$15.95
Soul Eyes	Wayne L. Wilson	$12.95
Soul to Soul	Donna Hill	$8.95
Southern Comfort	J.M. Jeffries	$8.95
Still the Storm	Sharon Robinson	$8.95
Still Waters Run Deep	Leslie Esdaile	$8.95
Stories to Excite You	Anna Forrest/Divine	$14.95
Subtle Secrets	Wanda Y. Thomas	$8.95
Suddenly You	Crystal Hubbard	$9.95
Sweet Repercussions	Kimberley White	$9.95
Sweet Tomorrows	Kimberly White	$8.95
Taken by You	Dorothy Elizabeth Love	$9.95
Tattooed Tears	T. T. Henderson	$8.95
The Color Line	Lizzette Grayson Carter	$9.95
The Color of Trouble	Dyanne Davis	$8.95
The Disappearance of Allison Jones	Kayla Perrin	$5.95
The Honey Dipper's Legacy	Pannell-Allen	$14.95
The Joker's Love Tune	Sidney Rickman	$15.95
The Little Pretender	Barbara Cartland	$10.95
The Love We Had	Natalie Dunbar	$8.95
The Man Who Could Fly	Bob & Milana Beamon	$18.95
The Missing Link	Charlyne Dickerson	$8.95
The Price of Love	Sinclair LeBeau	$8.95
The Smoking Life	Ilene Barth	$29.95
The Words of the Pitcher	Kei Swanson	$8.95
Three Wishes	Seressia Glass	$8.95
Ties That Bind	Kathleen Suzanne	$8.95
Tiger Woods	Libby Hughes	$5.95

Other Genesis Press, Inc. Titles (continued)

Time is of the Essence	Angie Daniels	$9.95
Timeless Devotion	Bella McFarland	$9.95
Tomorrow's Promise	Leslie Esdaile	$8.95
Truly Inseparable	Wanda Y. Thomas	$8.95
Unbreak My Heart	Dar Tomlinson	$8.95
Uncommon Prayer	Kenneth Swanson	$9.95
Unconditional	A.C. Arthur	$9.95
Unconditional Love	Alicia Wiggins	$8.95
Until Death Do Us Part	Susan Paul	$8.95
Vows of Passion	Bella McFarland	$9.95
Wedding Gown	Dyanne Davis	$8.95
What's Under Benjamin's Bed	Sandra Schaffer	$8.95
When Dreams Float	Dorothy Elizabeth Love	$8.95
Whispers in the Night	Dorothy Elizabeth Love	$8.95
Whispers in the Sand	LaFlorya Gauthier	$10.95
Wild Ravens	Altonya Washington	$9.95
Yesterday Is Gone	Beverly Clark	$10.95
Yesterday's Dreams, Tomorrow's Promises	Reon Laudat	$8.95
Your Precious Love	Sinclair LeBeau	$8.95